Praise for *Starcatcher*:

"Patricia Potter has created a lively Scottish tale that has just the right amount of intrigue, romance, and conflict."
—*Literary Journal*

"Once again, Pat Potter demonstrates why she is considered one of the best writers of historical novels on the market today . . . Ms. Potter scores big time with this fabulously fine fiction that will be devoured by fans of this genre."
—Harriet Klausner

The
Perfect Family

Patricia Potter

BERKLEY BOOKS, NEW YORK

THE PERFECT FAMILY

A Berkley Book / published by arrangement with
the author

ISBN: 0-7394-1564-6

BERKLEY®
Berkley Books are published by The Berkley Publishing Group,
a division of Penguin Putnam Inc.,
375 Hudson Street, New York, New York 10014.
BERKLEY and the "B" design
are trademarks belonging to Penguin Putnam Inc.

PRINTED IN THE UNITED STATES OF AMERICA

To Gail Fortune, editor extraordinaire,
who makes writing a joy.
Pat

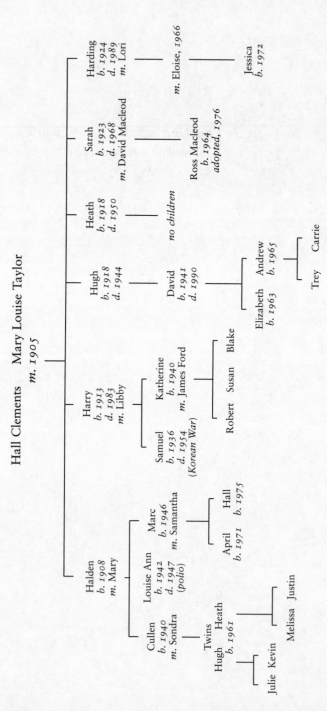

GENEALOGY OF THE CLEMENTS FAMILY

Hall Clements   Mary Louise Taylor
m. 1905

prologue

His gut burned.

Harding Clements reached over and touched the rifle he'd taken from the barn. Five more minutes. Five more minutes and he would face his wife.

His wife and her lover.

A long discordant blast jerked his eyes back to the road. Damn, he was on the center line. A monster truck bore down on him.

For a second, he thought about staying where he was. Betrayal was a poison eating through him, and he'd tasted it twice this day. He glanced down at the empty money bags on the seat behind him. He had gone to the bank this morning to pick up the payroll for the ranch hands, all of whom wanted cash. The money that was to have been deposited a week ago, the money that would see them through the fall and winter, was not there. His brother, Heath, had not deposited it. Instead, the account had been drained.

He had gone first to the guest cottage that Heath had been temporarily using. There had to be an explanation. But Heath was gone, and the cottage looked ransacked, as if someone had left in a hurry. He stood in the bedroom, looking at the pulled-out drawers and empty closet. Then he headed for the main house where he and his wife lived. He needed to think, to take a drink, or two. Thank God, none of the rest of his extended family were in the living room.

He had slipped quietly inside and walked up to the room he shared with his wife, Lori. He hesitated when he saw a suitcase near the door. Surprised, he started to go inside when he heard Lori's voice.

"Yes, darling. No, he went into town. He'll probably stop for a drink or two. I should be at the cabin in thirty minutes."

Harding slipped back out the door. He considered confronting her, but he had to know who she was meeting. Even as, deep in his heart, he knew.

He had to have proof, though. He couldn't accuse his brother without it.

The cabin! It must be the Oak Creek cabin. Damn them. Damn both of them.

He ran out to his car and drove around the other side of the barn so she wouldn't see him. He heard her small sports car roar out of the yard and after waiting several moments, he spun out onto the road. He didn't have to follow closely.

The truck's horn blasted again. At the very last minute, he swerved, and the truck missed him by mere inches. He pulled over for a moment, reclaiming his breath. And he prayed. He prayed to God he wouldn't find Heath there, because if he did he would kill his brother.

He thought about the car she'd taken. The little red convertible. She loved that car and now she was taking it to meet her lover. Probably to escape together in it. All Heath had was an old pickup, unless, of course, he'd used the family's money to buy a new vehicle. He saw that damn red car in his mind's eye. It had been yet another example of her selfishness, her reckless spending. But he had loved her and indulged her even when it took every penny he had.

She had been unsatisfied with that last penny. He'd tolerated her growing complaints, observed the restlessness that went with them. He'd tried to ignore the disappearances, the too-transparent lies, because he'd been addicted to her beauty and the unrestrained passion that transported him, at least temporarily. He had hesitated to question her too closely, knowing her quick temper. And there was always the fear she might leave him.

He knew, of course, that Lori and Heath had once been childhood sweethearts. But when Heath and his twin marched off to Europe, Lori had been hurt and angry. Heath hadn't written to her once while he was away, hadn't made any effort to make sure she stayed his girl.

So Lori had turned to Harding. He realized after their marriage that she'd been more in love with the idea of becoming a Clements than in actually being his wife. He'd tried desperately to make it work, though. He'd loved her for years and he tried to give her anything that might make her happy. Content to be his.

But then an embittered Heath returned from the war. And Lori's eyes followed him everywhere.

Harding had tried not to notice, not to care. Heath had gone through a terrible time and had seen their brother— Heath's twin—die. He had the right to flirt. But Heath was Harding's hero. He had never thought his brother would take the flirtation any further.

He should have known better. War had done something to Heath, something irreparable. He no longer cared about anyone but himself. In the last year, he had complained as bitterly as Lori about lack of funds. He wanted to sell his share of the ranch and get into the oil business with an army buddy. But no one in the family had the cash to buy him out.

Apparently, he had found his own way to take both the money and Harding's wife.

The fury built again. There had been six of them: five boys, all with names starting with H, and one sister, Sarah. They had quarreled, fought, competed, but they had all been loyal to the Clements ranch and to each other.

Harding pulled back onto the highway. A part of his heart died with every mile he traveled. He reached out and touched the rifle lying next to him, then took a drink from the bottle left in his car several days ago. It burned his throat down to his gut. He almost choked on it, but still took another swallow. He needed liquid courage. He needed it to face his brother and his wife.

The road narrowed and he turned off onto a dirt road that wound into the canyon. It was fall, and the leaves were vivid yellow or orange with a mixture of rust colors. He usually loved this season. Not today, though. Today, he scarcely noticed.

He parked his car away from the cabin and took out his rifle. He felt as if he were sleepwalking, as if he were a character in a nightmare, as he walked down the dirt road to the cabin. Oak Creek seemed to mock him as the water tumbled over rocks in its rush to the swimming hole where he and his brothers once swam in their birthday suits. Memories. So many memories. They crashed around him like the lightning-downed trees.

Harding approached the adobe and log cabin. Two vehicles were parked in front of the cabin. Lori's car. Heath's truck. The cabin door was open. So was the door to one vehicle.

The cabin itself was framed by the cottonwoods and maples and oaks. But the trees faded into the background as his gaze remained on the door. His brother appeared in the opening, carrying a briefcase.

Heath stopped when he saw Harding. His eyes went to the rifle in his brother's hand. His body stiffened.

"Darlin'?" Lori's voice came from inside the cabin.

Harding could barely see now for the fury in him. The mist in his eyes. His wife's voice echoed in his brain. "Going somewhere, Heath?" His voice sounded scratchy, broken.

Heath stared at him defiantly.

"Where is the cattle sale money?"

Heath's gaze flickered to his briefcase, then back again. "I took it for my share of the ranch," he said. "I never want to see a damn cow again."

"We need that money."

"So do I," Heath said lazily. "At any rate, it's gone. I bought bearer bonds in Off-Shore Drilling in exchange for a partnership."

Lori came out the door, her eyes widening at the sight of the two brothers. She moved to Heath's side.

Harding forced himself not to lunge at his brother. Not to tear him from limb to limb. Instead, he asked in what he hoped was a calm, reasoned voice, "Where are the bonds? I want the money back."

Heath shrugged carelessly. "It's too late. The transaction was completed yesterday."

"I could have you arrested."

"You could, but you won't. The family wouldn't permit it," Heath said. "Besides, it is just a loan and a good one for the Clementses. Those bonds will be worth millions some day."

"The hell they will. That company will go bankrupt just like all your other damn money-making schemes."

"Not this one," Heath said. "They know the oil is there. We just needed the money for equipment."

"The bonds?" Harding said. "Where are they?"

"Well hidden at the moment. I won't have you mucking this up for me. But I'll send you directions . . . in a book we're both familiar with. In time. Those bonds may be worthless at the moment, brother, but in another five years they will be worth millions. I've already buried them not far from here, and they will more than repay the money I've . . . borrowed temporarily. I swear it."

"Your promises have never been worth a damn thing. You stole from the family. You know how much we needed that money." Harding's gaze went to Lori. "You stole from me."

Heath shrugged. "Lori? You knew she loved me when you married her. You were nothing but a stand-in, Harding." He put his arm around Lori and went back inside the cabin. "Get your things, Lori."

The indifference in his voice enraged Harding. He followed them inside, repositioning the rifle from the crook in his arm to both hands.

Heath ignored him, instead keeping his arm around Lori while his other hand clutched the briefcase.

Her eyes seemed to waver, but she said nothing to Harding. Instead, she did as Heath instructed. Harding felt his blood heat as she picked up a small suitcase and her pocketbook, staying close to Heath as she did so. Then they started for the door.

Harding barred it with his own body. "You won't take whatever is in that briefcase and you won't take her," he said.

"Don't be a fool, Harding. She has never cared about you."

Harding's gaze went to her. She was so beautiful. So passionate. So treacherous. Her blond hair curled around her shoulders. Her dark blue eyes were wide. Her sensuous lips frowned at him.

He could barely breathe now. His heart pounded so loud he was sure both of them could hear it. "Is that true, Lori?"

Say no. Please say no.

"Don't be a fool, Harding," she said. "And don't ask questions you really don't want the answers to."

"Damn you," he said. "Damn you to hell." He levered his rifle at her.

Heath took a step toward her.

"Don't worry, Heath. He won't do anything." Her voice was laced with contempt. "He doesn't have the balls."

Harding felt as if he were suffocating in a dark noxious cloud. He took a step forward. His fingers instinctively tightened on the trigger, then stopped.

Heath reached out to grab the rifle. It went off, the sound resounding, echoing in the room. Harding's ears rung with it, even as his eyes tried to register what they were seeing. He barely realized that his brother was slowly, ever so slowly, sinking to the floor, crimson spreading over his shirt.

He leaned down next to his brother. "Heath . . ." he called. "I didn't mean . . . God help me . . . I didn't mean . . ."

Heath's lips were moving. Harding reached down to hear. "Bonds. Buried. Book. In . . . brief . . ." Then he groaned, and the color in his eyes faded.

Lori threw herself on Heath, then turned toward Harding in a fury. "You killed him. I'll see you dead. I'll see you electrocuted."

Harding pulled her off Heath and pushed her away. Harder than he'd intended. She stumbled toward the hearth. Her head connected with the brick fireplace, and she crumbled to the floor. Blood trickled from a wound in her head.

He rose, looking at the carnage around him. His brain tried to comprehend it, but couldn't. God knew he'd thought about killing his brother. Lori, too. But when it came down to it, he'd hesitated. If Heath had not grabbed the gun . . .

But he had. And Lori . . .

God help him.

He dropped to the floor, sick. He'd killed them both. Cain. He was Cain. And damned forever.

His eyes went back to Lori. She was right. He *would* be convicted of murder. He would die in the electric chair. Or spend the rest of his life in prison. A cage. That would be even worse than death. He had always loved the freedom of a ranch, of riding, of camping, of hunting.

A cage for the rest of his life.

And explanations to his family. His parents. His sister. He buried his head in his arms.

No one knows I'm here.

He leaned down and picked up the briefcase. He quickly looked inside. A package. And money. Not as much as the cattle sale would have brought, but enough to disappear. *Heath's traveling money. Heath's and Lori's.*

His eyes filled with tears. He had never cried before, at least not as long as he could remember. Not even when they heard about Hugh's death in France during the Normandy invasion.

No time for tears. No time for regret.

He took the briefcase, looked one last time at the two bodies, then ran out the door, down the road to his car. He started the engine and stomped down on the gas pedal. Leaving a whirl of dust behind him, he bounced along the dirt trail until he reached the highway, then sped down the road toward New Mexico.

one

Apprehension prickled along Jessie Clayton's spine as she drove into the tree-lined driveway of her small brick house. The front curtain was closed.

She would have sworn she left it open. She always left the curtains opened for Ben, her big shaggy mutt of a dog who usually spent his days surveying the world outside. Or just waiting for her return.

No Ben at the window, either. He would have heard her car pulling into the driveway. He would be wriggling with excitement. Something was wrong.

She hurriedly left the car, keys in hand, and nearly ran to the door. She tried the doorknob and felt it turn. *Unlocked.*

She hesitated. She never forgot to lock the door. *Never.*

She seldom came home for lunch, either. Usually her bookstore, located near a university campus, was busy at lunchtime. But she and her partner, Sol, had recently found a student who was both knowledgeable and reliable to fill in, and she'd reveled in having an extra hour of freedom. A trip home for lunch and to take Ben for a walk on a lovely day was a luxury she'd planned to enjoy.

But now she froze. Someone had been inside her house. Someone who shouldn't have been.

Even more worrisome was the absence of a welcoming bark.

She hesitated. *Run,* she told herself. *Run. You've always done that so well.*

But she couldn't. Ben was inside. Ben, her only family. What if he was injured?

Call the police. But whoever had been there was probably long gone. Her heart pounding, she pushed the door open. Then she saw a figure. Dressed in black with a ski mask covering his face. Tall. That's all she noticed before he sprinted toward the door, knocking her aside as he did so. Instinctively, she grabbed for him and caught cloth. He whirled around, one hand fending her off, the other smacking her face.

He was gone. She managed to get to her feet and started calling the dog. She heard a whine, ran to the bathroom and threw open the door. Ben was trying to get to his feet, his furry body wriggling with anxiety.

"What happened, Ben?"

He whined and seemed to have a problem walking. She hugged him for a long moment. He was infinitely dear, this nondescript furball she'd found abandoned. She didn't care if the burglar had taken everything she had as long as Ben was all right.

And he did seem to be all right. But she meant to keep a close watch on him the rest of the day.

Her face still smarting from the blow, Jessie looked around the room. The house—more of a cottage—had been ransacked. Her belongings were strewn around the room, one of her miniature carousel horses smashed, apparently when the burglar was searching for valuables. She'd painstakingly collected them over the past eight years and each was special. She leaned down and picked up the pieces of broken china. One of her favorites.

But no time to worry about that. She called the police and held a still-trembling Ben as she waited for them. She felt herself trembling. Her sense of safety had been smashed along with the china horse. And the books thrown over the floor. She wanted to gather them up, but she hesitated to do anything until the police arrived.

At least all but one of her carousel horses had survived. So had the flowering plants that gave the room a sense of warmth. *Think of your blessings.*

Jessie called Rob at the bookstore. "I'll be late. Just lock up if you have to go to class," she told him, still too stunned to elaborate. Her voice sounded amazingly normal to her own ears.

She wandered outside and stood on the small porch. The tree-lined street of homes looked as peaceful as always. Located near Emory University, the homes were mostly brick two- and three-bedroom cottages built in the thirties and forties. She'd loved their storybook look and flower-filled yards; they seemed to have so much more character than the new subdivision homes.

The azaleas had faded, but nearly every house had a colorful year-round garden, including her own. She'd constructed her own garden, a haphazard profusion of lilies, begonias, and impatiens. She'd even planted a magnolia tree.

It was everything she'd ever pictured, ever wanted, as a child.

And now it had been violated. She turned around and went back inside, wincing at the destruction.

She waited for what seemed like an eternity before the doorbell rang—an impatient, authoritative ringing, not that of a casual caller. She tensed, and then wondered whether she would always brace herself whenever she heard a loud sound. She thought she'd moved beyond that fear.

She put a hand on Ben, reassuring him, when she was the one who really needed reassurance. When she looked out the window, Ben stayed at her side, his tail between his legs as if he'd condemned himself for failing as a watch-dog.

Police. She opened the door.

Jessie settled in her chair at the bookstore and opened the mail she'd grabbed from the mailbox as she left the cottage after a very unsatisfactory meeting with the police. She was still fuming.

For the first time, she didn't take pleasure in being alone in the bookstore that had become her second home. Rob *had* been gone when she arrived, and Sol was off on one of his research trips. She looked around the book-crammed shop, seeking the familiar sense of contentment. Every inch of shelf space was taken, and boxes full of additional books blocked much of the floor. Sol couldn't resist an es-tate sale, and usually she couldn't wait to open new crates and discover new treasures.

The Olde Book Shoppe specialized in rare books, and it smelled of leather and old paper and mustiness; even the latter usually gave her pleasure. It denoted substance. Sta-bility. Books whose appeal lasted throughout decades, even centuries. She was seldom lonely here. These were the books of her childhood and youth and adulthood. They were closer to her than any human being had been.

But their comforting presence didn't help today. She reached down and touched Ben. He seemed to have shaken whatever had happened—or been given—to him. His tail wagged at last, and she felt better. A little.

She went back to the mail. Bills. Catalogs. Credit card offers.

Then she opened the odd-looking envelope that had been stuck in a catalog. It *looked* personal, but then she had previously received advertisements or pleas for money in deceptively benign packaging.

Her grumpy mood made her rush to that conclusion, and she held it for a minute or so before opening it.

Ben nudged her, as if aware her attention had wandered away from him. She reached down and touched him, and he settled under her feet again, happy with just that small touch.

She opened it, read the invitation, then reread the address on the envelope again. *Jessica Clayton.* Her name. Her address. It was obviously some kind of ironic mistake.

An invitation to a family reunion.

A family she'd never heard of.

She didn't need this today. She didn't need reminders that she had no family. Not even a distant cousin.

Even the words *family reunion* summoned up images. Warm, wonderful pictures of everything she'd once dreamed about. So many childish dreams. Whenever her father had stumbled into their rented quarters, smelling of whiskey or beer or cheap wine, she would close her eyes and wish for a mother, a sister, a doting grandfather. She would wish for the type of family she'd seen in television series or read about in books.

Her fingers stroked the envelope. No return address, but many invitations didn't have return addresses. And there was no phone number inside. It was an informal invitation, obviously computer-generated, with horses galloping across the top. There was no R.S.V.P.

It was, in fact, an announcement more than an invitation, obviously sent to people who knew the phone number, the address, the sender. She couldn't even tell the mail carrier to return it to the sender. The rightful recipient would never receive it.

As someone who had never received such an invitation, she felt regret for that unknown person, that person with her name. But probably she would be notified by another member of the family. Close families kept in touch. At least, she'd always thought so. Her imaginary family had.

For a moment, she let herself believe it was for her. She slowly released a breath, just realizing that she'd bottled it up in her throat. Her fingers had dropped the invitation and were stiff with tension. Or was it memories? Memories she'd tried to erase. But all of them had returned today. Fear had returned, and so had the insecurity.

Her family had never been more than a father. A father who was distant at best, an angry drunk at worst. This card was a mocking reminder.

She saw him now in her mind's eye. His defeated eyes. His blustering defiance when he was fired once again for drinking, his absences when she had to try to find something to eat in empty cabinets, the smell of alcohol when he returned late at night, mumbling words she didn't understand.

Still, she had loved her father. He was older than most fathers, having married late in life. Her mother had been a waitress, far younger than him. She had left them when Jessie was only two, and neither of them had ever heard from her again. Jessie had never tried to find her, but instead had steeled herself emotionally from the realization of being unwanted by one of the two people who should have loved her most, and being considered a . . . burden by the other. She never knew whether her mother's desertion had turned her father into the embittered man she knew, but sometimes she had seen grief, even longing, in his eyes. And each time he got that look on his face, he would disappear for a day or two or even three.

He would lose his job and they would move again. States faded one into another. New York. Maryland. Kentucky. Tennessee. As she grew older, she'd asked about her mother, but she never got an answer. She grew accustomed to the shadows that never disappeared. Or perhaps *he* had been the shadow.

The only thing that had saved them was his reputation as a horse trainer. He'd been able to extract every measure of speed from the horses under his tutelage. He understood them as few others did, and in return they gave him everything they had. But eventually he would be fired. They would move to another place where someone else was willing to give him still another chance.

She glanced down at the invitation again and tried to blink away tears. She never cried. Never. Ever. Not since the night that had led to his death. But today . . . today was too much.

Even the police had lectured her instead of doing something useful, like collecting fingerprints. She'd been foolish to go inside. She should have called the police. They had also been unimpressed with Ben, who, despite his timidity, had a huge heart. At that moment, however, he'd chosen to hide behind her legs, thinking himself invisible.

"Not much of a guard dog," one officer noted.

"He wasn't meant to be," she'd snapped.

"You might think about trading him in," the second officer said.

"I would rather trade you in," she retorted. "Aren't you going to do anything?"

"Make a list of your stolen items," he said indifferently, "and take it to the police station. Then file with your insurance company."

"That's it?"

"That's it," he replied without apology.

"No fingerprints?"

"Look, lady, we don't have the resources to investigate every small burglary."

But it wasn't a small burglary to her. It was one huge violation even if whoever had invaded her home hadn't taken much. Perhaps she'd returned before he'd been able to collect his booty. He had, however, obviously gone through her desk and bookcases, apparently searching for something of value. He'd left books on the floor, papers messed. The only thing she'd found missing, though, was a little cash she'd kept in her desk for emergencies.

The greatest loss was her precious illusion of safety.

She fingered the invitation. The burglary brought back so much. Snapshots flipped through her mind. A violent struggle. Pain. The soul-searing shame that followed. And Mills. Her hero. She remembered the contempt on his face, the icy triumph after he'd raped her. It happened long ago, but the mental photos were sharp. So were those of her father's face two days later when he was fired. It was the last time she'd seen him alive.

She hadn't told him why he'd lost his job, that this time it hadn't been his fault. It had been hers.

Jessie had lived with that for the past ten years.

She had fled all connections to that last farm in Kentucky. She'd tried to flee from her father's death, from the betrayal she'd felt from the one person she'd trusted. She'd found her refuge in books and finally in this small, barely profitable bookstore on the edge of a university.

Damm it. She had allowed that invitation to open emotional boxes she'd believed locked forever.

She read it over again.

The Biannual Clements Family Reunion
June 25–27, 1999
The Clements Ranch and Quest Resort
Sedona, Arizona

Then, most puzzling of all, a handwritten note at the bottom: "*Jessica, please come, Sarah.*"

Clements? She'd never heard the name before. But the invitation came to her. Jessica . . .

Another Jessica somewhere. She didn't think Jessica was a common name. And who was Sarah?

She reminded herself it had nothing to do with her.

Still, she suddenly realized that the shy, wistful girl she

thought had turned into a pragmatic adult had not disappeared. The books that had become her friends were cold comfort when she glimpsed a couple together or a lighted house at holidays.

She'd kept telling herself she was strong, independent. She could be as aggressive in business as anyone, and she had worked at conquering the insecurities lurking inside. But in a particularly honest frame of mind, she knew she was hiding among the books, that she'd wrapped herself in a cocoon that made few demands. It certainly didn't require any real courage, any risk.

She liked it that way. No risks, no danger.

And now . . . her cocoon had been penetrated.

Impatient with herself, she shoved the invitation out of sight under a pile of orders. She had no time for *what if*s. Still, for some reason she did not destroy it or toss it in her wastebasket. It remained on her desk like a burning brand, announcing over and over again her aloneness. Maybe tomorrow, she would try to find the telephone number and tell them the invitation went astray. Tomorrow when the memories had faded.

She dismissed it from her mind and turned back to the list a professor had e-mailed her. It contained three titles, all out-of-print books. Such books were the store's specialty and the reason for the survival of a small independent bookstore among the behemoths that had taken over the book business.

Sol had collected and cultivated book sources throughout the years. Since he had semiretired two years ago, he had taught her how to contact them, how to talk with them. Many were now long-distance friends, and she yearned someday to visit them. More dreams, but those were of a more realistic type than yearning after a family that didn't exist.

She leaned down and petted a sleeping Ben, then picked

up the telephone and dialed Dickens Books in London. No more daydreaming today. No more fanciful visions.

SEDONA, ARIZONA

They gathered in the sprawling main room of the ranch house. Tension vibrated in the room.

Ross Macleod leaned against the wall, watching.

Mentally, he counted the votes, as he had so many times before. He'd lost another voting member today. One more, and he would lose everything. He tried to keep the simmering resentment from showing. He was the poor relation. Always had been. Always would be. He meant nothing to them other than what he could offer in skills.

There were only two survivors of the original progeny of Hall and Mary Louise Clements. Sarah was seventy-six, her brother Halden, ninety-one. Then there were what he called "the first cousins"—the second generation. There were six: Marc, Cullen, Katherine, Elizabeth, Andrew, and Melissa. Between them—the first and second generations—they held the fate of the ranch in their hands.

Marc and Cullen, though, were the main players in the current drama. Brothers, they had talked their father, Halden, and the owners of two other shares into voting to sell the Sunset. Only Sarah stood firm against them.

"How in the hell did that invitation go out?" Marc Clements asked as he paced back and forth. Tall, lean, and charismatic, he looked every inch the congressman he was and the senator he wanted to be. He had been Ross's ally until the past year, when he needed money for his campaign. Now he had become one of the enemies.

Sarah, Ross's adoptive mother, grimaced. "I know we had an agreement," she defended herself. "We were all to wait until after Alex talked to this woman. But I thought he was going three days ago. I didn't know he would be held up with a court case. I did so want her to feel welcome."

Marc sighed. "Are you sure you just didn't want to get to her first?"

"Now Marc, I would never do that."

But she would. Ross knew it. The others knew it, too.

Cullen's eyes were angry. He had been the one to set the terms. No one would approach the woman before she arrived, until after Alex, the family attorney, had met with her. Otherwise, it was feared any number of the family members might camp on her doorstep with a varying assortment of bribes.

None of them knew much about the prospective heiress; nor did they know if she knew anything at all about the family. It had been decided at an earlier meeting that Alex would explain the situation, then ask her to come to the already scheduled reunion and meet the family.

If this woman knew even some of the hidden agendas, she would probably run like hell.

Marc's stern expression softened. "Probably no harm done, Sarah. Alex said he will fly to Atlanta right after the court hearing this afternoon."

Ross watched Sarah's face flush. She had called the family meeting when she realized that Alex had not contacted Jessica Clayton prior to the time she should have received the invitation. She'd protested that the invitation was to be an added incentive, a warm welcome. But Ross wondered about that. Sarah could be as Machiavellian as any member of the family, and that was saying a great deal.

Despite any protestations she might make, he suspected she'd wanted to ingratiate herself on Ross's behalf.

Dammit, he didn't need or want a champion. Yet he was the only so-called cousin without Clements blood. He was the only one not to have a share in the Sunset. He had only his sweat.

And now a newcomer no one knew could well splinter the fragile truce that held the family together. She could also take away the only livelihood he knew. He couldn't quite tamp down the resentment, or the thought of the emptiness that would cause. The ranch was the only home he knew. Even if he'd never quite belonged, it was the only place that held good memories. Dammit, despite opposition, he'd dragged it into the twentieth century. He'd squeezed out a profit when every other ranch in the Southwest was going broke or being sold out. He'd worked all his life for the Clementses, and now a stranger could step in and take it all away. His stomach churned at the thought of losing the Sunset and what it would do to Sarah.

Cullen, Marc's brother and the oldest of the second generation, looked at Sarah. "Do we know any more about her?"

Sarah shook her head. "Only that the detective is sure he's found Harding's only heir. The man he thinks is Harding died ten years ago when she was seventeen. We know that she is part owner of a struggling bookstore."

"Then she will want to sell," Cullen said with satisfaction. Cullen, an older, larger version of his brother, thought the end-all of life was money. No, that wasn't exactly true. Money *and* the Quest, his resort development that ate up the former.

Sarah didn't blink. "Sam Davis said she doesn't seem to care too much about money."

"Has he seen her?"

"She's twenty-seven, auburn hair, hazel eyes," Sarah said with great satisfaction. "Just like most of the family," Sarah said. "It has to be her."

"There's about ten million people of the same description," Marc said dryly. "We won't know until we have a DNA test."

Sarah stood. Ross reminded himself she was seventy-six now. She acted younger. She still rode daily, and her mind was quick. But her face looked older than her years; her skin was dry and wrinkled by the sun. She'd shunned hats, saying she preferred the wind in her hair, the sun against her face. "Perhaps Alex can tell us more in the next few days. He reads people well."

"Don't depend on her to side with you, Sarah," Cullen warned. "She won't have the sentimental attachment that you have."

"Don't you count your chickens before they hatch, nephew."

"I just want you to think about selling, Sarah. You can build a home at the resort and stare out at those rocks all day long. You can even board old Daisy there."

Sarah glanced over toward Ross. "It wouldn't be the same. Clementses have lived in this house for a hundred years. I don't understand how you can even think of selling it. Your grandfather would turn over in his grave."

"Now Sarah, you know the land is good for development."

"With a hundred little ugly houses every eighty feet. Over my dead body. And Ross is making a profit now."

"A damned little one." Marc turned toward Ross. "It's just not fair to the other members of the family. You know that."

"I know nothing of the kind, and I don't expect Jessica will either," Sarah retorted. "Not if she's a *true* Clements."

The old girl really knows how to place her daggers, thought Ross. But then she'd aimed enough of them at Ross. He knew she could usually bully all the other members of the family, but not on this one issue. She was alone in this.

Her only hope was the missing heir, which is why she'd commissioned the search. They had fought her on it, but in the end she'd won. Sarah had even insisted on selecting the search firm, afraid that the others might find one that wouldn't be diligent enough.

No one had thought she would succeed. It had, after all, been nearly fifty years.

Ross knew the terms of the trust better than anyone. The

founder—old Hall Clements—had left the ranch in trust
for his five surviving children, or their progeny. The ranch
could be sold only if four of the five agreed to it. At the
moment, three wanted to sell; Sarah did not. The fifth vote
remained in trust for the missing heir, Harding Clements.

But it was nearly fifty years since he'd disappeared, and
the others were ready to go to court to have that share divided among all the heirs. A majority could rule that share.

There had been past attempts to locate Harding, but they
had all failed. Sarah had hoped that with all the new tech-
nology, they might have more success. And so, it appeared,
they had. After a four-month search, investigators with the
search firm believed they'd located Harding's daughter.

And no one had any idea what she would do.

"The hell with this," Ross muttered to himself. He had
far better things to do than speculate on the possible actions of some strange woman. He'd had a hard enough
time figuring out what the familiar ones would do.

And there was work. There was always work. He
pushed his hands into his pockets and strode out to the stables. Let the others stew. There was nothing he could do
except pray, and he'd given up on that a long time ago.

two

ATLANTA, GEORGIA

Jessie closed the blind and turned the "Closed" sign toward the outside. Then she opened the door and whistled for Ben. The shaggy white dog rose lazily, shook himself, then followed her out. He didn't need a leash; he wasn't going to get more than a foot away from her. After being a stray, he wasn't going to risk losing his home.

A blast of heat hit her as she left the store. It was eight o'clock but still light, and the air was stagnant and heavy.

It had been a long day, with customers coming in just before closing and lingering. She usually enjoyed them. They were mostly professors and students from Emory University, who loved to browse through the history section. They always stopped to chat, and she would hear historical tidbits about this time or another. These were the hours she liked most, but it had been three days since the burglary, and she had still felt a compelling urgency each day to get home and make sure that no one else had invaded it.

She locked the door and then turned to see a well-dressed man approaching. She expected him to go on to the pizza restaurant next door, though he would look out of place there among the casual college and mussed professor crowd. His clothing, she noticed, was immaculate despite the heat, which meant his suit was very expensive indeed.

He stopped at her doorway.

"I'm sorry," she said. "We're closed."

"I'm not looking for a book," he explained, and she noticed that he had blue Paul Newman eyes that twinkled. "Are you Miss Clayton?"

Warning bells rang in her head. Odd things had happened during the past few days. "It depends on who's asking," she said.

He thrust out a hand. "I'm Alex Kelley."

Anxiety knotted her stomach. "That doesn't explain a lot," she said with unusual waspishness.

"*Are* you Miss Clayton?" He persisted.

"I'm not sure . . ."

Ben seemed to sense her disquiet. Uncharacteristically, he growled.

The stranger leaned down. "I'm not going to hurt her," he explained patiently to the dog.

Ben the optimist stopped growling.

Then the stranger straightened and grinned. "Are you not sure you're Miss Clayton, or not sure you want to admit it?"

She narrowed her eyes, then studied him from his tawny head down to the briefcase he carried. He oozed charm, and she was suspicious of people who oozed charm. But he did not look like a serial killer either.

"A business call?" she said. "We don't buy new books."

"Nope," he said. "I'm worse. I'm an attorney."

She looked down at Ben. "Bite," she ordered.

Instead, Ben pushed against the stranger's legs in a blatant plea for attention.

"Some protection," he observed.

"The police noted the same thing," she replied wryly.

"Police?" His voice was suddenly sharp.

"They were investigating a burglary several days ago."

"Here?"

Jessie was suddenly aware that she was divulging far more information than she intended. She decided to turn businesslike. "What is it exactly that you want? You don't look like a book collector, and I know all our bills are paid."

"Ouch," he said with that easy grin of his. "Although I take it you don't consider lawyers much of a step up from bill collectors."

"Not much. You didn't answer my question."

"I bring you good tidings."

Now she was really suspicious. "A condo in Iceland? An igloo in Chile?"

He laughed. "You really are suspicious."

"Cautious," she corrected. "And I really do want to get home."

"Will you have dinner with me?"

"I would sooner sup with a viper than an attorney." Jessie didn't know why she was being so viperous herself. It was the week. And Alex Kelley's manner. She had a grudge against good-looking men who acted as if they owned the world.

He looked taken aback. She easily imagined that he was rarely refused. He was one of the best-looking men she'd ever met, as well as being an attorney. Which made her doubly wary.

"You really *don't* like lawyers."

"I have good reason."

"All the same, hear me out. Just a few moments. Please. I really do have good news."

"Then why didn't you call and make an appointment?"

"I wasn't sure when I could get to Atlanta, then when I could get in from the airport. I have to leave in the morning."

"Leave to where?"

"Sedona, Arizona."

"Are there igloos in Sedona?"

He grinned again. "Some developers might try to sell you one. They are selling everything else."

"I've heard."

His grin disappeared. His eyes seemed to pierce through her. "What do you know about Arizona?"

She shrugged. "I read a lot."

"Have you ever been there?"

"No." Damn it, he was doing it again. Milking information as if she were a cow, and providing none in return.

She looked at the store. Did she really want to be alone with him? Then she scolded herself. She had never been a coward, except perhaps in relationships. She looked back up at him, and he seemed to read her mind. It was disconcerting.

"I'll tell you what," he finally said. "I'm starving. Why don't I go next door and order a pizza and bring it over? Then Buster can have a piece."

"His name isn't Buster."

"He looks like a Buster to me."

"He doesn't eat from the table," she said sternly. She didn't want the intimacy of sharing a meal in her store.

The lawyer raised an eyebrow. He knew she was lying. Bus . . . Ben's girth was testament to that.

She surrendered. He would probably follow her home if she didn't, and she didn't think she wanted him anywhere around her cottage.

"Pepperoni," she said, unlocking the door into the bookstore.

"And anchovies?" he said hopefully.

"Not on my side."

"Your wish is my command."

"At what price?" she muttered as she went inside the door. Ben hesitated for a moment, then followed, obviously reluctant to leave Alex Kelley.

She heard the man's laugh. Drat it. He'd heard her. But

who cared? She didn't. She would eat the pizza, then get rid of him and whatever scam he intended.

She wouldn't lock the door. She felt safer that way. She was often alone with browsers, salesmen, and the rest, and it had never bothered her.

Why did this man?

But if he meant any harm, he certainly hadn't needed to purchase a pizza first. She tried to busy herself with some paperwork as she tried not to think about what he wanted. But curiosity had always been one of her greatest vices, and now it nagged at her. Good tidings? She didn't believe in fairy tales or genies or dollars from heaven. So what on earth did he want?

All too quickly, it seemed, the door opened, the little bell tinkling.

The lawyer stood in the doorway. "They said it would take twenty minutes."

"I thought you would wait," she said ungraciously.

He shook his head. "You *really* don't like attorneys."

"How nice of you to notice."

"I, Miss Clayton, am going to change your mind."

She was wrong about Alex Kelley trying to sell her a condo in Iceland. Instead, he wanted to sell her a family.

Jessie just stared at him as he sat, then took a folder from his briefcase and passed it over her cluttered desk. "We think your father's real name was Clements."

"We?" Jessie replied incredulously. "Who is we? And that's absurd. My father's name was Clayton. Jon Clayton."

His expression didn't change at her denial. "Did you ever meet any members of his family?"

"No."

He obviously expected the answer, and that bothered her. More than a little. She didn't like the idea of someone

investigating her father, or her. It was obvious that someone had. She let the silence speak her displeasure.

He appeared unfazed by it. "Did you never think that
strange?"

"Why should I? He was an orphan."

"Do you have any proof of that?"

"Why should I need it?" Her anger was building now.
So was a growing dread inside. She remembered the times
she had asked about her father's past, and he'd changed the
subject or grown morose.

"You don't, of course," he said in a soothing tone. "But
my clients believe that your father is a man who's been
missing since nineteen-fifty. And there is no record of your
father prior to nineteen-fifty. No driver's licenses, no credit
reports, no school records, no anything."

She was stunned. She'd found few records when she
was trying to clear his affairs, but he'd never been a pack
rat like she was. He'd never seen the need to keep things
of no use. The memory made her suddenly defensive.
"And why is that anyone's business?"

"His sister has been looking for him all these years. It
wasn't until recently that computers made it far easier to
find people."

"Why would . . . this sister want to find someone who
obviously didn't want to be found?"

He looked at her with something like respect dawning in
his eyes.

"It's a complicated story," he said. "One the family
would like to tell themselves."

"The family?"

"The Clementses. They live near Sedona, Arizona."

The invitation. Jessie felt as if she'd just been struck in
the stomach by a two-by-four. She eyed him warily, trying
to judge the kind of man he was, but she couldn't get behind the surface charm. His eyes said little, and his smile
came far too easily. She wished he weren't so attractive,

but she had a built-in protection system against attractive men. One had charmed her, then violated her in the worst way possible.

She chewed on her lip. In just a few moments, the light had faded into dusk. In a few more moments, it would be totally dark outside. "Why do they care about someone missing nearly fifty years?"

"It's a close-knit family. His sister, Sarah, has been trying to find him all these years."

"How can you be certain my father is the man she's trying to find?"

"We are as sure as we can be without a DNA test. We were hoping you might consent to one."

Her eyes narrowed. "You want me to give you blood?"

"You make it sound much more ominous than it is," he said. "I'm really not Dracula, and neither is the family. In fact, they are all anxious to meet you." He hesitated, then asked, "Did you receive an invitation to a family reunion?"

She hesitated, then said slowly, "Yes. It had no phone number. No address. I assumed it was a mistake."

"The person who sent it—Sarah Macleod—thought I had already contacted you," he said apologetically. "I was delayed."

"Macleod?"

"She's Harding Clements's sister."

Jessie still didn't understand. "I still don't understand why they would care. Even if it is true—and I doubt it—I'm a stranger to them."

"They think you are related by blood. And that is important to them."

"Why?" she asked again.

He blinked for a moment, and she was pleased she had disconcerted him for even a moment. He had disconcerted her considerably.

She took a deep breath. "Things like this do not happen any longer," she said. She felt unsettled, confused, and she didn't care for those feelings. She had finally found her place, had dealt with the uncertainty and loneliness of her childhood. Something inside felt threatened now. The barriers she'd erected to protect herself were far too fragile to confront what this man was saying. A family meant her father had lied to her his entire life. "They went out with gothic novels. Long-lost families just do not materialize out of nowhere."

He raised an eyebrow. "You are the suspicious sort."

"Wouldn't you be?"

"I suppose I would. So let me tell you a story. Harding Clements disappeared without a trace in nineteen-fifty from the Sedona, Arizona, area. No body was ever found, no note ever retrieved. He just disappeared. No one has heard from him since. We think he changed his name to Jonathan Clayton."

"Why?"

"Harding Clements was a well-known horseman. He had magic with animals. When the Clements family started looking for him, they started with racing stables, hunting through employment records."

"That would be impossible."

"Not to those skilled at searching."

"Why would anyone think Harding . . . Clements would change his name, Mr. Kelley?"

He gave her that easy grin that she surmised had broken far too many hearts. "Alex," he said.

She ignored the invitation for familiarity. "Why?" she insisted.

He hesitated, and she knew intuitively that he probably didn't do that very much. He looked as if he were weighing her, trying to decide what to say. That sent a frisson of apprehension up and down her spine. Still, she also felt the stirrings of unrest, even unexpected anticipation. Could any of what he said be true?

After several seconds of silence, he appeared to make a decision. "Did your father ever mention Arizona?"

She shook her head. "He said he liked the East. I wanted him to take me west, but he never wanted to go."

"And I'm told he was very good with horses."

"I imagine you were also told he was very good at drinking."

He had the grace to nod. "Did he ever say anything about his childhood? His family?"

"Why should I tell you anything, Mr. Kelley, when you have told me so little?"

He looked nonplussed at her use of "Mr. Kelley," but he didn't repeat his invitation. "All right, Miss Clayton. Your father disappeared the same day his wife and brother were apparently caught in a forest fire. They were both killed. We think he heard about it and . . . just wanted to get away."

For a moment, Alex Kelley faded away, replaced in her mind by her father, by the grim look in his eyes when she had questioned him about his past, his family. A dozen questions came to her mind, all of them ominous. She choked them back. She was trying to absorb too much information too quickly.

He stood. "I know that I've thrown a great deal at you. And I think it's time to see whether the pizza is ready." He hesitated. "You will be all right here? Alone?"

"I am here alone a great deal of the time, Mr. Kelley," she said. Even she heard the strain in her voice, and she regretted it. For some reason, she did not want to show uncertainty in front of this man.

He glanced around the room, at the numbers of books shelved neatly. He looked at one shelf. "Among friends," he observed with more insight than she would have credited him.

"And with Ben," she added. At the sound of his name, the dog raised his head and thumped his tail against the desk. She leaned down and petted him, taking comfort in the familiar thick fur.

She was aware of the door closing behind the attorney and was thankful for the silence that followed, for the reassuring presence of her dog. *Harding Clements had disappeared the same time his wife and brother had died.*

Jessie felt sick. If her father was indeed Harding Clements, it would explain so many things. His reticence about family, the grief she'd seen in his eyes too many times. She had always thought it was because of her mother, the woman who had abandoned her as a baby. Now she wondered whether it went so much deeper. Another wife. Killed in a fire. She closed her eyes. "Daddy," she whispered. "I hope it wasn't you."

Mistaken identity. *He was very good with horses.* That, apparently, was the connection between Harding Clements and Jon Clayton. Not much linkage. *Unless there was more.*

Just days ago, she was wishing to be a member of a large family. Now she wasn't sure.

Ben got up, stretched and put his head on her lap. "Ah, you don't care who I am, do you?" she said. And suddenly she felt tears in the back of her eyes. Not for herself, but for her father. The man she might never have really known.

The little bell on the door jingled, and Alex Kelley entered with a big flat box and two Cokes. She wondered whether she'd made a mistake talking to him, particularly here. Particularly tonight. He filled the room with his presence, with his energy. And, dammit, with his charm.

He didn't say anything as he set the box down on the desk, offered her some napkins, then a soda. He opened the box, took a long sniff, then sighed with pleasure. "You have no idea how hungry I am," he said.

Strangely enough, or maybe not strangely at all, *her* hunger had disappeared.

He bit into a slice, then grinned at her with delight. She

was grateful that he was no longer pushing her, no longer dropping disturbing pieces of information.

She'd tried not to think of herself as a coward. Not a physical coward, nor even a mental one. She'd confronted too many crises as a child, had been a parent more than a child. But now she wasn't sure she wanted to go on with this, to probe further into a man named Harding Clements.

So they ate in silence, Alex Kelley obviously sensing her need for time, even for distance.

Ben sat, begrudging them both every bite, and she gave him several pieces of crust, then turned her attention back to Alex. *You can't run again,* she told herself. "Tell me why you think this Harding Clements was my father."

"Sarah Macleod, Harding's sister, hired an agency that specializes in finding people. I don't know everything they did, but they started researching horse farms and racing stables, looking for someone of Harding's age and general characteristics. Owners remember good trainers, even if they don't stay long. Using computers, they were able to narrow the list by age and physical features, then started checking out each of the remaining names. Your father had no history before nineteen-fifty. He seemed the most likely prospect."

"Is that it?" she asked. It seemed rather thin to her.

"They found a photo in a magazine. It was rare. He seemed to avoid photographs, but this was an informal shot of Jon Clayton at the stall of one of his horses, a shot he probably didn't realize was being taken. Sarah recognized him."

She bit her lip. Her father *had* avoided cameras, often finding excuses not to go into the winning circle when one of his horses won. "Tell me about them . . . about the Clementses."

"It's a rather large family . . . and powerful. Mary Louise and Hall Clements—Harding's parents—had five boys and one girl. Two of them are still alive: the oldest son, Halden, and the daughter, Sarah." He hesitated, then added, "All the boys had names starting with an H. Makes things confusing at times."

Jessie knew she was certainly confused. And angry. What remained of her pizza grew cold. Her stomach turned into knots. She'd so longed for a large family, had queried her father so many times. What could have happened to make someone abandon his family? Usually when people lost someone they loved, they turned to their family, instead of running from it.

If he was her father. She still couldn't accept that he would have kept something like that from her.

It was a betrayal. A betrayal beyond anything she could imagine. A feeling deep and bitter that quarreled with the occasional flashes of hope. *Could it be true? A family. A family that must have spent tens of thousands of dollars looking for her.*

She continued listening, even as her mind was elsewhere, recalling different conversations with her father, looking for hints. There were none.

Alex Kelley's pleasant Texas drawl lapsed into a silence louder than any scream, a silence she felt in her bones.

She felt schizophrenic. She didn't want it to be true. She didn't want to accept that her father had lied to her his entire life, that her life had been a lie. That her name wasn't really hers. And yet another part of her wanted it to be true. She wanted a family. A family like other people had. A home place. *Roots.*

"Sarah is convinced that you are her niece." He had started talking again. "She wants you to come to the family reunion in two weeks. She wants to meet you and let you meet your cousins. We will pay all your expenses, of course."

Alex Kelley waited. It was as if he knew that any pressure would affect her negatively.

She looked up at him, up from the cold pizza. "I don't know whether I can get away. I have the shop. And Ben."

"You have a partner, don't you?"

She narrowed her eyes.

"I'm afraid the search firm did some investigating of you, too," he admitted easily.

"How much?"

"Investigating?"

"Yes."

"Enough. We know your father left an inheritance that allowed you to attend Emory University with enough left over to buy part of this business. We know you are single and that you own this store with your partner."

She felt invaded again, just as she had after the burglary. Someone was looking into her life without her knowledge. She suspected that he also knew much more than he was admitting.

"Sedona is a marvelous place," he said, obviously trying to change the subject. "If you have never been there, you owe it to yourself to visit. The Clementses own a large ranch twelve miles north, and one of the family owns the Quest Resort. You can stay at either place. I think Sarah would like it if you stayed at the ranch."

Jessie tried to take it all in. "A ranch?"

"The Clements family as a whole owns the Red Rock Ranch, better known as the Sunset. They run cattle, though most of the grazing land is leased from the government. Ross, the manager, also raises cutting horses."

Images danced in Jessie's head of all the western movies she'd seen and adored. She'd not been able to budge her father past the Mississippi, or even as far as Kentucky until the end when he could no longer find a job in New York or Maryland or Virginia.

Now that reluctance took on new significance.

Still, she couldn't quite believe. She wasn't sure she wanted to believe. It was one thing to dream. It was another to have dreams come true. They never came true like the dreamer envisioned. *Be careful what you wish for.*

Ben wriggled next to her. She knew he had to go outside to attend to business. He'd had a long day inside.

Jessie stood. "It's time for me to go home," she said.

He looked rueful. "I haven't convinced you."

"Is that rare?"

He grinned. "Not as rare as I would hope."

That damnable charm continued to flow. He was the kind of man, she thought, that usually had a slim, blond beauty on his arm, but at the moment he made her feel like the most important person in the world. And she found herself recoiling from that. This was business for him, and it was his job to persuade her to travel to Arizona.

Mills had exuded charm just as this man had. And Mills had been the worst thing that had ever happened to her. A chill ran through her as she tried to banish him from her thoughts.

Alex Kelley seemed to realize he was losing her. "Any other questions?"

"A million," she said, "but first I have to . . . let this sink in."

"Perhaps you will meet me for breakfast. My plane leaves at noon."

She hesitated.

"Bright sunshine," he tempted. "No Draculas."

"But you still want my blood."

He looked chagrined. "I'm afraid it's necessary."

"Only if I accept the possibility that . . . this family could be my father's."

"And yours."

She wanted to retort. She wanted to say that accepting that fact would mean admitting that her father might have lied to her all her life.

She finally nodded. She'd made her point. The shop didn't open until ten. And tomorrow Sol would return from his latest pilgrimage to Andersonville. He was writing his own book on the former Confederate prison, but she suspected he would never finish. It was the research he loved. He'd spent the last ten years hunting for diaries from men imprisoned there and the guards charged with holding them.

Perhaps he could keep Ben for her . . . if she decided to go to Sedona. He and Ben had a fine relationship.

Deep in her heart she already knew she was going. How could she not? She had been curious all her life. She found it difficult to let a question go unanswered. And yet she had left important ones unanswered. She knew that now. She'd never pried deeply into her father's past. *Because she feared the answers?*

And yet for some reason, she was reluctant to let Alex Kelley know she'd already made a decision. She didn't want to make it easy for him. She'd worked too hard to be strong, to be wise, to protect herself.

"Any suggestions for breakfast?" His question jolted her back to the present and she suspected he'd read her mind.

"Where are you staying?"

He shrugged. "I don't have a place yet. I came here right from the airport. Apparently there was an accident on the freeway and it took me longer than I thought."

Ah, she knew about that. One accident on an Atlanta freeway and everyone was stalled for hours. "There's a hotel around the corner," she suggested.

"Thank you," he said solemnly.

She nodded. "You have a car?"

"Yes."

"Go to the intersection, turn right. It's two blocks on the left."

"And breakfast?"

"There's a restaurant next door. I'll meet you at eight."

"Thank you, Miss Clayton."

She smiled for the first time. "Jessie," she said.

• • •

Jessie searched the web for information on Sedona. Beside the computer were several books she'd located at the store before leaving. One was a travel guide of Arizona. The others came from the American West history section. There was an advantage of being part owner of a book-store.

There was very little about the Sedona area in the history books. It had been settled fairly late in the 1800s by white settlers, though it had a long and rich history with early Indians and then later with Apaches and Yavapai.

Ben whined for attention, something he seldom did. Usually, he was content with just her company. It was as if he knew something was puzzling her, that all was not normal with their usually complacent life.

"I'm becoming obsessed," she told him.

He licked her, telling her that obsession was just fine as long as it didn't interfere with him.

She turned the computer off and stood, going over to the fireplace and the mantel. She touched one of the carousel horses, the first of her collection. As a child, she'd saved for the longest time to buy it, though it was an inexpensive imitation. But that hadn't mattered to her.

"But Daddy, I want to ride the merry-go-round."

Her father sighed. "We don't have time, Jessica. Now stop whining."

But she wanted it badly enough to pull on his hand. "Please."

"Dammit, I have to look at the horses for Mr. Daley. Don't be a baby."

"But Daddy . . ."

He turned then, fury on his face. He bent down and slapped her bottom so hard she could barely keep from yelling.

He pulled her along then as she looked back at the chil-

*dren being put on horses by their daddies and wanted . . .
oh how she wanted . . .*

She'd never had that ride, but the dream stayed in her mind, and when she'd seen a carousel horse in a store, she'd very carefully saved every penny she had, the nickels and dimes that people around the track gave her. And she'd bought her own horse. Later, as an adult, she started collecting originals. She wondered once what a psychologist would think. Was she subconsciously reliving painful memories or triumphing over them?

Later, of course, she'd learned to ride. Her father hadn't taught her. An exercise boy had. It was the one time she remembered pleasing her father, the first time he had watched her ride around the track at twelve. He said she had a natural seat and good hands, and eventually she'd become an exercise girl herself.

Jessie replaced the horse on the mantel, and the memories in the attic of her mind. Too much had been dredged up today. Too many emotions. Too many memories.

She thought about Alex Kelley. She sensed there was much he had not told her, that he had picked carefully through information for what he wanted to say.

Sedona. She tried the sound on her tongue. Should it ring bells? Had her father ever let the name slip from his lips?

One of five brothers. And one brother died the day Harding Clements disappeared from Sedona. Had he witnessed his brother's death and that of his wife? And finally, the question that plagued her most. Had he had something to do with their deaths? She tried not to even entertain the thought, but it resounded in her mind. And in her heart.

She couldn't avoid the idea that going to Sedona might open a Pandora's box. That it *would* open one.

How many times, she wondered, had flies flown voluntarily into a spider's web?

• • •

Alex Kelley knew he had succeeded. He knew it when she consented to having breakfast with him.

He had wondered whether he should mention the possible inheritance. But he had wanted to take a measure of her first. And it was more difficult than he had thought.

Jessica Clayton had given away very little. And she seemed impervious to the charm that he'd cultivated. That had surprised and intrigued him.

Most people would have jumped at what he had offered. The fact that she'd not done so gave him pause.

Did she know more than she pretended?

Or had she just learned to keep her own counsel?

Her life must have been hell, according to the reports from the detective agency. A father who drank to excess, who hadn't been able to keep a job. The wonder was that he had left her anything at all, much less enough to send her through Emory. It was rumored he gambled heavily. On his own horses? Or on those running against his own horses? Harding was supposed to have been the brother with integrity. Until he disappeared, that is, leaving a number of suspicions behind.

Alex had been convinced by both the agency and Sarah that Jonathan Clayton was indeed Harding Clements. It was the others who demanded a DNA test. They were the ones who stood to lose millions of dollars.

He looked around his room. It was pleasant enough, and he was too tired to do anything but go to bed. The last month had been pure hell, and he was weary of twenty-hour workdays, but one of the companies he represented had been sued, and the case had come to court a week ago.

And Sarah had not been willing to wait. Not a week. Not a day. Too much depended on Jessica.

Perhaps he should have warned Miss Clayton. She would be walking right into the middle of a family feud.

He tossed his small bag on the bed, then took a quick shower. He couldn't get Jessica Clayton out of his mind.

She was attractive but not a beauty by any means. Her eyes were by far her best feature: an intriguing hazel with golden flecks. They were wide with rich dark lashes framing them. Her short auburn hair was prettily tousled, and yet it was the haircut of someone who didn't overly fuss with it.

He liked her. No nonsense. No games. And she'd evidently been singularly unimpressed with him. He'd noted she'd not replenished her makeup while he went out for the pizza. It had been a bit demoralizing. He usually did very well with the opposite sex—mainly, he'd always thought, because he genuinely liked women. He came into contact with some very smart ones, and he'd known instantly that Jessica Clayton was one of those.

She had a steady gaze that probed, as well as a patience that waited for someone else to make a mistake before she did. It was a rare trait.

Sarah, he thought, would be pleased.

But would Jessica Clayton? Particularly when he introduced her to the volatile mix that was the current Clements family.

three

Jessie tortured herself with questions as the plane approached Phoenix. She already missed the safety of the bookstore, the comforting smell of leather binding, old paper, and even dust. She already missed Ben. Guilt ate at her every time she remembered the accusation in his eyes when she dropped him at Sol's house.

In the three years since she had found him wandering alongside a major highway, she hadn't left him with anyone. She had made him her family. He and Sol had been all she needed. Or so she had told herself.

She looked out the window. Not many trees, not at all like Atlanta. It was more like an alien landscape. Mountains rose out of nowhere, then reclined back into flat earth. A few scattered clumps of green broke an endless tan carpet.

Jessie sat back in the plush seat. She had certainly not expected a first-class seat when Alex said the family would provide the airfare. But she had never flown that way before, and she enjoyed every moment of being pampered. Alex had also said she would be met by someone and driven up to Sedona, but she had insisted on renting a car. She wanted the independence of her own transportation.

The freedom to escape.

She really wanted to do that at this very moment.

She recalled the breakfast meeting with Alex Kelley. He'd added little real information about the circumstances of Harding Clements's disappearance, which was really what she wanted. Instead, he discussed the various relatives she would meet. Foremost, in his estimation, was Sarah, who was seventy-six, and the matriarch of the family. She had an adopted son, Ross, who ran the ranch.

Then there was Halden, Sarah's brother and the oldest of the family. He was ninety-one, still mentally sharp but irascible. He had two living children—sons. One was a congressman preparing to run for the U.S. Senate, the other a banker who was also the owner of the resort where she would stay. Alex had also mentioned a number of others, insisting they were all eager to meet her.

Why? Why would they try so hard to find, and meet, someone they had never known?

A nagging doubt persisted that something far more than a family trying to find a lost sheep could be in play. But then maybe it was all the books she read. She'd fantasized since she was a child and found comfort in the nearest library, especially when her father was on one of his drunken binges. She'd fantasized that she was part of the novel she read—the beautiful princess, the dashing hero whom everyone loved and admired, or the little lost girl reunited with loving parents. The books were her private world and when she didn't have one, she'd made up stories in her head.

She told herself she was making one up now.

And what better scenario than the one that had presented itself just a few weeks ago? A handsome lawyer. A new family. A ranch in Arizona. The only thing missing was being an heiress.

She looked at the book in her lap. She always had one with her, but for one of the few times in her life she hadn't been able to read. She wished the rumblings of apprehension would fade. If the visit worked out, then fine. If it didn't, well, then she hadn't lost anything. Except the peace she'd worked so hard for, except for the crumbling of the barricades she'd wrapped around herself.

She kept telling herself she had an ally in Alex, but she wasn't even sure about that. She couldn't escape the feeling that he had withheld important pieces of the puzzle. The question was why.

Nonsense. She was just creating problems in her mind. She would enjoy this adventure, the chance to see a part of the country she'd always longed to visit. Perhaps she would even ride again. Her heart pounded faster at the idea. Life was stirring back in her body, in her heart.

And she wanted to learn more about Harding Clements. She wanted to know if her father had indeed hid his past, and why. She wanted to know what had caused the sadness in his eyes, the detachment in his heart.

The pilot came on the intercom and announced their approach into Phoenix. She looked at her watch. About three or four hours until she reached Sedona. Perhaps then she would learn answers to some of those questions.

Ross felt his gut turn somersaults. Everything he had worked so goddamn hard for was at risk. But he tried to submerge those feelings now. Horses sensed turmoil, uncertainty. Particularly skittish youngsters like this one.

He snapped the rope in his hands. *Keep the colt going. Keep him at an easy trot around the ring.* By the end of the day, if he had no interruptions, the colt would be broken to saddle. Then the tedious work began. But it was work he loved.

How much longer would he have it?

The youngster had slowed. Ross moved, snaking out the rope, pushing the colt to speed his pace.

Keep your attention on the animal, dammit. His mind

kept wandering, though, to the command performance he had to attend tonight. He'd tried to squirm out, but Sarah had made it quite clear he was expected to attend.

He hated the biannual reunions. He'd always felt like an outsider, an interloper, a fraud. For various reasons, mostly Sarah, he had stayed at the Sunset long past the time he'd known it wise to go. Now he had his entire life invested in it. He'd almost come to think of it as home. The only real home he'd ever had. And yet he'd also realized he never really belonged here.

That knowledge had been a burr under his skin. God only knew he'd fought establishing an attachment to this land. To Sarah. He'd always believed it would be jerked away, just as so many other things had been. But now the Sunset was in his blood, the land his very soul, the horses his future. And the whole damn thing was about to be pulled out from under him.

And by an outsider just like him. Yet that outsider had the blood he could not claim.

The colt was quickly tiring. A few more rounds and he would halter the youngster, then allow him to grow used to the saddle. No violent confrontations between man and beast, merely a subtle building of trust between them, of understanding as to which was dominant.

Ross loved these sessions in the round pen. He enjoyed it far more than the spring and fall roundups of the cattle, and certainly more than the paperwork, especially that involved in leasing so much government land for grazing. Cattle, particularly in this country, were becoming a losing proposition. The value of a good cutting horse, though, was spiraling upward for reasons best not dwelt upon. What little profit the ranch produced now came from the horses. He wanted to enlarge the program, but he couldn't as long as the fate of the ranch hung on such slender threads.

Its immediate sale would bring millions to the Clementses, not just a promise of later profits.

But how could anyone even consider selling a legend?

He looked up at the red mountains in the distance. God, he loved them. He loved their secrets. The thought of turning this land into small lots made him physically ill.

The colt snorted, aware again of his lack of attention. Ross spoke softly, calming him, then approached with confidence, always keeping to the side or front. He slipped the lariat around the animal's head, waited as the youngster tested it, then stood quietly. "Good boy," he soothed.

The animal tossed his head but stood quietly as Ross placed a saddle pad on the horse's back. The horse bucked slightly at the unfamiliar object, then stilled again. After several more rounds, Ross saddled him and started him around the ring again, allowing him to become accustomed to carrying the weight.

He forced all his concentration on the animal, a buckskin with all the breeding, instincts, and natural moves of a champion cutting horse. Several such animals, and he could name his own prices for Sunset horses.

After several hours, the horse was accustomed to the rope, and the saddle. *The moment of truth was here.* He slowly lifted himself into the saddle. The horse danced nervously for a moment, then quieted, and Ross felt the supreme satisfaction of accomplishment. With a touch of Ross's heels, the horse circled the ring.

Ross tried to concentrate, but his mind kept returning to thoughts of the god-awful party tonight.

He heard Timber bark behind him. Even the dog was reminding him he was running late. The animal was uncanny. "Be patient, Timber," he said, and the dog lay down, putting his head between his front paws. Timber always knew what he was thinking. He might have looked like a hound from hell, but the part-wolf, part-dog mixture was the smartest animal he'd ever trained.

Timber didn't care if his master was charming.

But Sarah sure as hell did. She'd pleaded with him to be charming.

He grimaced at the thought. Hell, he didn't know a damn thing about being charming. He didn't care to know.

He would leave that up to Alex.

The ride up to Sedona was fascinating. Spectacular. If only all the *if*s didn't eat at her. If only her stomach hadn't turned into a South American forest full of butterflies. She drank in the vistas, the saguaro and other varieties of cactus. It was a world apart from the lush forests she knew. An alien world but beautiful in its own stark way.

She sped by places called Deadman's Creek and Sunset Point and Black Canyon, longing to stop and explore the small winding roads that led to those intriguing-sounding locations. But she was committed to a party tonight, a welcoming get-together.

An inspection, she feared. An inspection she was sure to fail. She was only too aware of her limited wardrobe. She'd bought several silk blouses and one elegant pantsuit for the trip. She'd added a skirt and several pairs of slacks from her own wardrobe. Inadequate, she thought, for one of the premier ranching families in Arizona, but she wasn't willing to pretend she was something she was not. Nor spend a fortune doing it.

She didn't have an awe of politicians or of wealth, having seen too much of both on the horse farms. She was, instead, wary of anyone with inherited wealth. She had believed herself in love with one young scion of a wealthy family, and he'd turned out to be both vicious and duplicitous. Since then, she'd been reluctant to trust many people. But she wanted to trust Alex Kelley. She really wanted it.

As her car climbed higher into the Colorado rim, she became enraptured by the strangely beautiful land. Was this her heritage? Was this land in her blood? Was that why she felt such a rising excitement? Yet, she had not agreed to a DNA test. It represented a commitment to her. She wasn't ready to make that commitment. She wasn't ready to believe that fairy tales really did come true. Neither could she quite concede that her father had lied to her all these years.

Maybe she wouldn't want to be related to this family.

She wished, more than anything, that her emotions didn't run amok, that she could be practical and measured and objective, as she'd tried so hard to be about her life. She'd sworn never to be ruled again by impulses, to allow them to overcome her good sense.

But now she was a squirming mess of conflicting cautions, hopes, and dreams, and nothing she did seemed to tamp them down.

A family. A huge family. And horses.

Could she bear being around horses again? Live ones. She'd been collecting china ones for years, her safe substitute for live ones. She had given up what she once loved best after the nightmare of her father's death. Given up? No, she'd run from everything that reminded her of that night.

She knew now she hadn't entirely succeeded. Her carousel horses were her substitute, steeds to take her off on adventures and away from her father's too-often drunken spells and later from memories.

Could she dare dream once more?

Alex lounged in the foyer of the Quest, waiting for Jessica to check in.

He debated how much warning to give her. He had learned far more about her than she'd ever guessed. Some he'd shared with the family, some he had not.

He had admitted to some investigation, but not to the extent of it. In fact, Sarah knew more than the others, and that was not all. It had been Sarah's money that financed the search, and he'd felt honor-bound to give all that information to her, but then he'd had reason to personally extend the investigation, and those findings belonged to him and only him. He too had a lot at stake in the upcoming family battle. He'd wanted to know everything there was to know about Jessica Clayton.

After learning what he had, he'd expected her caution. He'd made a few assessments from his conversations with her but unlike most women, she was accomplished at masking her feelings.

He knew that there was a bottle of champagne in her room, ordered by Congressman Marc Clements; a basket of fruit from Sarah; and God only knew what else from other members of the family. Even without the DNA results, they were all trying to position themselves. If they weren't careful, they would send Jessica Clayton running back to Atlanta. He didn't think she suffered fools lightly.

He wished for a cigar at times like this. He'd stopped smoking years ago, but the longing remained with him. Especially at stressful times.

He looked at his watch. She should have arrived in Phoenix four hours earlier. Depending on how she drove, she should be here shortly. Or had she changed her mind about coming?

Not for the first time, he wondered why he stayed with the family. Its various members and their enterprises constituted more than fifty percent of his law firm's time, as they had his father's practice but he knew he could do far better financially in Phoenix. Still, he stayed. He'd inherited the practice when his father died, and Alex, like his father, had become an extended member of the family. He was like Ross in that aspect. Almost a Clements, but not quite.

The work had been varied and challenging these past twelve years. He'd interpreted the provisions of a very complicated will, seen to the government lease contracts, and negotiated land sales for the Quest. He'd also bailed Cullen's twins out of jail, kept secrets no outsider should know, and tried to keep peace among the family members.

Now he would have to take sides, and he hadn't decided yet which side he would choose. He liked Sarah enormously, but she lived in the past. His firm stood to make a fortune if the ranch was sold, and he was never adverse to money.

Marc wanted the sale. With adequate financing, he was a shoo-in to be elected senator—and then who knew how far he would go? He had hopes, Alex knew, of running for president. Marc's friends would travel a long way with him, too.

Every pot was ready to boil. He just didn't know which would boil over first.

For the moment, Alex was keeping his options open.

He looked at his watch again. Should he keep waiting? Would she even want him to be here? But he was the one who had lured her here, and he felt a certain responsibility. He wondered whether he should even have reported the search firm's finding. Whatever else she'd had, Jessica Clayton had undergone more than her share of betrayal and pain.

The entrance door opened and the object of his thoughts entered.

She looked startled as he stood. "Are you the innkeeper, too?" she asked.

"Just the welcoming committee," he said, holding out his hand and taking hers. He looked over at the desk and the well-groomed young man behind it. "You don't have to check in. I have your key."

She nodded, her gaze steady but wary. She wore a pair of jeans that fit, but not too tightly, and a green knit shirt that brought out a compelling green in her changeable eyes. Nothing pretentious. Just comfortable, and he was reminded how much he'd liked her. He liked her challenging manner, her forthrightness, and her intelligence. He should tell her to turn around and leave.

Instead, he gave her his most charming smile. "I thought you might like to see a friendly face. I'll show you your room, then you can get a couple of hours of rest before the party tonight."

He saw doubt flicker in her eyes and reminded himself again to be careful. She had reason not to trust easily.

She finally smiled. But he saw the uncertainty behind it. "No signature? No credit card?"

"Everything is already done," he said. "The family asked you here, and the family owns this place."

She looked around the luxurious but informal lobby. A huge fireplace took up one wall. Comfortable little groups of chairs and loveseats were clustered throughout the room, interspersed by giant ferns. A glass cage filled with live colorful birds ran along one side of the room. The smell of leather and newly cut flowers permeated the air.

"Wine and cheese are served in the afternoon," Alex explained. "And the restaurant is very good."

"It's lovely," she said.

"It's Cullen's pride and joy. I'll drive you around to your room, then pick you up at six-thirty for the party tonight."

He knew from the instant question in her eyes that he'd assumed too much. Her back stiffened.

"You will never find the ranch yourself," he added, trying to smooth his blunder. "Even longtime residents can't find it. There are no directional signs and you have to wind around up into the hills."

She raised an eyebrow.

"Sarah says it keeps the salesmen away. Personally, I think Ross dismantled all the signs, hoping no one would find it."

She remembered the name. The cousin who ran the ranch. Alex, though, had said less about him than the others. "Tell me about him."

"Ross?" He shrugged. "He's a loner. He may not even be at the party tonight unless Sarah somehow talks him into it. He considers social events the next thing to hell. He might even consider them worse than hell. Just don't let him intimidate you."

"Intimidate *moi*?" she replied teasingly, a certain bravado masking the apprehension she felt growing with every new description of this family that apparently wanted to claim her as their own. "Not even an attorney could do that."

"I noticed," he answered wryly, then steered her toward the door. "But you haven't met Ross. He glowers at anything and everybody except his beloved horses."

She seemed to weigh that, cataloging the piece of information in her mind. He could almost see it working. Obviously uncertain and just as obviously hating that uncertainty, she asked hesitantly, "What should I wear tonight?"

"It will be very informal," he said. "The Sunset is a working ranch."

"The Sunset?"

"The Clementses' ranch is officially the Double R for Red Rock Ranch. But the founder's wife—Mary Louise Clements—arrived at the site at sunset. She thought it glorious and started calling the ranch the Sunset. Everyone just adopted it. But in answer to your question, no one dresses up much. A pair of slacks and shirt will be just fine."

She looked at him dubiously.

"You think I would lie?"

"You're a lawyer."

"You haven't gotten over that yet?" he asked, a twinkle in his eyes. "The worst thing about my chosen profession is all the lawyer jokes and misconceptions." He guided her out the door, then looked at her rental car. "Your room is really a casita, a small cottage. It overlooks a creek and you can sit outside and just listen to it gurgle if the family gets to be too much. It's peaceful, the perfect place to read a book."

She smiled, and this time it was real, even radiant. It transformed her from an attractive woman into an immensely appealing one.

Guilt started to gnaw at him. So did something else, and that startled him. He wouldn't, couldn't become interested in her. Too much was at stake.

She stopped at the car, and he reached for her keys. "Let me drive you down there and help you carry the luggage inside."

Jessie hesitated, then agreed. She gave him the car keys and got in on the passenger side without waiting for him to open the door. He backed the car up, then drove it to the end of the drive. He'd always marveled at the design of the resort, and he noticed that she too awed. The Southwestern contemporary-styled building blended perfectly into the red rock terrain. Red tile roofs gave it an expensive, sophisticated look.

Cullen had searched out the best architects for this resort and spent millions to create something unique. The cost overrides had been terrific, and the property still hadn't yet made a profit despite its popularity with tourists. Cullen would feel the financial yoke around his neck for years unless . . .

But that was Cullen's problem, not Alex's. He had warned the oldest of the Clements cousins about overreaching, a warning that had been ignored.

Alex drove his passenger to a small group of casitas, separate little cottages situated alongside a creek that tumbled merrily down from a cliff behind it. He suspected she would like the privacy it provided, especially with all the pressure Sarah would exert to get her to move into the ranch house. Sarah had been profoundly disappointed that

Jessica had decided to stay in Sedona at the Quest rather than at the Sunset.

She would soon discover that her probable niece had a mind of her own.

Alex parked the car in front of the first casita, then got out and opened the truck and lifted her suitcase from it. Then he unlocked the door of the casita and stood aside as she entered.

He heard the intake of her breath and smiled to himself. She wasn't quite as indifferent as she tried to be.

"I'll pick you up at six-thirty," he said again.

She merely nodded as her gaze continued to roam around the room, resting on a table laden with gifts.

A good time for him to disappear. She was already getting under his skin. Her spontaneous reaction to something he took for granted was surprisingly endearing.

He placed the suitcase inside, closed the door behind him as he went outside, and walked back to the main building.

He looked at his watch. A few hours before he would meet her again. He might as well return to his office. Maybe work would take his mind off her. Dammit, but he hoped so.

four

Jessie felt like an alien as Alex drove her toward her first meeting with her potential family. She thought of it like that. Potential. Not sure. Probably not even likely.

The sun was beginning to set, its glow appearing to ignite the red rock, turning it to fire. The sky itself was ribboned with magnificent colors ranging from pure gold to scarlet. The sheer beauty of it made her ache.

"I told you it was spectacular," Alex said.

"So you did," she said, grateful for his matter-of-fact presence. He had driven her from the resort, which itself had been an experience. Her room was large and equipped with any number of luxuries, including a Jacuzzi bath, fully stocked bar, fluffy white robes, and a gloriously comfortable bed. Even more amazing had been the assortment of items awaiting her: a bottle of expensive champagne, a huge bowl of fruit, crackers and cheese, and two fresh bouquets of flowers. At least someone was certainly trying to make her feel welcome. Several someones, according to the cards attached to the gifts.

She was beginning to feel like Alice in Wonderland. She only hoped she wouldn't be meeting some of the book's inhabitants. The Cheshire Cat, for instance. He'd lured poor unsuspecting Alice into a false security. Was Alex *her* Cheshire Cat, luring her into the same sense of security with his charming smile? She reminded herself that if something seemed too good to be true, it probably was. Little was ever as it seemed, and she'd be wise to keep that lesson in mind, unlike the headstrong Alice . . .

She folded her legs, betraying a nervousness she'd tried to hide. She prayed she was dressed correctly: a pair of gray tailored slacks, a peach silk blouse, and a silver necklace of twenty fine strands. She had been careful with makeup, using just a touch of powder and mascara in addition to her lipstick. Then she'd stood in front of the mirror, regarding herself critically. Nothing special there. No heiress. No princess. No Cinderella. Just plain Jessie who lived in a small book-crowded cottage and barely made a living selling her tomes.

She'd been unprepared for the appreciative look she saw in Alex's eyes when he'd picked her up.

"You look very pretty," he said, and she felt a flush of pleasure. She was glad he hadn't used grander words, because she wouldn't have believed him then. But his quiet compliment gave her a flush of confidence.

She'd made him go over the members of the family again, telling her about what each of them did. She remembered the congressman, of course, and after a few hours at the Quest felt she knew something of Cullen, the man who had built the hotel. She'd learned more about his children—twins. One apparently managed the resort. The other was a city councilman in a nearby town.

She had tried to inventory the others, but the one that intrigued her was Ross, possibly because of the way Alex avoided talking about him. She wondered if he would be present tonight. Jitters intensified inside her.

She asked questions as Alex drove from Sedona. He drove a luxurious sports vehicle, and she noticed that it was only one of many on the road. Nearly everyone, it seemed, drove either a sports vehicle, a Jeep, or a pickup truck. She turned her attention from the road to the land around them, searching for cattle but not finding any. The dry land appeared hostile to any type of life.

"Are there no cattle?" she asked.

"They've been taken up to higher pastures," he said. "In the fall, Ross will bring them down."

She found herself speaking to keep her nervousness from roiling too violently. "It doesn't look like it would feed very many."

"It doesn't. It takes twenty acres to feed a unit."

"A unit?"

"A cow and calf," he said.

Twenty acres for one cow and calf. She could barely imagine it. "But a ranch would require so much land."

"It does, but most of it is leased from the government. The Clementses have the original homestead claim of three hundred twenty acres, then bought out other ranchers. They own a total of nine hundred acres and lease thousands more from the government."

She mentally tried to total up the number of cattle that would support, but without success.

They started climbing, the road twisting and changing, bordered on each side by strands of wire. She wondered how wise she'd been to come with him as the sun started to fall and she still saw no sign of human habitation.

Alex turned off the main road onto a dirt road. After approximately five minutes, they rode over a rise and she saw a cluster of buildings sitting amid a clump of trees. A sprawling house of rock and wood was surrounded by several outbuildings, including a newly painted barn that was fronted by a riding ring. To its side was a smaller house. Then there were several sheds.

Horses grazed in a pasture just beyond the barn; even from here she recognized quality. Her father had taught her that.

Her gaze went back to what was obviously the main house. The building itself had little grace but looked as if it had been built in haphazard fashion, a new wing here, a new room there. Part of the structure was rock, part frame. A rocking-chair porch wrapped around the front and sides. Rosebushes brimming with coral and crimson blooms framed the house in well-tended beds.

The Sunset didn't have the grandeur of Southfork from *Dallas,* but it had a warm charm about it. She looked around. The sun was descending in an apricot sky and its rays hit the red rock cliff behind the house. She didn't even try to stifle an exclamation of delight as shafts of light turned the rock into flaming gold.

Jessie saw several figures around the corral and three more on the porch. They disappeared inside as the car drew up, perhaps to announce a new presence. Alex had already stopped the vehicle and gone around to her side. He gave her his hand, and she slipped out. He held on to it, as if he knew she needed this support.

She tightened her fingers around his for a moment, then let them go. She said a brief prayer as they approached the door, and it opened.

An older woman appeared at the doorway. Her hair was short and gray, and her skin was dark and weathered. She wore denim trousers, a tan shirt, and a suede vest decorated with what looked like turquoise. Lively hazel eyes, the same color as Jessie's, searched her face, then the woman's lips spread into a warm smile.

"Jessica," she said, reaching out with both hands. "Welcome to the Sunset. I'm Sarah Macleod," she said, without giving Alex a chance to introduce them. The older woman took her hand. "You don't mind, do you, Jessica?" she'd asked.

Jessie realized immediately she did not. She instantly liked the older woman, who looked as if she were in her mid-seventies but moved like a much younger person. Warmth exuded from her, but Jessie saw a flash of uncertainty in her eyes, and that made her clasp the woman's hand. They had something in common, both of them. Neither was as assured as she'd wanted to be. That realization made her like Sarah Macleod far more than certainty would.

The evening became a blur of names and faces.

Sarah was memorable, as was Halden. He was obviously the patriarch of the family and sat in what looked like the most comfortable chair in the room. He looked to be in his eighties or so, and he had a thatch of white hair over a face inlaid with wrinkled trails. Calm hazel eyes, like those of Sarah and her own, peered at her with interest. "You have the look of a Clements," he said in a surprisingly strong voice, though he didn't try to stand.

She wasn't sure whether the comment called for an answer or not, so she just stood straight under his searching gaze.

"That's a compliment, girl," he added, a slight twinkle in his eyes.

"Thank you," she replied.

"You have doubts?"

"I've never believed in fairy tales," she said honestly.

"Good for you. I never did, either. A good, healthy doubt now and then won't hurt anyone. Some in this family would be better off it they didn't count their chickens before they hatched." His gaze left her face to wander about the room, leaving her to puzzle over the remark.

She turned to look at Sarah, and was surprised at the expression that flitted across her face. Fear? But it disappeared quickly. Sarah tugged slightly on her hand. "Let me show you some photos."

But before they had moved two feet, they were stopped by a tall, distinguished man. That he was related to Halden was obvious, except he had spectacular eyes as blue as a summer's sky. Clear. Bright. Probing. "I'm

Marc Clements," he said easily, taking her free hand and holding it as if it were a treasure of some sort.

The congressman. She would have known it instantly, even if he hadn't mentioned his name.

He'd given her a smile even more charming than Alex's, and the room seemed to still with his magnetism. Jessie guessed his age at early fifties, but she couldn't be sure. She only knew that he made her feel like the most important person in the room.

"My cousin," he said as the lines around his eyes creased with warmth. His smile widened.

She was surprised at the depth of pleasure filling her. She'd felt at ease with Sarah and now with this man. It was odd because she generally was reserved, even shy, with strangers. Alex's easy manner had torn down some of her wariness, and now she felt caught in a glow of belonging.

"I'm . . . not sure," she said, almost stuttering. She had tried so hard to stay objective, but she found herself melting under all the acceptance she felt. *A family.* A family that seemed absolutely perfect.

"You look just like the pictures of Sarah when she was young," Marc Clements said. "She pulled them out before you arrived."

"I was just going to show them to her," Sarah said. Jessie thought she heard irritation in her voice. Or was it merely impatience?

If it was there, Marc Clements ignored it. "We've been hoping you would stay longer than this weekend. Family is important to us all." A very pretty blond woman came over to him, and the congressman put his arm around her. "This is Samantha, my wife and best political asset."

"Jessica," Samantha acknowledged, but her eyes didn't warm as her husband's had. Jessie had the sudden, unpleasant impression of being under a microscope, and the viewer was looking for a particularly obnoxious bug. But then Samantha smiled, and Jessie could see why the congressman had said what he had about her being a political asset. She also wondered whether she had been mistaken, whether she'd read something into a moment's hesitation that didn't belong there.

"Please call me Jessie," she said. "Everyone does."

"But Jessica is such a pretty name," Samantha said.

"Only my father called me that," she said in a voice tighter than she intended.

The silence was deafening. It was the first time, she suddenly realized, that he had been mentioned. He was, however, like a ghost in the room. She hadn't realized it until this moment.

"Don't you all monopolize her." The booming voice belonged to a tall, commanding figure of a man standing next to a tiny woman. He had blue eyes like the congressman, but they were a paler shade, almost gray.

Marc smiled wryly and turned to him. "Jessie, this is my brother, Cullen, and his wife, Sondra. Those identical images in the corner are his twin sons."

"She sure is as pretty as a Clements," Cullen said. "She looks just like Sarah . . ."

Marc had charisma, but this man was like a bounding Labrador retriever. He had an exuberance that made his brother look reticent and reserved.

He leaned over and kissed her on the cheek, making her feel indeed like the long-lost prodigal daughter.

Jessie felt almost inconsequential between the force of these two men, both of whom seemed determined to make her feel as if she belonged. She tried to reclaim part of herself. "You're the one who built the Quest," she said. "It's wonderful. Thank you for letting me stay there."

"Delighted, cousin." He looked at Marc. "I told you she would like it."

Marc glanced at Sarah, whose face tightened. Jessie felt a sudden chill as she noted the exchange. She was aware of a tension between the three, almost as if the brothers were claiming some kind of subtle triumph.

She felt a tug on her arm. "I am going to steal her away," Sarah said.

Jessie allowed herself to be led from the room, grateful for a moment's reprieve from that momentary discomfiture from the many faces, from the expectation she saw in them. Suddenly, she felt overwhelmed, caught in the eye of a storm she didn't really understand.

She was aware of eyes following her. Friendly eyes, mostly, she thought, but something else hovered in the air. She felt an edge, a watchfulness.

Sarah led her down the hall to a large bedroom. The hardwood floor was covered by a colorful woven rug, the walls by western paintings. A fireplace was framed by two large windows that looked out over the mountain she'd seen on the approach.

But she had little time to study the room. Sarah led her to a dresser and took from it a large framed photo of a man and woman seated in two chairs. Behind them were five young men and a girl.

"This was taken in nineteen-forty. I was sixteen. Halden, whom you met tonight, was thirty-two, and this is Harding." She pointed to a handsome young boy of around seventeen and handed the photo to Jessie, who looked at it wonderingly. "Is this your father?"

Jessie couldn't answer for a moment. Harding Clements had a wide grin on his face as if he'd just stolen cookies from a cookie jar or committed some other mischief. She couldn't remember ever seeing her father smile like that.

And yet she knew that her father and this man were the same. She'd recognized him immediately. The set of his eyes, the heavy brows, the tall, rangy form. She had never seen a photo of him as a young man, had never even been able to imagine him as one. He'd always been so much older than other fathers, so . . . severe, distant, forbidding. Her fingers went over the photo as if she were trying to capture his image. Maybe she was.

Her breath caught in her throat. She could barely breathe. And her heart thumped faster. Her father! She knew. She *knew.*

Then she looked at the girl standing next to Harding Clements. Her hair was caught in the wind, long and blond. A smile lit her face. The girl, frozen in time, *did* look much as Jessie had a few years ago.

She stood, stunned. The picture mesmerized her. Six siblings.

Why had the one brother left a group that looked so . . . pleased with each other?

She felt Sarah's arm go around her. "He was my favorite brother," she said. "He was a year younger, and we always looked after each other."

"Why . . . would he leave?" Jessie finally asked the question that wouldn't go away.

"I don't know," Sarah said, but Jessie instantly sensed that she did indeed know. Or suspected.

Jessie looked from her father's photo to the two young men next to him. They were identical.

"Hugh and Heath," Sarah said. "They were identical twins, just like Cullen's twins. Hugh was killed in Europe in World War II. They were together when . . . Hugh stepped on a mine."

"What happened to Heath?"

"He died a few years later," Sarah said shortly.

Jessie tried to recall exactly what Alex had said about the man they believed was her father. *Your father disappeared the same day his wife and brother were apparently caught in a forest fire. They were both killed. We think he heard about it and just . . . wanted to get away.*

"Heath? Was he the one caught in the forest fire?"

Sarah looked startled. "How did you know about that?"

"Alex."

The startled look disappeared, but Jessie saw something unsettling in the woman's eyes before she spoke again. "I didn't know Alex had mentioned that, but yes, it was Heath."

"And Harding's wife?" She could not let herself say *father*. Not yet.

"Yes." It was a flat answer,

Sarah then reached over and pointed to the second man to the right. "This was Harry, another brother. He ran the ranch until he died and my husband took over. Now Ross is in charge." It was obvious she was trying to change the subject.

"I haven't met Ross yet, have I?"

A shadow crossed her face. "No, he isn't here. I expect him later."

"He's your son?" Jessie was still trying to get the relationships in their right place.

"Yes," Sarah replied softly.

Jessie's gaze turned back to the man that now on one level she was beginning to accept as her father. He had been forty-eight when she was born and was in his midsixties when he died. She couldn't remember when he wasn't gray, when deep lines hadn't aged his face beyond his years. He had always been rangy, though. As lean as he was in the photo.

But the deep-set, piercing eyes were the same, even if the smile wasn't.

"Do you have any other photos?" she asked.

"Enough to exhaust you," Sarah said. She went over to a desk and picked up one of several albums sitting there, then sat down on a loveseat in front of the fireplace. She patted the empty seat beside her. Jessie went over and sat down.

Sarah opened one of the albums. The photos were mostly small, black-and-white, some of them turning brown with age. "I received a camera for Christmas when I was eight. I had wonderful dreams about being a photographer and roaming the world."

Jessie looked up at her. "What happened to that dream?"

"I married the foreman. My family didn't approve, of course, but I loved him, and no one could tell me anything." She pulled out a photo. "Both your father and I were married the same year." She pulled out a photo of a man and woman who were obviously posing in front of the house. *Harding*. His arm was around the woman. She was blond, her tresses falling over half her face. Her skirt was short for the time, her blouse more than a little snug. She was startlingly beautiful.

"Her name was Lori," Sarah said, a harshness entering her voice for the first time.

"She's beautiful."

"In some ways," Sarah retorted.

"Alex said she died the same time . . . that Harding disappeared?"

"I think that's why he left. He couldn't remain here with the memories. He loved her beyond reason." Sarah turned the page to another photo. A young Sarah stood next to a tall lanky man whose dark hair spilled over his forehead. He wore a jaunty smile. "That's David," she said. "I loved him beyond reason, too, so I quite understood how Harding felt about Lori."

Something unbearably sad tinged the words. They seemed to echo in the room.

Jessie couldn't speak, didn't know how to break through the sudden curtain of emotion. She had a hundred questions, maybe even more, but she felt it would be an intrusion into someone's dark place. She held herself still, though she was greedy for any piece of information about her father.

"He always had a way with horses," Sarah said after a moment. She was ruminating, her voice soft with what were obviously fond memories. "That's how we found you. We looked toward the horses." Then she looked up at Jessie. "Was he happy?"

Jessie weighed her reply. He had not been happy. He'd . . . endured. He'd spent most of his leisure hours in a bottle. Now she was beginning to understand the complexity of the demons that caused it. "He enjoyed doing what he was good at," she finally said.

"You are diplomatic," Sarah said, obviously seeing through her words. "Tell me about your mother."

Jessie had no good answer for that. "I never knew her," she said. "She left us when I was very small. My father never talked about her." Her gaze met Sarah's. "You've had detectives. Perhaps you know more than I do."

Sarah shook her head. "We picked up your father's trail just months ago. I had hoped that we would find him alive, but we were so pleased to hear he had a daughter."

"We still don't know it is the same man," Jessie said, even though she was now convinced it was. The photos didn't lie, regardless of the intervening years.

"I am," Sarah said. She reached out and took Jessie's hand. She hesitated, then asked, "Did he leave any personal effects? Photos? Books?"

It was a curious question, but then Sarah was apparently looking for any information about her brother, about how he'd lived. It was natural enough, Jessie supposed. She herself was hungry for information about her father. So why would she question Sarah's desire for the same? But she hesitated. "We moved a lot. We lived—I guess you would call it—light. His only interest was horses. I can't remember seeing him with anything but breeding books. Maybe a veterinary textbook. Horse magazines. Racing forms." It was the truth. Not the whole truth. She didn't know why she held back, perhaps because she didn't want this woman to know what she suspected about her father, that in the last few years he'd bet against his own horses.

It was the only way he could have accumulated enough money to leave her an inheritance. A start in life. She hadn't known about it until he was dead. The money had meant college, and he'd known how much she wanted that. But she also knew there had been only one way to get that much. Knowing he had done something that he detested so she would have a future, had been a wound never quite healed. She had thought about giving it back, but to whom? And so she had used it. She'd never been comfortable with that choice, though. She always felt as if she owed a debt.

There was one other legacy, a primer dating back to the seventeenth century. Her father had given it to her when she was sixteen, one year before he'd died. "This might be very valuable someday," he'd said. "Keep it safe." He hesitated, then insisted in a whiskey-edged voice: "Promise me."

And she had. She kept it in a safe-deposit box along with her birth certificate, her diploma, and a few other items. And thank God she had. The burglar had torn her house apart, tearing up precious books, pulling out drawers, even turning over the mattress. She was lucky she had no valuables that appealed to him, and even luckier that he'd left Ben unharmed.

She hadn't even thought of the book in years, and suddenly the cover flashed in her mind, a washed-out gray that might have originally been blue.

Keep it safe. For the first time she wondered about his words, wondered why she didn't just blurt out its existence. But his voice was insistent in her mind and for some reason Sarah's question made it even louder.

She turned the page of the photo album and saw a young, dark-haired boy staring defiantly at the camera. His hair was too long, his face too thin, and even in the black-and-white view of the camera, his eyes were resentful. "Who is that?"

"Ross. This was taken a month after he came to live with us."

She looked up. "Alex said he was adopted."

Sarah smiled stiffly.

Jessie had learned long ago to detect changes in mood. She'd had to. Her father had been mercurial. And now she knew that the mood in the room had been muddied. The easy familiarity was gone. Sarah didn't like Alex. Or maybe didn't trust him for some reason. The image of the Cheshire Cat returned.

She stored that in her mind for future reference. "Alex also said Ross runs the ranch."

Sarah's frown faded. Pride shone bright from her face. It was very clear that she adored her son. "He took over from his father. He might as well have had Clements blood. He has the same talent your father did with horses, the same instinct."

"How old was he when you adopted him?"

"Twelve. As you can see, he wasn't very happy about it at first. He'd lived with his grandmother before she died, and she'd let him run wild. He wouldn't be . . . civilized, he always claimed. And he wasn't. I still never know what he is going to do. I had hoped he would come tonight . . ." Her voice trailed off.

"I would only get him confused with another family member," Jessie said gently. Vulnerability. If Sarah had one, it was her son. And the fact touched Jessie. Sarah had a kind of indomitable grandeur. Not the kind that goes with beauty, but with a sense of knowing who and what she was, and being comfortable with it. Her trousers were of thick denim, the kind one might wear while riding, and her boots were clean but obviously scuffed from use. Her eyes were bright and curious and her body still limber and graceful.

"Tell me about the other family members," she said.

"There's not that many," Sarah said. "Heath didn't

have any children, and Hugh had only one before he died. I . . . couldn't have children. Harry had two children, but one died in the Korean War—Cullen served there too— and one of Halden's daughters died of polio. Sometimes, I feel we have a curse." Then she shook her head as if to shoo away the thought and changed the subject. "I understand you exercised horses for your father. Do you like riding?"

Jessie again felt discomfort about the way her life had been examined without her knowledge. She shivered inside as she imagined what else Alex's detective had discovered. She couldn't rid herself of the feeling of violation Then, or now.

Sarah put her hand on Jessie's. "I know," she said slowly, as if she'd read Jessie's mind. "It mustn't seem fair to you that we know about you and you know so little about us. I didn't mean to intrude. I just wanted to find my brother. I always felt as if I should take care of him. And I didn't succeed. That always haunted me. If only he'd come to me."

"What happened exactly?" Jessie tried again to exact information she sensed Sarah didn't want to impart. She wasn't sure whether she wanted an answer to the question, and yet it had burst forth. Too late now to reclaim it.

"I don't know. None of us do." Sarah looked away and Jessie knew she was lying.

"Then tell me about his wife."

Sarah shrugged slightly. "It was nearly fifty years ago. I don't remember much."

But she did. Jessie knew that the woman remembered those years as if they were yesterday. She had seen it in Sarah's eyes before she turned away.

Jessie also knew she would learn little else about her father tonight and tried to stifle her sudden, intense irritation. She had shared information. She wanted some in return. Certainly more than she'd received.

Sarah rose from the chair and put the album down on the table. "Perhaps you would like to borrow this tonight," she said. "You can have a chance to study *us*. Turnabout is fair play."

"I would like that very much," Jessie said. And perhaps she would learn more from some of the other family members. She had little seeds now. Perhaps they would grow.

She followed Sarah back into the main room. Alex suddenly materialized out of nowhere with his ever-present smile. "Can I get you a drink?"

Jessie looked around. It seemed everyone in the room had something in their hands. "A glass of wine?"

"White or red?"

"Red."

His smile widened. "Delighted to be of service." He disappeared over toward a temporary bar. Sarah had also disappeared. Jessie took the opportunity to hide in a corner and watch the others chatting in small groups. She tried to put names and faces together, but there were more than thirty people, many with the last name of Clements. In mental defense, she started giving them names from *Alice in Wonderland*. Fitting, she thought, when she felt as if she were inhabiting those pages. Marc's wife was the Duchess; Cullen Humpty Dumpty; and Sondra the Queen of Hearts. Others were the officious March Hare, the Gryphon, the sad Mock Turtle. Cullen's twins were Tweedledee and Tweedledum; even their wives and children looked alike. She still assigned the Cheshire Cat to Alex. There was also a Katherine and her husband. Several others she would catalog them later. Her gaze searched the room, wondering if the mysterious Ross mingled somewhere within.

The congressman was talking to a young man of about thirty or so. Jessie didn't think she had met him yet; he must have arrived late. Halden Clements was still sitting in the comfortable chair, observing the crowd with a satisfied look. Most of the younger people had disappeared to some other room. The normal division between generations, she guessed.

Then Alex returned with a glass of wine for her and something obviously stronger for himself. "How do you like Sarah?"

"I like her very much, but I'm not exactly sure what to call her."

"I think Sarah will do just fine. Everyone calls her that, even Ross. Are you ready to take the blood test?"

"Can't you just find a piece of my hair or something?"

"Surreptitiously?"

"You did everything else surreptitiously," she retorted.

"But that was before we met you."

She arched an eyebrow.

"You look skeptical," he said with a grin.

"Something about you does that to me."

"Now that really hurts." But his gaze remained steady on hers.

"Yes," she said, suddenly making up her mind. "I will take it. For Sarah's sake."

"You really enjoy puncturing my pride, don't you?"

She did, though she didn't understand why. Probably because she knew she wasn't really doing any damage. He seemed to enjoy banter. It had never come easy to her before, but now each retort flowed from her, and she enjoyed the easy camaraderie it seemed to forge.

"Is that possible?"

"You are doing a great job." Then he sobered. "I know a doctor here in town. We could run by his office tomorrow."

"Afraid I'll back out?"

The smile left his face. "No, I don't think that. But now that I have your agreement, let me introduce the other members of the clan."

She was beginning to feel like family. A sense of warm belonging filled her as she met first one Clements, then another, shared their smiles, heard their memories.

Her family.

For the first time, she dared to believe.

five

Jessie's fingers smoothed over the battered photograph of Harding Clements. *Her father?*

Photos didn't lie. The resemblances were stark. Unmistakable. And yet she still didn't want to admit that her father had lied to her. Nor did she want to explore what might have happened that would cause him to abandon all that should have been held dear.

A shiver ran down her spine. Then another. A chill crept through her bones.

Secrets? Her father? Sure, she knew he'd had some. But something this deep, this big?

Parents were infallible when you were young. You loved them because they were your world. They were safety, security. Even when they were not perfect, they were a known entity and therefore believed, respected, and treasured. Maybe it was belonging. Jon Clayton had been all she had. And though he'd had faults and often retreated into a demon-infested world of his own, he'd never been physically abusive. Emotionally abusive? At times. But she had loved him so fiercely, she'd accepted it, had tried harder to be everything he'd wanted her to be. She had accepted him as he was, had thought that drink had been his only enemy.

Had it really been his past?

She pictured him in her mind again. He was wiry, almost gaunt. His hair had thinned, and his lips seldom smiled. He usually wore an old pair of jeans, a plaid shirt, and a denim jacket. A cigarette frequently dangled from his lips except when he was in a barn. He was careful around horses. Always. She'd often thought he preferred them to people. And to her.

She looked back at the laughing figure in the photo. Carefree. Happy. And so young. It was difficult to think of her father ever being that age.

There were other photos of him in the first pages of the album, one with him on horseback, another as a boy with a dog at his side. He'd never allowed her to have a dog; they'd always lived in other people's houses, and it wouldn't be fair, he'd said, to get an animal, then have to give it up.

Anger simmered inside her as she stared at the picture, and she realized it had been building ever since Alex had appeared with his news. She had been cheated of a real home and everything that went with it: friends, support, family.

Belonging.

She'd always told herself it didn't matter. Her father could have dumped her as her mother apparently had. He'd never shown much affection, but he'd always been there. She'd always hoped deep in her heart that he loved her.

Why then had he kept her from his family?

Those questions, she knew, would haunt her until she knew every one of the answers.

She recalled every face she'd seen tonight, compared some of them to the photos in the album. She was also reminded of the tragedies that had touched the family: Hugh who had died in the Second World War, then Heath, who had died in a fire; Halden's daughter, Louise, who'd died of polio at five; and Samuel, who'd died in the Korean

War. There was something very sad about looking at faces of people long dead, particularly when they died young.

Cullen, too, apparently had his near disaster, she thought as she saw a photo of a much younger Cullen in uniform. A rifle cradled in his arms, he stood with a group of other soldiers on a Korean hill.

Too many for one family? Or was it normal? She had no way of knowing, but she found herself aching for each one of them.

She tried to wipe away the cobwebs in her mind, looking for similarities between these people and the quiet, stern man who too often turned into a maudlin drinker. Grief curled up inside her and took a seat next to her anger.

A cauldron of emotions turned her mind to mush.

Jessie finally turned off the light, but she couldn't rid her thoughts of the image of the five brothers and sister. Only two were alive now, but they had all looked so young and vital in the photo. But in her mind, time corroded that picture like acid through cloth.

Alex would pick her up at ten in the morning for the blood test. If things worked out as he obviously expected, she would soon become an official part of the family she'd met tonight.

Was that what she really wanted?

Of course it was. She had reveled in Sarah's warmth, in Alex's acceptance and the congressman's obvious approval. Sedona *was* truly a wonderland, but not so . . . nonsensical. This was reality. She kept trying to tell herself that.

And she found herself looking forward to seeing Alex again. She'd never been the type of girl who attracted the "hunks." Which was why, she supposed, she'd succumbed so easily to Mills, only to find her knight was nothing but the worst kind of knave. She'd become immune then. And, she hoped, forever. But still, Alex was disarming.

She wasted most of the night that way, pondering imponderables until finally she fell asleep.

Alex had breakfast with Marc at a small coffee shop in Sedona. Marc had driven in from the ranch, where he and his wife always stayed when they were in Arizona. Since they spent most of their time in Washington, Marc saw little need to keep a separate residence in town. And the ranch house was certainly large enough.

Alex had understood the decision. Marc had always enjoyed riding and hunting, and he liked the image it presented. Family man. Rancher. He also liked the economics. Members of Congress did not have large salaries.

"What do you think of her?" Marc asked Alex. "You've been with her more than any of us."

"I like her," Alex said.

"So do I," Marc said. "But what will she do?"

Alex shrugged. "I have no idea. I haven't told her yet."

Marc gave him a questioning look.

"It didn't seem useful until we received the DNA test results. I didn't want to scare her off."

"She spent a lot of time with Sarah."

"Sarah was bound and determined to talk to her. She gave her one of those photograph albums."

"And the girl never said anything about her father?"

"Damned little."

Marc's eyes narrowed. "You know how important this is?" It wasn't a question as much as a statement of fact.

"Of course I do. You've told me enough times."

"I thought she would be eating out of your hand by now." Marc's voice had an edge to it.

"You thought wrong."

"You must be slipping, Alex."

"She's agreed to the blood test. She needs time, Marc. You won't win her to your side if you push right now.

She's still grappling with everything I've thrown at her, and she doesn't know the half of it yet."

"Are you sure? Are you sure her . . . Harding said nothing to her?"

"Nothing is sure, Marc. You know that by now. But I would wager my Jeep that Harding never uttered a word about his past. She was completely stunned."

"Then we have to keep it that way."

"She deserves to know everything."

Marc raised an eyebrow. "Everything? We don't know her that well. Hell, she might have the clue to those bonds without knowing it. If we tell her, she could take everything herself."

"I don't think so," Alex said.

"Well, I'm not willing to risk it. And you *can't* say anything. You're bound by attorney-client privilege. The family is your client, and she's not a Clements yet."

"You're a fine one to be talking about ethics."

Marc shrugged. "Has she gotten to you? I didn't think she's quite your type."

"Are you through, Marc?" Alex started to rise.

"For now," Marc replied. "When are you bringing her back to the ranch?"

"This afternoon for the barbecue."

Marc nodded. "I don't want her to spend time with Ross."

"Hell, Ross didn't even show up last night, though I think Sarah expected him. He has little patience with greenhorns."

"She isn't exactly a greenhorn," Marc said. "You said she was an exercise girl for her father. She's probably damned good. I'll ask April to take her riding."

Alex couldn't keep the surprise from his face.

"I thought April was still in Washington."

"She arrived last night. I think she and my new cousin might get along well together."

"Maybe," Alex said dubiously. Marc's two children had been a handful when young, both vying for their father's attention. Unfortunately, he'd been gone much of the time and had spoiled them rotten on the rare occasions they were together. They still hungered for his favor, and couldn't seem to make a life of their own; both planned to work in his senatorial campaign. April had majored in journalism and at twenty-eight was Marc's press secretary. She was talented and ambitious. And, Alex knew, willful. She always wanted what she couldn't have. Still, Alex had always been intrigued by her. They'd even dated for a short time before April had left for Washington, and she'd left him with an itch he'd never recovered from. But he had learned to hide it well. If not, April would use it as a weapon. So would her father.

The one striking thing about April was her unquestioned devotion to her father. And his career.

Marc looked out the window at the tourists. "Smith needs an answer soon, or the deal will fall through."

"It'll also fall through if this whole thing is handled wrong," Alex said. "Be patient."

"I'm still not sure what side you're on."

"I'm the family's attorney. I'm on the side of the majority."

"You can sway that majority . . ."

"Can I?"

Marc's lips frowned in disapproval. "Don't play games with me, Alex."

Alex shrugged. "You give me too much credit. I don't care for the responsibility."

"You never have," Marc observed. "But I can tell she likes you."

"Perhaps, but she doesn't completely trust me. She doesn't like lawyers."

"Smart girl," Marc said. "But she'll be happy enough when she realizes she's inheriting a great deal of money."

"I don't believe money means that much to her. She's never once asked whether there is any kind of inheritance."

"That much money means a lot to everyone."

Alex shrugged. "Perhaps."

"I'm depending on you," Marc said. He didn't wait for an answer but rose, tossed a twenty-dollar bill on the table, and walked away. He stopped and talked to people on his way out, his face wreathed in a smile. The consummate politician.

And a good one, Alex knew. Marc had been careful to keep any stains from his record, and people liked him. But he needed money if he wanted to be senator. He hadn't been able to raise enough to compete effectively. At least Alex didn't think he had.

Jessica was the key to that money.

Alex picked up his mug and sipped the rest of his coffee. The next few weeks would be very interesting.

Jessie had breakfast at the hotel, then took a cup of coffee down to the creek. She sat on a boulder that overlooked the stream.

She looked up at the huge rock called the Coffee Pot, for obvious reasons. The sun dappled its side, pulling out the various shades of red. Not for the first time, she wished she were competent with a paintbrush. No wonder there were so many artists here.

The land had already grown on her. Grown on her and seeped into her very being.

Was that why she'd finally consented to the blood test?

She'd been hesitant before. It was a commitment of sorts. A negative result would destroy her feeling of being Alice in Wonderland or even Dorothy in Oz. She hadn't been sure she wanted to prick the dream. But after seeing the photos, she had few doubts that Clements blood ran through her.

The creek bubbled along, a musical accompaniment to

her thoughts. There had been so many questions asked that she hadn't been able to answer. So many more questions in her own mind.

"Jessie."

She whirled around to see Alex standing there. "I thought I might find you here after my knocks didn't work."

"I'm sorry. Am I late?"

"No. I'm a few minutes early. I thought we would get rid of the business early, then drive out to the ranch. They're cooking a side of beef. They probably started it last night."

"Sounds good."

"It is." He looked at her closely. "Having second thoughts about the blood test?"

"No. It's just still a little bewildering."

"They're really not that bad."

"I didn't think they were. They're just . . . overwhelming. I liked Sarah, though."

He raised an eyebrow. "No one else?"

"You're fishing."

"I am," he admitted shamelessly. "Are you ready?"

No. She wasn't. Not really. She nodded.

They walked silently to her room, where she picked up her handbag. She was wearing a pair of jeans and an embroidered shirt. Barbecue clothes. She hoped.

The morning went quickly. Once they arrived at the medical building, a physician ushered them into his silent office. He'd obviously opened it just for her, and he regarded her with more than a little interest. "And so you are Miss Clements?"

"Clayton," she corrected.

His eyes twinkled. "I think that's what we're here to find out."

Several minutes later, she and Alex were walking out of the office. "You must have influence," she said. "I didn't expect a doctor to do it."

Alex shrugged. "I didn't think you would want this to be public knowledge. I trust Phil."

She wondered whether it was the family that didn't want this to become public knowledge, but she quickly shoved the thought out of her consciousness. She was going to enjoy this afternoon.

Ross changed to a pair of clean jeans and shirt. He couldn't delay this any longer. Sarah had been visibly upset this morning, refusing to accept his excuse of a sick horse. "Maybe you want to lose the Sunset," she said. "I don't."

"Going to a party isn't going to change that," he said bitterly.

"It could. And you will like her."

"The heiress? I don't think so." He had already pictured a gold digger in his mind.

She frowned at him. "Don't always be a cynic, Ross. She's nothing like that. She doesn't even know about the terms of the will."

He looked at her skeptically. "I can't believe that Alex hasn't started working on her."

"You could be nicer to him."

"When horses sprout wings and fly."

"Just be pleasant."

"I'll show up. I can't promise more than that."

She gave him an anguished look before starting for the door.

"I'll try," he said, uttering a curse under his breath when she turned around and beamed at him. He didn't want to be a part of this, none of it.

He shaved quickly, and ran a comb through his unruly hair. Didn't really matter. It would be unmanageable again. It was coarse and straight and kept falling over his eyes. He hated taking time to get a haircut, and now he'd let it grow too long.

But there were far more important matters. Like a job.

He would never find another position like this one. He had
chosen a quickly shrinking career field. There was no demand for ranch managers, particularly one who had his
own way of doing things.

The family had left him alone as long as the Sunset was
making money. But profits had shrunk, along with the
price of beef, in the past few years. And meanwhile, the
price of land near Sedona had grown proportionally
greater. He'd responded by diversifying. The price of good
cutting horses had risen dramatically in the past few years.
But it took years to build a recognized stable that would
bring the prices he needed.

Two more years. Just two more years.

But the family wasn't willing to wait.

The family! Damn them. All but Sarah. He owed her.
God, he owed her his life.

And he knew he would do anything necessary to repay
her.

Jessie saw Ross Macleod and immediately knew who he
was.

Alex had parked the car near the corral. A man she
hadn't seen before lounged against a fence post, talking to
a very pretty woman dressed in a sky-blue silk blouse and
tailored dark-blue slacks. She was looking up at her companion, and Jessie heard her laughter.

For a moment her gaze lingered on the woman. She was
blond, like the congressman. Jessie couldn't see her eyes,
but she would bet a twenty that they were blue. Her gaze
moved to the man. In contrast to the well-dressed woman,
he was dressed in well-worn jeans and a faded blue shirt
with its sleeves rolled up. His skin was bronze. She realized that it was not altogether from the sun.

She was struck by his resemblance to David Macleod,
Sarah's husband. The way he leaned against the corral was
identical to the photo of his adoptive father. His mouth was

the same, and so were the deep-set eyes. His cheeks, though were more finely drawn, more angular. *He was adopted.* Then why the physical resemblance? More secrets?

Like David Macleod, this man's hair was dark, nearly black. A shock of it fell over his forehead, and she watched as his fingers ran through it, pushing it back in place. Even that movement had a grace to it, a quality common to good horsemen. He was not handsome in the accepted way, but there was a rugged attractiveness that appealed to her. More than appealed to her. It jolted her like a sudden streak of lightning.

"That's Ross," Alex said, touching her arm. She wondered if she'd looked as starstruck as she felt. She felt a flush rising to her cheeks. "And April. She's Marc's daughter."

Something intimate touched his words. She turned and looked at him, wondering if he had an interest there. She felt his hand guiding her toward the two. April appeared to be close to her own age, but looked as elegant as a film star. Her blond hair was pulled back into a French twist. Her face had the bone structure of a Grace Kelly.

The woman turned toward them, fixing her gaze on Jessie. Her eyes *were* blue, a gorgeous unfair blue. Jessie suddenly felt awkward and tall and not very well put together.

But the woman gave her a blinding smile and held out her hand. "You must be Jessica, our long-lost cousin."

Her charm was every bit the equal of Alex's. Jessie couldn't help but melt under the force of it as she took April's hand. "We're not sure of that yet," she cautioned.

"Sarah is sure and that's good enough for me," April said. "So welcome to the family." Then she looked up at her companion. "Have you met our recluse yet?" she asked in a light, teasing voice.

Jessie looked up into Ross Macleod's face and suddenly

was tongue-tied. His eyes were nearly as dark as his hair, a deep dark brown framed by thick black lashes. Unlike the other Clementses, there was no welcome in them, not even curiosity. If anything, she saw traces of hostility, and most certainly wariness.

He gave a nod of acknowledgment. "Miss . . . Clayton, is it?" His voice was deep, drawling but devoid of warmth.

"Jessie," she said. It came out more of a croak.

"How do you like Sedona?" April broke the silence that followed.

"It's very pretty," Jessie said inadequately, then blundered on. "I've never seen anything like it."

"I understand you live in Atlanta. It's an exciting city." April was doing her best to make her feel at ease, and yet Jessie felt like a lump of coal. Perhaps because Ross Macleod was studying her as if she were a horse he might consider buying, then found it wanting.

"I like it," she finally said.

"Daddy said you ride. Would you like to take some horses out this afternoon? I can show you some rather spectacular Indian ruins. Maybe even the bear here will go." She looked up at Ross again, a grin on her face.

One side of Ross's lips turned up slightly, bringing out an unlikely dimple in his chin. Perhaps it had been hidden in his scowl. "The bear?"

"The bear," April confirmed, obviously not at all intimidated by his manner.

Jessie suddenly wished she could tease out a real smile. Instead, she could merely observe.

Ross turned to her, and she felt her legs suddenly weaken. Again, his eyes seemed to probe her. "Perhaps Alex can accompany you later. I have a horse that's ready to foal. I don't want to leave now."

"You always have an excuse," April complained, and for the first time some of the charm was gone. "Oh well, we don't need a chaperon."

Alex's fingers tightened on Jessie's arm. It was an outright rejection of him. Jessie felt a sudden wave of sympathy. "I would like him to come," she said, gratified when she saw appreciation in Alex's eyes and surprise in Ross's. Something like irritation flashed across April's face, but then it disappeared as quickly as it came.

"We'll go at sunset," April said. "It's the prettiest time of the day."

Ross seemed about to say something, then turned away. "I'll have some horses saddled."

"I want Ladybird," April said. She turned to Jessie. "Do you ride well?"

Jessie hesitated. She hadn't ridden since she was seventeen, but then she could ride nearly any horse. She shrugged. "Adequately," she said.

April looked toward Ross. "Maybe Jessica would like Firebird. He's Ladybird's brother. He's fast and steady."

"No," Ross said. "I'll pick one." He nodded to Jessie, then strode off toward the barn.

"Charming as a rattlesnake," Alex muttered.

April's gaze followed Ross Macleod. Jessie couldn't help but notice the longing in her face before turning back to them.

"I'm hungry," April said lightly. "Come on, Jessica, I'll introduce you to the latecomers."

Alex watched Sarah take Jessica under her wing again, regaling her with stories familiar to him: how Hall Clements came to the area with his parents just after the last of the Apaches and Yavapai had been driven out by General Crook. Apache crops of squash, beans, and corn proved that the soil was fertile.

Like a handful of other pioneers, Hall's father had been seduced by Oak Creek Canyon and the majestic red rocks. He'd found a piece of land beside a creek and planted crops; within two years his wife died of a rattlesnake bite and he was killed a year later by a bear. Hall had been only fourteen, but he had stayed on the land they homesteaded, doing a man's work. Because he was a hardworking lad, and well-liked as well, no one had made a point of telling authorities.

He'd married at twenty-five, but his first wife and child died in childbirth. Brokenhearted, he waited ten years to wed again, this time to a strong determined young woman he met in St. Louis. She, so the story went, was sturdy enough to survive the hardships of frontier life. Mary Louise more than fulfilled his expectations. Practical in many ways, she'd loved her husband desperately, knowing that she had escaped being an old maid by his unromantic proposal. It was Mary Louise who started calling the ranch the Sunset, a name that forever replaced Hall's plain-spoken Double R Ranch, which remained on the deeds.

They had grown old together. Mary Louise died first, but prior to her death she'd insisted on the terms of Hall's will. She'd wanted two things: to keep the Sunset in the family, and to keep the family together.

Alex watched the rapt look on Jessica's face. She was being seduced by the family history, just as Sarah knew she would. The stories were many and for someone like Jessica, who'd never had much of a family, probably irresistible.

He looked around for Marc, but he had not yet arrived. God knew everyone would be aware of his presence the moment he appeared. He seemed to expect it and usually took care in making an entrance, even when it involved only his family. April, whom Alex knew had been told to keep Jessica busy, had disappeared. Probably to the barn.

He swore under his breath. He hadn't seen April in six months, the last time at Christmas. She'd been angry then, and she apparently hadn't forgiven him. The reason had been the same: Ross.

She'd always hankered after Ross, probably, he thought,

because he was the one man who'd never paid sufficient attention to her. At least, that was what he'd told himself. He thought perhaps if he tried the same tactic . . .

He thought about intruding on Sarah and Jessica, but hell, that was Marc's problem.

He turned around and headed for the door. He had other business in town.

six

The ranch house was pulsing with life late that afternoon. Jessie was beginning to put names and faces together. Perhaps the Duchess would always be the Duchess, but she was also Samantha Clements. Twins Hugh and Heath were Tweedledee and Tweedledum, but they were also Hugh and Heath.

A guitar player wandered about outside, and the aroma of cooking meat infiltrated every nook and cranny of the ranch. The sun was golden, the sky a deep royal blue, the land radiant. She not only heard laughter, but was part of it.

It was a giddy feeling. Every one of her senses had gone into high gear. She soaked up the history, the ambience, the warmth. She found herself reveling in the stories, the history of an intriguing family. And for the first time in her life she was the belle of the ball, and she was enjoying every moment of it.

She hugged the moments to herself, cataloging them in a mental scrapbook. She wished she had a camera, but she hadn't thought to bring one in the unnerving days after Alex's first visit.

Supper was going to be served on a long table that had mysteriously appeared in the front yard. She didn't see Alex. Nor did she see Ross. But April came over to her, bringing with her a young man who looked considerably like the senator.

"My kid brother, Hall," April said, ducking a teasing blow from her sibling. Another name with an H. Hall appeared to be in his early twenties, and he had a reckless gleam in his eyes. Now which Wonderland character was he? *The Cheshire Cat?* No, that was Alex.

"My father is delighted with you," Hall said. "You'd better watch out. He'll enlist you in his campaign like he has everyone else in the family."

"Everyone but Ross," April interjected.

"Ross doesn't count," Hall said. His voice dismissed his cousin with something like contempt. Jessie's back went rigid. She wondered whether she didn't count, either.

"He means that Ross doesn't care about politics," April said hurriedly, shooting a warning look at her brother.

"Of course." Hall recovered nicely, but his blue eyes were cool.

Jessie felt a chill run through her. For an instant, she felt she was an unsuspecting participant in a play produced just for her. Her gaze wandered around the room. Knots of people were talking, laughing. There *was* warmth. A sense of belonging. She brushed the unsettling thought aside.

"Where's your father?"

"He's attending a festival in Phoenix," April said. "He's flying back later this afternoon. He wouldn't miss this supper. He's the one who started these reunions about twenty years ago. The family seemed to be growing apart, spreading out throughout the country. He didn't want that to happen. He even wrote a book about the family history."

That surprised Jessie. Marc Clements appeared to be one of those people with too much energy to devote time to such a sedentary project as writing a book. "I'd like to read it."

"I'll get you a copy," April promised, "though Aunt Sarah has probably told you most of the good stuff."

Jessie wondered why Sarah had not mentioned the book, nor given her a copy, since she'd insisted on Jessie's taking the photograph album.

Hall was regarding her with amusement, and she wondered whether her thoughts were mirrored on her face. "You haven't heard about it? Well, Sarah wasn't exactly pleased. She said it had been expunged of all the good stuff, that Dad was using the family to help himself."

April frowned at her brother again, as if any criticism of their father were heresy. Jessie had thought earlier she'd detected some tension between Marc and Sarah. She wondered whether the book was responsible for it. Sarah had seemed to take pleasure in telling family stories—good and bad. All except Harding's disappearance. Jessie wondered what the congressman's tome had to say about that. She didn't think she would wait until someone sent it to her; she would check the library first thing. And the newspapers.

"April says you like horses," Hall said.

Jessie looked at April. She'd never said that, only that she could ride "adequately." Once more, she wondered how much the family knew, how much of her life had been torn open for strangers to examine. The sense of invasion replaced the warmth, even happiness she'd felt. Both April and her brother—and their mother yesterday—disconcerted her. Perhaps because they all appeared "perfect," and she didn't trust perfect. Mills had been perfect on the surface and scarred on the inside.

"Yes," she said shortly.

"We're going riding later this afternoon," April added.

Hall's brows furrowed together in surprise. He looked at his sister, then back at Jessie.

"Do you want to go?" April asked. Jessie detected a challenge in her question.

"Hell, no."

"Hall fell a couple of years ago," April said, and there was a slightest edge of contempt in her voice. "He hasn't ridden since."

Hall flushed. "You haven't been riding yourself very much."

"How would you know?"

Jessie was forgotten. The animosity seemed to be something more than sibling rivalry. She felt like backing away from the intensity of it.

Instead, she tried to change the subject. "Alex said you've just finished law school. Congratulations."

The grin returned to his face. "Thank you. I'll be joining Dad's campaign here next week."

"Hall just returned from Europe," April said.

"A graduation gift," Hall said. "Now I have to start working."

"That will be a change," April sniped.

Jessie was beginning to understand. Both brother and sister working in their father's campaign? She could virtually feel April's jealousy.

Jessie had always wanted brothers and sisters. She'd had a make-believe sister when she was a child. Now she wondered whether there was always this kind of tension between siblings.

"You are just envious, sister dear," Hall said.

April shrugged. "I hardly think so."

Then they were interrupted by still another Clements and, in minutes, April and Hall left, first one, then the other. Jessie saw them in a corner arguing.

She excused herself. She was feeling overwhelmed again, uncertain about the currents flowing in the room. She stepped outside, tasting the smell of smoke permeating the area.

Her Wonderland!

Was it like Alice's? Nothing as it seemed to be?

She was seized again with the sense of unreality. She had felt a sense of belonging, and yet there was also a detachment, a sense of looking into someone else's house.

Jessie went outside and looked over the scene in front. The smoking meat, the stretch of picnic tables, the horses in a pasture. Just as she had seen in the movies. Just as she had always wanted.

She walked over to the barn. It had been a long time since she smelled those odors. Fresh hay, horses, leather. She hesitated at the door, not sure whether she wanted to feel all those emotions again. She had not been in a barn since the day she'd found her father there. He'd been late, much too late, in returning home. She'd thought he might be at a bar, but his truck was still in front of their small house that was part of the Lynford Farms. She found him there, sprawled out over the hay, a hand clutching his chest. He'd been given notice the night before. And it had been her fault. Everything had been her fault . . .

She heard a soft, warning growl. It startled her out of the memory. Out of the nightmare. She turned.

"Timber. Down."

The growl stopped, and her eyes adjusted to the interior of the barn. An animal that looked more wolf than dog glared at her.

"Miss Clayton." The soft drawl was a counterpart to the earlier sharp command. Ross Macleod had approached silently. His dark eyes were quizzical but guarded. She wondered whether they were always like that.

"This is Timber," he said. "He's a bit . . . edgy among people he doesn't know, or like. I'll put him away."

"No," Jessie said. She stooped and held out her hand for the dog to sniff. "Timber?"

He looked down at the dog. "For Timber Wolf. It just

seemed to fit." Then he spoke to the dog. "It's okay," he said. Only then did Timber take a step forward and cautiously sniff Jessie. After a moment of tentative exploration, she ran her fingers behind his ear. He moaned quietly with pleasure.

She looked up and saw an astonished expression on Ross's face. "He doesn't usually do that," he said.

"I've never met a dog I didn't like," she said, taking liberties with Will Rogers. "They seem to know that."

"He won't let April anywhere near him. I have to keep him at the house or locked in the tack room when she's here."

"That doesn't seem fair."

"Timber doesn't think so, either," he said. He paused for a moment, then asked, "Family getting too much for you?"

She didn't have to ask what he meant. "A little," she said. "I'm not used to so many people."

His gaze was appraising. She felt as though she were under a microscope. She gave the dog one last pat, then stood, moving over to the stalls. A head poked out and she held out her hand. The animal sniffed it, then tossed its head.

"Firebird," he said from behind her. "He's more than a handful. April shouldn't have suggested you ride him."

She resented his assumption that she was either fainthearted or incompetent. Still, it had been years—it seemed a lifetime—since she'd been near a horse. She had consciously stayed away from them. Now all her old love for them flooded back. She was a horse-struck girl with a stable of animals to love.

"It has been a long time," she admitted.

"How long?"

"Ten years."

The horse extended his head, and she ran her fingers along the side of his head. He whinnied softly.

"He doesn't usually accept people that easily either," Ross said, moving to her side.

"I like horses. They know it. At least, that's what my father used to say. They can detect a phony in a moment."

"I think I would have liked your father."

"He probably would have liked you, too. He too was . . ."

"Was what?"

"A loner. At least, that's what everyone says about you."

"Do you always believe what everyone says?"

Her gaze met his. "No," she said. "But you do seem to be avoiding everyone."

The side of his lips turned up. "I'm the family skeleton. Hasn't anyone told you?"

"Only that you were adopted."

"I'm also part Apache," he said. "And my adoptive father's blood son. A bastard, in other words. The two aren't exactly what a family of this . . . stature really wants."

He looked at her steadily, obviously trying to gauge her reaction.

She met his gaze. "At least you know who you are."

"Oh yes, I know," he said bitterly.

"You manage the property," she said.

"Only because no one else wanted the job. Can you imagine our congressman cleaning out a barn?"

"Do you do that?"

"When we're shorthanded, which is today."

"I used to enjoy cleaning stalls," she said. And she had. She'd felt at home in the barns. She'd loved the shuffling of horses, the soft muzzles as they searched her hand for a piece of carrot. Because she and her father had moved so often, she'd never had time to make human friends, and so she made them of the animals. She'd loved some with all her heart.

"I'll remember that," he said, his lips turning up at the sides again.

She tipped her head slightly to look up at him. She was tall, but he was several inches over six feet, and all of his rangy body was whipcord strong.

Her gaze apparently disconcerted him. He turned around. "You want to meet the others?"

Meet. She liked that. It demonstrated a care for his charges, a respect.

"Very much."

"What kind of horses did your father train?"

The question surprised her. Everyone else seemed to know more about her than she did herself. "Thoroughbreds. Racing stock."

"You'll find ours far different. They're quarter horses, bred and trained for cutting and reining. They move suddenly and unexpectedly. They think for themselves. You have to be alert every moment."

"They're beautiful."

A hint of pride broke the stark angles of his face. "We're gradually earning a reputation," he said. "A few more years . . ." He left the sentence unfinished and walked down the aisle, mentioning the names, occasionally running a hand affectionately down a well-groomed neck. Then they arrived at a set of larger stalls. A mare nuzzled her colt. "He's going to be the best yet," Ross said.

Her heart speeded. She hadn't realized how much she missed this. How much the miracle of birth had always moved her. Her teeth bit her lower lip. She could almost see her father squatting next to a foal, eyeing it speculatively. She turned away blindly. Damn it. Ten years. And yet now it felt like yesterday, the memories illuminated by the photographs, the recollections.

All of Ross's attention was on the foal, his dark eyes warm for the first time. When he turned back, though, they were cool. She felt as though she'd been dismissed. Yet she didn't want to go. He apparently expected nothing of her, while the others in the house all seemed to have expectations. Here, there were no odd little currents, no competition. She felt at home here.

She'd thought she'd made the bookstore her home. Now she wondered whether she hadn't just been hiding.

"You had better get back," he said. "They'll be sending out a search party."

"Why?"

His eyes narrowed. "You really don't know, do you?"

"Know what?"

"Damn Alex."

"Why?"

He shrugged. "He likes games."

"Then you tell me."

"It's not my place."

"Because you feel like an outsider?"

"Did I say that?"

"In essence. Why?"

"Why what?"

"Why did you tell me what you did about yourself?"

He shrugged. "You'll hear it soon enough. It's just one of the family secrets. I thought you should know."

"Is that a warning?"

"Maybe."

"You're like Mouse."

His brows furrowed together. "Mouse?"

"In *Alice in Wonderland.* He doesn't finish a story. He just . . . intimates."

"I've never read it."

"Then that explains it."

"Explains what?"

"The scowl on your face."

"I don't see the connection."

"Read the book. You have to have a healthy respect for the absurd."

"Why?"

"Sometimes it's quite necessary to survive." She found herself confiding in him. "In fact the only way I can tell everyone apart is by thinking of them as a character from the novel."

"And I'm Mouse?" he said with an arched eyebrow. It was the first indication of humor she'd seen.

"It's better than Tweedledee and Tweedledum," she said. "Or Humpty Dumpty."

"I *have* heard of *them*," he said. "Now who do you think are Tweedledee and Tweedledum?"

"Can't you guess?"

"I don't have a clue."

"The twins."

"And Humpty Dumpty?"

"I don't think I should say," she said.

He grimaced. "So you think this is Wonderland?"

"It is to me."

His gaze bored into her, but she saw a glimmer of interest that wasn't there before. "Perhaps I *should* have read it. I didn't have much time to read as a kid."

She turned around. There was a quiet intensity about him that attracted her far more than Alex's breeziness. She'd felt struck by lightning when she first met him. She still felt heat, but it was no longer the sudden violent kind. Her body was tremulous, warm. Aware. She couldn't remember ever responding this way to anyone, not even to Mills.

Ridiculous. She remembered the seductive look April had given Ross.

How could she ever compete with such glossy perfection?

"How many secrets are there?" she asked after a brief pause. She heard the break in her own voice. She had always thought her life so ordinary, and now she found it wrapped in mystery.

He shrugged. "Probably not many more than other families."

"I don't know about families," she said.

He had moved closer to her. She smelled aftershave, and the aroma of horses and leather. Heat seemed to radiate from him, as well as assurance. An assurance that she didn't have, had never had. His proximity bombarded her senses. A trembling excitement reverberated inside like the beginning rumblings of an earthquake.

"It looks like you're going to find out about one," he said. His voice, she'd noticed before, was deep, and he spoke with a lazy drawl. But there wasn't the easy give and take she had with Alex. She had to draw every word out of a most reluctant mouth.

"Should I?"

"Having second thoughts?" he replied in a cool tone. He'd answered the question with a question, and that was disconcerting. It was obvious he was sparing with words, with thoughts, with explanations. No quick retorts as Alex produced, no quick smiles. He seemed to consider each word, weighing it carefully. He was probably impatient with her at the moment, her and her *Alice in Wonderland* nonsense.

She felt totally unsophisticated. Nothing like April's easy assurance. Her throat suddenly became tight.

Jessie thought she must appear cowardly. "No," she said.

He looked skeptical, as if he knew she was lying. "Just keep your sense of the absurd," he warned. "And now you had better go out to supper."

"Are you coming?"

"No. Someone has to keep the ranch going." A hard edge shadowed his voice.

"You can't be all alone?"

"No. Jimmy and Carlos are checking the tanks. Two others are riding fence. Dan'l usually feeds and waters the horses, but he's helping with the cooking today, so I'm doing it. I prefer that to cooking," he added wryly.

It also gave him an excuse to avoid the family gathering. She suspected that was why he was out here doing a hand's work. Instead of voicing her thought, she asked a question. "Tanks?"

"Watering holes for the cattle. We have to keep them in shape even when the cattle are grazing in higher pastures."

"Five hands," she said dubiously. "It doesn't seem like very many to run a ranch this big."

"We hire cowboys for spring and fall roundups. We can't afford much more. Cattle prices have dropped. Times are hard for ranches like the Sunset."

Jessie remembered the numerous grooms and servants at the big breeding farms in Maryland, Kentucky, and Tennessee, and she'd expected the same here. She was a voracious reader of newspapers as well as books. She'd read that ranchers were having difficulties, but she'd really not understood how severe they were.

He had already turned away, though, and she sensed that he regretted saying what he had. His back was straight, unyielding, even as his steps were uncommonly graceful. Her gaze followed him. Despite his disturbing presence, or perhaps, because of it, she didn't want to leave. For the first time since she'd come to Sedona, she'd felt totally at ease. For a few moments anyway. Until his obvious impatience drove away that altogether too brief feeling.

Ross muttered to himself. *A lamb.* She was a lamb, and one who could easily be sheared by some of the experts in the family.

Unfortunately she was an appealing lamb. He'd surprised himself at finding himself fascinated with her, though he winced at being labeled a mouse. He suspected he knew whom she considered Humpty Dumpty. He chuckled at the aptness of the description of Cullen. She had no pretensions, and he liked that. He liked her sense of humor and her lack of awe at the Clementses. He also liked her instant rapport with Timber. Most people backed away in terror. She treated him like a big pussycat, and by God, the beast loved it.

He thought about warning her, but then he might end up being one of the shearers. His motives would most certainly be suspect. His own future was at stake, and he would do nearly anything to protect Sarah.

He pondered over the selection of horses for Jessica's ride. She said she hadn't ridden in a number of years. He was having second thoughts about not tagging along, but he really didn't want to ride with April. She was pure poison for someone like him. He suspected that his attraction for her was his unavailability; she wasn't used to being denied.

He had known her as a child, and he'd not particularly liked her. She'd been spoiled and demanding. When he'd once scolded her for running her pony too hard, she'd slapped him and said he was only a servant and had no right to give her instructions. He'd never forgotten that. It was a constant reminder of his status in the family.

He didn't mind teasing her but he had no intentions of being used. Not now. Not ever.

And he didn't like her suggestion that Jessica use Firebird. The horse was still young and unsteady. And April knew it; God knows he had warned her about the horse enough. Perhaps she just wanted to show off her superior riding skills, or even scare the newest member of the family.

He didn't have the time to chase after sunsets and nursemaid two young women, but he didn't trust April.

He cursed under his breath. He would go if Alex didn't return. Ross didn't particularly care for Alex, but the lawyer was a competent horseman. Jessica would be safe with him. For now.

seven

Jessie knew she would pay for this adventure. It had been far too long since she'd been on a horse, and her muscles weren't prepared but, dear God, how she looked forward to it.

Pleasure surged inside her as she mounted a well-behaved sorrel gelding and settled onto a well-worn western saddle. It was heavy and clumsy, unlike the light racing saddles she'd ridden with her father's horses. She felt it a barricade between her and the horse, but the gelding had been already saddled. And when in Rome . . .

"His name is Carefree. Ross's choice," said a young dark-haired teenager who stood by the horses.

"You must be Dan'l," she said.

"Yes, ma'am," he replied with a shy smile.

"Thank you," she said.

"You're welcome, ma'am."

"Please call me Jessie. I don't feel like a ma'am."

His smile spread into a grin. "Yes ma'am—Jessie."

She had come out a few moments early. She'd wanted a few moments with the horse, to get acquainted with him. She tried to remember everything Ross had told her about cutting horses. *They can move quickly and think for themselves. You have to be alert every moment.* As if to prove his words, Carefree stamped restlessly. Jessie leaned over and whispered a few words to him.

April and Alex, a cellular phone stuffed prominently in his pocket, strode over from the house. Jessie watched as Alex helped April mount a large bay mare, then swung into the saddle himself. He was, she noted, an experienced but not a natural horseman. He was a little stiff, his hand tighter than necessary on the reins.

April, on the other hand, apparently had the family talent for riding or else she'd grown up on horseback. She looked graceful and natural. Jessie told herself she should have expected that. April was one of the golden people who did everything well.

It was April who took the lead, starting to move toward the mountain behind the ranch house.

The sun was already lying low in the sky. Jessie was mellow from the recent feast of beef and vinegary coleslaw and beans. Warmed by the banter during the meal, she dismissed some of the undercurrents she'd felt earlier. Every family, she supposed, had its competitions.

Her horse had a fine easy gait. Keeping pace with April, she moved to a trot, then a lope. Carefree held his head low and relaxed, and she knew immediately he was well trained. Unlike his name, he obviously had learned very good manners. *Ross?*

They'd ridden about thirty minutes when she heard a loud beep. Alex looked at her apologetically, then slowed his horse to a walk and pulled out his cellular phone.

The phone seemed out of place here. Almost obscene. She could barely see the house and they were surrounded by piñon, pine, juniper, and cypress. The red rock cliffs stretched ruggedly in front of them. She could well imagine herself in the past century, untouched by civilization. Until the blasted phone rang.

Alex said something into the phone, then moved toward her. "I have to get back. A client's son has just been arrested for vandalism, and the police won't release him."

Jessie would hope not, but she held her tongue.

April had apparently sensed they were no longer with her, and she'd turned around and was trotting back.

"We have to get back," Alex said.

April shrugged. "You might. We don't. What do you say, Jessica? Are you game?"

It was a challenge.

"I think we should all go back," Alex said.

April merely raised an eyebrow and waited for Jessie to answer.

Aside from the challenge, Jessie simply didn't want to go back. The pleasure of riding was too strong. She simply wasn't ready to return. She wanted to fly across the prairie. She wanted to feel the horse's muscles stretch under her as she had as a girl. She wanted to bring back all the joy she'd once felt.

And April apparently grew up here. She probably knew every foot of land.

"I'll go with April," she said.

Alex started to protest.

April put her finger to her mouth. "Don't be such an old man, Alex. We'll be fine. We can get to know each other better."

He shrugged. "Be back before dark, or Ross will be combing the entire ranch for you."

April nodded, then as if it were all settled, she turned her bay and started in an easy canter toward the mountain.

Alex hesitated, then said, "Stay close to April."

"I will," she said. "I can take care of myself. I've done it since I was a child."

Approval flickered in his eyes. "I know."

The answer was not altogether comforting. It indicated once again the extent of the knowledge others had of her. Just how much? Darn it. How much?

Alex had never given her a straight answer about that. She started to turn her horse back in the direction April had taken, but Alex didn't move. Instead, he seemed more than a little reluctant to leave her.

"I'll return in time to take you back to the lodge," he said.

"You won't have to worry about driving me after today," she said. "I know the way now."

"I don't worry about it. It's a pleasure."

She raised a doubting eyebrow. "Your duties as chauffeur?"

"But I have such a pretty passenger."

It would be nice to believe that. But she had seen the way he looked at April, and it was exactly the way April had looked at Ross. Currents again. Vaguely uncomfortable ones.

It was as if he sensed her discomfort. "You had best hurry if you want to see that sunset," he said. Then he turned and trotted away from her, his body a little stiff. She watched as he disappeared, and for a moment she enjoyed the solitude. She drank in the taste, smell, and sights of an area not quite a desert, but with the same stark beauty as one.

She turned the horse and with a light tightening of her legs pushed her sorrel into a trot. April was far ahead now, the silhouette of rider and mount beginning to disappear into the shadows surrounding the mountain of rock.

"Dammit," she said. She wondered about turning around and catching up with Alex, but she wasn't going to give up that easily. The red rock beckoned to her. She could catch up to April, she was sure of it.

"Come on, boy," she said, dropping her weight in her heels. She squeezed his side with her lower legs and rose into the two-point position. The horse moved into a canter, then stretched into a full gallop.

The dry wind brushed her cheeks and whipped her hair around her face. Pure joy surged through her as her body moved with the gelding's. She gave him his head, though she kept a steady grip on the reins, and for moments she just relished the feel of the wind and the horse and the clean air and cloudless sky and the bright orange ball that was the sun.

She looked for April, but didn't see her. At the moment she didn't care.

She had always loved the wind flowing through her hair, the freedom she felt. All those feelings came flooding back. Breezing a three-year-old at five-thirty A.M. while her father held a stopwatch on her. The exhilaration of speed, of muscles stretching beneath her, of being in control of so much strength. She tried to remember everything her father had taught her. *Relax your hips, drop your weight into your stirrups. Goddammit, that's not the way to hold the reins.* She heard his voice in her heart, his instructions in her mind.

She was racing the wind. And the past. It kept flooding back. As did other thoughts. Had her father galloped over this ground?

Jessie looked up. They were nearing a stand of junipers and pines, many of their trunks split by lightning. Fast. They were going to be hitting the trees in a moment. She knew what the branches could do to both her and the horse. It was too late to swerve out of the way, even if she knew which direction to take. She would stop, then try to find out where April had gone.

She pulled on the reins, yelling "Whoa." The horse slid to a stop so quickly he sat back on his haunches. Jessie kept on going, right over the horse's head. She reached out her arms to protect her head and rolled onto her shoulder, coming to a rest on her back. Unable to breathe and hurting like hell, she lay there. The horse limped several steps away, then turned and looked at her as if she were the world's stupidest human alive.

He was right.

Jessie tried to move. Slowly. One digit at a time. Her left

wrist, the one she'd thrust out to break the fall, was all grinding pain. She felt it gingerly. Not broken, but most certainly sprained. It had happened to her before, just as she'd fallen before. Now she felt like a total fool. And an aching one. Deep bruises were already beginning to color her arm, and her blouse was ripped beyond repair. At least she wasn't beyond repair. Or she didn't think so. She wasn't entirely sure.

She looked at the horse again, wondering why it had not wandered away. Then she remembered. She'd heard western horses were trained to stay still when the reins trailed the ground. *Ground tied.* This, apparently, was one of those horses. As well as one that took the word *whoa* quite literally.

But he was favoring his right front leg. She wondered whether he'd somehow injured it when she went sailing over its head, or had lost his footing when he sat back.

She leaned down and checked it. It wasn't broken, thank God. She'd been around horses enough to know a bad injury.

She bit her lip against the pain and, even worse, the shame. If she had injured the horse by letting her own pleasure overcome good sense, she'd never forgive herself. Neither, she suspected, would Ross.

She went back to her own wounds. She was already stiffening. She put her good hand down on the ground, then realized she had apparently put it on something that pricked, then stung.

Jessie turned around. Whatever it was had apparently fallen from some kind of cactus. She tried to stand, but didn't quite make it. Every bone in her body complained.

She looked out over the landscape. No sign of April. No sign of anyone. And the sun was setting. Its glow didn't look nearly as glorious—or as friendly—as it had the previous evening.

She considered her alternatives. She could sit and wait

for someone to find her, but no one knew where she was. And she didn't want to stay out here. She knew how easily a horse spooked. It was better if she got Carefree back to the stable where his leg could be tended.

And she should be able to find the way. There were, after all, roads, and people and tourists. She just wasn't sure in what direction.

And where did April go?

She tried again to get to her feet. She swayed for a moment. Then she limped over to the sorrel. He nickered nervously and she ran her hand down his neck. "It's not your fault."

Carefree tossed his head, as if agreeing with her, then eyed her warily. She partly leaned against him, then picked up the reins. Whatever had stuck in her hand burned, but her other arm was useless. She started limping out from under the trees and noticed, for the first time, how quickly daylight was fading. In the past few moments, the sun had dipped behind a faraway mountain. The sky had turned dark blue with a crimson edging. In minutes, it would be dark.

No city lights here.

She swallowed hard. She'd been told the country was alive with rattlesnakes. There were cactus—prickly pear— everywhere, the same kind already burning through her hand.

No lights on the horizon. At least the mountain was at her back. Or had she gone to its side during her mindless race?

She decided to toss away her pride. "April," she said in a loud voice. Then again in one several decibels higher.

An owl hooted somewhere. An evening bird answered.

Jessie bit her lip, trying to stifle a growing fear.

Surely, when she didn't get back before dark, they would send out someone. In the meantime, she would move along. She looked back at the huge rock. She tried to remember the angle she'd seen from the house. But now it looked different.

She wished she wore riding boots as she stumbled along the rocks and brush. Her loafers and slacks provided precious little protection. She ached all over, and shooting pain ran through her wrist.

But the horse was of even more concern. He continued to favor his foreleg. Jessie picked her way through some brush, trying to keep from falling. Then she stilled. Listening. Night noises. Different than those at home. No grasshoppers whistling, or dogs barking. No familiar, comforting sounds. Instead, she thought she heard things moving through the brush, heard the hoot of an owl. She wished Ben were with her. Except he would probably be as confused, and frightened, as she.

She was afraid that if she kept going she could tumble into a gully. Then she had an idea. Horses could usually find their own stable. They had an instinct that she didn't. Of course, Carefree could leave her behind, but probably not with the injured leg. Decided, she pulled the reins back and tied them on the saddlehorn. The horse stood there.

"Go home, love," she said.

The beast didn't move.

She gave him a slap on his rear. He turned his head around and looked at her. She couldn't see exactly what kind of look. It was too dark. She imagined it was an accusation, though.

But the gelding lifted his head as if listening. "Go home," she urged again. Carefree started to move, and she moved beside him. Now her muscles were screaming in protest, as much from riding as from the fall. Between the two, she wondered how she could keep going. How she could put one foot in front of another.

But she did.

She didn't know how long she walked. Concentrating on just staying upright. Wondering whether she should have just stayed put. She remembered hearing that. When you're lost, you stay in one place and let someone find you. She had taken care of herself too long to do that.

She also wondered how April had disappeared so quickly. But she really had no one to blame but herself. She had been the one to race recklessly over country she didn't know. And yet . . . it had given her such joy, such unexpected pleasure. How could she have left that part of her life for so long?

You know why.

She bit her lip, remembering. The night held too many memories, and it was very, very dark now. She could barely see the blur of the horse in front of her. She didn't know if she could go any further.

She felt like Alice in Wonderland again, but this time the unfamiliar world was dark and strange and frightening. One foot, then another. Finally she couldn't take another step.

"Whoa," she said. The horse stopped so quickly she almost fell into him.

She leaned against him for a moment, and then in the distance she saw moving lights.

"Hel—lo," she yelled as loud as she could.

She heard an answering bark, then a gunshot. The lights moved toward her. Not fast enough, but they came on. Then a running form stopped abruptly, sniffed her, then stood stiffly beside her.

"Timber," she whispered, putting her head near his large, furry one. He whined and lifted a paw. She just held on to him until a horse and rider reached her. The rider dismounted and walked over to her. She knew simply by the way he walked that it was Ross. Somehow she'd known it would be him.

She'd never been so glad to see anyone in her life.

He kneeled next to her. "Are you all right?"

"Barely," she replied.

He held up a lantern, and his dark eyes moved over her. "You fell?"

"I said *whoa*. It was a mistake. I didn't know he took the word so to heart."

She saw the barest smile on his face, then it turned stern again. He knelt beside her and checked all her body parts. His hands were gentle but impersonal. He lingered over her arm. "Sprained, I think," he said, "but nothing serious." Then he stood and walked over to Carefree, who was still favoring his right front leg.

Jessie watched as he leaned down and looked at the leg. She held her breath, praying nothing was seriously wrong with the animal. He spoke to the animal with far more gentleness than he had to her. She recognized instantly who was the more important delinquent. It wasn't her.

"I don't think he's badly hurt," she said.

"No thanks to you," he said curtly. "How in the hell did you lose April?"

She deserved every implied criticism. She couldn't even answer him. She didn't know how she had lost her companion. "I don't know."

"I thought you knew something about horses. Otherwise, I never would have let you go."

She started to get indignant. But she knew she shouldn't have let Carefree run as she had. Not in terrain unfamiliar to her.

"I'm sorry," she apologized. "I was . . . enjoying riding so much, I—" Her words faltered as she saw the tense set of his shoulders. He was barely containing his anger.

He finished with the horse, then came back to her, looming like some tall specter over her. "April came back an hour ago. She said she'd looked for you everywhere, that you just seemed to disappear."

By then, another rider had approached. It was a man she hadn't seen before. "This is Charlie," Ross said. "There's half a dozen other men out searching for you, including Marc and his son."

"I'm sorry to cause so much trouble," she said again.

He stood then, lifted the lantern and looked at her. She couldn't see his face in the flash of the light. "Can you stand?"

"Yep," she said, although not at all sure. She heard the unwanted tremble in her voice. In truth, she was not all right at all. In truth, she was close to tears. She wasn't about to shed them, though. "It was a small tumble."

He frowned, leaned down, and gave her a hand up. She stood for a moment, trying to gain her balance. Timber stood as close as he could.

"Try walking," Ross commanded.

She didn't think she could. But she wouldn't give him the satisfaction of knowing it. She took one step, then fell into his arms. She couldn't stop the soft groan that escaped her lips.

"I *have* been walking," she said defensively.

"Well, you can't now," he said. He picked her up as easily as if she were a burlap sack of potatoes. When they got to the horse, he asked, "How far have you come?"

"I don't know. I just let the horse go, and I followed."

He didn't reply, but his grip tightened. Despite his anger, she felt safe in his arms. Very safe. She found herself snuggling pleasantly against his chest. Too soon they were at his horse, and he was helping her onto it. She instinctively reached for the reins, and her left arm rebelled. Every part of her rebelled. Another groan escaped.

His hands gentled. For a moment, she felt as if she'd never known anything quite as gentle. Then he swung up behind her. His arms went around her. All the fear she'd tried to rein, to hide, to pretend didn't exist took one last sharp aim at her, a delayed reaction, then gradually faded.

She leaned back against him. All was suddenly right with the world, and Alice had found her way home.

April said she'd looked for you everywhere.
Had she?
She was found. That was all that was important. Not that she'd made an idiot out of herself. Nor what had happened with April.
She kept telling herself that.

eight

Jessie soaked in the Jacuzzi bath for an hour. It was a truly glorious luxury, especially now, and she thought she could stay there forever. She certainly didn't want to expend the effort to get out.

Her body was all shades of gray and purple and red. Her wrist was wrapped in a tight elastic bandage. That was on the outside. She winced when thinking about the inside.

Every bone, every ligament, every muscle in her body hurt.

So did her pride.

She recalled every ignominious moment of her return to the ranch house . . .

The entire Clements clan had gathered outside. Sarah had taken over and hovered over her like a mother hen, seeing to each of the open wounds, using a pair of tweezers to extract thorns.

Ross had looked at her wrist again. "You should have it x-rayed," he said. "I'll drive you to the hospital."

She hadn't wanted that. She knew he must be concerned about Carefree, and probably the last thing he wanted to do was nurse a minor injury of a careless rider. "Go see about Carefree," she'd pleaded.

It had finally been decided that Cullen and Sarah would

take her to the hospital. April, full of apologies, had decided to go along.

Jessie had been reluctant, but she'd realized they were not going to let her go without having the arm checked first. She'd felt swept away by a tide of concern. It was a strange, unsettling feeling. She'd always taken care of herself before.

An hour later, an emergency doctor at a small hospital confirmed what she knew. Nothing was broken. Not even a bad sprain. Wrap it with a tight bandage and she would be as good as new in a few days.

She'd apologized profusely for putting everyone to so much trouble. Part of her had appreciated the worry and concern and cosseting. Another part merely wanted to crawl into a hole and nurse her wounds by herself . . .

She sank deeper into the tub with its jets. Alex had heard about the accident and showed up at the hospital. He'd glared at April, then uttered his own apologies for having left her. Jessie felt she was drowning in recriminations— and self-recrimination.

Sarah had wanted her to return to the ranch, to stay there at least one night, but Jessie had wanted to come back to the peace of her room. She'd wanted to think, to sort out all the feelings that had lodged themselves in her mind. So many.

She ran a soapy washcloth over her face, then gingerly over her body. She remembered the strength of Ross's arms, even the comfort she felt in them. But she also remembered the humiliation of being so incredibly stupid. How *could* she have lost April?

For only a split second, she considered the possibility that perhaps April . . .

But no. There was no reason. Could be none. She was making up villains because she wasn't willing to take full responsibility. And it had been obvious that everyone had been worried sick over her mishap. It had warmed her, even though she'd been terribly embarrassed and filled with guilt at causing so much trouble. She remembered how everyone was waiting, the smiles when Ross had helped her from the horse.

A family. Worried about her. She simply didn't know how to react.

She moved. And groaned. At least no one would hear it here. A family was fine, but . . .

Jessie knew if she didn't get up now, she probably never would. She heaved her battered body up and wrapped a towel around herself, then went to the dresser where she'd put her clothes. The top drawer held a nightshirt, a robe, and her undergarments along with the liquid silver necklace she'd purchased for herself at college graduation. She'd had no one there to celebrate with her, so she'd marked the occasion by driving to a jewelry store and impulsively buying the necklace.

Jessie took out the worn but comfortable oversized nightshirt, then checked the corner where she kept the necklace. It wasn't there. Her heart dropped precipitously. Her hands searched the bottom of the drawer under the other clothes. Then she found it on the other side of the drawer. She stood straight, the necklace clutched in her hands. She knew she had left it in the left-hand corner.

She systematically went through the other drawers. Not sure exactly what might be required, she'd brought more clothes than she needed. Now she saw other things out of order. If she hadn't missed the necklace, she might never have noticed that the slacks had not been smoothed down, nor that the shirts had been disturbed.

Someone had been in the room and had gone through her possessions!

She couldn't prove it, but she knew it. She *felt* someone else's presence in the room. A sense of violation intruded through all the other emotions. She shivered, not from cold but from the feeling of being watched. Her mind flitted back to the burglary of her home. Coincidence?

Chills ran down her spine. There couldn't be a connection.

Awkwardly, she pulled on the nightshirt and buttoned it, then went to the windows of her cottage. Only her car was parked in front of her casita. She couldn't see the window or parking area for the next one. Trees separated them.

She could see the second story of the main lodge. She suddenly had the feeling of being watched. Or was it because someone had been in the room?

Why?

Jessie closed the curtains and painfully limped to the bed, punching on the television remote. She wanted noise. She stretched out on the bed, grateful that it was more comfortable then her own. Cullen had certainly spared no expense.

Cullen. He would most certainly have keys to each room. She tried to remember everything Alex had told her about him. He'd served in Korea with honor but, unlike his uncle, he'd never lost his sense of direction. He'd been successful in banking, then had put together the consortium to build the Quest. He most certainly wouldn't be interested in her possessions.

She ignored the television and her mind relived the day. Alex had left twice during the day. Marc had also been gone most of the day. So had, for that matter, Ross. How many others had an opportunity? But she kept returning to the original puzzle. Why would anyone want to go through her possessions?

She changed position and pain jabbed through her arm. Jessie repressed a few choice expressions, then rose painfully and went to the bathroom. Alex had stopped at a convenience store and picked up some double-strength aspirin before returning Jessie to the Quest. She gulped down several.

Her mind was still spinning. She wanted it to stop. There was no way she could solve any of the puzzles tonight.

Tomorrow was Sunday. The last day of the reunion. She had planned to leave on Monday, but now she might stay another day. Visit the library. And the newspaper if there was one. Even the courthouse. Perhaps she could learn more about what happened fifty years ago. Could that have anything to do with her? With the questions—and fear—whirling in her head? In the meantime, she would ask questions.

With that promise to herself, she started to drift off. She turned down the volume of the television, but left it on, comforted by the humming sound. She turned off the light.

She only wished she could turn off the questions. And warm the chill that replaced the euphoria she'd felt earlier in the day.

Ross ran his hands over the sorrel. He was usually reliable, well-mannered. And Dan'l had told him that Jessica had a good seat, that she seemed competent.

He blamed himself for not going with them. He'd thought she would be safe enough with Alex, and then the bastard had left them. After that, Ross wasn't sure what happened.

April had claimed that she thought Jessica was right behind her when she turned into a path that wound up into the rocky cliffs. When she had stopped to warn her of the steep path, Jessica was gone.

He was also angry with Alex. The damned lawyer had said he would accompany the women. Ross had expected him to do so.

He was equally angry with himself. He'd had errands that afternoon. Errands that couldn't be postponed. But he *should* have postponed them. He didn't like the fear that had knotted his stomach when April had come galloping in. It had already been dark, and he knew how easy it was to get lost in the hills and mountains that surrounded the ranch.

He'd found himself liking Jessica and her wry sense of humor. He hadn't liked thinking of her out there. Alone. Too much could happen.

It had taken several hours to locate her. He'd been amazed, though, to find her traveling in the right direction toward the ranch. She'd been thrown, which had to have hurt like hell, and yet she'd tried to get back on her own. It'd been foolish but game.

But one look at her, and he'd known she was operating at the limit of her endurance. He'd been surprised at the tenderness he felt when she'd rested trustingly against him.

Damn, he didn't want to feel tenderness. He didn't want to get involved with a woman. Particularly this woman, who might hold his future in her hands. He couldn't afford losing his objectivity.

He'd had many brief affairs in which both he and the woman understood it would be exactly that and no more. His Apache blood had proved an aphrodisiac to some and a deterrent to others. He hadn't cared much either way. He only knew he wouldn't brand a woman with that mark. Nor saddle one with a man with a police record.

He finished his inspection. He'd realized immediately that the limp wasn't serious. But he'd looked for something, an indication that the saddle or blanket had been tampered with in some way. From everything he knew of Jessica, she was a good rider. Of course, it had been a long time. Still . . .

He didn't trust Marc, not when the congressman really wanted something. Nor Alex. Over the years, Ross had had many dealings with him, and he knew that Alex took chances. Oddly enough, it had been the family outlaw—himself—who'd insisted they not stretch the truth on loan statements or lease applications. But then, he admitted, he'd never trusted anyone who had anything to do with the law. Justice had always been for families like the Clementses. Not for families with names like Sanchez, his mother's and grandmother's name.

He ran his hand down Carefree's neck. "Good boy," he murmured softly. He'd found nothing suspicious. For a moment, he wondered why he'd even looked.

It was a case of mixed signals. Nothing more. And Jessica had learned a lesson last night. If she was plucky enough to ride again, he would teach her something about cutting horses. If she stayed that long. Alex had said she planned to leave Monday.

But she would be back when she learned the details of the trust.

For how long?

To stay. Or to sell? So much depended on one woman's decision.

After this night, she would probably be only too eager to sell a tradition.

Hell, a tradition, and a losing proposition.

But dammit, all he needed was a few years to prove that the Sunset could make a good profit, if not a great one. That was all in the hell he needed.

He closed his eyes, wondering how badly he wanted those years. And what he would do—when it came down to it—to get them. How much of his soul would he trade for them?

Jessie took another hot bath in the morning and plotted her next moves. Then she changed her airline ticket, delaying her return to Atlanta for a few days. Because Alex, or the family, had paid top price for them, there was no problem.

Then she called Sol. He was obviously pleased—and relieved—to hear her voice. "Ben and I have missed you."

"I miss you, too. How's Ben coping?"

"He's pining. He sits next to me, but he's always facing

the door. His tail starts beating when the door opens." Then he added quickly, "But he's eating well."

"Ben always eats well," she said wryly. She hesitated, then added, "Would it be too much trouble if I stayed a few days longer?"

"No, of course not. You're more than due for a vacation, and Ben is good company." Then curiosity crept into his voice. "Is it true? Was your father Harding Clements?"

She had explained everything to him before she'd left Atlanta, and he'd been more than a little intrigued. He loved historical mysteries and this seemed to qualify as one.

"I think so," she said. "I gave them blood for the DNA test, but they have a picture of him, and I'm pretty sure it's my father. I also look very much like Sarah did when she was my age. She was Harding's sister."

"Ahhhhhhh." She heard the long sigh across the miles. Then he asked, "Did you find out why he left?"

"That still seems the big mystery," she replied. "That's why I want to stay. I want to do some research. Library. Court records."

"Then stay as long as you feel it's necessary, Jessie. I know how important this is to you."

"Thanks," she said. "I'll be back in a few days."

"And Jessie?" She heard a hesitancy in his voice. "I wasn't sure I should tell you, but in light of the burglary in your house, I think you should know. The shop was burglarized last night. I haven't done a complete inventory yet, but they ransacked our desks and got into the safe. Thank God, there wasn't much there. Just Saturday receipts. A few hundred dollars."

She stilled. Another coincidence? They were beginning to pile up. "Maybe I *should* come home."

"No, no, of course not. There's been other burglaries in this center. I probably shouldn't even have said anything, but . . ."

She smiled to herself despite her apprehension. Sol was open and honest, and couldn't keep any secret unless pledged to secrecy. Then he would go to his grave with it. "You'll let me know if you find anything else missing?"

"Of course. You have a good time. Solve those mysteries to your satisfaction."

"I will. Say hello to Ben."

"Of course. I'll tell him you said to give him an extra dog biscuit."

"Are you spoiling him?"

"Rotten," he answered.

"And you told me you didn't like dogs."

"Ben is different. And I didn't say I didn't like them. I just . . . never had time for them."

"Wait until Christmas," she threatened.

He chuckled. "We'll talk about that when you get back."

She said good-bye, and thanked him again, and hung up the phone.

Another burglary. And someone had searched her room. What could they be looking for? Or was it still another coincidence? She swallowed hard, wondering whether Sol might be in danger. And yet none of the invasions had been violent. Even the burglar at her home had obviously just wanted to get away. Still, Sol was like a father to her. He had given her a job her sophomore year, realizing from her constant visits that she loved books as much as he did. She had worked for him for three years until she received her degree in literature and discovered that it equipped her for few jobs.

Sol had an independent income from his family. He owned the store just because he loved books, but now he was in his sixties, and he had an itch to write a book, to add to the history he loved so well. When he'd offered her a partnership with a very low down payment, she'd seized the opportunity. She hadn't realized then that she was hiding from life, from risks, from painful commitments. A bookstore was the perfect place to do that. She lived vicariously, but safely, through books.

She hadn't known it, in fact, until she mounted Carefree yesterday, until she felt the old power of a muscled body beneath her, the thrill of the rushing wind, the warm caress of a hot sun. She'd forgotten how it felt to be so alive, to experience so many sensations and emotions, and plain unadulterated joy.

Jessie knew one thing now. When she did return to Atlanta, she would start riding again. Somewhere. Somehow.

Ignoring all the stiffness and painful bruises, she dressed, made a cup of coffee from the coffeemaker in her room and took it outside. The morning sun was bright, intense. It bounced off Coffee Pot Rock, the massive red rock formation shaped like its name. The hues were spectacular, and the raw rugged beauty filled her with awe. And something else.

A sense of belonging? A kind of rightness?

Could a place really be part of one's soul, or was everyone affected by the sheer magnificence of the area?

And loneliness. She had discovered that last night.

She shivered despite the heat. It was late June, and the day already hot. Not like Phoenix, but warm enough. After finishing her coffee, she thought about breakfast. A number of the family staying at the resort had planned to eat breakfast together. But she wasn't up to that yet this morning. April was staying here, and her brother, as were assorted other first and second cousins.

Jessie didn't relish seeing April this morning, not before breakfast. She didn't want either apologies or, she feared, a certain amount of smugness that Jessie had not only been thrown but had also gotten herself lost. She felt her face flush as she thought about last night.

She hadn't had any time to look around Sedona on her own. She would check out the local bookstores to see what they had in literature about the area, then find the library.

It would be closed today, but she planned to be there bright and early tomorrow morning. Her conversation with Sol had spurred her determination to find out more about the family. Independently.

She went back inside the room. It had lost some of its charm last night. She considered moving to another hotel, but the horse was already out of the barn. She doubted whether she would have another visitor.

Sighing, she turned off the coffeemaker and located the keys to the rental car.

Marc glared at his daughter. "What in the hell were you up to?"

April flinched, but he didn't relent. Dammit, she could have ruined everything.

"I didn't think you wanted her to get too fond of the Sunset."

"So you drove her into the arms of Ross. Her protector. Is that what you wanted?"

"How would I know that he would be the one to find her. It could have been my brother. Or you. Then you two could have been heroes."

"It was reckless and foolish. You might well have made her suspicious."

April shook her head. "She blamed herself. And well she should. I didn't plan it. I just saw the opportunity when she didn't keep up with me."

"And Ross?"

April shrugged her shoulders. "Who cares about Ross?"

"I've seen the way you look at him."

She shrugged.

"He doesn't want you. That's it, isn't it?" Marc said with a hint of cruelty. "You've always wanted what you can't have."

"I want what you want, Daddy."

"Then don't go off on your own. Jessica needs to be

handled very carefully. I want her to trust me. She won't if my daughter abandons her in the middle of nowhere."

"I'm sorry. I just thought . . ."

He sighed. "You thought you would outsmart your brother. You don't have to compete with him, baby."

Her eyes flashed. *Damn.* April had always been competitive, especially with her brother. For some reason, she thought she had to outperform him to win approval. She'd always resented Hall, the son who'd been named after their great-grandfather. Marc sighed. Great things had always been expected of Hall, little from her. A good marriage for April would have suited him fine.

But that had never suited April. She'd wanted to be his campaign manager when she wasn't anywhere near ready for the position. She resented the fact that Marc had brought Hall immediately into a prominent position with the campaign. He partially understood. She'd been stuffing envelopes for him when Hall was out playing baseball. She'd come to consider herself indispensable. And, in many ways, she was. But she was also too assertive, too abrasive with the others on the campaign staff. She'd never learned that a politician gathered more flies with honey.

He was convinced that her desire to best her brother had prompted her to lose Jessica. She wanted to show him up, to make Marc see that she could be as tough as any man.

Just how far would she go?

He didn't know, and that frightened him.

"Just don't do anything else without asking me first."

She bit her lip, and he wasn't sure whether she understood how important it was. It wasn't just the sale of the ranch at stake. It was those bonds. And if anyone had a key to them, Jessica did. They couldn't scare her off.

"Swear?"

"I promise."

"Good. Now let's go have breakfast. Perhaps Jessica will be there."

"Not another apology," April complained. "I made one last night."

"And you'll make fifteen more if necessary," he said.

"All right," she said reluctantly.

"How would you like to go with me to the meeting in Phoenix next week?"

Her eyes shone. The defiance faded from her face. She'd been wanting to sit in on some of the meetings with key supporters. He had recently taken Hall to several.

"It's done, then," he said. "And always remember there are many ways to trap your quarry. The best is not always the most obvious."

Jessie told herself that walking was the best possible cure for sore muscles. She wasn't sure she believed it. Not when every step was agony.

The car wasn't much better. Thank God, it was her left wrist that was sprained. She rested that arm on the armrest, using her fingers sparingly. Her right hand did all the work.

Armed with a good breakfast from a diner, she drove to the old center of town, stopping at the tourist center which, happily, was open on Sunday. After loading herself down with chamber of commerce information, she headed for the bookstore in the next block.

She spent an hour there, prowling over every book with even a hint of history in it, then wandered the short streets that made up what was one of three separate entities that composed the city of Sedona. According to the map, this was the old town. Further out was the government complex, including the library. Then there was Tlaquepaque, the arts and crafts village.

But these streets were lined with souvenir shops and storefronts hawking Jeep trip explorations and hot air balloon excursions. She saw a number of people getting into colorful Jeeps, and she longed to get in with them. She longed to be anonymous. But it was already getting late.

She was due at the ranch for the final reunion supper and to say her good-byes to those family members who were leaving tomorrow.

With her maps and books on the seat beside her, she drove out to the ranch. More food. More drink. More people. More puzzles.

And Ross Macleod.

Embarrassment burned deep inside her whenever she thought of him. How could she have been so foolish as to get lost?

Would he even be there? He seemed to make elusiveness an art.

Once again, cars were parked all over the yard, including Alex's. She decided to head over to the barn first and see how Carefree was. She would also beg the horse's pardon.

She had no more than slammed the door of the car shut when Alex emerged from the house and came directly to her. "I called this morning. You didn't answer." His tone was a little querulous.

"I wanted to explore. You don't have to take care of me forever."

"I wish I had," he said, reaching out and taking her hand. "If I had even imagined that . . ."

"That I would make a total idiot out of myself. Not your fault, Mr. Kelley."

"I shouldn't have left."

She tried to change the subject. "Did you get your client's son out?"

"He was out when I got there. I think they got impatient and contacted the judge directly."

"They can do that?"

"In a small community some people can do anything they want."

Jessie stored that piece of information in her mind.

"In any event, I apologize. Next time I will stay by your side."

Jessie wasn't sure she wanted that. She sidestepped the offer. "You have no idea how much I enjoyed that ride. Until the end," she added wryly.

He grinned. "Indefatigable, huh?"

"Well, I do have a few aches."

"I bet you do," he said. "But you look good."

"With all my new fine colors. Purple, mauve?" She asked the question as she looked ruefully down at the quite evident bruises and the tight bandage around her wrist.

Alex eyed it, too. "You shouldn't be driving with that wrist."

"It's my left. And I can use it slightly."

He shook his head. "At least we know you have the Clements stubbornness."

She nodded. "I want to see how Carefree is."

"I'll go with you."

At the moment, she didn't want that. She wanted a word with Ross if he was there. She wanted to apologize once more. She might not see him again. Although she was convinced in her own mind now that her father was indeed the missing Clements brother, the blood tests could still prove differently If so, she would not be returning. Even if it did prove to be Clements blood, her home was in Atlanta. Her brief visit in Wonderland was nearly over.

"I'll see you in the house later," she said.

He hesitated as if he wanted to say something. She didn't want him to feel guilty about last night, but he apparently did. Everyone was feeling guilty, and she hated that. It was her fault. No one else's. Still when she looked at him, she wondered where he had gone yesterday. Had it been to her room? And why? There was no one to ask, because there was no one she knew well enough to trust.

She knew that sad truth would color everything she did or thought or said today. The magic had left. An enigma remained. But she sought to reassure him. "Don't worry about me. I'm fine."

He grinned. "I hear even Ross was impressed with the way you found your way back."

"Partially back," she corrected. "And he didn't *seem* impressed. He was angry and had every right to be."

Alex frowned. "He thinks more of those horses than he does of people."

"I find nothing wrong with that," she replied tartly. "People should have sense enough to take care of themselves."

He ignored her defense of Ross. "All the same, you kept your wits when many wouldn't have."

And if she hadn't? She most certainly would have been found. This was no longer the wild west. She was never in any danger. There were roads and walking trails and markings. At worst, she would have spent a few uncomfortable hours.

"It was an adventure," she said.

He raised an eyebrow. "And you're going riding again?"

"Of course. Every rider knows you have to get right back on a horse."

"Not today. Not with that wrist."

For some reason, she took that as a challenge. "Perhaps."

Jessie gave him a brief nod, and headed toward the barn. There would be no nuances there. Ross was blunt and honest.

She thought. She hoped.

But during the day she'd told herself not to trust anyone. Not until she discovered who had an interest in her room. *She had to remember that.*

Ross wasn't there. But Carefree was. He nickered softly when she approached and ran a hand down the side of his head. Apparently, she was forgiven for yesterday's mishap. He was standing easily enough, though she saw that his leg was neatly wrapped. "Ah, Carefree," she murmured. "I'm sorry. You should be out, kicking up your heels with the other horses."

"Oh, I think he enjoys the pampering." The deep soft drawl startled her, and she spun around.

He had approached so quietly that she couldn't believe he was only two feet behind her.

"Here," he said, thrusting half a carrot in her hand. He was wearing a faded denim shirt and an equally worn pair of Levi's.

The gesture surprised her. She looked up into his dark eyes. She wished she could fathom them, to know what emotions lay behind them. But they were as enigmatic as before. "Thank you," she said and held out the carrot to Carefree. The horse took it carefully from her hand and chomped on the treat.

"He'll be fine," he said after an awkwardly silent moment. "No lasting damage." Ross regarded her critically, as if she were one of his charges. "What did the doctor say about your arm?"

"A minor sprain, just as you diagnosed," she said. "No more than I deserved."

"I should never have let you go without telling you more about these horses. They're trained differently from the thoroughbreds your father handled. They can stop on a dime and when you tighten the reins, they step backward rather than stopping. Carefree is a hold back horse, not a cutting horse, but he was trained in many of the same maneuvers."

"What's the difference?" she asked.

He looked at her carefully, almost as if he were measuring the stamina or worth of a horse. Jessie had seen owners and trainers scout horses with that same speculative look in their eyes. She had to fight to keep from squirming under his perusal.

"He's not quite as quick or quite as agile."

"I think he's agile," she said wryly.

The side of his mouth turned up in what could be construed as a half smile. He changed the subject. "I hear you're leaving tomorrow."

No offer to ride again. Just an objective, neutral statement.

"That's the plan," she said just as neutrally.

He raised a dark eyebrow, and she wondered whether he'd caught the significance of her wording. He didn't comment on it, though, and she felt a rush of disappointment. A word of regret would have been nice.

"I imagine you'll be back. You can try that sunset again," he said.

"Will you come with me?"

"Someone sure as hell will," he answered. "And it won't be April."

"It wasn't her fault," she protested. "If I'd stayed with her . . ." Her voice trailed off as she saw his expression. She could feel the heat of it. He'd not let it show before, but anger apparently had been simmering inside him. She wondered if some of it was directed toward her.

A muscle jerked in his cheek. "Don't be too trusting, Miss Clayton."

"Does that mean I shouldn't trust you either?" she asked. A shiver ran down her spine again, just as it had this morning.

"Hasn't anyone warned you about me?" he said with a small enigmatic smile.

She shook her head.

"I'm the black sheep. The wild one. You should be particularly wary of me. Alex would tell you that."

"Alex hasn't told me anything about you." It was only a small untruth. Alex had said very little.

He shrugged. "I imagine he will once the DNA match comes in."

"Why then?"

Ross Macleod shrugged. "I have to go," he said. "An appointment. I just came to look at Carefree, but he seems to be doing fine." He hesitated, then said with just a trace of irony, "Have a good trip home."

He walked off then. She hesitated a moment, then followed him to the door and watched as he strode over to the least imposing vehicle in the horseshoe-shaped drive: a dusty, blue pickup truck. He didn't look back as he got into the driver's seat.

She ducked back into the barn, not wanting him to see her staring after him.

An appointment? On Sunday during a family function. Or was he avoiding them all again. Avoiding her.

Don't be too trusting. She wanted to kick him. How could he say something like that, then leave so abruptly?

A warning? About who? Or what?

nine

"I wish you would stay longer," Sarah told Jessie as she was about to leave. "In fact, I wish you would move into the house."

Jessie felt like an ingrate, but she really didn't want to stay at the ranch. Not until she had confirmation that she had a right to do so. Not until she knew whether or not she was truly a Clements.

"I've decided to stay a few days," she said. "But I'm really comfortable at the Quest. I will come over, though."

A worry line seemed to smooth out in Sarah's face. "I'm so glad. Now that everyone's leaving, we will have more time to talk."

Jessie wanted that. She wanted it very much. Perhaps Sarah would tell her more about Harding Clements. About his childhood. About the events prior to his disappearance. Jessie had to know, needed to understand.

Especially now. The unwanted visitor of yesterday kept haunting her. So did Sol's report of the burglary, but neither were something she wanted to mention. Not at the moment. After all, nothing had been missing from her room. She had no reason to go to the police here. In fact, they would probably laugh in her face.

She nodded. "I would like that."

"I still wish you'd think again about staying here,

though. Marc and his family are leaving Tuesday morning. It will be only Halden and me in the ranch house then. Rosa is our housekeeper and cook, so it wouldn't be any trouble. Ross, of course, has his own house."

Jessie almost changed her mind at the thought of a nearly empty Sunset. The sprawling house was comfortable, and she would have access to the horses. And Ross. She doubted he shared her interest in proximity.

And safety?

Would the Sunset be any safer than her present lodging?

But she didn't want to have to account for every moment. "I'm already settled," she said as gently as she could, "and I want to do some exploring on my own. I promise to spend a lot of time here, though."

"Lunch tomorrow?" Sarah said hopefully. "Then we can go for a ride later."

"I would love it," Jessie said, wondering how her plans had gone so awry. Her time tomorrow was being whittled down.

"Good. We can get to know each other better without so much interference."

Interference? Jessie thought it a strange choice of words.

Just then, Marc and Samantha came in.

Marc came straight to her. "I'm so sorry about yesterday," he said. "So is April."

"She shouldn't be. It was my fault completely," Jessie said, saying the same words she'd voiced all day.

"She should have kept a better watch. She knew you weren't familiar with the area. Ross said you used your head, though." He grinned. "Big praise from him."

Too bad Ross hadn't told her.

"It was an . . . adventure," she said. "And I haven't had one of those for a while."

He nodded at her with approval. "Samantha and I are driving to Phoenix Tuesday. We'll be staying there a few days before flying on to Washington for some meetings. If you need anything, anything at all, call one of us."

"Thank you," she said. "Good luck with your campaign."

"Would you think about working with us, too?" he asked.

"I'm in Atlanta," she reminded him.

"But we hope to see you frequently. Cullen will always make a room available for you at the Quest." She noticed he didn't repeat Sarah's invitation to stay at the ranch.

He turned around. His brother was behind him. "Won't you, Cullen?"

"Of course. Any time," boomed Cullen. "You have only to let me know."

"She's planning to stay a few more days," Sarah said.

"Then of course she should stay at the resort as our guest," Cullen quickly replied, casting a look at Sarah. Jessie thought she detected something like triumph in it.

"I was going to pay for it," Jessie protested.

"I wouldn't permit any such thing," Cullen said. "You stay as long as you wish."

"Just two or three days. I have a business in Atlanta."

"Well, we'll have to have dinner together before you leave. I'll call you."

He leaned over and kissed Jessie on the cheek, and she felt a little ungrateful. They were all trying to make her feel comfortable. It wasn't their fault that they did the opposite, that she needed some time to absorb everything. It was hers.

The two men walked together toward the door, conversing intently, leaving her with Sarah to say good-bye to other members of the Clements family. Alex appeared from the living room with a glass in his hand and joined them out on the porch. In a few more moments, the room had emptied.

"It's always a little sad when everyone leaves," Sarah said.

"It must be a lot of work for you."

"Everyone pitches in. Cullen and his wife live in Sedona, not far from the Quest, and his twins and their wives always help."

"How did the Quest get its name?"

"Cullen wanted something unique. Many of those coming to Sedona are on a quest. They want to find beauty, peace, adventure. He tries to offer all of it."

"He's also a banker?"

"He was for a while, working with his father, Halden. But he always wanted something of his own. Korea changed him, just as World War Two changed Heath. I think war probably always changes the young men who fight. There's an impatience, a feeling that they've lost years of their lives. Perhaps they even feel that life is uncertain, fragile, and they have to live it to the hilt. In any event, the Quest became his dream. It took him years to get the financing, but it was something that was all his."

And the Quest *was* special. Jessie had recognized that. Everything about it spoke of perfection.

She nodded. "I can understand that." And she could. Like the bookstore was hers. Not entirely, perhaps, but Sol had made it more and more hers.

Her respect for Cullen grew. He could have followed in his father's footsteps. Instead, he'd taken risks.

"And the ranch?"

Sarah frowned. "Ranching is a twenty-four-hour-a-day job without much profit. It was never that attractive to him. And the house was never fancy enough for his wife."

"But Marc stays here," Jessie said, still trying to sort out the family dynamics.

"It's convenient for him. Congressmen don't really make that much, and he and Samantha have a town house in Georgetown, in Washington. The ranch gives him an address in his district. There's enough room that we don't see each other that much. April, though, usually likes staying at the Quest. She doesn't think the ranch is good enough, either."

Jessie wondered whether Sarah thought that about her, too. It wasn't that the Quest was more luxurious. Or more comfortable. She would have preferred the laid-back Sunset if she didn't still feel the interloper, if she didn't need the freedom to research what unquestionably were secrets withheld from her.

Perhaps she wouldn't feel that way if the DNA proved she was indeed a Clements. But she couldn't stay that long. Not when her home, business, and even hotel room had been invaded. She didn't want to believe that last night's misadventure might be part of a pattern, but neither could she discount it.

She found herself missing Sol and his good common sense. She also missed Ben desperately. She could never doubt his loyalty.

Jessie glanced out the window. The three men had left the porch. The sisters-in-law, Sondra and Samantha, also had their heads together.

Her eyes were still on the two groups when a blue pickup drove in.

Ross jumped down from the cab and approached the three men. His dog followed at his heels, sitting when Ross stopped. In the next few moments, she was mesmerized by the body language. Anger was obvious. On all their parts.

She saw Ross stiffen, saw his fingers bunch into a fist.

She glanced at Sarah, who was also staring out the large glass windows toward the quartet of men. Then she obviously tried to avert Jessie's attention. "Ross really was impressed with you last night."

"For getting lost and laming his horse?" Jessie asked dubiously.

"For keeping your head. Someone else might well have tried to ride the horse."

Jessie shook her head in disbelief.

"April did once. Ruined the horse."

"Was it destroyed?"

"Ross would never destroy a horse just because it was no longer useful. But the horse never regained the strength in his leg. He couldn't be ridden again."

"And Ross kept him?"

"Until he died of old age. He tries to hide it, thinks it's a weakness, but he has a soft spot for animals. He found Timber half dead. He was a part-wolf pup and had been shot by someone. Ross nursed him back to health. Ross is still the only person he'll take food from."

"I suppose Ross will be pleased that everyone's leaving."

Sarah sighed. "Most likely."

"He said something puzzling earlier."

"What?"

"That I should be wary of him, that someone would tell me why once the DNA results came back."

Sarah frowned. "Ross sees devils where there are none."

After the last few days, Jessie wondered whether Ross didn't see clearer than anyone. But she held her peace. She didn't want to accuse anyone of illegal entry of her room. Perhaps it wasn't even illegal entry. Perhaps it had been a maid who'd just had a moment's curiosity. Her mind cleared slightly. That was it. Why hadn't she considered the possibility before?

Because both her home and store had been burglarized? Because she didn't believe in coincidence?

Still it was an explanation. One she desperately wanted to believe.

Ross disappeared into the barn carrying a package, then, as she watched, he left again and strode down the path to his house. "Why did he tell me to be careful?"

Sarah smiled weakly. "When he first came here, he was as wild as a young wolverine. He got into trouble all the time. For the first time, he had controls, and he didn't like it. And I couldn't blame him. He'd never had any stability, any discipline. His father, who was married to another woman, had abandoned his mother, and now his father's widow—a stranger—was making rules for him to follow."

She hesitated, then added painfully, "The family knew he was my husband's natural son. Marc and Cullen were afraid of the scandal. Cullen's twins gave him a hard time. But Halden knew how much I always wanted a child, and he accepted Ross, particularly when he showed such an aptitude and interest in ranching. I think that upset everyone more.

"Marc was especially angry," Sarah added. "He hadn't liked my husband either, and he thought I was making a mistake all over again, especially when Ross got in trouble. But the will gave me and mine life tenancy at the ranch, at least as long as the trust held."

Jessie felt her heart go out to the boy Ross had been. Tossed from pillar to post, then obviously unwanted when brought into this house. How often had she felt like that? An outsider looking in?

She imagined the loneliness of the boy. She understood the rebelliousness.

She also realized that Sarah had held back something. "But Ross obviously grew out of it," she said.

"Once he got involved with the horses, yes. But he never felt he belonged here. He wasn't a Clements, and April and the twins never let him forget it."

"What about April's brother?"

"He always liked Ross. Ross was the only person who didn't expect something from him."

The relationships were whirling around in Jessie's head. Was this what it was like in every family? Competition, jealousy, suspicions? But then there was the open warmth she'd seen, too. The honest affection between cousins. That was what she'd wanted. What she'd longed for. What she was loath to relinquish before she fully knew it.

She moved without looking and her injured arm hit the side of a chair. An unexpected gasp exploded from her.

Sarah looked at her. "I don't think you should make that long drive with that arm," she said.

Jessie shrugged. "I drove here without a problem."

"Still, if you need to make an unexpected movement . . ." She hesitated. "Ross will drive you."

That was the last thing she needed. Or wanted.

But when she started to protest, Sarah was already at the phone, punching a button. Before Jessie could stop her, Sarah had started speaking. "I want you to drive Jessie home."

Jessie shook her head frantically.

Sarah made no sign she understood. Instead, she put the phone back into its cradle. "He's on his way."

Jessie closed her eyes for a moment. "What about my car?"

"We can get someone to take it to the Quest tomorrow," Sarah said, leading the way out the door onto the porch.

The sun hovered on the horizon, turning the sky into a blaze of colors. Crimson, peach, orange, and copper layered the sky. The last rays hit the red rock formations, turning them into molten gold. The sheer beauty made her gasp.

She had missed the sunset yesterday in all that had happened. Or at least had paid little attention to it. And now she was awed at the splendor, and yet it made her hurt, too. The vastness of the sky—the wild glory of it—revived an old unexplicable yearning.

A dampness fogged her eyes and she knew tears were hovering somewhere close. She wondered whether her father had stood here and watched the same band of fire around the earth, felt the depth of the blue in the sky. Had he felt awe at a sunset? Or had he always taken them for granted?

She felt herself shiver. Sarah moved closer to her.

"Did . . . Harding like sunsets?"

"Your father?" Sarah seemed intent on making the two into one.

Jessie nodded.

"I wonder if the male species ever admits they like sunsets," Sarah mused.

"He . . . Harding looked so . . . carefree in those photos. I can't remember my father smiling."

"*Cocky* was more the word," Sarah said with a slight smile. "He thought the world was his oyster. He could ride anything alive, and he knew it."

"But that oyster was crushed," Jessie said. It was a question as much as a statement.

Sarah's face suddenly looked far older. It seemed to crumple in front of Jessie's eyes. Jessie took her hand and held it tight.

For a moment, she thought Sarah was going to answer, but the door slammed and the room suddenly filled with Ross's presence. He went quickly to Sarah, putting his hand under her arm, steadying her. Then he looked at Jessie with an accusation in his eyes.

With visible effort, Sarah straightened. "Don't look at her like that," she ordered. "She only asked me if my brother liked sunsets. We dragged her all the way out here for her to learn about us. She has a right to ask questions."

Ross ignored her defense. "Are you all right?" he asked Sarah.

"I'm better than I've been in years," she said. "Just having Jessie here has been a tonic."

Warmth flooded through Jessie. She reached over and gave Sarah a quick hug.

Sarah grabbed her hand and held on as though for dear

life. "Jessie," she said in a broken voice. "Thank you for coming."

The emotion in her voice was deep. Jessie felt its echo. It was as if they'd shared the death of someone who'd died last week rather than years ago. The grief Jessie had felt at her father's death rose in her again, strong and alive and terrible. There was so much she didn't know, hadn't realized. She had thought her life was lonely. It couldn't have come close to the loneliness he must have felt. He'd had a family, a heritage, an identity. It must be far worse to know and lose such things than to have never known them at all.

She'd felt sudden, unexpected jolts of grief before. But they had faded, become rarer until Alex had appeared. Then they'd started again. But none had been as strong as this one, none as powerful. Her father hadn't been the best father ever created. He'd not been an easy father, or an easy man. But he'd been her world. All she'd ever had.

"Jessica?"

She looked up into dark, expressionless eyes. "Jessie," she corrected.

"I like Jessica," he said, his drawl deep and soft. So had her father. That was why she seldom used it. Jessica had been vulnerable. Jessie was tough. She'd learned to be.

But she wasn't going to debate the matter now.

"It doesn't matter," she muttered softly, still dazed by those intense moments of feeling.

Just then, Alex came inside. He looked surprised to see Ross there. "I thought you were boycotting us."

It seemed a strange observation for an attorney, a man who was not a member of the family, either.

But Sarah seemed not to take offense.

Nor, apparently, did Ross. "I'm taking Jessica home."

"I was going to offer to do just that," Alex said. "I didn't think it was a good idea for her to drive, either."

"Well, you're too late, now," Ross replied in a taut voice.

"I'm going into Sedona anyway," Alex said, his voice challenging him.

"I thought I would take her to supper."

The latter claim from Ross was news to her. She'd eaten earlier, and she wasn't hungry. She hadn't even been consulted, much less asked. All of a sudden, Jessie felt like a scrap of food being contested by two bully dogs. Testosterone was alive and well.

Unfortunately, she didn't think any of it was because she was irresistible.

"I will drive myself home," she announced.

Both men turned toward her, dismayed astonishment in Alex's expression, something entirely different in Ross's. Amusement. At least she thought it was amusement. It was difficult to tell with Ross.

"I'm sorry," Alex said, immediately contrite. "Of course you can go any way you wish."

"She'd already accepted Ross's offer," Sarah stepped in quickly.

Jessie was neatly trapped. She could either call Sarah a liar or accept. She didn't want to do the former. She nodded.

"Well, then I'll retreat gracefully," Alex said, but Jessie saw an angry glint in his eyes. "Cullen said you are planning to stay a few more days. Perhaps we can have dinner together, tomorrow."

Her dance card was filling up even more rapidly than she'd first thought. She'd never been in such demand. It made her more than a little suspicious. But perhaps she could extract something from Ross. She'd always been a good listener. And being a good listener often led to confidences. She tried to smile noncommittally.

Then she looked back up at Ross, and realized she was fooling herself. He was probably as enigmatic as his eyes. He nodded at Alex, but thankfully she didn't see any triumph in his face. Instead, he took her arm and guided her out the door as neatly as a dog might gather a sheep wandering in the wrong direction.

But as his fingers lightly met her skin, she felt his very touch burn through her. She glanced up at him, remembering how she'd felt the night before, when Ross had found her. Safe. But this was different. This was anything but safe. She'd received what amounted to an electric shock, and now it sizzled inside her, twisting and burning and making a shambles of her practical self.

He didn't seem to notice, except perhaps when he opened the door and she stumbled. It had been a long time since she'd felt so clumsy. Inadequate. The fact that two very good-looking men had been vying for her attentions didn't help at all. It only heightened her suspicions that something odd was going on, and everyone knew what it was but her.

The thought angered her, and she straightened her shoulders. Tonight, she decided, she would start batting the piñata of mysteries. She moved perceptively away from her escort. She didn't want the irresistible attraction she felt, especially since he didn't seem to feel the same. Did there have to be two magnets to attract? An interesting proposition.

She knew she was thinking nonsense as a safeguard. She hadn't been this attracted to a man since Mills. And she remembered exactly how much Mills had reciprocated the feelings. She cringed as she remembered how angry he'd been when she refused to sleep with him when he'd taken her to the barn after returning from her first prom, the first that she'd ever been invited to attend. "You're nothing but a cheap tease," he spat at her. "Why in the hell did you think I took you to the dance?" Then he'd torn off her clothes . . .

She'd stopped believing in princes.

She'd stopped believing in fairy tales then, too. Until now. But Wonderland wasn't really a fairy tale. It was a puzzle. Nothing was as it seemed; everything was nonsensical. She could accept that.

"Are you angry?"

The question startled her. She decided not to look at him. Perhaps that would help. "No. Sarah trapped you as well as me."

"Why do you think I was trapped?" He held the door of his truck open for her, closed it once she got in, then leaned against the door, looking at her through the open window. He was obviously waiting for an answer.

"Sarah called you."

"I often tell Sarah no," he said.

"Do you?" she asked curiously, losing herself again in those fathomless dark eyes.

"Just ask her."

All his natural intensity was focused on her. She really didn't understand why. She only knew her stomach was doing somersaults.

He abruptly left the window and walked around to the driver's side. She wasn't sure she was ready for him sitting beside her for the next thirty minutes or so. She found herself biting her lip, which she'd done a lot as a teenager. She thought she'd progressed beyond that. Apparently not.

Ross handled the truck the same way he handled horses—with efficiency, respect, and, she thought, even a bit of affection.

"Since you're going to be here so briefly, I thought you might enjoy a part of Arizona the others wouldn't expose you to," he said, his eyes staying on the road.

"That sounds ominous," she replied.

"I wouldn't take everyone there, but I think you might enjoy it."

"Is that a compliment or an insult?"

He chuckled. It had a nice sound, and she guessed its

husky quality might come from disuse. "A compliment, suspicious lady. But anytime you want to leave, you can."

She had the strangest feeling that she'd passed some kind of test, that he really did want her to come with him.

She only wondered whether he was going to pass her own test. It had everything to do with truth.

ten

Ross had lied, of course. He had indeed been coerced into driving Jessica home. He'd wanted to stay as far away from her as possible.

He didn't believe in forever. He didn't even believe in relationships of any duration.

And Jessica was a forever kind of lady. He'd learned to recognize those types immediately and to stay away.

And yet . . . there was a recognition between them, one he'd tried to ignore. He'd never felt this kind of awareness before. He'd always been attracted to earthy women, not to sleek beauties like April, although at one time in his life he'd lusted after her. He probably still did, at one level. But he liked women who didn't mind getting their hands dirty, who would drink beer from a bottle, and who didn't spend half a day trying to improve on nature.

He also liked women who enjoyed sex for sex's sake, who didn't expect a wedding ring at the end of a healthy coupling. He didn't want entanglements. He'd seen too many go wrong.

Unexpectedly, he'd found himself thinking far too frequently about Jessica. He liked the way she'd made so little fuss about her fall and, in fact, had taken the blame for it. He wasn't sure she deserved to be doing so, but he admired her grit. He also liked the way she appeared the next day, driving herself, asking for little. And, as far as he knew, she'd not inquired once about whether she had an inheritance due.

She had a quiet self-sufficiency. It was due, he expected, to her childhood, which Sarah had explained in detail. She too had been on her own much of her life. Perhaps that accounted for the attraction, or recognition, or whatever the hell it was that flashed between them.

He'd resolved to keep his distance. Until Sarah called. Then he'd found himself not only coerced but eager, and he thought he would take her to his favorite place. Perhaps she would turn up her nose at it, and that would end any reluctant interest he might have.

What he hadn't expected was to become embroiled in a battle with Alex for the privilege, and he'd astounded himself for acting as idiotic as he had. But Alex's possessiveness had struck him the wrong way. Alex had a reputation with women, and Ross didn't want Jessica to be one of his victims. Damn. He didn't like the sudden protectiveness he'd felt, or feeling like an adolescent kid vying for the favors of the prettiest girl in class.

The only thing gained from the stupid confrontation was the distaste in Jessica's eyes. She was obviously not one of those women who enjoyed being fought over. She'd found them both ridiculous.

That knowledge didn't help his pride, but it did make him like her more.

"I'm sorry," he said as he drove toward Sedona. He realized he couldn't remember when last he'd said those words. They knotted in his gut.

"You don't say that often, do you?"

It was uncanny. Exactly as if she'd read his mind. Uncanny? Hell, unsettling.

"No," he said.

She didn't say anything, and yet he felt comfortable. Even his anger at himself faded away. He gave her a fleeting look. The windows were open, and her short hair blew against her face. Her lipstick was gone, and her cheeks were blushed with the wind.

Warm air blew through the cab. He'd never liked air-conditioning and though the pickup had it, he seldom used it. He leaned down to turn it on.

"No," she said. "I like the air. It's different here. Fresh."

"Is it that bad in Atlanta?"

"I didn't think so."

"Didn't?"

"You grow used to it. You don't notice it until you come to someplace like this."

Except even here, the air was becoming polluted. Too many people. And there would be more if Marc and Cullen had their way.

"You raised some interesting subjects earlier," she said casually. So casually that it took him a moment before the words—and their meaning—registered.

He turned, sorry that he'd brought them up at all. Perhaps it hadn't been the time. But April's stunt had worried him. He knew how much was at stake. "I talked too much. I just wanted you to be careful."

"Why?"

He hesitated, but then he had started to open the box of secrets. It wasn't fair to her to slam it closed now. "Alex didn't tell you anything about the trust?"

"What trust?"

"Old Hall Clements's will—really it was Mary Louise's doing—put the Sunset in a trust. Equal parts to the ranch went to the surviving children or their blood heirs. Only Heath had died without children, leaving five shares."

He waited for a reaction, but there was none. Her face showed shock. He hadn't been sure how much he wanted to say. Whether he should say anything at all. Now he thought she should know it all. "The ranch couldn't be sold without agreement of the owners of at least four of the five shares. One couldn't stop the sale. Two could. That made it damned near impossible to sell the ranch since your father disappeared."

Grateful there was no traffic on this road, he turned his eyes from the road to her face. Color had drained from it. The news obviously came as a complete surprise.

His eyes returned to the road, and he waited for the questions. It was a moment before they came.

"I . . . don't think I understand."

"If the DNA confirms the relationship, then you are one-fifth owner of the Sunset," he said.

"One-fifth?" She replied, wonderment in her voice. Shock filled her face.

"Mary Louise died long before I came to the ranch," he said, "but I understand she was the driving power behind the will. She had a fierce love for both the family and the Sunset. She wanted to keep them together. That's why she talked Hall into adding the stipulation that at least four of the shares had to vote to sell."

"But my father—Harding—was missing for so many years. Why wasn't he declared dead?"

Jessica was smart as hell. She had found the one joker in the deck. "I don't think Mary Louise ever accepted his disappearance," he explained. "She made sure he could not be written out unless . . . there was proof he had died and had left no heirs."

"And so the ranch couldn't be sold unless it was unanimous?"

"Right."

Several moments of silence passed. He could almost see the thoughts running through her head. He waited for the next question. He was sure it would come. She was too bright not to understand.

"Does someone want to sell?"

"Everyone but Sarah."

"It would have been better then—for her—if Harding

was never found. No one could ever get the four-fifths approval."

"The others planned to file suit and have him declared dead."

"The *others*?"

"Marc, Cullen, Katherine, Andrew, and Elizabeth."

"Then that's why they were looking for Harding," she said, almost to herself. "It wasn't a sudden surge of familial affection."

He heard the disappointment in her voice. And a certain cynicism. But she'd deserved the truth. She had to know what was going on.

"Sarah did have a reason," he said. "She loves the ranch. But she also loved Harding. She often talked about him. You can't imagine how pleased she was when the search firm found you. And it wasn't entirely because of the ranch."

"And you?" she asked.

Ah, the final question. "I can never have a vote, nor can I inherit part of the ranch. I'm not a blood heir," he said.

"Then what happens when Sarah . . ." She couldn't quite say the word.

"Her share will be divided evenly among the others."

"That could get very complicated."

"Yes," he said simply.

She was quiet, obviously trying to absorb all the information.

He came to a turn and took a left. The road widened, and businesses began to dot the landscape. Ross turned into one of them. It was a cantina, one frequented by many of the Hispanic hands in the area and also local cowboys. The food was excellent, the music good.

Then he looked at her, suddenly ashamed of his high-handedness. He had used it as a test, expecting her to dislike it and thus strengthen his resolve to stay away from her. He realized now how completely unfair that was. But then he hadn't been acting rationally since he'd met her. "I didn't ask you if you liked Mexican."

"I do," she said. Her eyes sparkled suddenly, and he knew she wasn't just saying it for her benefit.

"We could go somewhere else." *Say yes.*

"No." She was already getting out of her side of the cab.

He swore silently. But it wasn't the first time one of his plans backfired. He just wondered how badly.

A will. Trusts. An equal share to each child and their blood heirs. The implications echoed in her head after the shock had worn off. She had never thought, never expected . . .

Inheritances were what happened to other people.

Why hadn't Alex said anything? An overabundance of legal caution?

The thoughts hammered at her. She'd needed the diversion that Ross provided when he'd pulled into the cantina. She'd automatically opened her own door, not waiting for him to come around, but he was there when she stepped down. His hand was outstretched and she took it, feeling the sudden warmth as his skin touched hers. Warmth? It was more like a red-hot poker and she dropped it that quickly.

She still felt the surge of energy reverberating through her as his hand went to the small of her back, guiding her toward the door. She had seen men do that in films, but never had experienced it before. Sure, they'd held her hand, or put an arm around her shoulder, but none had so naturally claimed her both protectively and possessively. There was a casual elegance about it that made her heart pound harder.

She loved the cantina. She'd always liked Mexican food and even had a predilection toward small, out-of-the-way authentic eateries that most people never found, or wouldn't frequent even if they'd heard about them. No tablecloths, no overly attentive waiters.

But the smells were wonderfully provocative, and the small dark interior was scrupulously clean. A singer was belting out a Spanish song on an old jukebox.

A hostess gave Ross a big grin. "Señor Ross," she said, "I have a table for you and the señorita." They threaded through a room packed with mostly Hispanic families to a table in a corner. Many of them nodded at Ross, and he stopped several times to speak and introduce her. She was obviously with a well-liked celebrity. She had never seen him like this before. He was totally at ease, a quick smile on his lips. Eyes flashed to her in surprise, and she wondered if he'd ever brought a date here before.

A date. She doubted he considered it as such.

She knew a little Spanish and caught some words, but all her attention was fastened on her companion as they were seated at a table. A candle in a small bowl provided dim light. It flickered, casting shadows across Ross's angular face, and seemed to make his eyes even darker.

When a pretty young Hispanic girl appeared and asked for their drink orders, Ross looked toward Jessie, an eyebrow raised.

She named a Mexican beer she often drank, and Ross ordered the same.

"Hungry?" he asked.

"I wasn't until I came inside."

"Everything is good," he said as the beer arrived, along with chips and dip. The music changed. A slow, sultry song drifted through the restaurant. Jessie understood enough Spanish to know it was a song about doomed love.

Her gaze met his, and she felt herself being singed by his lazy, appraising look. This time, she didn't try to look away. She felt as if every bone were melting, that under his gaze she was turning into one warm liquid puddle.

His lips had a crook to them and she was disconcerted by that dimple that appeared on the rare occasions when he smiled. Other than those two vulnerabilities, his face was all angles and planes. His dark lashes were thick and long, giving him a lazy languid look. Yet there was nothing lazy—or languid—about him. His fingers thrummed on the table with the restless energy that so attracted her. It contrasted with the patience she'd seen in him when he was with the horses.

He raised an eyebrow. "Made up your mind?"

She did something she'd never done before. "Order for me," she said.

"Are you real hungry?" he asked, then without waiting for an answer turned toward the waitress and in what she thought must be flawless Spanish he gave what seemed an endless order.

"Not that hungry," she said.

"But *I* haven't eaten yet," he replied with that rare, attractive smile. He seemed more comfortable here than any place she had seen him. An older Hispanic man came over and put a hand on his shoulder.

"This is the owner, Ramon. His son, Dan'l, works at the Sunset. Ramon, this is Jessica Clayton."

The man bowed. "I am honored. I try to get my son to work here, to take over the business, but no, he wants to be a cowboy."

"He'll outgrow it," Ross assured him.

"I am trusting you to make it so," Ramon said.

"I'm working his ass off," Ross said

"A conspiracy?" Jessie interjected.

"A very small one," Ramon said, holding up his two fingers and bringing them close together.

"I won't tell," she promised.

"I like this one," Ramon said. He wandered off then, stopping to talk to customers at one table, then another.

"*This* one?" She raised an eyebrow as he had.

He chuckled, a sound that was like a gentle earthquake, if that were possible. She realized the dichotomy of that description. Nonetheless, it fit. She stored it in her mind.

But now she'd allowed some of what he'd said to sink in. She had a million more questions. "Do you know why my father disappeared?"

Any hint of amusement left his eyes. "Not firsthand."

"But you've heard rumors," she said. "Suppositions?"

He was silent. His fingers thrummed again on the table. "Those are not for me to repeat," he said finally.

"I need a friend," she said. "I hoped I'd found one in you."

"Don't," he said. "I have as much to gain or lose as anyone in all this. You should know that."

"Why?"

"If the ranch is sold, I lose my job."

Jessie filed that away, too. "Why would they sell it?"

He laughed, but this time there was nothing warm and fuzzy about it. "Money. What else?"

"Don't make me fish this out, piece by piece," Jessie pleaded.

"The ranch is barely staying afloat," he said reluctantly. "An offer has been made for the land. Some moneymen want to create 'a planned development,' as they call it. The offer is very high."

"And Sarah is blocking it."

"For the moment," he said, his obsidian eyes watching carefully.

A chill ran down Jessie's back. He did have a reason to take her out tonight. He was telling her himself, before she found out from others. For a few silly moments, she'd actually thought . . .

She was suddenly glad she hadn't told him about the intruder. Or intruders. The one at the Quest. The one at home. The one at the bookstore. An ominous pattern was developing, and she had no idea whom to trust. But why would anyone be snooping into her life if all they wanted was her vote? They already knew everything there was to know about her. Probably more than she did, herself.

She also found it was useless to ask him more questions about her father. He wasn't going to answer. She was not going to be a supplicant. She would get the answers for herself.

The happiness Jessie had felt at being with Ross drained away. Sure, he had told her more than anyone else had, but not enough. He was hiding as much as the rest of the family was. She had believed the Clementses the perfect family, the family she'd dreamed of for so long. All her life. And now she didn't know who or what to believe.

The perfect family, indeed.

The food came. She knew it was probably very good. Yet it tasted like cardboard. Their conversation slowed, halted. The magic seeped away like sand through fingers.

He was still devilishly attractive. Her heart beat faster when she looked at him. She nearly melted under his gaze. But she couldn't trust him. And she would never let herself be used. Not ever again.

"Jessica?"

"There's more, isn't there? There's more to all this than you're telling me."

His eyes narrowed, but he didn't say anything.

"Dammit," she said. "I want to know."

"Jessica, I shouldn't have told you what I did. The family agreed that Alex would explain everything after the DNA results came back."

"Then why are you telling me now?"

"*I* didn't agree. I thought you had a right to know."

She was angry. And hurt. She felt like a puppet being manipulated by any number of puppeteers.

"You're not going to tell me more, are you?"

"I can't tell you, because I don't *know.*"

"I'm sorry I asked." She heard the stiffness in her voice, the chill.

"Don't be." But his voice had cooled, too. The distance between them was growing greater by the minute.

They finished in silence, she leaving much of the food. He looked askance at her.

"It's good," she said. "I'm just . . . not hungry."

He nodded. He pulled out a twenty and a ten without receiving a bill, put them on the table, then stood. She wonder if this was his usual practice, but she had little time to consider it. His arm again guided her to the door. He stopped to say good-bye to Ramon, and then they were outside in the warm air.

His touch was just as firm, just as confident. Just as warm. Just as enticing. She wanted it so badly. She wanted to trust it.

She couldn't.

He opened the truck door for her, and she stepped inside. She watched as he walked around, got in on his own side, and started the engine. He didn't say anything else until they reached the resort.

"Where to?" he asked when they got to the entrance.

She felt a momentary relief that he hadn't automatically driven to her casita. Or was he just too intelligent for that?

She gave him directions, then opened the door of the pickup as he stopped. But if she thought to outrun him, she didn't. He was at her side, taking the key from her hand and opening the door to the casita.

He stood to one side, but his hand caught her as she started to walk in. "Jessie, you're right not to trust anyone, but . . ."

Then she was in his arms, and he was looking down at her. His eyes weren't enigmatic now. They were intense and sexy as hell. She saw that much before his lips touched hers. Searching at first, then with a beguiling laziness that sent waves of desire radiating through her. His fingers touched her cheeks with a softness and gentleness that were more persuasive than any more determined seduction. Her blood warmed, her senses danced.

He swept her closer, and her body pressed against his.

She could hear the beat of his heart, feel the hard, muscled strength of him. Her breath caught in her throat, and she opened her mouth. His tongue entered. Exploring. Seducing. An ache started deep inside, a deep, intense yearning for something more.

Could she trust *this?*

She'd closed her eyes, but now she opened them and looked up. His eyes were partially curtained by those thick lashes, as difficult to read as ever. He was a man who'd learned to control his feelings. Her hand went up and touched the back of his neck, the thick dark hair curling slightly around her fingers. The intimacy was so strong she thought she would drown in it.

His kiss deepened and she responded in a way she'd never done before. Emotions surged through her as did acute physical reactions. The enchantment she'd felt earlier wrapped around her.

The warm breeze quickened and brushed their bodies. She was only slightly aware of that new sensation. It was an added aphrodisiac when none was needed. All she needed at the moment was Ross Macleod.

Even if she didn't trust him. Or his motives.

That didn't matter at the moment. Her cautions, her good sense, were swept away by his nearness, by the intoxication of his touch, the promise of his fingers, the sweet seduction of his lips. She found herself melting into him, her mouth responding to his, her body wantonly clinging to him. She felt his body change, grow hard and wanting. Expectation built furiously inside her.

His hands moved from her face to her hair, then to the back of her neck, playing with nerve ends she didn't know existed as his kiss deepened, became harder, more demanding, more searching. She could barely breathe under the onslaught. Her body felt like a willow, bending to him, depriving her of all will of her own.

She felt she was drowning in him, in the intensity that

was so much a part of him. Piercing need ripped through her. Not just physical need, but something far stronger, far needier. She had been alone so long.

But even as she felt the painful need, a delicious warmth started to move through her. His mouth gentled suddenly, surprising her. His lips moved, brushing kisses against her cheek, and strangely, those kisses were far more sensuous, far more arousing than his lips had been against hers. Her entire body trembled and ached and tingled.

Her hips arched toward his, and her breasts strained and hurt. She wanted to stretch against him, to feel the growing bulge under his jeans, to . . .

Dear God, what was she doing? Thinking?

He groaned, a growl deep in his throat. She thought she heard the beat of his heart, a loud thunder in her ears. The sound was erotic and irresistible. He was feeling it too, this need, this want that was more intense than she'd thought possible. The power of it astounded her. Her breath caught in her throat, and she looked up. His eyes were like dark flames. Hot. Brilliant.

His lips captured hers again and moved lazily, sensually. Then he released them and stepped back. She felt him take a deep breath. "Good God, lady."

This time she didn't question his sincerity. She knew he was fully aroused. So was she.

A muscle flexed in his cheek, and his face looked drawn. His lips were tight. One of his hands had clasped hers and held it tight. He looked down, apparently surprised, then let it go and touched her cheek again. "I didn't mean for this to happen."

Her entire body ached. Her brain felt fogged. Her body didn't want to obey. She could only stare at him like a zombie, wondering what had happened. How it had started? And then ended so abruptly?

But it hadn't stopped. Her senses were burning, tingling.

Her legs felt rubbery. She knew she had to go in before she made a total fool of herself.

"Good night." She forced the words out of her mouth.

His fingers were still on her cheek, still burning a trail along her skin. Then he dropped his hand, moving away, moving toward the truck.

The door was open. But she couldn't move yet. She waited until the engine of his pickup started; then, like a sleepwalker, she took the steps inside. She closed the door and went to the window.

The pickup was still there. A moment passed, then another. Finally, it moved. She watched as it disappeared into the darkness.

eleven

Ross almost didn't leave. God knew he didn't want to leave.

But he saw the distrust—along with the passion—in her eyes. He knew he'd helped plant it there, but it hurt nonetheless. He wanted her, but he wanted her after she knew everything. Not now. Not when she was still swimming in confusion. Not when she was trying to find her way.

She was vulnerable, and he was damned if he was going to use that.

But he wanted to. Oh, how he'd wanted to ravish her then and there. He'd also wanted to kiss away the doubt in her eyes. The questions.

He knew it was all wrong. And he'd broken away, though it took every ounce of his strength, his willpower. So he sat in the cab of his pickup, thinking about how much he wanted to knock on her door and go inside.

Instead, he started the pickup and drove out of the resort parking lot. He hated the damned place. It was one of the causes of Cullen's sudden desire to sell the Sunset. Cullen had poured everything he had into the Quest. If rumors were true, he was near bankruptcy. So he'd joined forces with Marc, who needed funds to seed his Senate campaign. Both men had talked their father into supporting the proposal. At ninety-one, the older Halden was no match for their joint campaign. He just wanted peace in his family.

They had cajoled the others, children of Harry and Hugh and their offspring, into supporting their bid to sell the Sunset. Sarah was the only holdout.

Jessie's share would be more than a million dollars if she agreed to the sale. For a young woman who'd never had much, it would represent a fortune. Invested wisely, it would support her forever. Certainly, it would present opportunities she'd never had before.

Damn. Of all the women in the world, she was the one he least wanted to become involved with. Their interests were divergent. If it were only himself, it wouldn't matter so much. But Sarah *did* matter. The Sunset was her life.

If only Marc would change his mind. If only Ross could persuade him in some way . . .

Frustrated, he fought his way through tourist traffic. It was at its heaviest at this time of year. All Sedona needed was another development. More homes. More resorts. A golf course, for God's sake. Who cared if it reduced the water table another inch or so. Who cared as long as more money was to be made?

He was working himself up to a fine rage when he hit the road to the Sunset, driving far too fast. He caught himself. He did that crap as a kid. He slowed, trying to harness his anger before he got back. Sarah would probably come over to the house if he didn't report to her first. She would want to know all the details.

He cursed long and hard.

Jessie's car was in front of her casita when she woke. She didn't know who had brought it or when, but she was grateful.

Her wrist felt better, not as sore. It didn't matter, anyway. She had things to do today. She looked for the keys. They were under the floor mat. Easy enough for someone to steal, but apparently no one was overly concerned about that in Sedona.

She drove out and found a family-type restaurant where she ate breakfast. She was at the library when it opened its doors.

Her first stop was the computer to see if there was any book available about the Clements family. Finding none, she next went to the newspaper on microfiche. It was a bi-weekly paper, more about community doings and person-alities than hard news. She went to the year 1950. The Clements name was mentioned frequently. One had been a city board member; another had received a civic award. The Clementses had hosted a barbecue to raise money for the community hospital.

Clementses, in fact, were everywhere. Then finally in June, she found what she sought: an obituary of war hero Sergeant Heath Clements. Note was made of his twin brother, Hugh, who'd died during the war.

No cause of death was named. No details listed. Just a notice that he had died on a Monday and that the funeral was on Wednesday. The only survivors mentioned were his father, his mother, Sarah, and the remaining brothers. Harding was among them.

She found nothing about Lori Clements, Harding's wife.

The article posed more questions then it answered. She'd noticed that there were few controversial items in the paper. Had the owner buried any questions about the death? Had he or she bowed to the wishes of the Clements family?

She wondered whether the Flagstaff paper would have any more information. She obtained microfiche for that date, too, and looked. Same type of item, but smaller.

Did the Clementses really have that kind of influence? *Hell's bells.* She sighed in frustration.

She finally gave up. She looked at her watch. *Eleven.* She had promised to have lunch with Sarah. Which meant she would probably see Ross. She closed her eyes. She didn't know how she would face him. She'd practically invited him to bed last night. And he hadn't wanted her. She flinched at the memory of his rejection.

Well, she would be leaving Wednesday. Early. She would have to find out what she wanted to know before that.

Tomorrow she would go to Flagstaff, the county seat, and see if she could find records of the deaths of Harding's wife and brother. There must be a death certificate or record of an inquest.

Harding. Her probable father. She still couldn't quite believe it. She still couldn't quite call him that. Her father was Jonathan Clayton. Horse trainer.

And when Sarah asked her what she was doing today? The truth? Jessie wasn't sure.

She made a copy of the obituary of Heath Clements, tucked it into her pocketbook, and left. She walked quickly to the door, then across the parking lot. Her gaze moved around as it always did. She'd taken a self-protection course, and she always made a point of being aware of what was going on around her. She also always had her keys in her hand, grasped tightly in her fingers.

Her gaze lingered only a second on a blue sedan with a young man sitting inside. He must be waiting for someone. She really didn't think anyone was lurking outside the Sedona library with mayhem in mind.

Still, she kept her eyes on the door of the car as she unlocked her rental and climbed inside. As she turned into the road, then took a right on 89A, she noted that the sedan pulled out, too. But then she lost sight of it as she slipped into the right lane. The sedan passed on the left.

Her imagination. She was seeing ghosts where there were none. She was even beginning to wonder whether she'd overreacted about her room. Perhaps she hadn't put the necklace where she thought. Perhaps the whole situation had unnerved her more than she'd realized.

Glancing occasionally out the rearview mirror, she drove to the ranch. She thought she saw the blue sedan once on the highway. When she turned onto the road to the ranch, she slowed, even stopped. She looked behind her. No blue car on the highway.

Jessie breathed slowly, not realizing she'd been holding it. She felt her body slowly relax. Calling herself all sorts of a timid fool, she pressed her foot down on the gas pedal. The car jerked forward.

She found herself further loosening the tight ball of nerves. The ranch house would probably be mostly empty by now. Marc and his wife hadn't left, but she suspected he would be off campaigning somewhere. Ross would most likely be working. This would be her one chance to really talk to Sarah.

When Jessie arrived at the ranch house, it looked a little forlorn without cars parked in all directions. There was only a rather serviceable-looking Jeep she'd seen before. She looked toward's Ross's house. His pickup was gone. A flash of disappointment ran through her. But there was relief, too. She still felt pangs of rejection.

Before she reached the stone steps, the door opened and Sarah stood there, her weathered face wreathed in a smile. She was wearing Levi's today, and a checked shirt. A blue scarf was knotted around her neck. Jessie could barely believe she was in her seventies, despite the wrinkles around her eyes. She moved with a lighter step than Jessie.

"Jessie, I'm so pleased to see you. We'll eat, then go for a ride. I promise not to lose you." Then the smile faded. "If your wrist is all right, that is."

"I've been looking forward to a ride," Jessie said.

"Good. Lunch is ready. I hope you like salad and cold chicken."

"Sounds wonderful," Jessie said. And it was true. She'd been eating enough for a horse lately.

"Come on into the kitchen," Sarah said. "Everything's ready. Would you like tea or a soda?"

"Tea sounds good," Jessie replied. Then she asked curiously, "There's a Jeep out there."

"It's Cullen's. His wife's car is at the garage and she's using his so he's using the Jeep. He came over to see his father about some business. I asked him to join us for lunch but he said he's scheduled a late business lunch."

It was just as well. Jessie had wanted to spend this time with Sarah.

Jessie followed Sarah into the kitchen and greeted Rosa, whom she'd met over the weekend. In minutes, Rosa served them both a salad topped with grilled chicken and a glass of iced tea, then disappeared.

Jessie was relieved. She wanted to talk to Sarah alone. "I went to the library today," she said, feeling her way. "I wanted to see whether there was anything about the . . . deaths fifty years ago."

Sarah stilled. "Why? That was so long ago. It has nothing to do with you."

"Doesn't it?" Jessie replied.

"It shouldn't," Sarah insisted.

Jessie wanted to say something about the will, but the words disappeared somewhere in her throat. She should wait, listen. It might never affect her. She might not be Harding's child. Still, she thought it time to drop a few bombs and see what scattered.

"My home was burglarized just before I received the invitation to the reunion," Jessie said. "Then my shop several days ago. And I think someone was in my room on Saturday while I was gone. Coincidence? Or is something going on I know nothing about?"

It was as frank as she knew how to be. Jessie usually didn't confront people. Oh, she could play word games, as she had with Alex, but she'd always had a problem with anything that might hurt or anger someone else. She would go a hundred miles out of her way to please people, a habit formed when she tried so hard to please her father. But now it was time for her to be an adult.

She waited for an answer. For a moment, she didn't think she would get one. Several emotions passed over Sarah's face. The first was disbelief. The second, anger. Jessie saw it in the flashing of her eyes. Then she covered both up. A mask settled over her face. But her hands betrayed her. Her fingers curved up into fists.

"Sarah?" she prompted. Then after a moment's silence, she added, "I plan to go to the county seat tomorrow. There must be death certificates, an inquest."

"Can't you leave it alone?"

"No," Jessie said. "You opened the past, you and your family. You should never have done that if you weren't willing to let me see everything. Not just what you select."

"We don't even know yet if . . ." Sarah's feeble protest trailed off.

"Don't you?" Jessie asked softly.

Sarah shook her head, as if to remove cobwebs there. "I'm sorry. Of course I know." She bit her lip, just as Jessie often did when nervous. "All right," she said. "If you are so determined . . ."

"I am," Jessie said. "Tell me about my . . . about Harding."

"There's not that much to tell," Sarah said. "No one really knows what happened."

"Tell me what you *do* know."

"Heath . . . well, Heath was never the same when he came back from Europe. I told you his twin brother was killed by a mine. I don't think I told you Heath saw it happen, was wounded by the same mine. He was a hero when he came home, and girls threw themselves at him. Including Harding's wife. I think he started believing the world owed him."

Sarah sighed. "Lori and Heath had been sweethearts before he went off to war. Lori hadn't wanted to wait for him, though. She was furious that Heath wouldn't marry her before he shipped out. She came from nothing, and this family represented everything she wanted. Instead of waiting for Heath, she went after Harding. We tried to warn him, but he was crazy in love."

She hesitated, then continued. "We all saw Lori teasing Heath, baiting Harding. She made it clear she thought she married the wrong brother."

Brothers in love with the same woman. Pain struck Jessie like a knife. All her life, she had wanted family. Now she was learning that having family could be as painful as having none. Maybe even more so. How had this betrayal affected her father?

"What happened?" Her voice was little more than a whisper.

"No one really knows. Harding might have suspected something. Perhaps he followed his wife. Perhaps he heard that both were lost in a fire and assumed the worst. No one will ever know now. All we know is that all three disappeared on the same day, and the bodies of Heath and Lori were found in a burned-out cabin that belonged to the family. There was no indication of foul play. That's what the court ruled."

But her voice sounded like a recording of something that had been repeated so many times it was almost rote. There seemed no substance, no truth, no conviction in it.

Jessie knew, though, she was being told that further investigation would tell her no more. She was being discouraged from going to Flagstaff. Would it be a wild-goose chase? Or was there another reason?

The other questions clouding her mind were more

painful. Could her father have been at the cabin? Had he been a witness? More than a witness?

Her blood chilled at the thought. In any event, what would those events so many years ago have to do with today?

"So you see," Sarah was saying, "there is no reason to spend time in musty files. As for those burglaries, what possibly could they have to do with us?"

Jessie's instincts were tingling again. She hoped it was merely the accumulation of recent events. She could not believe Sarah was lying, not about something that concerned her safety. She merely nodded. But she knew she was driving to Flagstaff in the morning.

They finished their luncheon in silence. They both put their dishes in the sink, then Sarah started for the door. Jessie followed her and together they walked to the barn.

The boy Jessie had seen Saturday night had two horses saddled.

"Dan'l." Jessie acknowledged him.

The boy gave her a grin. "Miss Sarah said to give you Rose."

Jessie looked at the mare. She was afraid she would be given a child's horse after Saturday's fiasco, but Rose, a gray, looked fit and pleased at the prospect of an outing.

Sarah winked at her. "Ross said you were a good rider."

Jessie couldn't stop the jolt of pleasure that ran through her. Still, she raised an eyebrow in disbelief.

"His bark is far worse than his bite," Sarah said. "He tries to scare everyone off. He respects those who refuse to be intimidated."

"I don't think the latter includes me," Jessie said wryly.

"Where did he take you last night?"

"A Mexican restaurant."

"El Cantina?"

Jessie nodded.

"He likes you then," Sarah said with satisfaction.

For a moment, Jessie wondered why Sarah cared whether Ross liked her or not, particularly in a romantic way. He could be a cousin. *But not by blood.*

She decided not to explore that particular thought any longer. He had more than indicated his disinterest in her. Because her left wrist was still sore, she let Dan'l help her mount. The mare took a couple of steps, and she enjoyed the feel of the animal beneath her. She was still sore from her earlier ride, stiff in places she'd forgotten existed, but it was a small enough price for the exhilaration she felt at being in a saddle again. She looked over at Sarah. The older woman swung into the saddle without help. Her back was straight, her hands relaxed. She was as at home in the saddle as Ross.

Sarah smiled over at her, sharing the same spontaneous pleasure as Jessie. It was written all over her face. The mask was gone. "Come on, Jessie. I'll make sure you don't get lost again."

That sounded like a fine idea to Jessie. She guided Rose to Sarah's mare, then kept apace of the older woman as the horses broke into a trot, then a canter.

The sun's rays looked like darting flames across the red towers of rock. The wind blew gently. For a moment, all was right with the world. The blue sedan disappeared from her mind. The image of her burglarized apartment faded.

She felt free. She was finally doing what she'd always been meant to do.

Ross finished inspecting the water tank as Timber watched carefully. The tank would be vital to the cattle when they were brought down from higher ground. It had been leaking, and it was one of the jobs he didn't like leaving to someone else. These watering places were too important.

It could have waited until tomorrow. He knew it. But

Sarah had told him this morning that Jessica was expected for lunch and a ride. He knew it was a measure of her pride that she was going to ride again after her mishap. It took guts to do that, especially with an injured wrist. He'd always believed in getting back up after a fall.

All morning, he'd fought an urge to return to the ranch and ride out with them. But she would be safe with Sarah. He had no doubt of that. He was dismayed, though, that he *wanted* to see her again. He kept remembering her light scent, the softness of her face, the passion that had roiled in her eyes. Even worse, he recalled how much he'd enjoyed her company. She was bright and inquisitive. She'd enjoyed the cantina as much as he always did, and he'd liked her immediate responsiveness to his friend Ramon.

Dammit.

He found the leak and realized he would need help to repair it. Well, he had weeks before they would be bringing the cattle back down. He climbed into his pickup and found himself driving back to the ranch. Maybe he would take a ride. He knew exactly where Sarah would take Jessica.

He returned only to find Dan'l frowning.

"What is it, Dan'l?"

"Mr. Marc took Hellfire out."

Ross swore. Hellfire was his best sire; no one rode him except Ross—except for the few times Marc had commandeered the big stallion. Ross had told him repeatedly that he didn't want the horse ridden by other members of the family. Marc ignored him, just as he had when Ross was a kid. Ross was still the poor relation as far as Marc was concerned. Someone to be used, but most definitely not someone to obey.

Marc was an adequate rider, but not a good one. He did not ride enough to be expert at it. Like many riders, he thought he was better than he was.

If Ross had been there, he could have stopped Marc. Hell, he would have used his fists if he'd had to. But Dan'l was defenseless against him. Ross would bet his last cent that Marc had waited until he knew Ross was gone.

"Did he say where he was going?"

"No, but he took his rifle."

That was nothing extraordinary. Marc usually took one with him. So did Ross. This was rattlesnake season.

Ross went into the barn and took out one of the horses, a quick and smart young stallion named, quite simply, Ginger. He saddled the animal himself, then mounted. He too took a rifle. He often did when he was riding, particularly in the summer because of rattlesnakes and other occasional varmints. In another minute, Ginger was trotting toward the rock tower, Timber running joyously behind him.

Jessie had thought she'd gotten a sense of place in the past few days. But as she followed Sarah up through steep trails and along rock cliffs, she knew she had not. Not until now. It was in the sweet smell of wildflowers, the plants with exotic names like Spanish bayonet and catsclaw, the cypress trees sculpted by lightning. It was in air so fresh and pure and sweet that it hurt. It was the views of the vermilion cliffs and red rock vistas, in the brief glimpse of a pronghorn elk, the sight of a soaring bald eagle.

And even rattlesnakes. Sarah had warned her to keep a sharp watch.

Nothing, not even rattlesnakes, could dim the exultation she felt, the pure joy she felt. They had not seen any other human beings since they left the ranch. There had been rustles in the grass, some shy creature scurrying out of the way. Some birds startled from their perches in trees. But Jessie felt she was a million miles from civilization.

Sarah didn't say much. Neither of them did. Jessie was in awe of everything. Sarah just seemed comfortable with it. It seemed almost a part of her. She needed no words. Neither did Jessie. It was enough to share.

They finally stopped. Sarah dismounted. Jessie slid down. It was easier on her still-sore thighs. They tied the horses to a pine and walked over to the edge of the cliff.

Sarah pointed. "We call this the Saddle," she said. "It's a ridge between two peaks. Down there is the Sunset."

Jessie could barely see the ranch house and barn nestled at the base of another jutting tower of rock. She saw the road leading to it. A dark-colored car was inching toward the buildings.

"They want to develop that land," Sarah said softly. "A goddamn golf course and lots of little look-alike houses."

Jessie started. She had never heard Sarah swear before. But it wasn't even the words as much as the emotion behind it.

"Did I tell you I was born there? In one of the bedrooms? All of Hall and Mary Louise's children were, except the twins." Sarah appeared lost in the past now. Jessie looked down again, and she saw what she knew Sarah was seeing. Not just buildings. Not even just land. *A homestead.* There was something about the word that was fraught with meaning. It sent a shiver through her.

Sarah didn't say anything else. They both stayed there another moment, then started for the horses.

Jessie found a rock to help her mount, and they started down, the two horses carefully picking their way over the rough path. Sarah went first, and Jessie followed. She continued to think of the ranch below, what Sarah had said. There'd been so much feeling in the words, so much pain. Well, she would feel pain too, if she was forced to leave the house where she'd been born and where she'd lived all her life.

A golf course? What an obscene idea.

They reached the bottom of the path. Sarah started talking again. "The land looked different fifty years ago, before developments dropped the water table." Tears were in Sarah's eyes. Jessie suspected such emotion was rare.

As if to disclaim it, Sarah pressed her mount into a trot, then an easy canter.

Hoping she would have Sarah's energy and strength at seventy-odd years, Jessica followed. She felt more of a bonding with the land, a connection with all around her. The wind blew through her hair and kissed her cheeks, and her mount stretched in strong powerful strides that ate up distance. Her mind cleared to all but pleasure.

Then Sarah slowed, and Jessie slowed her own horse. She caught up with Sarah, and saw her own pleasure reflected on her aunt's face. *Her aunt.* How easily she accepted that now. They walked their horses, comfortable with silence, content with the raw, jagged beauty of the country.

The sound of a rifle shot shattered the quiet companionship. It echoed in the warm air.

Jessie's horse pranced nervously for a moment, then quieted under her soothing hands. She looked at Sarah, who pulled up on her horse. They both listened.

"Hunters probably," Sarah said. "Poachers. The season hasn't started yet."

Another shot rang out. This one closer.

"Some fool with more gall than sense," Sarah remarked.

The last shot sounded too darn close to Jessie. But it was difficult to tell out here. It could be a mile away.

Another rang out, and this time she saw dust shoot up not far from where the horses had stopped.

"Hey," yelled Sarah. "There's people here."

They both looked around. No one was visible. But then the rough terrain made it possible to hide an army. A new volley of three shots ripped through the valley. Rose made a quick, darting nervous movement, but this time Jessie was prepared.

"Let's get out of here," Sarah said. She pressed her mount into a fast walk, a trot, then a gallop.

With another quick look around, Jessie followed.

twelve

Ross was not there when Jessie and Sarah returned. Dan'l told them that he had gone out looking for them.

Concern crossed the teenager's face when Sarah told him they'd heard shots.

"Both Mr. Marc and Ross had their rifles with them," he said.

"Did they leave together?"

Dan'l shook his head.

Sarah looked ready to go back and search. But for all her earlier energy, she suddenly looked tired.

"They'll be back soon," Jessie said. "They must have heard the shots."

"Danged hunters," Sarah said. "I'm going to call the sheriff, have a deputy sent over. We don't usually have problems like that. People around here respect posted property. It's considered worse than rustling to hunt on someone's property."

"Rustling?"

"There's still some going on," Sarah said. "Though mostly it's done with trucks now rather than horses."

Jessie slipped off from the horse, grateful to be on solid ground. Her muscles were all complaining again. She barely suppressed a groan.

Sarah followed, hopping down with ease. But she didn't

start toward the house. Instead, she put the side of her hand to her forehead, shading her eyes as she looked out toward the direction where they came. "I don't like it," she mumbled.

Her voice was so low Jessie barely caught the words. "Sarah?" she asked.

"Oh, never mind an old woman," Sarah replied.

"You are anything but an old woman," Jessie replied honestly. Sarah had as much energy as someone twenty years younger. She probably felt better than Jessie did at the moment.

Sarah seemed to revive at the words. A slight smile replaced a frown. "You have the Clements blarney," she said.

"There's a Clements blarney?"

"You mean you haven't been treated to it? Marc's probably the best at it."

Somehow, the words didn't sound as light as they were intended. There was a bite in them.

But Sarah didn't give her a chance to digest that observation. "Come," she said, "Let's get a cool drink while we wait for them."

Wait for them. Jessie wasn't at all sure that she wanted to wait for them, that she could keep her feelings as contained as Ross did, that she wouldn't look flushed and flustered. It was immensely disturbing that he was the first man to do that to her in years. It was even more disturbing that he was the type of man who was so difficult to read. He hoarded his feelings like a miser held on to his last penny.

She had some of the same tendencies—which she supposed came from their backgrounds, a lack of any real security as children. Which wasn't promising for any relationship. Not that it mattered. Ross Macleod obviously had little interest in her as a woman. He'd taken her to supper as a favor to his adopted mother, the only person he really seemed to like.

And yet she knew she couldn't leave Sarah alone. Worry had furrowed her forehead and her lips were pinched in a tight line. Those shots had obviously disturbed her more than she'd said. So she followed Sarah to the house and into the living area.

She tried to hide her own worry. But it nibbled at her. No, gnawed. She didn't know if she could bear it if anything had happened to Ross. In just a few short days, he'd become important to her. And she knew how much he meant to Sarah. "Should we call the sheriff?" she asked.

"I'll wait a bit longer," Sarah replied, her two hands fussing nervously with each other.

"I'll get you that drink. What would you like?"

"Just a cola," Sarah said. "You?"

"Sounds good to me," Jessie said. She went into the kitchen and returned with two cans of cola. "Where's Samantha?"

"Probably at one of the galleries," Sarah said. "She does a little painting and likes to see what others are doing. She likes Sedona far more than Marc, who loves the excitement of cities, of Washington."

For some reason, that surprised Jessie. It shouldn't, she knew. But Samantha had struck her as someone who enjoyed social activities and being a politician's wife. That's what you get, she told herself, when you make assumptions about people. "I'd like to see some of her paintings."

Sarah turned and pointed to a painting in the living room. It was a scene of one of the towering red rocks with the sun hitting against it. The red rock was reflected in a body of water beneath. The use of color was breathtaking.

"She's very good."

"I think she could have had a very fine career had she kept at it," Sarah said. "Being a politician's wife is very demanding, and they move between Arizona and Washington frequently."

"Does she approve of Marc's running for the Senate?"

Sarah sighed. "I think she's given up being anything other than being Marc's perfect wife. Just as April and Hall try to be perfect children."

Just as Jessie had tried to be the perfect daughter. She knew that was a road to disaster. "Is that what Marc wants?" The thought disappointed her. She'd liked the congressman.

Sarah shook her head. "I don't know. Samantha certainly has never faulted Marc or expressed any resentment."

Just then, she heard a shout. Both of them ran to the door.

Marc was riding in. He was slumped in the saddle, obviously barely hanging on.

His checked shirt was red with blood. When the horse came to a stop, he slipped from the saddle and fell on the ground. Dan'l ran to him, followed by Sarah. Jessie was immediately behind them.

Dan'l bent over him, pulling aside his shirt. "What happened, sir?"

"I . . . was shot."

"Who?"

"I didn't see anyone."

"I'll call an ambulance," Jessie said.

Sarah shook her head. "I'll drive him to the hospital. It will be faster. You stay here with him, see if you can stop the bleeding. I'll bring a car around."

Jessie didn't have a chance to answer. Sarah was already heading into the house, probably for the keys. Dan'l had taken off his shirt and was pressing it against the wound in the shoulder.

She felt useless, helpless. She stooped next to him. "Can I help at all?"

"Find Samantha."

Sweat had beaded on his forehead and a muscle moved

in his cheek. She saw the pain in his eyes, in the set of his mouth.

"I will," she promised, reaching down and taking his hand, giving him something to squeeze, to control.

He tried to smile. "A hunter, I suppose. A stray bullet."

"We heard several shots."

"So did I. I rode that way to see whether I could find out who was doing the shooting. Damn fool thing to do."

She was startled at the sound of another rider returning. She turned. *Ross.* Timber was running behind him. Ross was off before his mount had stopped, taking quick steps over to Marc, kneeling beside him. "What in the hell . . . ?"

She was surprised to see the sudden enmity in Marc's eyes. "Were *you* out?"

Ross's dark eyes curtained. He nodded.

"Someone shot me," Marc said, his gaze intent on Ross. Ross's lips firmed into a tight line.

Jessie felt the tension between the two men. She realized that Marc was blaming Ross, even accusing him. Her gaze went to the scabbard on Ross's saddle, then to his face. A chill ran through her. She'd caught some of the currents between Ross and the others, but nothing indicated they were strong enough that one might think the other meant intentional harm.

"No!" The exclamation left her mouth before she could stop it.

A car jerked to a stop next to them and Sarah jumped out. When she saw Ross, she nodded slightly. "You can help me get him into the car."

Without a word, Ross nodded. "I'll drive him into town." He looked down at the dog. "Stay here," he said. Timber sat obediently.

"I'll go with you," Jessie said.

She immediately wished she hadn't. Ross tossed her a cynical look, as if accusing her of actually believing he had something to do with Marc's injury and suggesting he might do something else on the way. But he only shrugged. "If you wish. You can keep the cloth tight against the wound."

He leaned down and clasped Marc under his arms. Marc rose awkwardly, a moan slipping from his throat as he stood, swaying slightly. Then he shook himself away from Ross and took several steps toward the car. Jessie hurried in front of him and opened the door, offering her own arm to help him get into the seat. Then she went around to the other side and got in beside him.

"Where did it happen?" Ross asked from the driver's seat. Sarah was climbing into the front seat next to him.

Marc's lips clenched. "Near the three soldiers," he said raggedly, and Jessie knew he was referring to a formation with three peaks. "Where were you?"

"I thought Sarah might take Jessica up to the Saddle. I was halfway there when I heard the shots."

Why then, Jessie thought, had they not met him on the way back? Unless he'd veered off to see where the shots came from. *That's it. That's the explanation.*

But she saw the doubt in Marc's face. *Why? Surely he couldn't think . . .*

The questions pommeled her as Ross drove rapidly toward town. He was far exceeding the speed limit, and yet she sensed his control as she maintained the pressure on Marc's shoulder.

Marc leaned back on the seat, his eyes closed, his hands rigid against the seat. "Jessica, will you call my daughter in . . . Phoenix?" He rattled off a number that she tried to memorize. "Tell her to get here as fast as possible. The news media . . ."

Sarah broke in. "I'll call Alex. He can pressure the hospital not to make any announcements."

"Good."

They were all silent then. Ross reached the main highway and darted in and out of traffic, blowing the horn when he felt trapped. They reached the hospital where Jessie had been taken only two nights earlier.

Ross helped Marc inside, although it was obvious Marc was accepting his assistance only because there was no one else. Inside, a staffer at the emergency desk took one look at the bloodied shirt and rang a bell. In seconds, a white-jacketed physician's assistant had Marc in a wheelchair and had hurried him into a small room. A doctor and nurse soon followed.

Sarah made several phone calls from the public telephone, trying to locate Samantha. Jessie tried to reach April in Phoenix. No one was at the number Marc had given her. She left a message for April to return to Sedona as soon as possible.

Then Jessie sat with Sarah. She watched as Ross wandered over to the other side of the room and leaned against a window. He always looked alone, isolated. His jaw was set, his lips grim. She couldn't see his eyes, but she would wager her last cent that they gave nothing away. Marc had as much as accused him of the shooting, and he'd not raised one word in defense.

Well, she wouldn't have either. It was so obviously wrong.

She looked at the clock and wondered why hospital clocks were always slower than other clocks. Thirty minutes seemed like an hour, even two. Time crawled by.

She rose and went over to Ross. She didn't say anything, just tried to tell him by her presence that she didn't believe Marc's accusation.

He gave her a crooked smile, and her heart jumped. She wanted badly to reach out and touch him, and yet, despite the electricity that crackled between them, there was something about him that warned her off. A sign saying, "Keep away."

Because of Marc's silent accusations?

She saw a doctor come out. Sarah went to ask the questions. Marc was Sarah's nephew. Maybe Jessie's cousin. But she found that her concern was more for Ross than Marc, and that made her feel guilty. Shouldn't she care for them all equally?

Sarah finished the conversation and approached them as the doctor left the room. The older woman's gaze caught Ross's. "They called the police because it's a gunshot wound," she said.

"It *was* an accident," Jessie said.

"Of course it was," Sarah replied, "but the law requires that all gunshot injuries be reported, accidental or not."

"How is Marc?" Jessie asked, realizing that no one had asked that question.

"The bullet just grazed his shoulder. It didn't hit anything major and it's a clean wound. He'll hurt for a while, but there shouldn't be any lasting damage. They'll fill him with antibiotics and release him." Then she added wryly, "I imagine that he'll find some way to use it to his advantage."

Jessie was at a loss for words. She still didn't understand all the twists of the relationships or the history behind them.

More moments passed. Then two men in uniform came in, went to the desk, then disappeared into the small room where Marc was still being tended. Jessie saw fear flit across Sarah's face, felt tension radiate from Ross's body. Her heart clenched. She wondered how—and when—she had come to care so intensely about Ross. And Sarah.

The two uniformed men came out. Jessie realized from the insignia that they were sheriff's deputies. County officers.

They went straight to Ross. "Mr. Macleod?"

Ross nodded.

"We would like to ask you some questions."

Ross shrugged, but Jessie knew him well enough now to

sense the anger in him, even the tautness of strain. "Where?"

"At our office."

He nodded.

"I'll go with you," Jessie said.

"No." His voice was low, firm, absolute. "You drive Marc back."

"Sarah can do that."

"Sarah is the world's worst driver. I don't want anything else to happen to Marc."

She hesitated.

"Please, Jessie."

It was the "Jessie" that did it. Until now, he had called her Jessica despite her invitation to call her Jessie. Jessica was formal, a name used to keep her at a distance. Jessie was a friend. She wanted to be more, but for the moment it would do. "All right," she said. "Should I ask Alex to meet you?"

"Sarah called him earlier. I'm surprised he's not here yet. But I don't need a lawyer. I'll probably be back before you are."

"What about a car?"

"They can take me back to the Sunset."

Jessie noted that he did not refer to the Sunset as home.

She wanted to protest again, but he didn't give her a chance. He led the way out the doors, the deputies following in his wake.

"Don't worry about Ross," Sarah said, touching her arm. "He'll be all right."

"But why would Marc . . . ?"

Sarah sighed. "They've never cared for each other. There's a history there. It doesn't help that April has been aggravating the situation by chasing after Ross."

"What kind of history?"

Sarah's mouth clamped down, and Jessie knew she

wasn't going to get an answer. Not to that question. "Surely, Marc doesn't really think . . ."

"I don't know what he thinks," Sarah said. "I just know Ross isn't responsible."

More questions than answers. The main one was why Ross still managed the Sunset if Marc disliked him so much. But before she could ask it, Marc emerged from the small room in a wheelchair, his shoulder bandaged and his arm in a sling. His face was pale, but he managed his charismatic grin.

"I'll live," he said.

"I never doubted it," Sarah said acidly. "You set them on Ross."

"I just told them what happened. I was riding alone. I didn't see who was shooting. I said I thought it was a stray bullet from some hunter."

"Then why did they want to question him?"

"So that's where he's gone. I simply mentioned that he was out riding today, too. They probably want to know if he saw anything."

Sarah looked at him for a long moment, then turned away. "Let's go home."

The tension was as thick as smoke from a forest fire. Marc turned to Jessie. "Did you contact my daughter?"

"I couldn't find her, but I left a message for her to drive back."

"Good. There will be a lot of press inquiries. We'll have to decide how to handle them."

"Tell the truth?" she asked with some cynicism.

His smile faded slightly, then returned. "Of course, Jessie."

He followed Sarah. Jessie kept pace with him. "Is there anything else I can do?"

"You've been wonderful," he replied warmly. "There is a prescription . . ."

She looked over to him again. She felt guilty. He must

be in pain, and he would be in more pain later. "I'm sorry," she said. She wanted to add that she'd been angry for Ross, but how could she judge, or even question, the merits of Marc's suspicions. She was a stranger to the family, and she was discovering that this family, at least, had their share of secrets.

She shivered, and his good hand took hers. He'd noticed her unease, of course. That was another thing. She apparently was as readable as a first-grade primer while everyone else seemed firmly masked.

First-grade primer. Jessie had given little thought to that part of her father's legacy. But now she recalled all those questions about her father, whether he had left her anything. She thought then they meant something that would confirm her identity. Now she wondered.

She immediately called herself a fool. Yet for some reason the idea nagged at her as Sarah drove down the main road toward the ranch. So did the idea of Ross at some office, defending himself against an accusation that he might have tried to kill his cousin. Her stomach knotted at the very thought.

She would wait at the ranch until he returned. And where was Alex? He always seemed to be around. But not apparently when he was needed. And whose side would he take in this? Would he also suspect Ross?

After a short stop at a pharmacy, Jessie drove them back to the ranch. Marc was silent and so was she. Until now, she'd liked him. Now she felt like an adversary.

Samantha was waiting on the porch. She'd obviously been informed about the accident. She swept down the stairs and into Marc's embrace. His good arm went around her, and Samantha saw him wince. It was a nice gesture, comforting her despite the fact that her embrace obviously pained him. She also saw another side of the aloof Samantha. Warm. Worried.

Had she been wrong to blame Marc? Perhaps he did have reason to . . .

Timber was also waiting. He had watched steadily as people left the car. When Ross did not, his head drooped. Jessie went over and stooped beside him. "He'll be home soon," she said. The animal's tail wagged halfheartedly.

"He won't let anyone else do that," Sarah said. She looked tired, even a little defeated.

"I've always been good with dogs," Jessie said. "I like them and they seem to know it." She put an arm around Sarah's shoulders. "You need a cup of coffee."

"I need a whiskey," Sarah corrected. "And so do you."

Marc thanked Sarah, then disappeared with Samantha into the bedroom they used. Jessie poured a glass of whiskey for Sarah and a glass of red wine for herself.

Sarah slumped into a chair. "You don't have to stay, Jessie."

"I want to," she replied. "Why would Marc even suggest Ross could be involved?" She'd asked the question to no avail earlier. Now she wanted to know. She was tired of mysteries.

Sarah hesitated. "They've had heated battles about the ranch. Marc believes that if Ross leaves, I'll agree to sell the ranch. And Marc hunts on this land. Ross doesn't like it. The truth is they've never liked—or trusted—each other, and now they both are a danger to what the other wants."

Another reason to like Ross. Jessie loathed hunting. "How has Ross managed to keep his position here?"

"Now that's complicated," Sarah said with a smile. "For one thing, the others realized they couldn't do any better than Ross. He's superb at what he does. He made a fine profit before the cattle market went to hell, and Halden was only too happy to let someone else be responsible for the ranch. In fact, that's one of the problems between Ross and Marc. Halden always liked Ross, admired his skill with horses. Said he had the Clements touch even if he wasn't one. Marc always craved his father's approval and he resented Ross. Marc felt he never measured up no matter how high he climbed in politics. I think he's jealous that his father puts so much faith in Ross."

Sarah took a sip of the whiskey and continued. "Halden and I had the votes to give Ross a long-term contract—which, considering the family rivalries, he demanded. Marc was not happy about it. It wasn't until the last few months that my brother started to bend on selling the ranch and that's because he doesn't have the strength to fight both his sons."

Jessie thought about everything that had been said. "Do you think Marc was hunting today?"

"I doubt it. It's out of season and he's been careful about his image in the past few years."

"Then why would he take a rifle?"

"Target practice. Protection against snakes." She shrugged. "Ross usually takes a rifle himself for that reason."

"Why would he possibly think Ross could be responsible for that shot?"

"Jessie, there's nothing Marc would like better than to get Ross fired. He believes Ross is the only chance the Sunset has to survive as a working ranch, that I'll vote to sell if Ross goes."

Jessie absorbed that. "Wishful thinking on his part?"

"Could be. He might really believe it. Marc has a tendency to believe what he wants to believe."

"Not a good trait for a senator."

"Oh, Marc would probably make a good senator. He pays attention to polls, and he has an instinct for what people want."

Jessie raised an eyebrow. "Damning with faint praise?"

Sarah chuckled. "I really didn't mean to be uncharitable. He does have some principles."

Jessie shook her head. "I'm confused."

"We're a confusing family. But I suppose all families are."

"I wouldn't know," Jessie said.

Sarah sighed. "I know. We must all seem a bit strange. But we do all care about you. We want to make it up to you . . . everything your father lost."

Jessie was wondering whether she wanted anything made up. Since she'd been "found," she'd been burglarized, lost in the mountains, her store vandalized. Her privacy had been invaded, and she'd felt that someone had been watching her.

Perfect family indeed.

And yet . . . she was beginning to feel just a tiny part of it. And that part felt natural. Right.

She walked over to the window. The land called to her in a way nothing had before. Because it was a part of her, part of her heritage?

Timber was still waiting. Head alert. Looking out toward the drive. She suspected he would sit there until Ross arrived.

And so would she.

thirteen

Ross had felt this way before. Rebellious. Angry. But now he'd learned to control his temper.

Or at least he thought he had.

"Do you have a rifle?" the cop asked.

"Of course I do," he shot back. "Name me someone over sixteen in the state who doesn't."

"Can we see it?"

"If you want to know whether it's been fired recently, yes it has."

A raised eyebrow met his declaration.

"Not at the congressman. You'll find a headless rattler near the Saddle. And a shell."

"That's real convenient."

"If I'd meant to shoot Marc Clements, he would be dead," Ross said.

"We can't be perfect all the time," one of the deputies said acidly.

"I didn't say I was perfect. I said I'm a good shot."

"Yeah, we know that," the other deputy said. "We also know you were a real hellion as a kid."

"Juvenile is the key word," Ross said. "I'm sure you checked and know damned well I haven't picked up as much as a traffic ticket since."

"Let's see if I remember right. Car theft. Assault, including one on the congressman."

"He wasn't a congressman then."

"Oh yeah, and a rape. You were a busy boy."

Ross had known that would be revisited. "The charges were dropped."

"They often are when the victim is threatened."

Ross didn't reply. They wanted to think he was guilty. He wondered what Marc had told them.

"Nothing to say?"

"Nothing you want to hear."

"Maybe a night in jail will make you more talkative."

"Are you going to charge me with something? Otherwise, I'm walking out of here. Now."

The cop frowned. "Don't clean that rifle. We'll be out later to look at it."

"Bring a search warrant." Ross knew his temper was ready to explode. Damn Marc anyway.

"We'll do it."

Ross rose. He needed to get the hell out of there.

He also knew he'd become a prime suspect.

Walking out of the office, he recalled Jessie's startled look when Marc as much as accused him of the shooting, remembered the exclamation she'd made. For an instant, she'd believed it.

But then why shouldn't she? He was part Apache, wasn't he? The son of an alcoholic ne'er-do-well? Bad blood. Marc had been saying that for years. Ross had wanted to do real damage to Marc years ago when he'd called Ross a rapist. Only Sarah's intervention with both the law and family had saved him then, but not until he'd spent several weeks in jail. Sarah had believed him and convinced everyone else. Everyone except Marc.

He owed Sarah.

And now the old story of the rape had surfaced again.

And probably so would the rumors. It was all he needed now.

Jessie was looking through a window when an unfamiliar, run-down truck pulled up in front of Ross's house. Ross stepped out and with his own unique grace took the few steps to the porch. Timber, who had been waiting patiently, made a dash to his side, but Ross paid no attention. Neither did he look toward the larger ranch house. He seemed only intent to get inside his own.

She turned toward Sarah. "He's back."

"Of course, he's back," Sarah said. "The police had no reason to keep him."

But despite her words, Jessie saw tension ease in her shoulders. "I'll go, then," Jessie said. "I think I have a dinner date with Alex."

"Rosa said his office called. He's in court in Flagstaff. He's coming by here as soon as he's finished. Why don't you wait here for him?"

"I'm not dressed for dinner," she said. At least not with Alex. She would be just fine for Ross. The realization did not endear Alex to her. Even after Marc's insinuations, she wanted to be with Ross. She wanted it very much.

Marc was in the bedroom he shared with his wife. Samantha hadn't appeared since they'd climbed the stairs to their wing of the house, and neither had Halden.

Jessie tried to think of something other than the earlier ugly scene. She turned her attention to the kitchen. Rosa was cooking something that smelled wonderful.

Jessie couldn't care less about Alex or about cooking. She wanted to go over and talk to Ross, to let him know she didn't believe a word of Marc's garbage. But why would he care?

The unfamiliar truck that had brought him disappeared down the road. Some friend, she supposed. Friends like those she'd met last night. Friends she wished she knew more about. Because then perhaps she would learn more about him.

"Will you ask Ross to come over for supper?" Sarah said.

Jessie looked at her suspiciously. "Why don't *you?*"

"Somehow I don't think I would have the same influence. I'm his mother. And you . . ." Her voice trailed off.

"And *me?*" Jessie asked dubiously.

"He likes you."

"How can you tell?"

Sarah finally smiled. "It's difficult at times, but I *can* tell."

Jessie hesitated. Although his face had been turned away when he'd arrived, she could sense his glowering mood even from a distance. Resentment had been clear in the taut set of his shoulders. She didn't blame him. What had happened was unfair. It had not been right. Indignation on his behalf flooded her.

The only problem was that she didn't think he would appreciate her indignation.

She looked at her watch. They had gone riding at noon, returned about two. It was after seven now. So much had happened in a few hours. So many . . . feelings unveiled. More secrets. "I'll tell him about supper. And that Alex is on his way," she said, finally deciding to err on the side of action rather than caution.

Sarah sank down in a chair. "Thank you," she said. "He will probably tell you to leave, but . . . he needs someone who believes in him."

The statement surprised her. Ross Macleod didn't seem to need anyone. Much less someone who believed in him. He didn't seem to care what anyone thought. Which was, she supposed, why he had put in so few appearances at the family reunion.

Reluctantly, she opened the door and took the path.

She'd never been inside Ross's house and she wondered now how he lived.

She knocked at the screen door. The other door was open, and she heard the rush of Timber's feet and his ferocious bark. As the dog lunged against the door, she thought Ben could certainly take lessons from him. *Her* burglar would have been in a different county instead of rummaging among her belongings.

"Timber!" Ross's voice was sharp. The dog stopped immediately and sat.

But his master didn't appear at the door. Only his voice emerged from the interior. "Go away, Sarah."

"It's not Sarah."

There was a silence, then footsteps. Ross stood at the door. "Only Sarah isn't afraid of Timber."

"Is that why you have him?"

He weighed that question for a moment, then the side of his mouth crooked upward. "No, but it's a fringe benefit."

He stood there in jeans and bare feet and nothing more. His cheeks were darkened with just a hint of a shadow. His jaw was set, emphasizing the hard angles of his face. And his eyes seemed to burn with anger. He was all masculine energy. Simmering, masculine energy. He looked dangerous and predatory.

Her heart beat frantically against her ribs.

He was splendid. His chest was bronze as if he'd spent time working without a shirt. His shoulders were broad, his muscles well-defined, and his body obviously whipcord strong. His jeans, worn to a soft gray, fit like a second skin.

The heat of late afternoon grew hotter. Sizzling.

"But he doesn't frighten *you*?" Ross's question startled her. She wondered if he'd caught her staring.

"Nothing with four feet and a tail frightens me."

"Then you should be afraid of *me*."

"Why?"

"Marc hasn't told you?"

"No one has told me anything," she said. "Except Sarah, who wanted me to invite you for supper. She also said Alex was on the way."

"I don't need Alex. And as for supper, she knows better than that. Marc and I in the same house? Not a good idea."

The door still stood between them. His gaze raked her as if he were trying to make a decision. She shifted on her feet, wondering whether she should leave.

Ross hesitated a moment longer, then opened the door. Timber stayed at his side.

"He missed you," Jessie ventured. "He wouldn't move from the porch."

"He senses when something is wrong," Ross said.

She entered the room. It was unlike any other bachelor's home she'd visited. Decorated with Indian rugs and artifacts, the room exuded warmth and character. Shelves filled with books, except for one shelf lined with kachina dolls, stretched across the one entire wall. She went over to the dolls and admired them. "These are wonderful," she said sincerely. She'd seen a private collection of kachina dolls at Emory University and knew they had to represent a great deal of money. "That's a valuable collection."

"To me," he said simply.

"To many people."

"I don't care about 'many people,' especially those who just collect."

"Isn't that what you're doing?"

"Only temporarily. I want to keep them from going into private collections. They're a heritage that's being lost to the people who created them," he said, passion creeping into his voice. "One day these will go back to them, once I know they'll be safe."

The answer astounded her. As did the sheer complexity of this man. Would she ever really know him? Understand him? She swallowed hard, then asked, "How did you get them?"

"I've found them one at a time. Usually when an old one dies. Their children sell anything they think is of value. They often don't know its true worth." He looked at her. "They don't care about the heritage, their meaning. Someday, they will."

Heritage. Belonging. Jessie realized that the dolls had everything to do with that, and nothing to do with the accumulation of wealth. He would never sell those dolls, just as she wouldn't sell her carousel horses.

Her gaze met his, and his eyes changed, softened. "You understand, don't you?"

She didn't have to ask what he meant. "Yes." She didn't elaborate. She didn't tell him about her horses, her magical steeds that could take her away to wonderful worlds where there was no loneliness.

There was none now. Not with Ross beside her.

Instead, her heart beat a steady tattoo in her chest as she looked up at him. His eyes weren't masked now, nor was his face. She saw a yearning in him, a vulnerability she hadn't seen before. He'd been wounded today in some way she really couldn't understand. She also knew it was a new tear across old scar tissue.

That understanding struck like a knife through her.

She lifted her hand and her fingers touched his cheek. She did it without plan, even without intent. The touch was all impulse. Instinct.

Necessity.

She wanted him to know she didn't believe Marc's insinuations. She wanted him to know she believed in him.

She raised her eyes to him. His eyes were smoldering.

Or was it she who was smoldering? Her legs felt boneless, as his hands touched her shoulders, the fingers splaying against her skin. The thin cloth of her blouse might not even exist as heat from his touch ignited flames beneath his hands, then spread deeper. She felt as if she'd moved into an energy field.

He bent his head and his lips touched hers. They moved hesitantly at first, then with increasing intensity. She found herself rising on tiptoes, her body instinctively moving closer to his. Her hands went to his face, feeling the roughness of his cheeks, her fingers exploring the crevices that so intrigued her. Then they moved to his neck, those same fingers tangling in the thick, dark hair.

Her heart thundered now. As if he could hear every accelerated beat, he pressed the kiss, his mouth opening to hers and his tongue seducing its way into her mouth. Her body was suddenly alive with sensations. Tremors shook her body. Desire. Want. Yearning. They all welled up inside the core of her, building to a hurricane of need. She was swept up in it, her blood rushing, her emotions racing.

His tongue explored the tender, sensitive parts of her mouth. Shivers of pleasure ran through her, leaving residues of a glowing warmth. Her body snuggled deeper into his, and she felt his body respond, grow hard and taut.

One of his hands slipped to the nape of her neck, playing with her hair, his fingers massaging the sensitive areas of the back of her neck. His tongue moved deep, exploring, teasing softly. Inviting her to join him. She did. She remembered the feel of him, the incredible sensations he'd aroused before, but this kiss had a desperation that touched her as nothing else had. She'd never known a kiss could be so intimate, so arousing, so soul-searing.

His hand moved from the back of her neck and touched her cheek, exploring it even as his tongue explored her mouth.

Suddenly he removed his lips and looked at her. "Dammit, Jessie, you shouldn't be here."

"Why?"

"A number of reasons."

"There's only one that would mean anything."

His face was close, his breath like a warm breeze against her face. "What would that be?"

"That you don't want me here." She felt naked with her answer. She had never been confident with a man. Mills had seen to that. And now she was less sure than ever. Ross was so much more than she'd ever thought she would have. Even for a moment in time. He was everything she'd ever thought she wanted when she'd daydreamed. A hero straight out of the pages of a book.

Just like a perfect family had been.

A sharp-edged lump formed in her throat at the sudden silence.

His fingers touched her chin, forcing her gaze to meet his. "I want you too much, Jessica."

"How could that be?"

He made a noise deep in his throat. She would have thought it a chuckle if his mouth wasn't so grim. "I've just been accused of attempted murder. That should give you some pause."

"Marc didn't mean it."

"Oh, he meant it all right." He chuckled but there was no mirth in him. "But he's a politician above all. On reflection, I think he decided not to pursue it because it wouldn't look good on his résumé. A bad seed in his family trying to do him in. Wouldn't do at all in a presidential campaign."

"Presidential?"

"He has aspirations. I doubt that he has a big enough hunger in his belly, but he likes the sound of it. At the moment, he has all he can handle running for Senate."

She was bewildered. A moment ago they had been caught in a whirlwind. But just as quickly, he'd called a halt to it. Aching inside, she sought to sound as normal as he did. "Will he win?" She hoped it wasn't as much a croak as it sounded to her.

Ross shrugged carelessly. And that hurt. More than he

would ever know. How could he sound so normal after her universe had been turned upside down?

"Who knows?" His voice remained matter of fact. As if they'd just shared a cup of coffee. "If he had the money, he might well have a good chance. He tells people what they want to hear." He shrugged. "And people like him. *You* like him, don't you?"

She met his gaze. Nodded. Tried to sound as normal as he. "Sarah told me he felt you were standing in the way of selling the ranch."

He shrugged. "He's wrong. *Sarah's* standing in the way. She won't let go of it. Not as long as she breathes." He hesitated, then added, "He also thinks I've been a bad influence on Hall and April."

Jessie wondered whether Marc's concern was more April than Hall. So she asked. "April doesn't seem to agree."

A small humorless smile finally lit his face. "Marc's afraid she might want the forbidden fruit. It's a pattern with her. She loves her father. Sometimes, I think too much. When she feels her brother is getting too much attention, she pulls some stunt to bring it back to her."

He didn't elaborate. He didn't have to. April used him. Or did she just want him? Jessie felt a chill creep up her back. Had he wanted April too? He hadn't indicated as much, but then he revealed very little.

"There's so many currents," she said.

"All families have conflicts," he said objectively. Stepping back as she'd seen him do before.

"Not the family I used to dream about."

"Didn't anyone ever warn you about dreams?" His voice took on a note of cynicism. She wondered what dreams he'd had.

"Oh yes," she replied dryly. She hesitated, then asked, "But why are you forbidden fruit? You're not a blood cousin."

"You keep asking questions. Are you sure you want answers?"

"Yes," she said. "Along with why you said you wanted me too much."

"I'm trying to be honorable, Jessie," he said. "I'm not very good at it."

Frustration made her knot her fists. "I'm tired of riddles."

"You have only to ask the police." His voice was suddenly bitter. She could sense he was withdrawing into some dark place.

"I don't understand."

"They just reminded me of my juvenile record. It should have been closed years ago, but the cops have long memories. Every time something happens, they come to me."

"Sarah told me you were . . . unruly as a boy."

He raised an eyebrow. "Unruly?"

"She didn't exactly put it that way."

"I don't imagine she did. Nor, I suppose, did she say anything about the rape."

Jessie stilled. She had never forgotten the night of the prom. She took a step back. She knew her eyes must be disbelieving.

He didn't say anything. His hooded eyes only watched.

"No," she said.

"You would have heard about it sooner or later," he continued, his voice cool. Contained. Even as she felt something inside her dying.

How could it? She hadn't known him that long. Hadn't really believed that someone like him could . . . be attracted to her.

She could barely breathe. She thought she would suffocate. Panic struck her as it had that night years ago, as it had in so many nightmares since.

He just stood there. So blasted tall. So overwhelming.

Rape!

The ugliest word in the English language. She felt as if she'd just been shredded by a cannon. She found herself backing away. Just as she had impulsively reached for him moments earlier, now she instinctively retreated.

He didn't say anything. A muscle in his neck moved. His eyes were curtained, his mouth grim.

She couldn't believe it. Surely, she would have heard something, been warned. Something. He wouldn't be manager of this ranch. He wouldn't be standing here watching her so intently.

"Go away, Jessie," he said wearily, as if he'd seen everything in her face he'd expected to see. "Remember what happens when you play with fire."

He turned away and went into another room.

She was still rooted to the floor, her emotions in turmoil. Even the familiar panic. Images flashed through her mind. The barn. The odor of alcohol. The cruel words. Then . . .

Jessie closed her eyes for a moment, just as her stomach heaved.

She ran out the door, out to her car. She started it, then, nearly blinded by unshed tears, pressed down the gas pedal and roared out the driveway, raising dirt and dust behind her.

fourteen

Ross stood at the window and watched her go.

Good riddance, he told himself. That would teach Sarah to try to matchmake.

For a moment, she had looked like a deer, caught in the headlights of a car. Unable to move. Stunned. Terrified.

Frozen.

She'd been horrified. She'd believed.

And why not? Still, it had hurt as much as anything in his life. More than the death of a mother who'd never been a mother. More than losing a grandmother, who'd tried so hard to instill a love of Indian customs in him. More than those lonely days when he'd first come to the Sunset, knowing no one wanted him here. No one but Sarah.

He'd rebelled at first. Fought them all with every weapon he had. He'd known they would abandon him as his mother and grandmother had, as the subsequent foster families had. That first moment of seeing the Sunset had always been a piece of magic he could never quite believe or accept. Why would any woman want her husband's bastard son?

So he'd done everything he could to push the issue. He wanted to leave on his terms, not theirs.

But Sarah countered his every move. She supported him, believed in him, and finally, through the horses, made him believe in his own value. But not before he made everyone pay a heavy price for it.

So why had he reverted to form? Why had he chased her away?

For all the reasons he'd given her. For once he'd tried to be noble. She was a match to the tinderbox that was this family. Sarah didn't realize the danger she was courting. Jessica was asking too many questions, insisting on too many answers. She wasn't going to quit.

Except perhaps now.

Perhaps he *had* scared her away now. He just wished that he felt better about it, that he didn't feel he'd just lost something very good. He'd never been so attracted to a woman, not in so many ways.

The passion that had erupted between them had . . . stunned him. Hell, it had terrified him. The sexual stirring was explainable. The emotional one was not.

He'd never believed in love at first sight. He'd never believed in lifetime commitment. He was the imperfect result of an imperfect marriage. His father had cheated on Sarah over and over again, and she'd continually forgiven him. His birth mother had been more than a little careless with her body, and his grandmother had watched her daughter die of alcoholism. Not much of a background to offer someone.

He didn't see much good in other marriages, either. Samantha lived only as Marc's wife. She'd given up every part of herself to be his shadow. Cullen's wife was perennially dissatisfied; she'd always wanted more than he could give her, which had guided him into overly risky ventures.

Ross had often counted himself lucky not to be infected by the emotion people called love. He'd always been able to put any woman from his mind.

Until now.

He wanted to be with Jessica, spend time with her. Hell,

who was he kidding? He wanted a lot more than that. She'd awakened something in him, had made him yearn for more than he had.

But Jessica could topple Sarah's house of cards. He couldn't let that happen, no matter what *he* wanted. He only wished Sarah understood that, too.

Timber whined.

He reached down and rubbed the animal behind the ears. "It looks like it'll be just the two of us," he said, then wondered why he'd ever thought anything else.

It was more than time to go home. She wanted to fold her arms around Ben, to receive his unconditional love. She wanted Sol's equally unconditional friendship.

Why did she ever think she could fit into a family? Especially a family like the Clementses.

No wonder Harding had run like a scalded cat.

She buried her head in her hands. She'd barely, just barely, managed to keep tears from streaking down her cheeks. She kept hearing Ross's words over and over again. *Rape.* Seeing Marc's eyes as he accused his cousin of attempted murder. Feeling Sarah's tension. Sarah had known far more than she'd ever divulged, even as she'd pushed Jessie into Ross's arms.

She hadn't had to push very hard.

The phone rang.

Jessie debated a moment on whether to answer it. She just wanted to pack, bury herself in the bed, and leave early in the morning. She would get the first available flight home, whatever it was.

She could be home tomorrow afternoon. She didn't really ever want to hear the Clements name again. She no longer wanted to know their secrets.

The phone continued to ring.

She finally reached for it.

"Jessica?" Alex's voice was concerned.

"Yes," she said.

"I'm at the ranch. Sarah said you tore off like the hounds of hell were after you."

They had been. She wasn't going to admit that to Alex, however. "I wasn't feeling well," she said instead. It was partly true, anyway.

"What about supper?"

She remembered that she had agreed to it. One last meeting. She would make it clear she didn't want anything from the Clements family, that she just wanted to go home and retrieve her quiet but safe life. "All right," she said.

There was a pause. He obviously heard her lack of enthusiasm. "I'll be there in thirty minutes," he said.

"I'll be ready." She tried to force a more positive note in her voice, yet she doubted she could eat a bite. She was still sick to her stomach.

After she replaced the phone in the cradle, she sat on the bed several moments. So much had happened today.

She recalled how Ross had looked. How grim his mouth had been. How shuttered his eyes as he had admitted to rape.

Or had he?

She tried to remember everything he'd said, and how he'd said it. *Police record. You would have heard about it sooner or later.*

Don't, she told herself. *Don't analyze everything. Don't hope. Don't expect.*

How many times had she told herself those things in the past?

You have a good life. A safe life. A comfortable life. You have Ben and Sol and friends and peace.

But is that enough now?

It would have to be.

She went to the bathroom and looked at herself in the mirror. Her eyes were red, her hair mussed, her cheeks without color. She looked terrible. Muttering to herself, she splashed cold water over a thick washcloth and washed her face. A start. Not much of one, but a start.

She leaned against the door. The image of Ross's face wouldn't leave her mind. If only she could separate him from the flashbacks of her own rape so many years ago. She'd been too afraid to say anything, even when her father was fired, even when he died. Who would believe her over the heir apparent of a prominent family? Who would believe that her father, known for his drinking, was fired because that young scion of her father's employer was afraid of what she might say?

She'd lived with both shames all these years, the shame of violation and the shame of saying nothing.

Jessie closed her eyes. She didn't want to think of it. She'd shut it away in a closet for so many years. The nightmares had faded. The panic attacks had grown fewer and then disappeared. Until this afternoon.

She opened her eyes again, then saw to her face. Lipstick. A little blush. A touch of mascara. She seldom used more. But she still looked pale.

Pale would have to do.

She ran a brush through her short hair, then went to her closet. She'd used most of her wardrobe. But tonight was not a date. Tonight was a good-bye.

Jessie selected the pale-blue silk blouse she'd worn before and a pair of slacks. She looked at her watch. She still had fifteen minutes before Alex was due to arrive.

She opened the door and went outside. A thin coral ring separated a dusk-blue sky from the earth. She shivered, though the evening air was warm. Her brief journey in Wonderland was over.

She remembered the last words of the tale: "Ever drifting down the stream— / Lingering in the golden gleam—"

Sedona was a golden place. But like Alice, she didn't belong.

She walked to the back, to the creek that bubbled merrily along. She sat on a big rock, knowing that Alex would check back here if she didn't answer his knock.

It was more than thirty minutes before she heard foot-falls. She turned and looked up at him. One of the hotel lights framed his figure.

"Hi," he said.

There was something very simple about his greeting that made the tears come back to her eyes. It denoted friend-ship. Acceptance for who and what she was.

"Hi," she replied.

He gave her his hand and helped her to his feet. The touch didn't scorch her as Ross's did. He didn't arouse her emotions, either. Her nerves didn't tingle at his nearness, nor did her belly grow hot with yearning. But she was sud-denly grateful for his presence.

"Are you all right?" he asked.

"No," she said honestly.

"Should I ask why?"

"Not now."

"All right," he said. "What would you like to eat?"

"Something informal," she said.

"Will Italian do?"

She nodded. In truth, she didn't care. She would get through this night, then leave.

His hand still around hers, he led her to his car. He knew when to be silent, and she appreciated it. She also appreci-ated the fact that the silence wasn't awkward.

She peered out the window, taking her last looks at a place that was part magic. They went by the New Age stores, the trading posts, then past several new housing de-velopments. She was reminded of what Sarah had said ear-lier. "What do you think?" she said.

"About what?"

"About all the development? Weren't you born here?"

He nodded. "I'm one of the few natives, along with the Clementses."

"Do you approve?"

"I don't approve or disapprove," he said. "I don't think anyone could have stopped it."

She didn't answer. There *was* a way. People could stop selling land. But he already knew that.

He stopped at a Mediterranean-styled building that looked sleek and expensive. It wouldn't be Ross's idea of informal. *Dammit. Stop thinking of him.*

This time she waited for him to come around and open the door. She needed that small courtesy, that touch of grace. He gave her a cocky grin, just as if he knew what she was thinking.

He touched her elbow lightly as they walked to the door and were seated immediately by a maître d' who obviously knew Alex.

Alex ordered a bottle of wine, then they both ordered their entrées. After the waiter had poured a glass of wine, she played with the glass. "What happened at the ranch?" she asked.

"Ross, you mean?" he replied with his own question.

"Yes."

He shrugged. "Nothing. I doubt if this will go any further. Marc doesn't want the publicity and I doubt whether he really believes Ross was responsible."

"Do you believe he could be?"

"No," he said, to her surprise.

"He told me he had a record."

Alex shrugged. "That was a long time ago."

She wanted to ask about the rape, but something held her back. An invasion of Ross's life? Her own? Or didn't she want to know? She changed the subject. "He also told me about the will," she said. "Why didn't you?"

There it was. The question. She'd asked it. She hadn't known until this moment that she would.

His gaze met hers. "I'm the family's attorney. They wanted it that way. And I agreed. We didn't know if you

were actually the heir or not. And personally—" He hesitated a moment, then continued. "I thought it better you get
to know them without the will clouding your judgment."

"You thought it would?"

"I didn't know."

An honest answer. One of the few she had received.

"I don't want anything," she said. "And I certainly don't
want to be part of a family fight."

His glass of wine was halfway to his lips. He very
slowly lowered it. His gaze studied her. After a moment, he
asked, "Don't you think you should wait until you get the
results of the DNA test to make that decision?"

"No," she replied sharply. "I want everyone to know up
front. I don't want to be involved with all the . . . games
going on."

He raised an eyebrow. "Games?"

"The secrets, the accusations, the one-upmanship."

He was silent for a moment. "Because of what happened
today?"

"Oh that's just one of several things," she said. "In addition to a congressman almost getting killed and accusations that Ross did it, there's silences when I come into a
room, history that no one wants me to know about, getting
lost at night when my companion disappears, a few burglaries in Atlanta and an intruder here." It all came out in
a rush of words.

"Burglaries? Intruder?" His surprise, and dismay, was
evident.

She hadn't meant to mention them. But now . . . perhaps
it was time. "The day I received the invitation to the reunion, my cottage was burglarized. A few days ago, the
bookstore was."

"And the intruder?"

"I believe someone was in my room," she said.
"Some . . . of my things were not as I left them."

"Could you be mistaken? About your room, I mean?" His lips were grim. So was the expression in her eyes.

"Yes. That's why I didn't say anything. But I don't think I'm wrong." She continued to watch him carefully. He could well have been in Atlanta during the burglary at her home. But not the second one at the shop.

"It could be coincidence," he said after a moment.

She regarded him steadily. "It could," she agreed cautiously.

"But you don't believe it?"

"I don't believe in cheap bridges, either," she said. "But I can't understand what anyone would want of mine." She waited a moment, then fired. "Do *you?*"

Something flickered in his eyes. "No," he said. But she knew he was lying. Well, he'd lied before. At least by omission.

"I'm leaving in the morning," she said.

"I'll let you know when the DNA test results are in." She noted he didn't try to dissuade her.

"I'm not sure I want to know now," she said.

He smiled, the old easy grin. "Well, the machinery has started. If it matches, and I'm sure now it will, you will have to take some action about the inheritance, even if you do decide to decline it."

"I wish that firm had never found me."

"No, you don't, Jessica. You're too smart not to want to know. You're too curious. I know it's all overwhelming. But there's a lot of good things about the Clements family."

"And what side are you on?"

He raised an eyebrow in question.

"To sell or not to sell?"

"I don't have a side," Alex replied.

"You're just an objective onlooker? Why don't I believe that?"

"It's my job to be objective, to represent the collective will."

"And no personal opinion at all?"

"A good attorney doesn't have those."

"Isn't that what a good attorney does? Advise?"

"Only when asked," he said, his lips quirking up in an attractive smile.

"Why do I doubt that, too?"

"Because now you are suspicious of everyone."

"Shouldn't I be?"

"Ah, Jessica. There are problems and disagreements in every family."

"But usually you grow up knowing what they are."

"You have good instincts."

"That's why I want to run like hell."

Alex raised an eyebrow. "Maybe I misjudged you. I thought you had more gumption than that."

Her hackles rose, even though she knew exactly what he was doing.

"Think about it, Jessica. For Sarah's sake, if for no other reason."

But Sarah had lied to her, too, or at least had withheld some important truths.

She nodded reluctantly. Just thinking about it held no promises.

"Now tell me, how do you like Sedona?"

Alex delivered her back to the casita, then went to his own home.

After persuading her to at least think about having a role in the family, he'd steered the conversation away, to the history of Sedona, the different peoples who'd lived there. He saw the interest in her eyes, and fanned it. He wanted her fascinated with Sedona. He wanted her in the mix.

He wanted her trust. Today's events had made her lose some in Ross. Perhaps even in Sarah.

He wasn't sure whether he had built it tonight or destroyed it. But he hadn't questioned the determination in her eyes when he'd picked her up. She'd been ready to give up everything. Perhaps he'd delayed that decision for a few days. As long, he hoped, as it took to get the DNA tests. And long enough to find out whether she knew anything about the book.

Alex sure as hell hoped so.

Jessie packed everything but the clothes she would wear in the morning and the nightshirt she would wear tonight. Then she found herself restless.

Alex had stirred something in her tonight. He'd surprised her with his knowledge, because it indicated an interest she hadn't known existed. Oh, he'd previously talked about the recent history of Sedona, about the people who had founded it, but now he talked about the people who'd inhabited the land prior to white settlement.

She wondered whether he was doing it just to pique her curiosity in Sedona, to deflect any additional questions, or because of any real interest in the subject. Or in her as a person. It was a measure of her newly cultivated skepticism that his motive was the immediate question that came to her mind.

She'd also been surprised at his defense of Ross.

Maybe there was more to Alex than she'd first thought. Perhaps he, like the family he served, was adept at hiding behind a facade.

He'd also expressed more than a little fondness for Sarah. Suddenly, she realized she had not said good-bye to the older woman. She looked at the clock. It was after eleven. And she wanted to leave at sunrise.

Regret over her thoughtlessness flooded her. But she wasn't going to change her mind now. She would call Sarah from the airport. She would send a bouquet of flowers as a thank-you.

Right now, all she wanted was to get home to all that was familiar, all that was safe.

But still, she couldn't sleep.

She put on the slacks and knit shirt she'd planned to wear to the airport and went outside. The rock formations were framed by a hauntingly beautiful full moon. Wispy clouds wandered past it, trailing tiny pieces of lace. The stars were so bright she felt she could reach up and touch them.

Familiar and safe.

Exotic and dangerous.

She needed one. She feared being seduced by the other.

fifteen

Jessie unlocked the door to her cottage in Atlanta and went inside. She closed the door, locked it, and leaned against the wall.

Home.

But it didn't feel like home. Not now.

Everything was quiet. Too quiet. Ben was still with Sol. That would be her next stop. Once he was home, everything would be back to normal. She could retreat back to a safe and tranquil life. Or would she ever feel safe here again? She remembered coming home only a couple of weeks earlier and finding the place in shambles.

Her gaze traveled over the interior, to the furniture she'd gradually accumulated. Nothing out of place. Her remaining carousel horses still sat atop the mantel. Her plants still looked healthy despite days of neglect. So did the garden outside. She ached to go out and work in it, to bury her hands in the dirt and her thoughts in physical activity.

A few days. *A lifetime.*

Was this how Alice felt when she woke up from her adventure?

Except she didn't know how she felt. She wondered whether she would ever sort out the past several days and her instinctive affinity for the Southwest and her ambiguity toward the Clements family. Her compass had gone awry, and the needle was spinning. She had worked hard for a place to belong, and had convinced herself that Atlanta, and the shop, were it. She'd shoved aside those shadows of loneliness and doubt and told herself she was content, and that was all she needed. But the cottage no longer seemed like home. Even the lush green she'd once loved seemed overblown after the stark, dry beauty of northern Arizona.

Perhaps she would feel . . . easier when she had Ben.

She went to the phone and called Sol at the bookstore.

He answered on the first ring.

"Sol?"

"Jessie." His voice sounded good. Normal. Familiar.

"I'm home. Is Ben with you?"

"Of course. He won't leave my side. Until you arrive, of course."

"I'll be right over. I'll stay until closing time. You deserve a break."

"Me? If anyone does, you do. That was a short vacation."

She hesitated, then asked, "Any more trouble?"

"No. Did you expect more?" His voice was different, concerned.

"No. Of course not."

"We will have tea when you get here. I'll put it on."

Familiar ground again. Sol loved tea. They had a little hot plate just for that reason. He would have made a great Englishman with his wont for tea, his love of books, and even his dress.

"I'll look forward to it."

Jessie replaced the phone in the cradle. Sol would also be full of questions. He took his role as surrogate uncle seriously.

She bit her lip. Why did she still feel this restlessness?

Why did she feel a loneliness stronger than ever before? She had been lonely in the past. Many, many times, but not like this. Not a piercing, stabbing pain. She'd had a taste of something more, of something she'd always wanted. The need for more petrified her.

The store, when she reached it, looked reassuringly normal. The scent of some exotic tea greeted her, along with frantic barking and a warm tongue washing over her.

"He doesn't say hello to *me* like that," Sol observed mournfully.

Jessie kneeled and buried herself in Ben's fur coat. *A rug with a head on it.* That was the apt description that one customer had given the dog.

But it was such a beloved rug, and such a dear head.

"I missed you," she whispered.

"What about me?" asked a grumpy voice.

Reluctantly, she released Ben and stood. She went over to Sol, who was sitting behind his desk. She leaned down and hugged him, too. "You don't feel as furry," she observed solemnly.

"Thank God for that," Sol said.

Jessie smiled.

He looked at her carefully. "Do you want to tell me about it?"

She sat in the cheap second chair. The store was small and crammed with books. There was no leisurely sitting area like some of the large bookstores. Customers who wanted to scan a book simply took a seat on the staircase, which led up to an equally book-crowded upper room. Since most of the customers were regulars from the university, they felt comfortable doing just that. Jessie weighed what she wanted to tell Sol. "It was . . . interesting."

"Just interesting?"

"Complicated," she amended.

"Is that good? Or bad?"

"I don't know. It's a very complex family. There's even someone running for the Senate."

"I know," he said. "I've been reading about him."

She should have known. Sol was a walking encyclopedia. He read everything, and even the mention of a Clements would have sent him to a computer to investigate.

"What do you think?" she asked.

"About the congressman?"

"Yes."

"He has a conservative record," Sol replied in a noncommittal tone.

In Sol's world, that was an insult. He was proud to be a liberal. He bore her middle-of-the-road independence with a soul-weary patience, convinced that one day he would lead her onto the path of righteousness.

"He's very personable," she offered.

"Most politicians are," he mumbled. "What about the others?"

"Sarah, who is Harding's sister, is very nice."

"And the attorney who came here?" A gleam was in his eye.

"Nice, too."

"Just nice?"

Sol had been trying to matchmake since she'd first started working for him. "Are you trying to get rid of me?"

Something like dismay crossed his face. "Never. I just want you to have a life other than the store. You can't keep hiding forever," he said quietly.

His words were like a hammer hitting her in the chest. "I haven't been hiding," she defended herself.

"I know it when I see it, Jessie," he said. "I've been hiding since my wife died. But at least I had her for twenty years. I had my taste of love. Now I'm content enough, but you've never had your chance."

Jessie dug her fingers into Ben's fur and tried to change the subject. "How has business been?"

Sol sighed. "Good. And no, I'm not going to let you change the subject. Tell me about the Clementses."

"I don't even know that the Clementses are my family," she argued, as much to herself as to him.

"You told me on the phone you believed so."

"That doesn't make it so."

"When will the DNA tests come back?"

"This week, I think."

He was silent, waiting in his own patient way for her to continue.

Her hands dug deeper into Ben's fur. "There's an inheritance," she said finally.

He lifted an eyebrow.

"It's a share in the ranch."

"You don't sound happy about it."

"I'm not. I'm not even supposed to know about it. Not until it's proven I am a Clements."

He shook his head. "You must be the only person in history who's unhappy with finding out she's an heiress."

"Most of the family wants to sell the ranch. One doesn't. If I inherit, I have the deciding vote."

He blinked.

"I don't want it, Sol. I liked Sarah, but I don't feel a part of the family. I don't have the right to make a decision like that."

"And so you came back."

"Yes. I can't help thinking that the burglaries must have had something to do with it, but I can't imagine what."

"You said there were mysteries," he said.

"And I'm no closer to solving them. I was going to the county seat today but . . . I wanted to come home."

His eyes told her that he knew she had come running home. "Why don't we close early tonight, and I'll make you and Ben supper?"

She knew he would squeeze more information from her. He was a fine listener. She wasn't sure how much she could tell him, or how much she would hold in her heart. But she didn't want to be home alone tonight. And Sol was a very good cook. He had a way with spaghetti sauce that would make an Italian matriarch green with envy.

"I would love that," she said. "Now tell me about the burglary."

"I think I told you everything. You should check your desk and see if anything is missing."

The bell on the door tinkled, and a customer entered. She let Sol handle it while she went to her desk in a cluttered corner behind Sol's. Ben went with her, huddling as close to her legs as he could manage. He whined with contentment.

She opened the main desk drawer. She'd never locked it for the simple reason that she never put anything there she wanted to keep secret. Now she wished she had, although whoever burglarized the shop probably would have forced it open.

The interior was a mess. Papers crumpled. Containers of paper clips spilled, business cards torn. She looked in the back of the drawer. She kept a separate set of keys there. It was gone.

Her heart stopped for a moment. The set included keys to her house, car, shop, and safe-deposit box.

She waited until he finished with the customer, who left happily with a rare book on the Boxer Rebellion in China. Jessie remembered when he'd ordered it weeks earlier and how difficult it had been to locate.

She tried to think of anything but what she'd just discovered.

Sol returned to the back. "What's wrong?"

"My keys are missing." Her voice was strained.

He frowned, and she realized he probably didn't even know she had kept a spare set at the office. She'd once misplaced her keys in the shop when a customer came in right after she unlocked it. She'd spent half a day trying to find them, and the next time she'd seen a key duplicating machine, she'd had several copies made.

"Your house key?" he asked.

"That among others."

"We'll have those locks changed this afternoon," he said. "I'll cook over at your house."

She nodded. "There was also a key to the shop."

"Whoever took it obviously didn't need it to get in," he said wryly. "But I'll have the locks changed here as well. Anything else?"

"There was a key to the car, the file cabinets, and a safe-deposit box."

"Safe-deposit box?"

"The old primer," she said. "The one you advised me to protect." That was, in fact, how she met Sol. She had brought the book to Sol, and he'd told her that while it held a moderate value now, it could someday be worth a great deal more. It hadn't mattered to her. She had not planned to sell it in any event, but her father's words had lingered in her mind. He had told her to protect it. She'd wanted to know why. Sol's assessment had satisfied her. Maybe her father had not realized that something that old would not be as valuable as he'd thought.

But she had put it in a safe-deposit box. It had been the last thing she could do for him.

She saw the question in Sol's eyes.

"It's just an old book," she said. Then she remembered the odd question from Sarah. *Did he leave any personal effects? Photos? Books?*

For some reason, she hadn't mentioned the primer.

Her home. Her business. Her hotel room. All invaded.

"You don't think anyone could be after the primer?" She finally put voice to the question in both their minds.

"I can't understand why," he said. "It's not worth

enough to commit a crime over. And you say you might receive an inheritance. They looked for you to give you something, not to take it away."

"Did they?" she asked, suddenly in doubt. Had they looked for her father because they wanted a vote on the ranch? Or an old book? She felt chilled.

"Why don't we look at the book again?" he asked. "I'll get a friend who specializes in that field to join us. In the meantime . . ."

For the next few minutes, they called locksmiths until they found one willing to come first to the shop, then to her house. Sol reached out and put his hand on hers. "I'll get some groceries while you wait here. Then we'll both go with him to your house."

Ben barked.

Sol chuckled, breaking some of the tension. "He approves. I actually think he's trying to talk to me."

And Ben was, Jessie knew. He would sit and make little growling, grumbling sounds as if he were carrying on a perfectly natural conversation. If she didn't understand, well, that was her loss. He would keep talking anyway. How she'd missed him.

She also knew that Sol was trying to make her relax. She realized then that her hands were locked together, her fingers intertwined. They were pressing down on the desk.

"Will you be all right?" he asked.

"Yes, of course," she said, unwinding her fingers. She wasn't entirely sure of that, but she didn't want him to know it. He'd said she'd been hiding. Perhaps she had. Perhaps it was time to come out of the shadows. "I have Ben," she said.

"That's what worries me," he said. He went to the door, then turned around to make sure. She nodded.

He left for the grocery store down the street. She started to straighten the top drawer of the desk. A customer came in, one she hadn't seen before, and for the first time she felt apprehension. She pushed it aside and went over to him. She wasn't going to succumb to fear.

"Can I help you with anything?"

"A friend told me you had a fine selection of Civil War books," he said.

She showed him those shelves, then retreated to her desk. Ben had moved with her, right on her heels. She watched the customer out of the corner of her eye. He somehow looked out of place. He didn't have the laid-back, casual air of most of their customers from the university. He had the look of a bodybuilder, not the sedentary slouch of a professor, and his blue eyes were a little too sharp, as if they'd been trained to notice everything. She also noticed they didn't smile when his lips did.

He picked out a volume and brought it to her. She looked at it, a rare memoir of a confederate officer under Colonel Mosby, the gray ghost of the Confederacy. It was expensive. She named the price, and he pulled out a wallet that looked thick with bills.

"Do you wish me to wrap it?"

"No," he said. He looked around again. "It's an interesting shop."

Did she hear any nuances? Or was her imagination running wild?

Her gaze followed him out the door. There was no satisfaction in the sale, as she wondered whether she would have a cold chill every time the door opened.

The week passed slowly. The new locks did not give her a sense of security. Nor were any of her questions answered. Sol's friend was out of town, and they decided to wait until he returned to retrieve the book from its place of safety.

Her thoughts continually returned to the sun-kissed red formations of Arizona—the clean, clear skies and the untamed beauty of high desert. Her nights were haunted by thoughts of Ross and all of his complexities. She thought of the two times she'd seen him relax: the restaurant and those brief moments in his home. She remembered the kiss and her body tingled and ached.

Good girls always like bad boys. Where had she heard that? Probably the same place that she'd heard such relationships never work. She told herself that people can't change others, not the core of them. The essence of their soul. But women kept trying.

Ross, even if he was innocent of rape, was a loner. He would always be a loner.

She kept trying to banish him from her thoughts, but he wouldn't stay vanquished. His arresting face kept appearing in the oddest places. The car. The shop. A restaurant. She would see a dark head and her senses would reel. Then the head would turn, and it was someone else, and her heart plummeted.

She found herself reaching for the phone with more eagerness than before, hoping against hope she would hear the low lazy rumble of his voice . . .

Jessie shook her head as she bent over the account books. She knew he wouldn't call. He thought she believed him capable of rape. And she had, for the briefest of time, when the shock of his words had stunned her and carried her back to a long-ago night. Until she had time to think about it, and exactly what he'd said.

She tried to concentrate on the account books. That was her job. Sol's was the acquisition of books, and even now he was at some estate sale and she was alone at the store. It was empty, as it usually was on a weekday morning. Ben, who always accompanied her to the store now, was at her side, his head resting on one of her feet.

It was Friday. Saturday would be busy. She would work in her garden on Sunday. The thought usually made her happy, but instead she just felt . . . empty. She hadn't realized until now how much she'd isolated herself, how hesitant she'd been to make deep friendships. Except for Sol, she'd been afraid to trust anyone.

Maybe she would go riding Sunday. She had started to look in the Yellow Pages for a riding stable when the phone rang. She bit her lip for a moment, trying to keep her hand from reaching for it too eagerly, then picked it up.

Before she could say the name of the store, she heard Alex's voice. "Jessica?"

"Alex?"

"The same," he said with that soothing confident tone of his. "I have news. The DNA results came back. You are a Clements. Your father was Harding Clements."

For some reason, the news stunned her. She had come to believe it in her mind. The photos of her and Sarah were too similar, the younger and older ones of her father too telling. And yet her heart hadn't yet accepted it. She didn't realize that until this very moment. It was proof positive that her entire life had been a lie. That her father had a secret so terrible that he had deprived himself, and her, of a heritage, of roots, of family.

"Jessica?"

"I'm here," she replied, knowing her words were strained.

"Can you return for a few days? There are things that must be discussed, papers to be signed."

She couldn't speak. She felt as if a huge weight had been placed on her back. She wasn't sure she was strong enough to carry it. Or even wanted to.

"I'm . . . busy right now," she finally replied.

He hesitated for a moment, then said quietly, "I didn't want to tell you this, but I think I should. Sarah's ill."

Jessie's hand balled into a fist. "What? How?"

"She has a bad heart."

"No one said anything to me about it."

"I don't think anyone knows but me. I didn't know myself until the DNA test proved you were a blood relative. She came to me because she wanted to make a new will."

Jessie waited. She knew whatever was to come was not good.

"I can't go into it now. She needs to tell you. Please come, Jessica. Just for a few days."

"I can't just up and leave whenever you call. I have a business. A dog." Even to her own ears, it sounded weak. She frantically tried to think of other excuses. She wasn't ready for this. She hadn't entirely accepted the fact she had a new family, and now she was being told that one of the two members she really cared about might be dying. The other didn't want anything to do with her.

Alex's voice became soothing, coaxing. "Hell, we'll fly the dog in. Marc is gone. There's plenty of room at the ranch house. It will mean everything to Sarah."

Jessie wavered. That damn impulse to try to please everyone. In truth, she found she didn't want to say no. Something in her hungered to return, despite all the emotional warning signs frantically waving at her.

The Sunset was her roots.

"I'll have to talk to Sol," she said, even as she knew he heard the surrender in her voice.

"Call me back as soon as you can," he said. "I'll make the arrangements."

"No," she said. "I'll do this my way." She hadn't figured out yet what *her* way would be, but she knew she had to fight for her independence, to remain neutral, even apart. She feared being torn asunder if she did not.

"But you will call me?"

"Yes."

She hung up the phone very carefully. As if sensing her careening emotions, Ben whined beside her.

"Ah, Ben," she said. "What have I done? I really thought I was finished with Wonderland."

She leaned back in her one extravagance in the shop, a

cushioned swivel chair, and looked around. It was everything familiar, everything comfortable.

But she hungered for the high desert, the spectacular scenery, the clean air and the clear nights. She'd felt from the first sight of it that she belonged, that it was the home place she'd always missed.

And Ross?

She hungered for him, too. Or did he just represent the land that had so enchanted her? The lonely splendor that touched her soul as nothing else had.

Jessie wondered whether she was willing to risk everything to discover whether it was all a mirage, a siren song that only meant disaster.

But she would never forgive herself if she didn't find out.

sixteen

Sarah put down the phone receiver. Jessie was returning.

She sat down heavily. She wished she weren't so tired. Sometimes her heart hurt so badly she thought she wouldn't live through another day. She wanted to live long enough to ensure the safety of the Sunset. She wanted even more to leave her son a piece of it.

An era was disappearing. A way of life fading into something called progress. The Sunset was one of the last remaining working ranches in the area. The rest had been redesigned into dude ranches, or bed-and-breakfast inns or resorts.

Was it so wrong to keep alive just one? Somehow she had to persuade Jessica to help her do that.

Sarah didn't know what had made Jessie flee days earlier. She only knew that the girl had done exactly that. Fled. From her. From the Sunset. From her heritage.

And she wasn't a tender shoot easily bruised. She had strength. Sarah knew that when she hadn't panicked the night she'd lost her way. The family hadn't daunted her. But what most impressed Sarah was that she'd never asked for a thing.

She'd known then what she had to do. She'd kept her

failing health from the family. Now she wasn't above using it to bring the girl back. She'd didn't have enough time to play fair.

She'd realized that she could die at any time. Unfortunately, Ross couldn't inherit her share of the ranch. But a blood relative could. And there was only one that she would trust with the Sunset. She had meant to tell Jessie the moment the DNA tests were confirmed, but the girl disappeared into her other life. She'd sent yellow roses to Sarah, though, a thoughtful thank-you.

When the DNA results came in, Sarah had asked Alex to plead with Jessie to return, to use her health if necessary.

She had expected an argument. Strangely enough, she didn't receive one. Instead, he'd merely suggested that she would probably outlive them all. It was then, and only then, that she told him there was some urgency to the matter. His subsequent phone conversation with Jessica, as related to her, had been disappointing. She hadn't refused to come, but she hadn't caught the first plane, either. Maybe she was wrong. Maybe the girl wasn't as enchanted with the Sunset as Sarah had thought.

Sarah thought she'd seen that glimmer of belonging in her eyes when they'd ridden together up to the Saddle. But then Marc . . . damn him.

She'd never had a chance to reassure her, to tell her that Marc's accusations were only a reflex reaction against what he considered an obstacle in the way of something he wanted. Marc and Ross had always been like oil and water. Despite the fact that Marc, the golden child, had been much older, he'd always resented Ross, and particularly his father's trust in him.

But he must know that Ross would never hurt him. He'd also known that even the slightest inference would set the police on Ross. Her son had never recovered from the accusation of rape, even after the girl recanted.

She sighed. She hoped Jessie would return. Perhaps

they—she and Jessica—could go for another ride, a less eventful one. She looked at Jessie and saw herself, though she hoped Jessie wouldn't make the same mistakes she'd made.

Or were they mistakes? Was loving too much a mistake? She'd forgiven her husband so many times she'd stopped counting them. She'd loved him so much that his son became her son, and she'd loved Ross with every fiber of her being. He made up for the children she hadn't borne, that she'd so badly wanted. God had not seen fit to bless her. Because of what she'd once done?

She'd tried to protect the people she loved, no matter what she'd had to do. She'd forgiven their faults, made excuses for them, covered for them. Perhaps she'd shouldn't have always done that with Harding. Perhaps then . . .

Sarah fought back tears. So many losses over the years.

Jessie offered her another chance. A chance to save the Sunset, to keep Ross here, even to save the entire family from tearing itself apart. If only she had the book . . . or knew where it was.

She often wondered whether Harding had thrown it away. Or perhaps Jessie wasn't aware of what she had? She had hoped to gain her niece's trust, but Marc and his accusations had obviously spooked her.

This time she would make sure everything went well. Thank God, Marc was back in Washington.

Jessie missed the anticipation she'd felt on her first drive up to Sedona. Her pleasure was now muted by a certain wariness.

There had been myriad reasons for her return so soon: Sarah's health, the growing necessity to get answers to questions. The fear invading her life.

She had been stunned by it, by the apprehension she felt now when strangers entered the store and every time there was a knock on her cottage door. Her safe, quiet world had been disrupted. She wanted to know why. She'd worked too hard to conquer the fear that had haunted her after the rape, after the death of her father. She wasn't going to surrender to it again. Not without a fight.

She didn't want an inheritance, not if it contained the strings she was beginning to feel were attached. But she *did* want information. She wanted to feel safe again.

Sarah had the answers.

At least, her safe-deposit box was secure. She'd checked that before leaving, had even changed boxes although she'd been assured by a bank officer that she had nothing to worry about. They had safeguards. Still, she felt better.

She tried to relax as she fought the heavy traffic out of Phoenix. She'd been nervous the last time. But then she was going to meet a family she could either reject and accept, and its members could do the same. Now she might have the power to make a difference in its future.

It was a power she didn't want.

She reached down with one hand and ran her fingers through Ben's fur. She had decided to bring him, partly because of the disquiet that gnawed at her. He had survived one burglary. He might not survive another. There was another reason. She needed a friend, and he was the only one she was sure didn't want anything from her. At least nothing but an occasional demonstration of love.

He'd endured the flight well, although he had given her an indignant look when she'd fetched him at the luggage department. She'd worried then that she'd made a mistake bringing him, but he was *her* family, and Alex *had* extended an invitation. She wanted him safe at her side.

She only wished that she'd had time to wait on Sol's friend to study the primer. But that would have been another week. And after Alex's call, she'd felt an urgency to return.

Be truthful. It was Ross as well. She hadn't taken the time to pick apart his words that afternoon before she'd left. Now she had. She realized what he'd said and what he hadn't said. She'd reacted to one word.

Perhaps because she knew the route now, it seemed no time at all until she drove up to the ranch house. The front drive was empty except for Ross's pickup. Her heart thumped loudly. She wondered whether he was out on a horse or nearby.

Her question was answered immediately when she saw him emerge from the barn. Timber was at his side. Their eyes met. He hesitated, then started toward the car.

She got out, keeping Ben inside the car until she knew how Timber would react. Her breath caught in her throat as he walked toward her. He wasn't wearing a hat, and his thick dark hair looked as if his fingers had combed it. She'd almost forgotten how tall he was, how he turned her insides to quivering jelly.

He's dangerous, she reminded herself. Even if the rape charge was not true, Jessie knew she should be cautious. He'd told her what he had for a reason. He'd tried to scare her off.

Still, she couldn't minimize the impact he had on her, the sheer jolt of electricity, the burning want he ignited in her.

She braced herself. "Ross?"

"I heard you were coming back," he said. There wasn't much welcome in his words, but she saw a momentary warmth in his eyes. His gaze was intent, studying her.

"Sarah wanted me," she said simply.

"Sarah's good at getting what she wants," he said.

"And you?"

He shrugged.

Jessie suddenly felt tongue-tied, unsure. She hated that feeling. They had been so at ease with each other the night they'd had dinner. Tension radiated between them now, tension and energy and ambivalence. The conflicting emotions paralyzed her.

Ben barked from the interior of the car.

"You can let him out." There was a touch of weariness in his voice, as if he knew what she was thinking. "Timber won't hurt him." *I won't hurt you.*

She didn't question his claim, either the spoken or silently conveyed. Instead, her skin seemed to prickle, even as she felt warmer than she should, even on a July day. She opened the door and Ben tumbled out with all the grace of a pregnant elephant. For a moment, his button eyes seemed to panic at the sight of Timber, and he edged close to her.

Timber started toward Ben.

"Stay," Ross said. "Sit." Then as the big dog sat, Ross went over to Ben and kneeled, whispered something to him, and scratched him behind his ears. Then he held out his hand to Timber. "Come."

The next second the dogs were sniffing each other, tails wagging.

"Timber knows he's a friend now," Ross said. "He'll protect your dog with his life if necessary."

Her eyes widened.

"I meant that to be comforting," he said with a wry turn of his lips.

"Ben is . . . shy," she said.

"Perhaps he has reason."

Nothing could have endeared him more to her. No snide comments about being a rug. Or timid. No comparisons with Timber. Just . . . acceptance.

"He does. I think he was badly mistreated until I got him. But he's very smart. And gentle."

His gaze rested on the dog for a moment, then returned to her face. "Does this mean you plan to stay awhile?" he asked.

"There's still my business. I'll have to get back to Atlanta soon. I just couldn't leave him again."

He nodded, not questioning the wisdom of bringing a

dog two thousand miles. Still, his next words were a little stiff. "I understand congratulations are in order."

She knew exactly what he meant. "I'm not sure about that," she said lightly. She hoped it didn't sound like a croak.

His eyes seemed to bore into her. "It's not every day one becomes an heiress."

"I'm not sure I am."

"Aren't you?" The wry cynicism was back in his voice. His raw disbelief was almost a slap in the face.

She stepped back, anger and hurt filling her. "Think what you want," she said. She started to turn away, back toward the house.

He blocked her, and she had to look up at him. She could feel the heat of his body. Her own skin was sizzling. But warmer yet was the core of her. Energy radiated between them. Then his fingers touched her cheek. No, caressed. Her legs became boneless. Her belly tensed with a gnawing want. She recalled what he'd said the last time they were together. *Remember what happens if you play with fire.*

And he *was* fire.

Irresistible fire.

His fingers dropped, and he stepped back as if burned himself, as if he found himself doing something he hadn't wanted to do.

Her fingers knotted into fists. She remembered the last time, when he was deliberately trying to chase her away, remembered the cold, objective words. She simply could not equate them now with the man who stood there.

"I only know what you told me," she said in a late answer to his question. "Alex is to explain everything."

"I'm sure Alex will do that very well."

"I'm sure he will," she said. "How is Sarah?"

He looked surprised. "Fine. Indestructible. She'll outlive all of us."

Alex had said that Sarah didn't want anyone to know she was ill. Had her son not noticed any changes? Or had there been changes?

For the briefest of seconds, she wondered if this wasn't a ploy of Sarah's. Then she felt guilty at the thought. But there were so many damn undercurrents, so many discordant notes.

Ross stood there, his eyes narrowing slightly. "Is there something I should know about Sarah?"

She shook her head. "I've just grown to like her enormously."

His lips smiled slightly. "She can be Machiavellian."

"I never would have guessed," she replied.

His smile broadened. "You recognized it?"

"Yes."

She loved that smile. She'd seen it so rarely.

Jessie knew now she hadn't returned simply because of Sarah, and certainly not because of an uncertain inheritance. She had come back to see Ross, to see whether his pull was as real and powerful as she'd believed it to be. She also knew with all her heart that he would never have purposely hurt anyone.

"Good," he said. "Be wary of Alex, too."

"He likes you. He defended you."

He stiffened. "Is that why . . . ?"

"No," she said simply. She didn't have to ask what he meant.

His gaze seemed to search her face, searching for truth. After a moment, he relaxed slightly. "I've known Alex a long time," he said. "You never know quite where he stands."

"I'll remember that," she said.

A muscle flexed in his cheek. "You'd better go see Sarah. She's been anxious ever since Alex said you were coming."

"Will you be here later?"

"I have work to do."

He didn't move, though, and neither did she. The energy was still wrapped around them, as if they were standing in the eye of a hurricane. They were talking calmly, and yet every word was forced. She wanted to reach out and touch him. She wanted to ask him why he'd mentioned the rape charge. She wanted to know why he'd wanted her to leave.

The smile had left his lips. "Take care," he said simply, then turned and walked away to his pickup. Timber followed him, and so did Ben.

"Ben!"

He turned back and sat next to her, looking up forlornly. He didn't want to give up a new friend. Well, she felt the same way. She wanted to follow Ross, but that air of isolation still hovered around him like some ominous cloud.

Only then did she see Sarah standing on the porch. "Come on, Ben," she said, and started for the house.

Sarah looked as elegant as she had the first time Jessie had met her. Her color, though, seemed less . . . robust. Or was it just the suggestion that her health was not good? Surely Ross would have noticed if there had been any changes. Or do you see them less when you are with someone day after day?

Sarah held out her hands, and Jessie took them. They felt strong enough.

"I'm so glad you came back," she said. "And this must be Ben."

"He's a bit shy," Jessie said as Ben pressed against her left leg. "Alex said you wouldn't mind, that he was invited, too."

"Of course, he was invited. We used to have a lot of dogs around here, and now there's only Timber. I miss having more. I'm sure Ben and I will get along very well." She glanced at her empty hands. "Luggage? You *are* staying here?"

"For several days," Jessie replied. "My bag is in the trunk."

"I'll have Ross bring in your luggage," Sarah said.

"No!" Jessie said in a voice sharper than intended. She didn't want him anywhere near her at the moment. Her reactions to him were too visceral. "I'll do it," she said.

Before Sarah could protest, Jessie was down the porch step, opening the trunk and taking out the suitcase. Setting it down on the rollers, she rejoined Sarah on the porch and followed her inside, wondering whether she was making one of the worst mistakes of her life.

Her room was upstairs, right over Sarah's room. Jessie hadn't seen the upstairs before, and she noticed that the wide hall led to five doors. Her room was large, sunny, and bright. Hardwood floors were covered with a bright Native American rug, and the walls with Southwestern paintings. A huge tester bed dominated the room.

"When Marc and Samantha are here, they have the rooms down the hall," Sarah said. "You have a private bath next door. There's another guest room across the hall, but we rarely use it."

She hesitated, then added. "I hope you'll consider every part of this ranch your home. Use the living room or kitchen whenever you wish." She reached out and took Jessie's hand. "Thank you for coming. I know . . . that we must have overwhelmed you the last time." She sighed. "We probably shouldn't have invited you that way, but everyone was so anxious to meet you."

Jessie was tired of hearing that. She also doubted whether it was true. Some would have been perfectly happy not to meet her. Including April.

But instead she told a partial truth. "I had to get home," she said. "I hadn't expected to stay any longer than the weekend."

"I hope you can stay longer this time."

"I want to learn more about my father. I hope you can—

will—help me now." She'd said it. Thrown down a challenge.

A fleeting emotion, something like dismay, flickered through Sarah's eyes, but she didn't let go of Jessie's hand. "We'll have a talk later," she said. "Alex wants to meet with you in the morning. I'll be glad to come with you if you like."

She shook her head. "Ross told me a little about what to expect. He said I would inherit a share of the ranch, and that my vote could control what is done with the Sunset. Is that true?"

Sarah nodded.

"I don't want that kind of power," Jessie said. "This family owes me nothing. My father surrendered any right to it when he left the ranch."

"Not according to the will. My father hoped he would return."

"He was still alive then?"

"Yes. He was nearly eighty then. I think losing two more sons . . . killed him. He died ten months after Heath died and Harding disappeared. It broke his heart, what was left after Mother died."

"Mary Louise?"

"Yes. She was always the strength of the family. She was so determined to keep the family together, she insisted early on the terms of my father's will."

"When did she die?"

"Just a few months before my father. She'd been ill, or she might have found a way to prevent . . ." Sarah stopped abruptly.

"Prevent what?" Jessie asked impatiently. "Don't you think it's time for me to know?"

Sarah went over to the window and looked out. "For years," she said with a sigh, "we lived together. My husband was foreman when we were married, and I moved with him into the house Ross has now. Your father and Lori lived in this house, as did Halden and his wife and children.

"Then Heath came home a year after Lori had married your father. He'd been badly wounded and was in a hospital in England for months."

Jessie saw Sarah's hand tighten on the windowsill. After a moment of strained silence, she continued, "When Heath came home, he was angry and bitter. He didn't want to work on the ranch. He didn't want to do anything. He drank and raised hell. One time he almost set the barn on fire, and our father told him to straighten up or get out. He got out. No one heard from him for three years, then he returned home, said he wanted to settle down and take his place in the business. My father was happy. The prodigal had returned."

Sarah sat down. Her mouth was grim.

Jessie waited silently. She wasn't sure she wanted to hear the rest of the story.

Finally, Sarah continued wearily. "Harding was happy, too. He'd felt guilty about marrying Lori, but she'd told him that Heath had broken it off."

She looked up at Jessie, her eyes begging her to understand. "Heath and Hugh had been your father's heroes. He worshiped both of them, and when Heath first came home, it was your father who kept making excuses for him. He was so pleased when Heath returned the second time, he was willing to give up his own position on the ranch. But Heath wasn't home to work. He was home to get money. He wanted Father to sell part of the ranch and give him his share. *His share.* He didn't care about the ranch or anyone on it. When Father wouldn't agree, Heath decided he would take what he felt was due him.

"He was asked to make delivery of a herd and pick up the money. Instead of bringing it back, he secretly invested it in an offshore oil company started by a war buddy; he'd been promised a partnership if he could come up with some financing.

"A week later, your father went to the bank to get the payroll—the hands all wanted cash—and discovered that not only was the money from the herd not deposited but most of the funds left in the account had been withdrawn."

Sarah leaned against the windowsill. "We knew your father went to the bank. We knew he talked to the manager. That's the last time anyone saw him. I can only imagine that he tried to find Heath. No one knows what happened then."

Jessie's heart was beating loud. She knew that a major part of the story was not yet told. "And Lori?"

"She was gone. Her jewelry, some of her clothes. She left a note, saying she was going with Heath."

Jessie slowly expelled breath she hadn't realized was bottled in her throat. She felt tears welling in back of her eyes. Her father. Betrayed by a brother he trusted and a wife he loved. More than life, Sarah had said.

"Go on," she said as Sarah faltered, her words dying away.

"We found a note from Heath saying he was leaving with Lori," she said, "just as the sheriff came and told us there had been a fire at our Oak Creek cabin. Two bodies had been found there. They identified Heath by his class ring and Lori by her wedding ring. We never saw Harding again."

seventeen

Jessie couldn't do anything but stare at her, the last words ringing in her head. *We never saw Harding again.*

Jessie didn't ask the question that came to the forefront of her mind. She knew that it had been pricking around before. But now she couldn't disregard the implications.

Had her father had anything to do with the fire? She couldn't force herself to put it any other way. She couldn't allow herself to consider the word *murder.*

But the words didn't come, and Sarah had looked very tired. For the first time, she looked every year of her age.

"You'll have to excuse me," Sarah said. She had leaned against the wall for a moment, obviously steadying herself. "I think I need some rest."

"Of course," Jessie said, feeling shaky herself.

"I had hoped we could go for a ride, but perhaps . . . tomorrow."

"I would like that," Jessie said, wondering whether the older woman would be up to it then, either.

"Why don't you go ahead and take a horse," Sarah said. "Ross can go with you. Supper will be at seven."

She started to leave, then stopped at the door. "Thank you for coming, Jessie. You can't know how much it means to me."

Jessie sat down on the bed as the door closed behind

Sarah. While she'd known that something terrible must have happened to make her father leave everything he knew and loved, she'd tried to avoid the notion that it was anything *he'd* done. Now she wasn't so sure. Could he have had something to do with the fire? With the deaths of his wife and brother?

She shivered and felt herself crying inside for the young man her father had been. *He loved her more than life.*

Betrayed not only by a wife he adored, but also by an older brother he'd made into a hero.

She realized now why he'd never smiled, why he'd preferred the bottle to life. She only wished that she'd been . . . more important to him. Perhaps he hadn't been able to let anyone be that important again.

Ben whined, and she remembered he hadn't been for a walk. She took him down the steps to the front and walked him over to the paddock. There were several horses munching grass. None of them paid any attention to either of them. She wondered whether her father used to walk over here and lean over the fence.

Grief swelled inside her. She felt as if she'd just lost her father. His death was as fresh to her now as it had been the day of the funeral.

She looked out over the rock formations. It was afternoon; dusk was several hours off.

She wanted to ride back to the rock formation called the Saddle and look below as she had with Sarah.

Ross's pickup was gone. She didn't know whether Sarah had known that. It didn't matter, though. In fact, she preferred riding alone at the moment. She *had* to be alone. She wanted to see the Sunset as her father had seen it.

Jessie took Ben up to her room. She'd brought his favorite blanket and she placed it on the floor. "I'll be back soon," she said. She hated to leave him, but she feared that his thick fur would pick up needles from cactus. Or that he might have a personal encounter with a snake. As long as he had the blanket, he'd know he was safe.

She changed into a pair of jeans and a shirt, pulled on a pair of boots she'd purchased in Atlanta, then reassured Ben once more. She took the steps two at a time, eager now to be on a horse.

Dan'l was in the stables.

"Sarah suggested I go for a ride," she said, fudging the truth only a little. "Can you suggest a horse?"

"Carefree is fine now," he offered. "Like to try him again?" Then he hesitated.

She knew he was thinking of Ross and didn't want to give him a chance to think about it. "That would be great," she replied. At least, she would know this time what to expect.

She watched as he saddled the horse. He offered to help her mount, but she easily swung up into the saddle.

"I'll be back in a couple of hours," she said. "Before dark."

"I'll come looking for you if you're not," he said.

"Not to worry," she said, adjusting her body to the saddle. She guided the horse out of the barn and down the road. Carefree didn't need much urging. In several moments, they were cantering toward the Saddle.

She felt the breeze against her face, fully aware it was cooling moisture on her cheeks. Her eyes hurt, but the wind was cleansing. She wondered if her father had ever wanted to come back, whether he missed the red rock and the yucca and the junipers.

Following the route she and Sarah had taken days ago, she rode toward the Saddle and found the path upward without trouble. She guided the horse up the steep trail, letting him do most of the work. This time she knew not to yell *whoa,* and to hold the reins lightly. Carefree knew what to do far better than she.

Jessie reached the top and dismounted. She went to

where she and Sarah had stood and looked down at the ranch below. She used a hand to wipe a tear from her face. "I'm here, Daddy," she said. "Part of you came back."

She tried to see him as a young man. A man in love. A man doing what he loved, and that apparently had been ranching. Where had all that youth and hope gone? Because it had been long gone when she knew him. How much courage had it taken to keep her when her mother deserted them? Had he ever even loved her mother? He'd never mentioned either her mother or Lori.

She wished she'd known him better.

"I loved you," she whispered to the wind. "I will always love you."

Then she saw movement below. A truck pulling into the road to the ranch. Ross. She suspected he wouldn't be happy that she'd taken one of his horses. Well, that was his problem. She turned and looked in another direction, at the vast panorama. The clear sky was darkening as it often did in late afternoon, and the sun looked like molten gold.

Her roots lay here in the rough soil, the rocky terrain, in the splendid hills and glorious red rock formations. For the first time, she felt close to her father, as if he were looking down at her with an approval she'd never received as a child.

She knew then that she could never vote to sell the Sunset.

She didn't know how long she lingered. An hour, perhaps. So many memories flashed through her mind, so many images. She was filled with feelings and emotions so tumultuous, so strong that they physically hurt.

She turned to go when she heard the whinny of another horse. For a moment, she felt a shiver of fear. She was out here alone. But any apprehension faded when she saw Ross appear on the trail. For a moment, her chest tightened, but then she slowly relaxed. She reminded herself that she wasn't going to run any longer. Not from fear. Not from uncertainty.

Ross's expression, though, was enough to put the fear of God into anyone. He glowered at her as he slid down from the horse.

"Dammit," he said in a low, furious voice. "Don't you have any sense?"

She bristled. "Sarah said . . ."

"I don't give a damn what Sarah said." He stalked over to her, his eyes furious.

"Your horse is perfectly fine," she defended herself, thinking he was afraid she might hurt the horse again. "Dan'l said . . ."

"I'm not worried about the horse," he said, interrupting her for the second time.

The admission stunned her. That was all she thought he cared about. Her chin lifted. "I can take care of myself," she said. "I've been doing it since I was seventeen."

"Yeah," he said sarcastically. "That's why you got lost last week." His lips thinned as he added, "And there's some maniac running around with a rifle. I'm sure Sarah did *not* mean for you to go riding alone."

"According to you, I'm a part owner," she said stiffly. "I have the right to go riding whenever . . ."

She didn't have a chance to continue. He was looming over her, his eyes angry, and his body tense. She was going to step back when his hand reached out. His fingers were like steel around her wrists.

"Dammit, Jessie, watch it."

She looked behind her. The ground behind her sloped to a steep decline. She had unconsciously stepped back further than she'd thought.

He drew her away from the edge, and she was in his arms, his lips pressed down on hers. Hard and hot and angry. Her own lips responded, partly out of the realization of how she'd nearly tumbled off the side of a cliff.

Whether it was fear or grief or passion, her entire body responded to his touch. She felt as if he'd sparked a thousand tiny charges inside her.

She found herself clinging to him, to his strength. His hard-muscled thighs pressed against hers and strong, tanned arms still held on to her.

He took his lips from hers. "Ah, Jessie," he said, his voice a husky whisper.

Her heart started beating strongly. The very air was suddenly electrified. It crackled. Hissed. Sparked.

Then his lips brushed against hers, and his fingers ran up and down her arms in caressingly sensuous trails. The air around them turned as molten as that in the heart of a volcano.

The grief she'd just felt, still felt, turned into desperate need. She'd grieved alone as a girl. More than grieved because she'd felt so much guilt. And she'd never cried. She'd held it all inside until today. And now Ross was here, and somehow she felt connected to him in a way she'd never known before.

Yet he was fighting the attraction between them. She could tell it in the tension of his body. She didn't understand why. She only knew she needed him at this moment, needed to fill the emptiness she'd felt since hearing at least part of her father's history. His lips slipped away, and her head somehow relaxed against his chest, against the solid strength.

She heard his soft sigh as his arms tightened around her. For the first time in her life, she felt protected.

An illusion?

Her gaze met his, and for a moment his mask slipped. She saw a kind of hopelessness, a pain that ripped into her. His chest quivered as he held her, and his eyes looked away as if trying to hide some emotion.

His lips touched hers again and he deepened the kiss with a slow sensuous tenderness that reached down into the deepest part of her soul. Her mouth opened to his, and the tenderness became something else altogether. Something explosive.

She traced her fingers along his back as if she couldn't get enough of him, even as his hands dug themselves through her hair. She closed her eyes, and she felt as if she were being transported to a magical place full of marvelous sensations.

She found herself doing things she'd never done before, her body molding itself to his. These new feelings enchanted her. She wanted to kiss him, touch him, feel him.

Tremors ran through her, even as his fingers trailed fire wherever they went.

A groan came from deep within him, then he released her lips. "Damn," he muttered. "Not here." With what seemed supreme effort, he pulled away, but her hand caught his, and his fingers wrapped around hers.

Her body ached. It was a mess of writhing nerve ends.

She leaned into him, looking out over the valley below, trying desperately to regain some equanimity. She forced herself to concentrate on something else, not on the proximity of his body.

"Sarah told me about my father, today," she said after a moment, hearing the strain in her own voice. "Did you know about Lori and . . . ?"

"I've heard the rumors," he said in that low drawl.

"Do you think my father could have . . ."

"I don't know, Jessie. It's all speculation. I don't think anyone really knows." His fingers tightened around hers.

"I never thought he loved me," she said. "I was a burden, someone who slowed him down, kept him from being all he could be."

"If he had a burden, it wasn't you," he said gently. "He must have loved you a great deal to keep you with him."

Jessie stood there, stunned. She'd never thought of it

that way. She swallowed hard. "Thank you," she whispered.

Obviously uncomfortable, he shrugged, but his fingers tightened around hers.

They stood there several moments. Then she struggled to change the subject. "Sarah mentioned that Heath had stolen money, that he'd invested it in some company."

"True enough, according to family legend," Ross said. "Heath had just sold a herd of cattle. He'd received a cashier's check, a substantial sum. Money needed for feed, stock, salaries. Heath apparently used it to buy bearer bonds in a new company. That company is now worth billions, and the bonds millions."

"What happened to them?"

"No one knows. They've never been found. I personally think they were destroyed in the fire."

She turned around and looked up at him. "Does everyone believe that?"

"I don't know," he said simply.

Her blood chilled. Harding could have been the last person to see Heath. But if her father had the bonds, surely he would have cashed them by now. They wouldn't have lived hand-to-mouth so many years. Or maybe the bonds weren't worth much until recently?

His arms went around her again, but this time they offered security, comfort, even as she felt the heat from his body, the hardness of it. "I don't think anyone really believes they still exist," he said, amending his last statement.

She didn't believe him. All of a sudden, the burglaries, the intrusion into her hotel room, the questions about whether her father had left her anything started to make sense.

"It was a long time ago," he said, his hands going up to her shoulders and massaging the area around her neck. Her body reacted, but her mind was spinning.

He let go and stood watching her for a moment, his eyes veiled. Then he held out his hand. "I think we had better go."

The sun was low, dropping quickly in a sky darkening to a rich fine royal blue. The last, lingering rays bounced off the red rock, making the walls glow with almost mystical light. She felt torn apart, lured by the beauty, repelled by the story she was piecing together bit by bit. Anger. Grief. Betrayal. She felt them all. As well as the lingering desire that Ross always kindled in her.

She didn't take his hand. She had to sort out the emotions, the suspicions gathering in her mind, the feelings in her heart. He had the power to blind her. It was something she couldn't afford now. Jessie walked over to her horse, aware that he was right behind her. She felt the heat of his body, the pull of his presence.

She took the reins, but he stepped in front of her and took them.

"I want you to promise me you won't ride alone again," he said.

"No," she replied. "I won't make a promise I don't intend to keep." Her body was still humming, still warm from his touch. But now the magic was gone. "And don't blame Dan'l. Sarah said . . ."

"I can imagine what Sarah said," he said. His voice hardened. "Don't you realize what she's doing?"

"Trying to bind me to the land?"

A muscle reacted in his cheek. "Yes," he finally said.

"And you don't approve?"

"I don't want to see you manipulated."

Her heart fell. And ached. It was obvious he didn't think much of her intelligence or abilities. "And you think I can be manipulated so easily."

His dark eyes bore into her. "No," he said. "But you may not have been exposed to a family like the Clementses before."

Her back stiffened. "It's not really your business," she said, forcing a coolness into her voice.

He didn't answer. Instead, he turned back to his original attack. "I thought you would have realized on your own that it's dangerous to ride alone."

"Because I might get lost or because someone might shoot me?"

"Both."

"I know the landmarks now. I remember everything you told me about a cutting horse, and I don't think there will be another hunter prowling around after injuring a congressman."

"And me?" he asked in a neutral voice. "Do you think I'm safe?" It was a challenge.

It was a question she couldn't answer. He *wasn't* safe. Not at all. But not in the way he meant. *He* didn't frighten her. Her feelings did.

A muscle jerked in his cheek. He took her silence as a negative.

She lifted her chin. "I'm not afraid of you, if that's what you mean."

"Aren't you? You couldn't run fast enough the other night."

She wished he hadn't thrown that up to her. "I didn't run," she protested. "I had to get home."

"You don't lie very well, Jessica."

She could hardly refute that. She knew she was a bad liar. Instead, she reached for the reins. "I think you said we should get back."

He stared at her intently, then put a finger to her cheek. "I'm just trying to make you aware of the dangers of trusting people you don't know."

She turned away from him. That touch was far too explosive. "Did they ever find out who shot Marc?"

"I think I'm still their prime suspect."

"That's ridiculous."

"Why?"

"I don't think you would miss."

Astonishment crossed his face. Then he chuckled." I suppose that's a compliment."

"Kind of. I suppose."

"Does anything frighten you?"

You do. "People breaking into my house." She hadn't meant to mention that. It just popped out.

His eyes studied her. "Has anyone done that?"

"Yes."

"Recently?" His expression was dark, unfathomable.

"Yes," she said. "Do you know why anyone would do that?" Why hadn't Sarah mentioned it to him?

"It couldn't have been a random burglary?"

"It could have, until it happened to my bookstore as well."

He turned away from her and looked down at the ranch house, then back at her. "Now I *insist* you don't go riding alone again."

She bristled at his tone. "Do you know what's going on?"

"No," he said.

"But you know more than you've told me," she accused, taking a stab in the dark. He stiffened, and she knew she was right.

He hadn't moved a muscle, nor had anything changed in his eyes. But she just knew.

"Damn you," she said. She was tired of pulling out one small fact after another. It was like a giant jigsaw puzzle with half the pieces missing.

"That night . . . you tried to frighten me away." Her frustration turned to anger as she realized he was part of the conspiracy of silence. "Did you know you picked the best possible way?"

His gaze was steady. "What do you mean?"

"The Clementses seem to know everything about me,

even as they keep everything about themselves from me. Did they find out I was raped when I was seventeen?"

He stilled. Everything seemed to still around her. Even the rustle of a breeze through the scrub. It was the first time she'd ever mentioned that night to anyone.

Pain flitted over his face, and his eyes closed for a moment. His head fell back so his face looked up toward the sun. After a long silence, he opened his eyes. "I'm sorry," he said. "I never imagined . . ."

"I knew almost immediately after I left your house that you couldn't have done anything like that."

"Why?"

"You wouldn't have used it as a weapon to frighten me away. And I just . . . *knew.*"

He walked over to a rock and put his foot on it. His posture looked relaxed, but the cords in his neck were strained, his jaw clenched. "I didn't rape her," he said. The words seemed torn from his mouth. "But I spent a month in the county jail for it. Her . . . father caught us in her bedroom. I was an Indian to him, a 'breed.' A breed who had already been in trouble for stealing a car. Tara was terrified of him. He was supposed to be in town, and she'd said we would have time to . . ." Ross shrugged. "He came back unexpectedly. When Tara heard him come inside, she screamed." He hesitated, then gave her a crooked smile. "I was strong for a kid, but he pulverized me, then called the cops."

Some of her anger faded, replaced with horror for him. Her gaze had not left his face. "What happened?"

"Sarah came riding to the rescue again. She hired a detective who discovered that Tara had been sleeping with nearly every boy in school, then she offered a hefty sum for Tara to leave Sedona. She recanted, then disappeared. The charges were dropped. But some folks have long memories."

"And the rest of the family? Did they believe you?"

"Halden did. Marc . . . well, Marc was afraid it would hurt his fledgling career. He was running for the Arizona house then." He hesitated, then added, "God, I was scared. And angry. But I never would have . . . used that if I had known that you . . ."

There was so much guilt, even agony in his voice, that she went over to him and touched his face. "You had no way of knowing." She paused, then asked, "But why?"

He shrugged. "Someone would have told you. And after April's escapade and the shooting, I thought it would be best if you left until they knew for sure whether you were Harding's daughter. Just think about it, Jess. You went riding and were abandoned. There was a rifle shot when you were out riding. Now you tell me you had two recent burglaries."

"Whoever did the shooting wasn't after me."

"No," he agreed. "But nothing like that has happened before. No stray hunters. No stray bullets."

A frisson of fear darted up her back. She'd had too many of the same thoughts herself. "You're saying I've stirred something up."

He looked grim. "Something like that."

"But wasn't there friction about the ranch before I came?"

"Yes."

"Then why . . . would anyone burglarize me? I don't have anything. Not worth stealing."

"Someone must think you do."

Her throat tightened.

"Jess?"

She tried to keep the panic down even as she noted his shortening of her name. No one had ever called her Jess before. She dwelled on that. She didn't want to think about the other thing, that there could be some malevolent person out there.

His eyes narrowed. "Have you thought of anything?"

She hesitated. She hadn't told anyone about the book except Sol. She wanted to tell Ross about it. She wanted it with all her being.

But the caution inside was too deep, the habits she'd learned as a girl too strong. *Protect yourself.* She'd already handed him part of her soul when she'd told him about the rape. She was hesitant to give him any more.

"No," she said.

His eyes told her that he knew she was lying. That she didn't trust him. He went over to the side of Carefree, obviously waiting for her to mount.

She felt a sudden loss. She wanted to grab his hand, hold on to it.

Stop him.

But she couldn't.

She mounted. Wordlessly, he handed her the reins, careful not to let their fingers touch. Then he mounted, and they guided the horses down the steep path as the horizon turned bloodred.

eighteen

Jessie's body ached from the wanting. So did her heart. She felt as if she'd tried to hand it to him, and once again he'd rejected it. Or had he felt she rejected *him?*

It all came back to the ranch, to the shares, to money, to power.

She hadn't looked at him nor tried to talk on the way back. She was surprised then when she discovered several cars parked at the ranch house. They must have arrived while they were riding down.

The government plate on one showed it belonged to Marc. She also recognized his daughter's sports car. Three others were parked nearby.

Jessie glanced over at Ross. "I thought Marc had gone to Washington."

"He apparently decided to come back," he said shortly.

"And the others?"

"Ask Sarah."

A ball of confusion knotted in her stomach. Sarah had said no one would be here this week. It was why she'd decided to stay at the house. It would give her some time to spend with her aunt.

Was she being manipulated again, as Ross had charged? Was she being ambushed? Or was Ross himself manipulating her?

She rode the horse to the barn. Dan'l was there waiting for them, but Ross quickly dismounted, then stepped over to her while she slid down. His hand went to her elbow in a steadying gesture. Unnecessary but welcome. His body warmth flowed through and burned right down to her core.

He held on a moment longer than necessary.

"Thank you for coming after me," she said, "but it really wasn't necessary."

"I meant what I said, Jessica. I don't want you riding alone."

"Is that an order?" Her back stiffened again.

"A suggestion," he said.

Dan'l took the reins of the two horses. He looked from Ross to her, and back again, before coughing. "Comp'ny," he said laconically, glancing quickly at Ross as if they shared the same disdain.

"I noticed," Ross said.

"Did you know anyone was coming?" she asked, trying to shake that attraction that always hovered between them.

"No, but I'm not usually consulted."

"Sarah?"

"She would have known. I don't know if she planned it. I imagine it's a 'welcome to the family' party."

"Will you come?"

His gaze bored into her. "I doubt whether Marc will welcome my presence."

"If it's my party, I can invite who I want."

He hesitated, then nodded. "All right," he said, then followed Dan'l into the barn.

Jessie watched him go, the confident walk, the innate pride. She bit her lip as she remembered the tight look on his face when he told her about the girl and her father's reaction. She wondered whether that was a reason he always held himself apart from the family, refusing in advance any rejection that might come his way.

When he disappeared into the barn, she looked at the

porch, the door, the house. She wasn't sure she wanted to go inside now. She was beginning to feel it was a lion's den.

Ross swore silently to himself as he rubbed down the horse. He'd wanted her more than he ever wanted a woman, but neither the location nor the situation had made lovemaking palatable for longer than a few moments.

Her halting confidence about the rape made such a move that much more reprehensible. That the rape still haunted her was obvious. He cursed himself for being so determined to chase her out of his life, that he'd used such a weapon. He wondered if anyone else knew what had happened to her.

It accounted for a lot, however. It explained her reaction to his kisses, as if she were astounded that she enjoyed them. That had surprised him. Even pleased him. As so many things about her pleased him.

He liked the way she asked questions, listened, weighed. She hadn't accepted everything he'd said. He knew that.

The strange thing was that she seemed to trust him, even when he'd given her every reason to do the opposite. He'd been . . . humbled by that. Which was why he agreed to supper. She needed a friend and if nothing else he could do that for her. He owed it to her after his stupid confession.

Sarah, he knew, would be amazed, but happy. Marc, well, he would probably glower. April would probably flirt with him to show her father her independence. Halden would be oblivious to everything, and Cullen anxious.

Ross finished with the horse, then headed for his house. He needed a shower. And a good stiff drink.

•   •   •

Wonderful aromas filled the house when Jessie entered. Marc was in the main living area, sprawled over a chair, reading something in a spiral notebook and sipping a whiskey. He must have arrived in the past hour, but he looked as relaxed and at home as ever. He rose when he saw her, a smile creasing his face and filling it with that charismatic warmth she remembered. "Hello, cousin. I hear it's official now."

"So they tell me," she said.

"My daughter will be here soon," he said. "Cullen is with our father. And Elizabeth is coming. You haven't met her yet. She was out of the country during the reunion. We all wanted to welcome you to the family."

"Elizabeth?" she said. Jessie knew the name. She'd gone over the family tree with Sarah, but she'd concentrated on those at the family reunion. "She's the granddaughter of Hugh, the twin that died in the war."

He nodded. "Hugh's son, David, married a girl in Chicago, and went into insurance. He had two children—Elizabeth, who's a librarian, and Andy, an attorney. Elizabeth had already planned a trip with a friend when we learned about you, so she didn't make the reunion."

A librarian. That hadn't been mentioned before, or she would have taken notice. Someone else with a love of books. She suddenly looked forward to meeting another member of the family.

"Sarah didn't mention a party tonight."

Marc beamed. "It was my idea when Alex called a few days ago. I didn't have anything essential for the next two days, and I did want to welcome you. I knew some of the others did, too. I swore Sarah to secrecy. We wanted to surprise you."

In advance of Alex's meeting. The thought came immediately to mind, and she scolded herself. She was becoming paranoid.

"You flew here from Washington?"

"It's a regular commute for me, Jessica and it's not often I gain a new cousin."

She met his gaze. It was warm and sincere. But she didn't want to be disarmed. "How is your arm?" she asked.

"Almost healed."

"I heard the police decided it was an errant hunter." She heard the challenge in her own voice.

"That's the common consensus," he replied cheerfully.

"And Ross?"

Marc shrugged. "A coincidence. I shouldn't have said anything. It's just . . . well, we haven't seen eye to eye about a lot of things recently."

"He's coming to supper tonight."

Surprise flickered across his face before he schooled it. "Good," he said jovially.

"We were out riding just now," she said, testing him further. "He was telling me a little more about the history of the ranch. And the family. There seem to be some mysteries."

He shrugged. "I imagine every family has them."

"Some more than most, I suppose," she said. "I had better go and see how Sarah is. I don't think she was feeling well earlier."

"She seemed fine when I saw her."

She remembered what Alex had told her. *Sarah's ill . . . I don't think anyone knows but me. I didn't know myself until the DNA test proved you were a blood relative.* Did her aunt feel a new urgency now? Was that why she told Alex?

"I'm going to find Sarah," she said.

"Don't be hard on her. We just descended on her."

"I won't," she said.

She turned and went down to Sarah's room, rapping lightly on the door.

There was no response for a moment. She rapped again.

"Come in."

Jessie opened the door. Sarah was seated on a sofa and had turned toward her. Her face was pale, but it broke into a smile. "Jessie, come sit next to me."

Jessie did so. "I didn't know Marc was coming."

"Alex told him you were coming," she said. "He called me this morning from the airport and said Elizabeth was coming too. I should have told you but he asked me not to, and I didn't know what to do." She brightened. "You'll like Elizabeth."

"How does she feel about selling the ranch?"

Sarah looked away. "If it were only her, I think she would probably vote to keep the ranch, but her brother wants to sell, and they're very close. He's an attorney in Chicago and has never much cared for the ranch. Elizabeth, though, has been visiting here since she was a youngster."

Jessie absorbed that particular piece of information.

"How are you feeling?" she asked.

"Better. I'll be ready to go riding tomorrow."

Jessie wasn't so sure, but she merely nodded. "I'd best take a shower. I smell like horse."

"Everyone is leaving tomorrow. We'll have time to talk about your father then."

"I would very much like that," Jessie said. "Oh, and Ross said he was coming tonight."

Sarah's eyes opened wide. "Ross?" A smile came to her lips and speculation to her eyes.

"I think it's probably to irritate Marc."

"I doubt he cares that much about Marc to bother," Sarah said. "But for whatever reason, I'm glad."

Jessie reached over and touched her hand. Sarah patted it. "I'm so glad we found you. I think Harding would be pleased."

Jessie hoped so. She excused herself once more and headed out the door, down the hall. Before she reached the opening into the large area, she heard her name mentioned, and stopped.

"She doesn't know anything." Alex's voice.

"Have you asked her?" Marc's voice.

"Yes. I've asked whether her father left her anything. She said no."

"There *has* to be something. Something she's not aware of. Heath said he left that note in a book."

"It probably burned with the cabin."

"Dammit, I'm not ready to give up."

There was a pause. "Maybe we should look at Heath's note again." Alex's voice. "Is it still in the files in the attic?"

There was a silence, and she could only guess that one of them had nodded.

She continued, her shoes making clicks on the hardwood floor. Alex turned, saw her and came forward. "Jessica, I'm glad to see you again."

She regarded him carefully. A few moments ago, she would have greeted him with pleasure. Now she wasn't so sure. What note? What was she supposed to have? The book? Could he mean the old primer?

But she had no time to pursue that line of thinking because a tall, attractive, dark-haired woman came in the door. Jessie surmised that it was Elizabeth.

The newcomer immediately came over to them. She grinned. "You must be the famous Jessica. Have you felt overpowered yet?"

"How did you know?"

"This family can do it to you. But they really aren't so bad." She gave Marc a big hug. "Are you, Marc?"

The affection between the two cousins was obvious. It stirred the longing in her to have similar relationships. That was what she'd dreamed about. Not suspicion, nor manipulation, nor accusations. Could she have been wrong? Was she really just plain paranoid?

In a matter of minutes, the room was full: Halden limped painfully from the hall on the other side of the room. Cullen appeared with his wife, Sondra. His twins were there with their wives. Samantha arrived several moments later with April.

Marc served as bartender. Every time the door opened, she turned her head to see whether it was Ross strolling through the room as if he owned it.

She accepted a glass of champagne as Sarah entered. No trace of fatigue was obvious in her face. She walked with a spring to her step and took a glass of champagne.

"Now that we're all here," Marc said, "I would like to offer a toast."

Ross walked in then. All the eyes turned toward him, surprise in most of them. Jessie saw deep pleasure in Sarah's eyes, then she turned back to Ross.

He looked magnificent. He was wearing charcoal slacks, a light-blue dress shirt unbuttoned at the collar, and a gray sports jacket. He looked casual yet unexpectedly elegant. His hair was still damp and curled slightly.

Elizabeth went over and hugged him. "I'm so glad to see you. Take me riding tomorrow?"

Ross turned to Jessie. "Ah, a woman with rare intelligence. She knows not to go riding alone."

She wanted to kick him. But she could tell he liked Elizabeth and she felt a lurch in her heart. Elizabeth was about his age, and totally at ease with him.

"I always used to read books in the barn, and he could never understand it, until I picked out a few I thought he might like. I created a monster."

Ross didn't say anything, but she wondered at the one person who apparently had the affection of both Ross and Marc.

Supper was surprisingly cordial, although she noticed

that Marc and Ross said little to one another. Sarah beamed at Ross, Elizabeth looked at him fondly, and Jessie wondered how she looked at him. Not as hungrily, she hoped, as she felt or as openly as April seemed to ogle him. But though he was polite to Marc's daughter, he made little attempt to engage her in conversation. Mostly, he talked to Elizabeth.

Jessie tried to relax, but she kept hearing those words earlier. *She doesn't know anything. There has to be something.* And a letter in the attic. It all sounded like some gothic novel. But she decided then and there she was going to see that letter.

The meal was very good—Chateaubriand and more champagne. Lots and lots of champagne. Ross, she noticed, was the only one who was scarcely drinking.

It was ten before dessert was finished, and the crowd started to disperse. Ross was the first to leave, saying he had work to do. Elizabeth was staying at the resort, and she decided to leave with Alex and April. Tweedledee and Tweedledum left with their wives, followed by Cullen and his wife.

Sarah retired with apologies.

Jessie had mellowed with the champagne. The normalcy of the dinner, the efforts of everyone to be pleasant, disarmed her. But she needed air. And time to think. She excused herself, went up and fetched Ben, then walked him around the paddock.

The quarter moon looked fragile, almost transparent. The night was warm and a small, tender breeze made it sensuous. Or perhaps anything would seem sensuous after this afternoon. She couldn't stop remembering the feel of Ross's lips on hers, and the lightning that streaked through her at his very touch.

Her gaze wandered over to his house beyond the barn, the small but well-tended manager's house. Ben kept close by, happily sniffing the intriguing smells of other animals. He barked at the soft whinny of a horse.

The door of the house opened, and she saw Ross standing in the doorway, Timber next to him. He was still wearing the dress shirt but the tails were loose, the sleeves rolled up and the neck unbuttoned. The dog's ears were cocked, his body alert.

She would dearly love to have a photo of them together like that.

Jessie tried to resist and turn away, but then Ben with a loud happy bark tore off toward them, his tail wagging frantically. Her shy dog. Her cautious dog. *Her Judas goat.* She followed.

Ross appeared bigger than life in the moonlight. His deeply tanned skin stretched over high cheekbones with an austerity lightened only slightly by thick dark eyelashes. Those lashes were half lowered, giving him a lazy look. But there was nothing lazy in his stance, in the energy that radiated from him.

Her gaze studied his face, the slight dent in his chin that gave him just the faintest hint of vulnerability, the lips that were sensual, too sensual. They were curved into a question now. She wondered what they would look like in an honest-to-God smile. She'd never quite seen one.

Timber sedately flicked his tail in a semblance of welcome as Ben wriggled ecstatically. He seldom saw other dogs and now he was making an abject idiot out of himself. She was afraid she would do the same.

She hesitated at the bottom of the two steps that led up to the porch. "Thank you for coming tonight."

He watched her for a moment, then stood aside, inviting her inside. The dogs followed. "I ended up enjoying it. I like Elizabeth."

"I noticed." She wished he'd said he liked *her.* But then his eyes were saying it. They were roaming all over her, apparently approving. "I liked her, too," she added hurriedly, afraid he'd detect a hint of jealousy.

He didn't smile, but he took a step closer.

All her senses began to react again. Traitorous body. Her heart pounded harder. Her nerve ends tingled. Desire eddied deep inside. She feared that she was standing there like a fool, staring up at him.

But he had a gleam in his eyes, too. *Not now*. He'd said those words earlier, and they echoed in her mind. Had he meant never? Or just that moment this afternoon? She sought frantically for something more to say. She did know she didn't want to leave. "Do you see her often?"

Ross shrugged. "Not recently. She used to come here on vacations as a girl. She read every single minute she wasn't on a horse."

Words. Questions. They always seemed to resort to that, Ross and she. They'd been protection against deeper feelings, against the heated recognition that always played between them.

"She never married?" She continued to play the game.

"She was engaged. Two days before the wedding, her fiancé died in an automobile accident. I don't think she ever got over it. She rarely comes here anymore," he said.

Feeling like a three-year-old under his gaze, she reminded herself of her suspicions that he was hiding something she needed to know. She tried to summon up the anger she'd felt earlier but it melted under his gaze.

But now she had another little tidbit of information, thanks to eavesdropping, and she couldn't stop herself from probing again. "Have you ever heard of a book connected to my father?"

His eyes narrowed. "I don't know what you mean."

She hesitated. He was not relaxed any longer. She saw the tension in him, tasted it. Felt it. Why? "I heard Marc and Alex talking."

He hesitated, obviously trying to decide what to say.

Finally he shrugged, and she knew she was going to get part of a story. If not all of it.

Ross looked resigned. "The family legend has it that Heath supposedly left a clue as to where the bonds were located, that he meant them to belong to the family once the company succeeded. The money was only a loan, a way to get him inside the oil venture." He paused. "I think he was just trying to justify a theft."

Her legs swayed under her. Her heart seemed to stop for a moment, then beat frantically. Breath caught in her throat until she felt she was suffocating.

"That's why they came looking for me," she said after a moment. "I thought . . . it was the ranch." But she had hoped a little bit had been for her. For her father.

"Not Sarah," he said gently. "Nor, I think, for most of the others."

"Most?" she asked. "Whom do you not include in 'most'?" Her mind was spinning ahead. The feeling of betrayal deepened. "You knew this when I told you about the burglaries. You didn't say anything."

"It's legend, rumor, God knows what," he replied slowly. "I've never seen the letter. I don't even know if it really exists."

She turned away from him and fought back tears. She had never felt so alone. It was as if a starving man had been handed food, then had it snatched away as he was putting it in his mouth. She hadn't realized until Alex contacted her how strong, how deep, her longing was.

How much she'd hoped she'd found a family.

And now the dream had exploded. It was all lies. No one had been completely honest, not even Ross. Her throat constricted until she couldn't breathe.

She'd realized, of course, that her vote on the matter of the ranch was important to everyone. But this . . . lost treasure or whatever it was far outreached that. Her home had been burglarized, her office ransacked, even her hotel room searched. Too much to be coincidental. She felt a sense of danger, even of evil, wrap around her, and she shivered. Could she ever believe any one of them again?

The scars on her heart were tearing open. How many birthdays had she waited for her father to come home? How many times had he returned after she was asleep on the sofa? There was only that one good day, her sixteenth birthday, when he'd given her a locket and the book.

And now she'd been waiting again. Expecting. Hoping. She felt like that child on the sofa. Eyeing the door, knowing that after a certain hour her father would return drunk, that he would stagger to the bedroom without seeing her.

She felt a hand on her shoulder. "Jess?"

She turned and saw his blurred figure through tears that hovered in her eyes. "Don't," she said.

Concern etched lines in his face, but she dared not believe them. She tried to turn to go, but he didn't let go. His hand was like steel around her wrist. The other touched her face and wiped away a wayward tear.

"Jessica, don't go now, not like this."

"Everyone has lied to me about everything. Except you. You only *omitted* a few crucial details."

"It wasn't my place," he said, but his voice was low, even uncertain.

"And you make sure it isn't your place, don't you," she said bitterly. "You make an art of being uninvolved. Why do you stay if that's the way you feel?"

A muscle quivered in his cheek, and his eyes hardened. He let her go.

"Damn you," she said suddenly. "Don't you care about anything?"

His hand jerked out and pulled her into his arms. He bent his head and his lips sought hers, his mouth violent with need.

She felt the depth of that need, and her own, as desire

swirled deep inside her and the very air was sucked from the room.

The need, the loneliness, the fear went with it. And they were the only two people in the universe.

nineteen

Ross hadn't meant it to happen.

Or maybe he had.

He only knew he couldn't let her go with so much pain in her eyes. He'd experienced the agony of betrayal himself. He knew she felt that, and worse, now . . .

And so he'd wiped the beginning of a tear from her face. And then he'd sought to silence the bitter words with a caress that turned into something else altogether.

He just hadn't realized how dangerous that was going to be. The electricity flared again, raw and bold and irresistible. It flashed between them like an exposed, snaking wire ready to strike and burst into flames. He knew he should move away from it, but he couldn't. *Not now.* He'd said those words because there had been no place up in the Saddle to make love. But it had also been self-protection. He'd meant *never.*

But never was here, and he didn't have an excuse. He didn't want an excuse. He wanted her.

And she wanted him. That was an aphrodisiac he couldn't resist.

He tightened his arms around her. He wanted to comfort. But he knew comfort would lead somewhere else. The desire between them was too explosive, the emotion too thick to disperse. They'd already stepped off the parapet into the abyss.

She shivered in his arms, and he was filled with a tenderness he didn't want, had tried to avoid. Tenderness led to commitment. Tenderness was weakening.

But now tides of it washed over him, through him. Reining in his own desires, he softened his kiss, seducing rather than taking.

Her lips parted then. Offering. Inviting.

He deepened his kiss, his tongue inching its way inside her mouth, searching, exploring, arousing. Need and yearning danced in a sensuous courtship.

His hands played with the back of her neck, and silken curls wrapped around his fingers. He wondered at their softness. There was nothing artificial about any of her. She was real and enchanting and challenging.

And hurting. *Remember that.* Remember that he knew things he could never share with her, and she might never forgive him if she ever learned of them. So why was his mouth pursuing the forbidden taste of her?

Yet he couldn't stop. He was lost in a sorcery he'd never known existed. Just as he'd never given tenderness, he had never received it either. Lovemaking had usually been a hot, frantic release between two consenting adults. Nothing more. But now he realized the magic of it, the sweetness that caring brought to a kiss, to a caress. He wanted to prolong every moment, relish every touch.

She snuggled against his body, and her arms clung around his neck. Her fingertips massaged the back of his neck in slow exquisite movements that ignited tiny explosions throughout his body. Heat radiated through their clothes, and they merged into one as much as their clothes allowed. Piercing streaks of raw need thundered through him.

He rained kisses on her face, tasting the saltiness of her tears. That touched him as nothing ever had before. She was such a intriguing combination of vulnerability and courage, of tenderness and toughness.

His hands moved to her back, massaged it in slow, sensuous movements. Then as her body burrowed even deeper into his, his hands pressed her hips up and tighter against him. The heat intensified between them. Match and kindling.

She trembled, and he remembered the rape. He took a step back. Jessie groaned in protest and looked up at him, her eyes glazed with desire.

"Jess?" he asked achingly, so soft he wondered whether she even heard.

She did. The word went straight to her heart. "Yes," she said, the word trembling on her lips. She had not been intimate with a man since the rape. She just hadn't been able to do it. She'd thought she could, but when the moment came she'd always turned to ice.

But now she felt herself responding. Not only responding, but becoming an eager partner. There was no ice now, no hesitation, not even fear. Perhaps because he *knew,* and then he'd *asked.* Perhaps because his touch was so tender, and his fingers light and gentle. Perhaps because she'd never had this hunger inside before. The compelling cry of her body. She'd hadn't realized how strong desire could be, how irresistible.

"Yes," she said again, hearing the hoarseness in her own voice.

He stared at her for a moment, his dark eyes boring into her as if they reached into her soul, still trying to decide whether she really meant it. Then he smiled, a crooked, wry sort of smile.

There was nothing at this moment but his head bending down to meet hers, his lips playing with hers with a sweet delicacy spiced by just a hint of restrained passion. But even as he obviously reined back the need in him, she felt it radiate in the shiver that ran the length of his body. The kiss intensified as their lips melded again in eager contest.

She found herself responding in ways she never thought

she would, her body swaying against his, her lips playing against his. She felt his swelling manhood against her and wasn't repelled. She sought it. She sought *him.*

His hands moved again, touching, sparking blazes wherever they went. She was consumed with wanting and feeling, the anticipation of something grand and glorious. His lips left her mouth and nibbled her ear, his breath sending shivers of pleasure through her. He kissed the pulse at her throat, and she thrust her head up, feeling the tenderness in each caress.

Tremors ran through her body as his hands continued to stoke it, his fingers trailing heat wherever they moved. An odd pressure grew inside her.

His hands left her, and she felt bereft. But then they were unbuttoning her blouse, not hurriedly, not violently, but with a care and restraint that made *her* want to rush it.

Her blouse slid easily off her shoulders, then her bra. His head bent and his mouth touched her breast, his tongue teasing and nibbling. Her breasts hardened, ached, became so sensitive that the merest touch of his tongue sent shivers of want reverberating through her.

He straightened, and her gaze lifted to his. His eyes smoldered now, like dark fire. No mask now. No enigma. Just need.

He took her hand and led her into another room. His bedroom. She hardly noticed. All her attention was on him, on the way her hand felt in his, of the internal echoes from his touch.

Ross guided her to the bed, and she sat down. He disappeared for a moment behind a door and quickly returned. He stood before her. She saw the tension in his body, the strain in his face. "Are you very, very sure, Jess?"

His tongue lingered over the shortened version of her name. She was glad no one had ever called her that before. She wanted it only on his lips. She nodded.

Still, he hesitated, and a thousand thoughts ran through

her mind. The accusation of rape against him, her own confession.

She reached out and unbuttoned, then unzipped, his jeans. It was shocking to her that she did so, that her fingers did such a bold thing. It was also exhilarating. For the first time, she felt free of the shadows that had kept her from intimacy, from trusting, from giving.

She trusted now, and it was as if some giant anvil had been lifted from her shoulders. She leaned her head against his hard stomach as her hands shoved down the trousers. She heard a small groan come from deep inside his chest, and then he lay naked next to her.

His hands caressed her, his lips touching hers again as if she were the most fragile piece of crystal. But now she didn't feel fragile. She didn't want to be crystal. She was all feelings, sensations, want.

She felt his hands at her slacks, undoing the clasps as she had undone his. Then she was naked, her body next to his, the friction of their skin setting new fires, and the pressure inside building to an inferno.

His mouth went to one of her breasts again, as his hand slid down to the triangle of hair, his fingers sparking new waves of sensation. She strained against him, her fears only a faint memory, her reservations trickling away like sand in a hourglass.

He guided her down, one hand still at the sensitive opening between her legs. His fingers teased, aroused until she was nearly mad with need for him. He moved slightly, positioning himself above her, his swollen manhood probing but not invading. He was waiting again, asking. In reply, her body instinctively reached for him, arching upward until she felt the marvelous warmth of him. Her arms went around him, urging him down, wondering at the strength and restraint of his body, the feel of him as he entered ever so slowly. She'd never known anything could feel this good, this . . . exquisitely painful friction that made every nerve come alive.

Her arms tightened as she needed more, had to have more, had to quench the aching, insatiable need spiraling in the core of her body.

Ross moved then, ever so slowly, igniting ripples of warm, expectant sensations. His slow, languorous movements stroked, then provoked, and she felt herself moving with him as his rhythm increased. Her body moved to his, danced with his in a primitive orgy. Streaks of exquisite pleasure rushed through her, and she felt her body quiver as the tempo increased and finally exploded in a burst of splendor.

He rested on his elbows, keeping them linked without having his weight on her. He rained kisses on her face, even as she felt the sumptuous aftershocks as tides of gratification continued to run through her.

She heard her own breath, felt his on her skin. "Oh my," she said, though it was more a wondrous sigh than words.

He chuckled. She felt it in the flat belly that was melded to hers. It sounded fine in her ears.

"I think it was more a *wow*," he said as his mouth reached down and nuzzled her neck.

"Definitely more," she agreed. Her fingers played with the dark, springy hair on his chest, then traveled lightly over his muscles, feeling the hardness of them. He rolled over, taking her with him until she was on top of him. She put an elbow on his chest, propped her head on her hand, and regarded him.

His eyes had a lazy, satisfied look, and his lips were curved in a slight smile. His hands ran up and down her body possessively. "You're so beautiful," he said.

"So are you," she whispered.

He chuckled again. "Men aren't beautiful."

"Yes, they are. You are." She couldn't keep her hands off him.

"Then I like it," he murmured. He was more relaxed than she had ever seen him.

She felt satisfied, fulfilled. Sensations still echoed inside her. For a moment, she felt nothing but bliss. Then gratitude that her fear of intimacy had dissolved, ecstasy at discovering she could respond to the right person.

She played with his hair. Thick and unruly and sexy. In fact, everything about him was sexy. And he made her feel sexy. She leaned down and started nibbling on his ear, amazed at herself, astounded at the ease she felt with him.

Her fears had faded in his tenderness. Since she'd become an adult, she'd told herself she didn't need protection; she could take care of herself. She still could. But she liked the warm protectiveness she felt in him. It felt good and right. A part of belonging.

He groaned as she continued her exploration. "You don't know what you're starting," he complained, in a voice that seemed tinged with hope rather than censure.

"Now I do," she said. She leaned down and touched his lips with hers. She was the aggressor now, and it delighted her. She was pushing away the last of her fears, the last shadow of a decade-old event that had haunted her ever since. She still didn't know why she had trusted him. But she had. And she'd been right.

He moved slightly, dislodging himself with obvious reluctance.

She watched him rise with the graceful ease she associated with him. She had an idea where he was going, and she appreciated it, even though she was reluctant to lose his warmth even for a moment. She stretched out. Her body felt different. It felt loved.

When he returned and sat down, a rush of fur joined him on the bed, jumping into his naked lap.

He yelped.

Surprised, Ben barked from his new perch on Ross's lap. Timber put a paw on the bed, obviously concerned that one dog was on the bed, and it wasn't him, but he was too mannered to make the leap. Still, he wasn't above sneaking another leg up onto the bed in hopeful exploration.

Ross disentangled himself and laughed. He leaned back and howled, and at that very moment Jessie knew she loved him.

"Foiled by a dog, and not even my own," he finally managed. Timber was still trying to find his way up on the bed without anyone noticing. Like an elephant dancing on a bar table.

"Timber," he said. The dog immediately put down both paws and stood at attention. Ben, however, was lolling all over the bed, trying to lick Jessie's face, then Ross's.

She giggled. She never giggled. She'd never lain naked in a man's bed. She'd never even kissed one back. Not really. Not with shameless abandon.

"My dignity's been destroyed," Ross protested, but amusement danced in his eyes. She'd been intrigued by him, fascinated, attracted, but now she discovered how much she liked him. "As well as the moment," he added.

She gave Ben a hug, then pushed him off. "Down," she said and, oddly enough, he obeyed. Then she turned back to Ross and held out her hand to him. Her fingers touched his cheek. "I don't think so," she said.

"What? My dignity or the moment?"

"Depends—which is more important?"

"I'll have to think about that."

She batted at him, still amazed at her lightheartedness, her absolute lack of self-consciousness at her lack of clothes. He turned and caught her in his arms, and the amused curl of his lips zoomed straight into her heart.

Ben whined. Timber joined him.

Ross shook his head.

"Perhaps you had better put them outside."

"Excellent suggestion."

In seconds, the dogs had been reluctantly ejected. He

was back on the bed, on sheets thoroughly mussed, and for a moment they stared at each other in a kind of wonderment. Then he bent his head, and she was whirled back into a world of sensation and wonder.

Ross watched her dress. He had watched other women dress, some obviously doing it slowly for his benefit. She was not. She was obviously uncertain. Hesitant.

He didn't want her to go. He wanted to go to sleep with her in his arms. He wanted to wake up next to her.

He'd never wanted that before. It stunned him.

He rose from the bed and helped her with buttons. Her own fingers were fumbling, her eyes not quite meeting his. The one thing he did know was that she wasn't used to doing this. He had felt, sensed, watched her bloom under his touch, realized that her first tentative responses were both shy and uncertain. He was sure he'd been the first since the rape.

The trust humbled him. It also filled him with guilt.

Still, he couldn't help but run his fingers across her cheek and meet her hazel eyes with their specks of gold. So solemn. So unsure.

She needed promises, and he had none to give her. Not until she knew who and what she was, not until she'd had time to understand the currents in the family. Even then, he wasn't sure he could offer her anything. Part of his heart had closed down years ago. He wasn't sure it could ever be whole again, and certainly not as long as he played around the edges of the Clementses.

Sarah had tied him to them as surely as if he'd been a bond servant two hundred years ago. She'd claimed what was left of a soul and placed upon it a burden and debt that could never be erased.

He leaned down and kissed Jessie. It was a tender gesture, but he knew it didn't answer the questions in her eyes.

"I had better get back," she said, and he knew she was disappointed when he didn't demur.

He walked her to the bedroom door. Two dogs were just outside, waiting. Ben jumped on her with pure joy at her appearance. His own dog regarded his master solemnly; it obviously didn't cross his mind to make such an undignified show of canine affection.

The little vignette said something about the two of them, of how different they were. He had perfected discipline and kept his emotions in tight little boxes. Hers were more open, spontaneous. She was obviously more willing to take chances.

He wasn't sure whether he was capable of that. It was not fair, not to any woman. Especially to someone like Jessie.

He walked her to the door, her Ben at her heels. He wanted to take her in his arms, but he resisted. He had done enough damage tonight.

Instead, he leaned over and kissed her cheek. He knew instantly it was the most wrong, most clumsy thing he could do.

She turned, the glint of tears in her eyes, and skipped down the steps, the bundle of fur on her heels.

Jessie knew she had no reason to expect more than he'd given. He'd made no promises, uttered no expressions of love. Or even affection.

Despite the sudden realization that making love hadn't meant to him what it did to her, she was not sorry. She'd learned tonight that making love could be tender and wondrous and even magical. She knew she *could* respond. For that, she would always be grateful. And she was also grateful he had not made promises he had no intentions of keeping.

She made her way back to the house. It was late, probably well after midnight. There was a light on in the living area. Jessie hoped no one would be there; she felt as if she wore a scarlet letter. Her clothes were mussed, as probably was her hair. She was sure new knowledge shone from her eyes.

Her body continued to feel the effects of his lovemaking. Heat rose in her when she thought of his arms around her.

Damn and hallelujah.

No one was inside the great room. She went to her room, refilled Ben's water dish, then looked to the clock. Two A.M. She wondered whether anyone noticed she'd been missing, but then dismissed the worry. She was an adult; it was her business. Still, she was new to this, and she knew her face flushed when she thought about it.

She also knew she couldn't sleep now; too many thoughts were like hammer blows on an anvil. She tried to get her mind off Ross and onto something else. *The book.*

Jessie knew where the stairs to the attic were—on the other side of the hall, near the room Marc and Samantha occupied when they were in residence. Perhaps she would go exploring.

Trespassing? No. She was legally a member of the family now. She would soon become part owner of the Sunset, whether or not she wanted it.

She gave Ben one last hug, then opened the door. She listened for a moment. Silence.

Jessie went back, put on a pair of tennis shoes that wouldn't make any noise, then closed Ben inside the room. She went to the stairs and listened again. Light filtered up from the room below. She hadn't turned it off, not knowing whether it had been kept lit for her or for someone else.

Still nothing. She walked down the hall, hearing the floor creak as she moved. Wishing she didn't feel so darn guilty, Jessie reached the narrow stairs that wound upward to a door. She took the steps and wondered whether the door was locked. Her heart bounced into her throat as she put her fingers on the knob and tried it.

It gave under her hand. Hinges squeaked as she opened it and looked inside. The attic was dark, lit only by the faint light that filtered in through the door. She looked for a light switch.

She couldn't find one. She looked at the half-opened door. If only she knew where a flashlight was. Perhaps she could buy one tomorrow and return tomorrow night.

Yet she was strangely reluctant to leave. She looked around. Boxes everywhere. They were piled up to the ceiling in some places. Old furniture. Her eyes slowly adjusted to the dim light. There was a window, one she'd seen from the outside. The part moon seemed to hang in the middle of it.

She moved carefully. The further she went, the mustier the air. She wondered what was in the boxes, who'd sat on the discarded furniture. The first Clementses? Her father? Had he rummaged around up here?

The floor creaked again. She estimated that she was right above Marc's room and, for a moment, she remained absolutely still. She felt like a thief in the night. Why hadn't she waited until daylight and told Sarah she wanted to explore the room?

Because Sarah seemed to have secrets of her own.

If she could find the letter Marc and Alex had discussed, perhaps she would know whether *her* book was involved. Perhaps she would learn what she should look for, if anything.

Her gaze wandered about the room and finally settled on several file cabinets lined up against the far wall.

She carefully made her way through the clutter, then pulled the handle of one of the drawers. It was locked.

For a moment, she wished mightily that she were a skilled safecracker. Since she wasn't, she turned her attention from the cabinets and toward a box at her feet. At the moment, she knew only what the Clementses wanted her to know. Were there more clues in these boxes? Perhaps something of her father?

The boxes were taped. To break them open would be an invasion. But then *her* life had been invaded in so many ways. She looked around for something sharp and found some clothes hangers. She used the hook to open the first box.

Paper. Letters. But she couldn't read them. The writing was too faint, and the light too poor. She went to another box. Clothes. An evening dress. Even now she could tell it had once been elegant. She closed both boxes, then went to a third.

The light dimmed even further then, and she turned toward the door. It had swung closed, and as she stood she thought she heard a noise behind her.

Pain cascaded in her head.

twenty

"Jessie? Jessie."

The repeated call pulled Jessie back to consciousness. Her head felt as if a dozen devils were hurling coals into a fiery furnace.

She slowly opened her eyes, then closed them again. Someone had turned on the lights.

She tried again, this time making out some of the figures above her. She closed them even quicker.

"Jessie." The first voice was Sarah's. The second was Marc's. They seemed identically worried.

She tried to move, and groaned instead. Even the slightest twitch made her head ache. "I'm taking her to the hospital," Marc said.

"I'll call Ross," Sarah said. "Neither you nor my brother can carry her."

"What were you doing up here?" Samantha asked.

Marc didn't wait for her to answer. "We heard a loud noise and I decided to investigate," he said. "Apparently a box fell on you," Marc interrupted. "You have to be careful up here."

Then who closed the door?

Someone in this room?

"I heard someone," she said, unwilling to let the questions go unasked.

"What do you mean?" Marc said.

"I couldn't find a light, and then the door closed. I heard someone," she repeated.

Samantha looked at Marc.

"It was only a few moments after I heard the crash that I reached the stairs. I . . . had to put some clothes on." Marc reddened a little. "I didn't see anyone."

"It could have been a breeze or anything," Samantha said. "And it does look as if a box fell on her."

Jessie tried to move again. She touched the back of her head and felt something wet and sticky. Blood. Then she looked around. Papers had scattered over the floor, apparently from a box that lay partially open. She tried to remember everything, but the last moments in the attic were a blur.

Marc offered his hand, and she took another look at him. He was wearing a pair of slacks, and a shirt half tucked in. It was the first time she hadn't seen him look immaculate. If he had been with Samantha, then who . . . ?

"I'm going to go get Ross," Sarah said.

Besides Marc and Samantha, there was only Sarah and ninety-one-year-old Halden in the house. And Ross, who was nearby. Ross who was the only one who knew about the conversation she'd overheard.

She suddenly felt very cold.

Sarah had started to go out the door.

"No," Jessie said sharply.

Sarah stopped, waited.

"I'm all right," Jessie said, moving again. At least her head had stopped spinning. The devils were still in there, though.

"You're going to the hospital anyway," Marc said. "I felt that bump. You might have a concussion."

Samantha sighed. "I'll drive. Marc's arm is still stiff."

"Ross . . ." Sarah started.

"No," Jessie said. "I'll go with Samantha." She didn't

want to go at all. But she knew that was foolish. A concussion could be serious, and she didn't want to stay in the house tonight. She needed to be away from it. Away from Ross. Away from all those feelings he invoked in her.

Away from the seed of suspicion.

And thoughts of tomorrow. Tomorrow she would hear the terms of her inheritance.

At the moment, it was the last thing she wanted to hear. She wanted to run again. But this time she wouldn't. This time, by God, she was going to stay. No one was going to frighten her away again.

"Ben . . ."

"Don't you worry about that dog," Sarah said. "I'll take care of him."

Jessie didn't want anyone taking care of Ben except her. He was already scared enough. Of everyone but Ross.

Don't think about him. But she felt her cheeks grow hot, and probably red.

"Can you stand?" Marc asked.

"I . . . think so."

He held out his hand and gently pulled her up. Her head pounded. She looked at the box and its spilled contents. Wouldn't she be hurt elsewhere if a box had fallen on her? Wouldn't she have bruises? Then a flash of intense pain blocked out any thought, and only Marc's steadying arm kept her upright.

"Let's go," Marc said worriedly.

She didn't protest any longer. She leaned on him, grateful for his strength. He was using the arm that hadn't been wounded, and that brought back memories of that day.

Ross had been around then, too.

Dear God, don't even think it.

She leaned on Marc as they went down first one set of stairs, then the other. She felt dizzy, unsteady. She wanted to stop at her room and reassure Ben, but she felt she would probably do the opposite.

Then they were in the car, and Samantha was screeching out of the driveway. The lights at Ross's house were dark. She closed her eyes and tried not to think.

Jessie woke with a raging headache and a drugged feeling. For a moment, she couldn't remember what had happened or where she was. Then it all flooded back, along with a heaviness of spirit.

She was in a hospital room. She remembered the stitches in her scalp. Thank God they didn't have to shave any of her hair. They'd explained that now they believed it best not to do that, that wounds were more prone to infection with bits and pieces of shaved hair.

The emergency room doctor had urged her to stay overnight. Since overnight was just a few hours, she'd consented. Sometime in the early morning, she'd fallen asleep.

But it had been a ragged, uncomfortable sleep, frequently interrupted by nurses who had come to check on her. She couldn't have any drugs because of the head wound, and her mind kept going over the events of last night. She *knew* there had been someone in that attic with her. The worst thing was realizing there were only five people on the ranch last night.

Either Marc and Samantha were both lying, or Halden had had a miraculous dose of the fountain of youth, or Sarah or Ross . . .

She could not bear the thought that either would have been involved.

A knock came at the door, and she tried to comb her hair with her fingers. She didn't want to see anyone until she had a chance to at least look presentable. She winced when she looked down at the shapeless hospital gown.

The rapping on the door came again. She sat up, and waves of pain assaulted her head. She yearned for a simple aspirin.

"Who is it?" she said.

The door opened slightly and she saw Alex's tawny hair.

"Give me five minutes," she said.

"I'll bring up coffee," he replied cheerfully.

She didn't like cheery at the moment. But he didn't wait for an answer.

Jessie put her legs over the side of the bed and stood. The pain faded to an ache. She took a few steps to the bathroom, opening a closet on the way to find her clothes and handbag. At least she'd have a comb and lipstick.

She took one look at herself, closed her eyes, and then, better prepared, looked again.

Her face was pale and her hair stuck out at peculiar angles. As she touched a particularly sore spot on the back of her head, she felt the recent stitches. She combed her hair as best she could, avoiding the tender area, then applied just a touch of lipstick. Then she quickly exchanged the hospital gown for her slacks and shirt.

Another knock, but this time the visitor didn't wait before entering. A doctor. One she hadn't seen last night.

He smiled when he saw her. "Ready to go?"

"As soon as you can release me."

He looked over a chart, then checked the wound in the back of her head. "We'll want to look at it again in six days."

"I don't think I'll be here then."

"Then get it done by your doctor. How does your head feel?"

"Like it's been stomped on."

"It's bound to ache near the wound, but if you feel any dizziness, loss of balance, or new pain, call your doctor or come back in."

She nodded. "Am I discharged then?"

He nodded. "I'll do the paperwork and send someone up for you. I'm going to write a prescription, but I'd rather you didn't use it for another few hours."

She nodded. She had no intention of using anything that would make her groggy. She had to keep her wits about her. "Thank you."

"And take it easy for the next few days. Get lots of rest."

"I will," she promised.

"You have someone to take you home?"

She nodded.

He almost bumped into Alex as he came into the room, a loaded tray in his hands. "How is she?"

"Ready to go. Just a few formalities." Then the doctor was gone.

Alex gave her a crooked smile. "Can't let you out of my sight for a moment." The smile faded. "Sarah asked me to pick you up. She knew we had an appointment this morning. Everyone wanted to come see you, but I told them I would have you back at the ranch before late afternoon. Can you tell me what happened?"

"What did Sarah tell you?"

"That a box fell on you."

"A box did fall," she said. "I'm not sure that's what hit me."

"What do you mean?"

She decided to tell him the truth. She was tired of all the evasions, the lies, the half-truths. She was not going to be a part of it.

"I heard you and Marc talk about a letter in the attic. I couldn't sleep last night, so I decided to look for the letter."

"Sarah would have taken you there," Alex said.

Jessie wasn't so sure. "I didn't want to wait. I . . . just get bits and pieces about my father. No one seems willing to tell me what happened fifty years ago, or at least everything that happened." She hesitated, then asked, "Did my father kill Lori and Heath?"

There. It was out. The damning words.

"I don't know, Jessie. And I don't think anyone really knows."

"And the bonds?"

"Ah, someone told you about them."

"I should have thought *you* would," she said. "I recall you asking whether my father had left me anything."

"I was going to tell you everything this morning," he said, "or at least what I know. I had no right to discuss past events if you weren't Harding's daughter."

"Not even when you knew there had been burglaries at my home and business?"

"Not even then. I couldn't know for sure they were connected with your father's estate."

She raised an eyebrow. "For sure?" she asked. "Does that mean you suspected?"

"No," he said. "I've known the Clementses all my life. I wouldn't suspect any of them of burglary."

"Not even Ross?" The question barely squeaked out.

"No," he said. "Probably especially not Ross."

"Why?"

"He would do nothing to hurt Sarah. He doesn't show it, but he loves that woman. And Sarah cares very much about you."

"Because I'm the key to holding on to the Sunset." Again it was a statement. She'd been badly disillusioned in the past few weeks, and she felt the wounds deep inside her heart.

"No," he said sharply. "Sarah loved your father. She feels that she failed in protecting him. She didn't tell you everything because she wanted to protect you. She didn't want you feeling exactly as you feel now. I don't think she ever thought Harding murdered his brother. Or Lori. She *wants* to believe they were caught in the fire."

"But you don't?"

"I didn't know him. I wouldn't even try to guess."

"And the bonds?"

He hesitated.

"The letter. What did it say?"

"I've not seen it. I just know it exists."

"Do you know what it says?"

"Marc told me that it was from Heath, a rambling letter justifying his theft of family money."

"What else?"

"It said that he'd repay the family once the oil firm was successful, that he had bought bearer bonds and one day they would be worth a great deal of money. No one thought they ever would, though. Everyone believed it was just another one of his schemes."

"But that's not what happened?"

"No, it became American Exploratory Company. Those bearer bonds could be worth millions."

"Could?"

"*If* they exist at all," Alex said. "*If* they didn't burn in the fire. *If* they are what Heath said they were. And no one knows how many bonds were exchanged for the money."

"Everyone keeps asking me about a book. Why?"

"I'm told that Heath said in the letter that he'd buried the bonds in a location easily accessible to the family, that he marked the location in an old primer."

Primer. She stiffened, then tried to relax. She didn't want Alex to know it meant anything to her. Not yet. Not until she knew more. But now she wondered if everything was beginning to make some kind of sick sense. Did someone suspect she had the primer with the location of the bonds in it? It didn't. She'd leafed through it a hundred times.

"Why would he do that?" She tried to keep her voice even.

"Damned if I know. Except each of the children were given one of a set of old primers that dated back to the sixteen hundreds. They'd belonged to Mary Louise and I think it was her way of reminding them of their heritage. It was kind of a legacy, part of Mary Louise's plan to keep them all attached to the family.

"Since I didn't know Heath, I can't even speculate on why he used the book, except that in some odd way it might be a form of apology, or even recognition of what he was doing. But it doesn't matter. No one ever found it."

"And my father's book?"

"It was in his room. He left everything. Wherever he went that afternoon, whatever he saw, he never returned to the house. I suppose now it should be yours. And that," he said, "brings me to official business. We can wait and go over everything at my office, or at the ranch."

Her eyes went to his briefcase then. "I don't want to discuss anything at the ranch, not with Sarah and Marc there," she said, wary now of everyone's motive or intentions. "Can we do it here?"

He looked. "Of course."

He sat down in the only chair in the room. From her perch on the bed, she had to look down at him. It gave her just a small sense of power, and that was something she felt dearly in need of.

"I think you know some of it," he said. "The Sunset and its assets were left in trust to the five surviving children and subsequently their heirs. Each of the original five had one vote in case of a sale. If the one share was divided among several heirs, such as Elizabeth and her brother, they have to agree together how they want to vote that share. Only blood relatives can inherit. As you know, that excludes Ross. It wasn't aimed at him; he wasn't born when the will was made. But Mary Louise and Hall had wanted the ranch to remain with the bloodline."

"What happens if one of the children dies without blood heirs?"

"It depends. The share could be left to the family to be divided, or left to a specific member of the family who would then have full voting rights for that share. Or it can be left to a non–family member. In that event, though, the trust kicks in. The share would have to be offered to the family for its market value."

She absorbed that. "So if Ross inherited, he couldn't keep the share himself?"

"No."

"That's not fair—he's her adopted son."

"Fairness doesn't have anything to do with it," he said, pulling out some papers from the briefcase. "The family has accepted the DNA tests as proof of your relationship, and so when you sign these papers and I file everything, you become one-fifth owner of the Sunset."

"What if I don't want it?"

"Then you will create one hell of a mess," he said. "You realize that there's been an offer for the Sunset. If you agree to the sale, you will receive in excess of a million and a half dollars. Three members of the family—Halden; Katherine, who is Harry's only heir; and Hugh's family, Elizabeth and Andrew—have all indicated they would vote for the sale. Only Sarah has voted no."

"So I have a choice of going against all but one of the family, or seeing Sarah's heart break?"

The side of his mouth twitched slightly. "That about says it."

"So everyone wants something from me. My vote."

"To be fair, they also like you, and family really is important to all of them. Harding's a legend in the family. He had a magic touch with horses. Everyone liked your father."

"He looked so young in photos. And without a care," Jessie said. "I don't remember him like that, and it makes me unbearably sad."

Alex didn't reply.

"He never smiled, and he drank too often, and then he would get sullen," she said. "He was so . . . dissatisfied."

"Your mother?"

"She left us not long after I was born. But you must know that," she added a little resentfully.

"No," he replied. "We only knew she wasn't with him those last years. It must have been hard for him, raising a child alone." Alex's voice was kind.

"It was. I don't know how he managed when I was a baby, but later I remember any number of baby-sitters." She shrugged. "We moved frequently, then there would be a new one. It's strange but I can't remember any of them now. They were never with us long enough. I just remembered how . . ."

She stopped, and he didn't press. She was grateful. She didn't understand why she was babbling on. She seldom confided in others, but her emotions were like raw nerve ends. Too much had happened in the last twenty-four hours. And now someone was throwing sums around, sums like more than a million dollars. She added it up. Even after taxes, she would have enough, if properly invested, to never worry about money again.

She saw Sarah in her mind's eye, recalled her words when they rode together up to the Saddle. The Sunset was her aunt's life. But was that more important than what the money could do for the lives of the other members of the family?

"And the bonds?" she asked. "It's not just my vote everyone wants. They also want to know if I have the key to some . . . hidden treasure." She looked into his eyes. "Everyone wants something and it's not me."

"That's not true. You'll be welcome no matter what you do. Marc and Cullen and others would like you to sell, yes. They have asked me to explain the benefits. But Sarah refuses to sell, and they still love her."

"And how would she feel if I voted with them against her? She was born in that house."

"She could do anything she wished," he said. "She could buy almost anything she liked."

"Except the Sunset." She stared at him until he looked away. She knew what she was going to do. It was probably foolish, but she'd never expected an inheritance. She couldn't regret losing something she'd never had, never earned. But she wasn't ready to make that declaration yet.

"What do *you* think I should do?" she asked.

He grinned. "Not a fair question to ask me. My fees would be astronomical if the sale is closed."

"That's not the way to convince me."

He shrugged. "I didn't think so. I suspect you don't want to sell."

"Why?"

"Because material things don't seem to mean a great deal to you."

"If you grow up without a lot of things, then you don't miss them. I can't even imagine what I would do with that much money."

"Well, there *are* taxes, though the trust was designed to avoid some of them."

"I suppose I also feel that I don't have a right to do anything," she admitted. "The easiest thing seems to be to do nothing."

He passed her some papers. "You don't have to make a decision immediately. In fact, I would prefer you didn't."

"I'll take them and read them. Carefully," she said.

Alex looked at her with new respect. "We have another week before the offer will be withdrawn. Once you were found . . . Cullen requested, and received, an extension."

"What happens to Ross if the ranch is sold?"

"He'd get another job, I suppose. He shouldn't have a problem. He's a good manager. Even Marc admits that."

A knock came at the door. A hospital staffer entered, along with a man pushing an empty wheelchair. "I think the doctor told you to have the stitches removed in about ten days," the woman said. "Here's a prescription if you need something for pain."

"The bill?"

"Already been taken care of," the woman said.

"Who?"

"I don't know," the woman said. "I just know there's no balance."

Jessie looked at Alex. He shrugged. "I imagine Marc took care of it. It happened in the family home." Then he grinned, "And yours."

It didn't feel like *her* house when she walked inside. Except, of course, for Ben's ecstatic barking. She realized the dog had probably been waiting at the door, and she knelt beside him, giving him a huge hug as Ben squirmed in a frenzy of happiness. She lost herself in that welcome for a moment, not really wanting to face everyone else in the house.

But she had to.

She still felt a shiver of fear. It was probably foolish. No one had actually hurt her, or threatened her. The blow on her head *could* have been from a falling box. The bonds probably were only a half-forgotten legend with just enough truth to be a mystery.

Sarah was hovering nearby. She looked as if she hadn't had any sleep, either. "How are you feeling?" Sarah's words came in a rush. "I think you should sit down. Or should you be lying down? And you must be hungry. I'll have something fixed for you."

All Jessie really wanted was to disappear into her room and study the documents Alex had given her. She wanted to be alone to mull over what Alex had said. And hadn't said.

There had been no pressure, which surprised her. But then pressure would have made her stubborn. Could they know that?

They. Her family. She wanted nothing more at the moment than to be back in her shop in Atlanta, among the books that had been her friends and family. Undemanding friends and family. But, like Alice, she was in a world she didn't understand and where danger lurked in unknown and unexpected places.

But she'd already decided she wasn't going to run again, and she meant it.

She had glanced over at Ross's house, but she saw no movement. His truck wasn't there, either. She felt a stab of disappointment that he hadn't visited her, nor apparently been concerned enough to see how she was.

Sarah's face was drawn, her expression apprehensive. "Are you all right?" she asked. "I wanted to go to the hospital this morning, but Alex said he needed to talk to you."

"He explained everything about the trust," Jessie said.

"Good. If you have any more questions, just ask me."

Jessie had a bunch of them, but she didn't expect to get any answers. And now was not the time. The elderly Halden was sitting in a chair, watching.

"Jessie," he said, his face crumbling with concern.

She went over to him and sat on a footstool nearby. He held out a hand and took hers, patting it. "I heard what happened last night," he said. "I am so sorry you were hurt."

"At least I discovered I have a hard head," she said with a smile. He did seem genuinely concerned about her.

"It's a very pretty one," he said, a twinkle in his eyes.

She started feeling mellow again. Certainly neither he nor Sarah had asked for her vote. They *were* concerned. About *her.* Not her vote, not some bonds that probably didn't exist.

She found herself smiling, despite the continued pounding in her head. "You must be prejudiced." And it felt rather nice that someone was prejudiced toward her.

Jessie felt herself relaxing. Ben was crowded next to her. Her uncle kept his hand on hers. *Uncle. Aunt.* Both words still felt strange, and yet they remained a siren's song to her despite everything she now knew.

Alex had followed her inside and over to where she sat. "The doctor advised her to keep quiet and get some rest." He took a prescription bottle out of his pocket and handed it to her. He had stopped at a pharmacy on the drive home. "And now I have to get back to the office."

"Thank you," Jessie said. "For driving me home."

The qualification was obvious. He grinned, acknowledging it. "Let me know when you're ready to sign those papers," he said. "Or if you have any other questions."

A sudden silence descended on the room.

Then Ben barked. He'd heard something outside. *Ross.* Just the thought made her heart beat faster and a flush rise to her cheeks. Even as niggling strands of thoughts wouldn't go away.

She stood, her hand sliding from Halden's grasp, and picked up her handbag and the file of papers Alex had given her. Her fingers tightened around them. "I will," she said, trying not to notice that Sarah and Halden were obviously listening intently. She wanted to run for her room, for haven. In seconds, Ross might be coming up the steps outside. Into the room.

So why was she going into a panic?

Remember, you said you weren't going to run again. Not from choices. Not from the Clementses. Not from Ross. No more running. No more shadows.

Besides, she felt rooted to the floor as Ben's barks grew more excited.

Her gaze turned toward the door as it opened, and Ross stood there. Ben went running over to him, dancing around him with nearly as much enthusiasm as he had with her.

But Ross didn't lean down and pet Ben. Instead, his gaze went directly to her and in their depths she saw something she didn't want to see.

Guilt.

twenty-one

Ross saw Alex's sports vehicle in front of the house as he drove up. He'd left his house early to trailer one of his horses to an anxious buyer near Phoenix. He'd stopped in Sedona on the way back to deposit the check. Then, anxious to see Jess, he'd driven back, only to hear from Dan'l that she was at the hospital. The boy told him she had been hit by a box in the attic.

He'd driven to the hospital, but too late. She had already left. Why in the hell hadn't Sarah come for him last night? Why hadn't Jess asked for him? Because of the way he'd left things last night?

Sarah had said only that Jessie had asked her not to wake him. He'd been furious with her, and furious with Jess for making such a request. Neither did he understand why Timber had made no noise, but then he remembered that the dog had been restless at some time during the night. He also remembered hearing a car, but then Marc often came home late from some meeting or another.

Dammit, but the woman turned him into knots. He'd known he should stay away from Jessie, that he'd made a bad mistake last night when he'd allowed lust, or whatever in the hell it was, to take over his common sense and usual self-control. It was a mistake that could eventually be disastrous. He only wished that he had said something, or done something, when Jessie told him about overhearing something about that damned letter. He'd never suspected that she planned to go rummaging around in that attic.

The best-laid plans. And now as he looked into her face, he saw a mixture of emotions, ranging from a quick blush to suspicion.

"Jess," he said, "I was just at the hospital, but you'd already left."

The rose in her cheeks deepened. "Alex picked me up."

"I didn't know what happened until noon today. Sarah didn't tell me last night and I left early this morning to take a horse down to Phoenix. Dan'l said a box struck you?" He didn't have to ask what she was doing in the attic.

"Or something," she said with just a small edge to her voice.

He didn't miss the edge to her voice. And he didn't like the way she'd phrased her answer. But neither did he wish to ask questions with others in the room. Then he saw the papers in her hand. *Clutched* in her hand.

Ross knew what they were. The key to the Sunset, to Sarah's life, to his future. To Jessica's safety.

And the look in her eyes made him feel as if he had just been sucker-punched. "I had better get back to work. I just wanted to know if you were all right."

She nodded, her hazel eyes appearing a little moist. Damn, but he wanted to take her in his arms. Instead, he went over to Sarah. Her face softened, some of the tension fading. He reached out and touched her shoulder, then forced himself not to look at Jessie again. He turned and retraced his steps out the door and to the barn. He wished he had something to strike, words strong enough to dislodge the lump in his throat.

Instead he turned his thoughts to the horses. He needed to work with one of the young colts. The price he'd received—the *ranch* had received—for a green broke three-year-old had been just what he needed to show everyone they could make a good profit. He'd hated to let the colt go, but Ross knew he had to produce some revenue. Now he had others coming up, a reputation to sustain.

He went back to his house to let Timber out. Unlike Jessie's Ben, Timber greeted his master with dignity. Ross found himself missing the spontaneous joy of Jessie's Ben. But then she herself had a spontaneity. She also had fire under that quiet reserve, a glow that often transformed her face.

But there had been no glow today. Had the "accident" been no accident at all? And if not, who might have caused it? He remembered the suspicion in her eyes, the fact that she'd not asked for him last night. Surely she couldn't believe he might harm her.

The thought was like a knife wound to his soul. She certainly had no reason to trust him, not even after last night. He had kept things from her, and she sensed it. He felt as if he were walking a tightrope, and the slightest misstep would destroy Sarah. Unfortunately, Sarah didn't seem to be as aware of the dangers as he was.

He went into the barn, saddled a colt named Black Jack, and led him out. He would spend the rest of the day working him, then go to the cantina. He wished he could get drunk, but he didn't drive when he'd been drinking. One beer, yes. Two, maybe; three, no.

He tried not to look at the ranch house as he put the horse through the paces, talking, always talking. He took him out into the pasture where he kept several head of cattle just for this reason, to teach the horse the maneuvers necessary for a cutting horse. Much of it was instinct, and Black Jack was a natural with plenty of heart. That meant more than stamina or speed.

Heart. It was something he always felt lacking in himself. Perhaps because he'd walled himself off. He'd been afraid to trust, afraid to feel. He had damned little to offer anyone.

Don't think about it.

Work.

Don't think about a young woman who was probably afraid, hurt, and bewildered.

She has Alex.

Why did that notion hurt so much?

Jessie watched him from a window. She'd pleaded exhaustion and retired to her room, Ben in tow.

Her head still hurt. She thought about taking one of the pills Alex had bought, but then opted for a couple of aspirins instead. She didn't want her judgment clouded any more than it already was.

A knock on the door. She went and opened it. Sarah stood there with a tray loaded with hot chocolate and hot cinnamon bread.

Sarah smiled. "I always like hot chocolate and cinnamon bread when I don't feel well."

No one had ever brought Jessie hot chocolate, much less cinnamon bread. "Sit with me for a few moments," she said.

Sarah's smile widened as she put the tray down on a table. She suddenly looked younger, and yet there was a bluish tinge to her skin. Jessie knew that Alex had not been lying or exaggerating. Sarah *was* ill. Spontaneously, Jessie reached out her hand and touched her aunt's.

A family. Perhaps for the first time, it became real. Despite last night, a sense of belonging flowed into her. No one had asked her how she would vote when she'd returned from the hospital. They'd just embraced her, hurting for her.

That's what families did. Didn't they?

"Eat while it's hot, Jessie," Sarah said, and Jessie obeyed. She *was* hungry. Starved. She sipped the chocolate, then nibbled on the toast. It was wonderful. It was the ultimate comfort food, loaded with fat and calories and other things that were supposed to be bad. But it was nectar. She started to relax. The ache in the back of her head seemed to fade away.

"I hope . . . the accident won't make you decide to leave," Sarah said after a moment.

"I don't plan to go anywhere. Not yet."

"Good for you. You're a true Clements."

A true Clements. Jessie wasn't sure at this moment whether that was good or bad. But she knew it was meant as a compliment, and so she decided to take it that way. "Tell me more about my father."

Sarah smiled. "Harding was a year younger than me. Being the youngest, we looked out for each other. He was a hellion, though, just like most boys around here. They grow up around guns and horses and are raised to believe the world revolves around them."

The remainder of the cinnamon toast lay uneaten. Sarah had an expression on her face that told Jessie she had gone back fifty years and was seeing exactly what she was telling. "He didn't like school and wasn't good at it, mainly because his interests were elsewhere and he saw no need for 'book learning.' He loved the land, the hills. He would camp out for days and explore the cliffs and cave dwellings used by the Indians. He knew more about this land than any of us, probably loved it more. And when his brothers left the ranch and he knew it would be his, he settled down and learned all he needed to run the ranch."

Jessie felt her eyes water, but then it seemed they'd been doing a lot of that in the past couple of days. How little she'd known her father. How much had he given up to keep her? He could have handed her over to the state, or left her in a church, but he had dragged her from position to position, probably losing some because he'd had a child tagging along. What had happened to that boy who had loved the desert and the stars? The boy who had apparently so loved his family. Was that why he'd kept her when it would have been so much easier to give her up? Because he'd never quite lost that deep, abiding respect for family, for belonging.

"I would like to see those caves," she said.

"Then you will," Sarah said. "Ross knows them all, too."

"I don't think . . ."

"Or I can," Sarah said. "I have a few more rides in me."

Then Sarah must have seen something in Jessie's eyes because she continued, "The day I stop riding is the day I'll lie down and die," Sarah said. "I have no intention of sitting in a rocking chair, knitting. My greatest happiness would be showing you more of this country. I think your father would expect it of me." Sarah stood then. "Listen to me prattling along like an old woman while your food gets cold and you need rest. Now don't you feel you have to come to supper."

She stooped to pet Ben. "You take good care of her," she ordered the dog who waved his tale in frantic consent.

"Sarah," Jessie asked, stopping her.

"Yes?"

"I overheard Alex and Marc talking about a letter Heath might have left. Can I see it?"

Sarah's face clouded again. "Is that what you were doing in the attic?"

"Yes. I didn't think there would be anything wrong . . ."

"Of course there isn't," Sarah said. "I told you this house is as much yours as mine now. I'll see if I can find it."

But Sarah's eyes avoided hers, and Jessie wondered whether the letter would ever surface.

Then Sarah was gone, leaving the fragrance of lavender in the room.

Jessie slept for a while. When she woke, she still felt as if her mind was fogged. She wanted a cup of coffee, or something else to clear it, but she wasn't ready to see anyone yet. Instead, she took out the sheaf of papers Alex had given her and tried to read the small print. There was a copy of the original will, her DNA test results, an affidavit that she would have to sign declaring that she was who she was. Then there was a copy of the offer for the ranch. It was for an astronomical amount of money.

Money that wouldn't be needed by anyone if the bearer bonds were found and divided. Finding those bonds would reduce the pressure for selling the ranch.

Her head pounded harder.

So did her heart.

Regardless of whom a sale would benefit or destroy, she felt to her bones that selling this land, subdividing it into little parcels of look-alike houses, would be a tragedy. *He loved the land.* Jessie realized her father would never have wanted this land sold, sacrificed. He'd always been true to her, in his own way. He'd kept her. Now she had to keep the land intact for him. It was the least she could do.

And then she would return home, look again at the primer, and see whether or not there really were clues to a fortune in bearer bonds.

She felt better now that she had determined in her own mind exactly what she wanted to do. And the sooner now that she told everyone she would not approve the sale, then the sooner everyone could go about their business. She felt wary enough, though, not to mention the book yet, not until she determined whether there was really something to it.

Jessie knew enough about bearer bonds to understand that whoever had possession could cash them in. She wasn't entirely sure that whoever was searching for the bonds planned to share.

Ben crowded next to her, and she gave him a hug. "Are you ready to go home?" she asked.

Ben's tail wagged eagerly.

"I know," she said. "Home is good." But there were still things she had to know. She wondered if last night had been more of a warning than a real intention to hurt her.

She looked at the clock, then the late afternoon sun filtering through the window. No one had knocked, apparently deciding to let her sleep, but now she was hungry. She went to the window. No Ross. But there were several cars in front. More of the family was back, and it was probably the best thing to tell them all her decision. Then maybe they wouldn't be so eager to claim her.

Pleased that she'd made a decision, she quickly changed into slacks and a knit shirt and regarded herself critically in the mirror.

Her eyes looked sleepy, a little bloodshot. Her hair around the stitches seemed to stand straight up. She had no idea what to do about that. Spray wouldn't be wise. Then she decided it didn't matter. She applied a little lipstick, then a touch of powder to give her some color.

"You can come," she told Ben, who undoubtedly needed a trip outside. He followed happily as she descended the stairs. The room was full. Marc and Samantha were both there. So was Halden, the eldest Clements, in his usual easy chair. Cullen with his wife, Sondra. Elizabeth. And Sarah.

But Cullen's sons weren't there.

Nor was Alex.

Or Ross.

His hand wrapped around a highball glass, Cullen rose and came over to her. "I'm not going to ask you how you are because I'm sure you're tired of the question. But you certainly look fine. I want you to know we were all very worried about you."

"Thank you," she said. "I hope you haven't been waiting for me."

He put his hand on hers. "Elizabeth decided to stay over another day to make sure you were all right."

Jessie felt a small glow. She tried not to, but it was there all the same. She remembered what Ross had told her about Elizabeth, that she'd lost her fiancé. There were few people she'd connected with as easily as she had with her new cousin. She wondered how Elizabeth would feel about her decision.

Best not to wait, she thought. "I've made a decision," she said. Everyone looked at her. Sarah had gone absolutely still. She suddenly felt as if she were in a tableau, in which everyone was frozen in place. She hadn't needed to elaborate.

"I don't think my father would have wanted me to vote to sell," she said.

The tableau didn't move for a moment.

Then Marc rose. "Don't you think you should think about it a little longer?"

Sarah didn't say anything, but a smile lit her face.

Cullen moved closer. "I hope you haven't ruled it out altogether. It's a great deal of money, and the buyer might even offer more."

Then Elizabeth came over to her and put an arm around her. "Don't bully her," she said.

"Have you told Alex yet?" Marc asked.

She shook her head. "I thought I should tell you first."

Samantha's face was tight-lipped. Sondra frowned, anger flashing in her eyes.

"A lot has happened in the past few days," Marc said soothingly. "It might be wise if you didn't make a decision so quickly."

"It's not quick," she said. "I've had time to think about it. I just don't think this land should be sold."

"You don't even know this land," Sondra said, a tight look spoiling the lovely face. "It's not fair to the rest of us."

Jessie met her angry eyes. "Perhaps not," she said levelly, "but apparently Hall Clements wanted to preserve the ranch, too, or he never would have made that provision."

Cullen went over to his wife and put his hands on her shoulders, but she angrily shook out of them, rose, and stalked away.

"Just think about it," Cullen pleaded. "And give Roy Smith a chance to make another offer."

She wanted to say yes, to equivocate, but she knew she wouldn't change her decision. "It wouldn't change my mind," she said. "I would still vote no."

"That's your right," Marc said smoothly. "You don't owe us anything."

Something about that statement didn't strike her right, but she ignored it. "I think I'd better let Ben out."

Seven pairs of eyes went down to Ben, who seemed to notice. He retreated behind her legs.

Sarah spoke for the first time. "We'll have a buffet ready in just a few moments."

"I need a drink," Jessie heard Marc say as she went out the door.

She closed it quietly behind her. Ben went running over to Ross's house. She should have realized that he would. His truck was parked in front, so he'd arrived sometime in the past hour.

"Ben," she called. She didn't think she was ready for another encounter with Ross Macleod. She knew he would be pleased with her decision, but that wasn't why she'd made it. Her father had come alive for her in the past weeks, strangely more so than when he *was* alive. Now he was a man with dreams and passions, not one drained by life and drink. And she knew to the depths of her soul exactly what he would want her to do.

Ben returned reluctantly, went about his business, then started once more for Ross's home.

She wanted to follow. She wanted to tell him that the

ranch would continue as it had for nearly one hundred years.

But she couldn't do it. She still felt too raw. Too uncertain of his feelings, his motives. Everyone's motives. She felt that what she'd done had been right for her, for her father. And she would receive small payments over the years from profits of the ranch, though it certainly wouldn't be millions of dollars. It was far more than she'd ever expected.

She did feel good about her decision, and it had nothing to do with Sarah or Ross. It had all to do with her. And now, she knew, it was time to go home. Then perhaps she could find the answer to the final mystery. And cope with the fact that she would probably never know exactly what happened that day fifty years ago that tore apart a family.

She lingered for a moment, hoping perhaps that Ross would come out. But he might well be out riding. He often did in the evening, she was told. She wanted to be with him, astride a horse and watching the sun recede behind a mountain. How could she feel that way if she thought he might have struck her? Because part of her knew it couldn't be true?

Then who?

She returned to the house before she lost her resolve. Rosa was laying out food on the table, and she was reminded how hungry she was. No one had left after her announcement, and with the exception of Samantha, everyone was cordial. Elizabeth grabbed a plate and sat next to her. "That was gutsy," she whispered in approval.

"How do you feel about it?" she asked.

"I have mixed feelings," Elizabeth said. "I spent a lot more time here than my brother and I love it. But Andy never comes. I told him I would agree if he really wanted it," she added with a sigh. "It would mean I could travel, but deep down I would always miss the Sunset."

Jessie nodded, more sure than ever that she'd made the right decision.

An hour later, everyone who didn't live at the Sunset left. They all gave her a kiss, and none indicated any resentment over what she had decided, but she also had the feeling that they had not given up yet.

Finally, Marc and Samantha also left, heading for a party at a local home. "A political party," Marc said. Halden went to bed, leaving Jessie alone with Sarah.

They went out on the patio in back and settled down in chairs. A part moon and a million stars lit the spectacular rock formations. "It's beautiful," she said.

"Thank you," Sarah said softly.

"There's no need. I think it's what my father would have wanted."

"He would," Sarah said. "I imagine he's smiling now."

"I hope so."

"Would you think about staying?" Sarah asked. "Becoming a part of the ranch? I've been doing a lot of the bookkeeping, but my . . . eyes and concentration aren't what they used to be. And you belong here."

Ben stirred next to her. Perhaps he sensed her sudden excitement. Living here in such raw rugged beauty. Riding every day. Working with Ross. It was an incredibly appealing thought. Too appealing.

Everything she owned was in Atlanta. Her life was in Atlanta and in the Olde Book Shoppe. The Sunset was a rather unsettling fantasy, something still not quite real. Just as Ross wasn't quite real. She had never attracted anyone like him before, someone who exuded confidence and competence and pure masculine sensuality. She knew it couldn't last.

You belong here.

But she didn't. Not really. She still felt a stranger with most of them, and she still knew that someone had struck her in the dark. Like a coward.

That was why, she suddenly realized, she couldn't believe Ross was involved. He wasn't a coward. Someone else then. But who?

"Did you look for the letter?" she asked Sarah.

"Yes," she said. "It wasn't where I thought it should be."

"You didn't find it then?"

"No," Sarah said slowly. "But I don't think you would find anything helpful. The only reason it was kept is because Halden has a horror of throwing anything away. So did our father. I haven't seen it myself in forty years."

"And it was from Heath?"

"Yes," she said reluctantly.

"What exactly did it say?"

"That he considered the money a loan, that the bonds that had purchased him a share in the business would be worth far more than what he had taken."

"And he didn't say what he did with them?"

She was obviously reluctant even to remember, though Jessie sensed that the content of the letter was engraved in her mind. "Sarah?"

"He said he'd buried them, that he would send us directions in the primer when the company became successful."

"Why a primer?"

She shrugged. "Maybe it was part of the promise, his commitment. He knew how important those primers were to the family."

"Why doesn't everyone believe it was destroyed in the fire?"

"I think they do," Sarah said. "But it's the stuff of legend. Buried treasure. Every kid in the family has been out there trying to find it. They just can't seem to give up hope."

Jessie pondered that. "Marc and Cullen," she finally said. "They seem close."

"They are, always have been. Up until lately, though, they disagreed on the ranch. Cullen never cared about it.

Marc, perhaps because he lived here so long, wanted to keep it. It was just lately that Cullen persuaded him to sell. The offer was a very high one, and Marc is having problems raising money for his campaign. He's convinced he can win with the right financing."

Jessie absorbed all the information. Had Marc mentioned the letter to Cullen? But then Cullen wasn't at the ranch last night.

Sarah broke into her thoughts. "You didn't answer my question about staying here."

But Jessie couldn't let her suspicions go. "Someone was in the attic last night," she said. "Someone who didn't want me to find that letter." It was the best answer she could give. She didn't feel safe here. There was something . . . at work that she didn't understand.

Sarah didn't try to contradict her. "Will you at least come back often?"

"I *will* do that," she said. Then she voiced the other decision she'd made today. "I'll be going home the day after tomorrow."

A moment passed. Jessie sensed the regret in her aunt. She was still hiding something. Or protecting someone.

"I had better go up to bed," Jessie said.

"How's your head?"

"It aches a little. Other than that, I'm fine."

"Would you like to go up to the cliffs?" Sarah said.

Her hesitation prompted Sarah to add, "I would be riding anyway, Jessie. I was riding this morning. Like I said, I'll ride until the day I die. And," she added with a mischievous expression, "it would be much safer if I rode with someone."

"Ouch," Jessie said. Sarah knew exactly how to manipulate her. Just as Ross had charged. Still, she surrendered because she wanted to explore more of this country before she left. "Will you take me to some places where my father used to go?"

"I would like that," Sarah said quietly. "Thank you, Jessie. Thank you for being your father's daughter."

Jessie rose, and Ben lazily got to his feet. He wasn't going to let her out of his sight. "I'll see you in the morning." She didn't wait for Sarah to go inside with her. Instead, she stopped in the kitchen, got a glass of water, and went upstairs. She looked at the stairs up to the attic, and shuddered. No more such expeditions for her. She suspected that the letter, if it had been there, was now long gone. But why? Particularly when so many seemed to know the contents.

Once in her room, she settled down with a book, knowing she wouldn't sleep after today's nap. Unable to concentrate, she went to the window. The lights were on in Ross's house. After several moments, she saw Sarah coming out of Ross's house.

So Sarah had told him about her vote. He had no need to charm her now, or court her. And in two days she would be back home. Jessie's magnificent adventure would end.

twenty-two

Jessie woke up just before dawn. She glanced at the clock. Six A.M. She thought about burrowing back within the bed.

But her movements had roused Ben, who was sleeping beside the bed, and he jumped up on her, his body wriggling in eager anticipation of a trip outside. *Just as well.* She could see another sunrise.

She dressed hurriedly in a pair of jeans and sweater, ran a comb through her hair, and applied just a touch of lipstick. Then she went down the steps at a jog, Ben trailing behind her. She felt far better than she'd thought she would and looked forward to the ride ahead. Decisions had been made, and she felt as if she'd finished at least one chapter of the book that was becoming her life. Now a cup of coffee and a view of the sunrise were exactly what she needed.

But as she headed for the kitchen, she nearly ran down Sarah. Her aunt was wearing riding clothes and looked healthier than she had anytime in the past several days. Jessie wondered whether it was because she knew she could live on in the house, or whether she was just having a good day.

Sarah's face brightened and Jessie's heart contracted. She was just beginning to realize how much she had come to care for Sarah, manipulation or not.

"I'll fix breakfast for us," her aunt said. "Marc and Samantha didn't get in until late and probably won't be up for a while. Halden is having breakfast in his room."

"He's all right, isn't he?"

"Oh yes, but he just wants toast in the morning and he likes to eat and read the paper in his room."

They went into the kitchen and the aroma of coffee was lovely. "What would you like?" Sarah asked. "Rosa isn't here yet, but I can whip up something."

"Anything."

"Fresh fruit and an omelet? Mine aren't as good as Rosa's but . . ."

"Sounds marvelous." It sounded better than marvelous, in fact. The ache in her head had almost disappeared, and she found herself unexpectedly hungry. "I'll have to call Alex and make an appointment to sign those papers of his," she said. "I want to leave tomorrow."

"Have you made your reservation?"

"It was open-ended. I'll check on that later, too."

"I can ask Alex to come over here."

"Thanks, but I think I would rather go to his office."

Sarah nodded. "We'll go to the cliffs this morning, and you'll have all afternoon. I'll ask Halden to call Alex and make the appointment. In the meantime, why don't you go out and tell Ross we'll take Carefree and Daisy?"

"Will he be up?"

"Ross? As sure as the sun rises. This is midmorning for him."

Jessie wasn't at all sure that she wanted to see Ross this morning. *Liar.* It wasn't that she didn't want to see him. She wished it were that simple. It was herself she feared. She turned insensible when he was around.

"Go, Jessie," Sarah said.

Jessie went, Ben romping beside her.

The barn door was open. Jessie told herself to control her roaring hormones.

She heard a soft nicker and went down to the end of the barn. Ross was talking softly to one of his charges as he poured oats into a feed bucket. She saw him run a hand fondly along the neck of the horse. It was a horse she didn't know yet, but he nudged Ross with his handsome head.

Ross turned, obviously sensing her presence. "Jess," he said in a cool voice.

His hair was still damp from a shower, his shirtsleeves rolled up. He was wearing the usual well-worn jeans. She'd never seen anyone look quite as . . . lethally attractive in them. But the coolness in his voice made her take a step back.

"Ross?"

His expression didn't mellow. "Congratulations, I heard that you're officially an owner now."

She was baffled. "That sounds as if you don't approve."

"I don't approve or disapprove." His voice remained cool. She wondered whether Sarah had told him of her decision. "It's none of my business."

"I voted against the sale," she said.

"I heard."

"Isn't that what you wanted?"

"I didn't want anything from you," he said.

"Your mother . . ."

"She's not my mother," he said abruptly, and she knew he was angry. White-hot angry.

"She thinks she is."

He turned to her. "My mother was an alcoholic who slept with a married man. Among others. I'm not even sure David Macleod was my father." His voice was flat. But despite the lack of emotion, he seemed alone and exposed.

"Blood isn't the only thing that makes a mother," she said. "Mine left me when I was still a baby. She didn't want to be burdened with a child."

"Is that what your father told you?"

"No, but then I never heard another explanation, either."

Ross didn't say anything.

"Sarah said to tell you that we would be taking out Daisy and Carefree. Or do you think it's okay for Sarah to ride? She looks . . . a little tired."

"Neither you or I can keep her off a horse. She's been riding since she was four. She won't stop now."

"That's what I thought," she said as she continued to watch his face. The reserve was still there, gathered around him like a cloak.

She started to go, then hesitated. "You're angry."

He stared right through her. "I'm just the hired help, ma'am."

"You're anything but just the hired help."

"Ah, but not good enough to call when you were hurt."

"I didn't want you bothered. Everyone else was awake and . . ."

"And you'd told me about the letter." He hesitated, then continued bitterly, "Elizabeth told me that you thought someone had hit you. Is that why you didn't want Sarah to get me? Did you think I would ever hurt you?"

He'd figured it all out. And she saw the pain in his eyes. The pain that went hand-in-hand with his anger.

"No," she said. "I *don't* think so. I was confused yesterday morning. I hurt and I was scared, and I didn't know what was going on. But whoever did it was a coward. And the one thing you're not is a coward."

He stood absolutely still for a moment, then slowly seemed to relax.

"I had better get back," she said. "Sarah's making breakfast."

He nodded.

She found herself reluctant to leave, unwilling—or unable—to flee those searching dark eyes. The barn suddenly seemed very close. She shivered inside her skin but she couldn't seem to move.

Ben barked, and both grateful and resentful for the interruption, she looked down. Although he stayed at her feet, his body wriggled frantically. He'd just seen Timber, who had come out of one of the stalls and stood next to Ross.

"I'll miss him," she said. She really meant she would miss both of them.

"Then don't go."

His words stunned her. And obviously from the look on his face they stunned him, too.

He turned his back as if to deny his words.

Left speechless and confused for a moment, she didn't know how to answer. So she didn't. She escaped instead into something easier. "We . . . we'll be here in about a half hour," she said.

"I'll have the horses ready," he said curtly.

She left while she could. He always sent her senses spiraling in storm-tossed confusion.

Breakfast was ready when she got back. Orange juice, berries, and a Southwestern omelet. But her appetite was gone, lost in that maelstrom of emotions Ross always stirred in her. Why couldn't her heart beat faster when she was with Alex? He seemed so simple compared to Ross's complexity. Yet never once had her heart jumped at just seeing him.

But neither had it felt fear.

She forced down some food. She knew it was good, but it still tasted like cardboard. Her enthusiasm for a ride had dimmed, also. Sarah, however, filled the silence with stories about the peoples who once lived here, and the pictographs they would see. "I hope Ross will go with us," she said. "He knows far more about them than I do."

That didn't surprise Jessie. She remembered the intensity with which he'd talked about the kachina dolls, the rare enthusiasm she'd caught in his voice. But she doubted whether he would accompany them—though she suspected he was more concerned about Sarah's health than he'd indicated.

Her heart pounded harder with expectation even as she helped Sarah clean up the dishes. Then she put Ben in her room and fed him. She'd told Sarah she would meet her at the barn.

When she arrived there, Ross was holding the reins of three saddled horses and she knew he intended to accompany them. "I don't think you two should be out there alone," he said simply as he handed her the reins to Carefree and watched as she lifted herself into the saddle. Sarah appeared then, refusing Ross's offer of help. She mounted with the ease of someone who'd done it for a lifetime.

The morning was already warm. Heat radiated off the high desert. Jessie felt a denser heat, though, as Ross fell into an easy pace between Sarah and her. Timber ran behind them. Sarah, Jessie noted, wore a satisfied smile. Jessie suddenly wondered whether she'd planned this trip very carefully, using her health as a spur to both her and Ross.

Jessie reminded herself that she would be gone tomorrow, away from the manipulations, the emotional uncertainties and the dangers—real and imagined—of the Clementses. She shouldn't feel so desolate about the prospect. She should feel relieved. Happy that she would receive some pittance over the years, and knowing that she had helped preserve this small piece of God's garden.

They rode past the Saddle, the rock formation she'd visited before, and on toward a mountain. The sun crept higher into the sky as the horses passed several roads. Sarah explained that they were on federal land now, and Jessie saw Jeeps full of tourists heading up one steep road.

The three of them rode another fifteen minutes or so before stopping at the foot of a twisting trail. Sarah stopped. "I'm going to wait here," she said, pointing to a large rock under a large pine tree.

Ross's brows furrowed in concern. "Do you feel all right?"

"Yes indeed," she said, "but that is a long ride up, and I think I would like to just sit in the shade."

"We should go back," Jessie said.

"No," Sarah said sharply. "I want you to see this. Your father used to prowl all over these cliffs. I like to think that a little of him is still here. I'm fine, really I am. I love this spot."

Jessie looked at Ross, who was regarding his adoptive mother with affectionate bemusement, but not worry. Jessie realized that she had planned the trip exactly this way.

"Jess?" he asked. "It's a rough ride."

It was a challenge. One she wasn't going to give him the satisfaction of refusing.

She nodded.

"Follow me, then. Call out if you have any problem. The trail will take only one horse at a time." His weighed her with his gaze.

"What about Timber?"

"Oh, he'll do some exploring of his own. He won't go too far away."

She simply nodded again. Sarah, a satisfied look on her face, slid down from the horse and went to sit on the rock. Jessie had a momentary pause, wondering whether they should really leave her, then she saw Sarah's wink. She turned her horse and started to follow Ross up the steep trail.

They seemed to climb forever. She had to focus all her attention on the trail ahead, though she let the horse do all the work. Ross rode in front of her, his body easily adapting to the sharp incline. It was far different from racing a horse around a level track. When they finally reached the top, he stopped until she reached his side. They rode around a rim, skirting prickly pear cactus, yucca, and bladelike needle-pointed agave plants. There was odorous evidence that elk and other wildlife were frequent visitors. From here, there was no sign of civilization, only a heavily wooded canyon framed by mountains. The land was wild and untouched, and the view was breathtaking.

"It's beautiful," she said.

"This is all national forest land," he said. He slid from the saddle, then went over to her and held out his arms. She slid naturally into them, and their faces were inches apart. "You know Sarah planned all this," he said.

"I do now."

"You could have refused to come."

"And miss all this? I want to see as much as I can while I'm here." She wanted to say something else, that she relished the time spent with him. That she wanted to be with him. But the words went unsaid, exchanged only through the exquisite bond that always seemed to connect them. Exquisite and painful.

There was a sudden uncertainty in his face. He bent over, his lips touching hers very, very softly.

Her lips parted. She knew it wasn't wise, but his mouth was searching, hesitant, almost achingly desperate. All the feelings she'd tried to subdue came tumbling out, the wreckage crashing around her. All she cared about was how much she wanted his touch. Her feelings were as intense and fiery and raw as they ever had been.

The almost fragile, hesitant quality of the kiss deepened, became something fierce and needy. His very touch singed her to the core. It always would, she knew. Just as she thought he would never be comfortable with it. She saw that knowledge in his eyes, in the desperation of his lips.

He held on to her as if she were his last link with life. He released her lips but cradled her body as if she were a butterfly that would escape once freed. Then he let her go. Physically. Emotionally he had her tied in knots.

He took her hand and led her carefully to the edge of

what looked like a cliff. She looked down. The bottom was a long way. He let go, took several steps down, then held out his hand to help her. She tried not to look as she gingerly followed him. A few more feet, then they crawled over a tree and edged along a narrow ledge. For a moment her throat seemed to close. One false step could send her tumbling down the cliff. If Ross had ever meant her any harm, then this would be the place. But all she felt in his hand was confidence, power, and security. Finally, they stopped at a sheer piece of red rock.

His fingers were tight around hers as he showed her a series of pictures on the wall. Stick men and animal figures.

"They could be as much as three thousand years old," he said. "This one was just recently discovered. We think it tells of an antelope hunt. Mind-boggling, isn't it?"

"We?"

"I belong to an archeology group." Yet another side to him, this man who seemed such a loner.

"You're full of surprises," she said.

"So are you," he said. "I never thought . . ." He stopped.

"That I would vote to keep the ranch."

"Yes."

"Easy come, easy go," she said lightly.

"It's much more than that," he said in a husky voice.

"I just don't feel that any of the Clements money should be mine," she said. "The others . . . they were born here, grew up here, worked on the ranch. They had a stake in it. I don't think I do."

"Your father gave up more than anyone else for this ranch," he said, surprising her. Another little tidbit dropped. But never enough. Would there ever be enough?

"We had better go back," he said.

She nodded. "I know Sarah will be ready, and I have to go into Sedona."

"I think Sarah is prepared to wait," he replied.

"You knew she was planning to disappear," she accused him.

"I suspected, but if I hadn't come, she would have brought you here herself and that would be far too dangerous for both of you. She's not always steady on her feet but no one can tell her that. I try to keep an eye on her."

She heard the affection in his voice. It seemed to contrast with his flat statement earlier. *She's not my mother.* Whatever she was to Ross, it was important. She recalled the bitterness in his voice when he talked about his blood mother, and she wanted to know more about the boy in that picture in Sarah's room. The thin, rebellious boy with a cowlick.

They moved along the ledge again, and she felt a moment of fear again. It faded quickly as she felt his reassuring presence, the way he placed himself between her and the emptiness below. It took them another thirty minutes or so to get back to the top of the rim. She'd squirmed over trees and scrambled across rocks and she wondered how Sarah could ever had made it. *She* almost didn't.

But then she had seen Sarah ride, racing breakneck across the valley. Her aunt. And Halden, her uncle, who was still going strong in his nineties. At least she apparently had good genes.

A sense of pride filled her. She'd always been afraid of heights, and now she'd triumphed over several fears.

Ross took her hand as they walked to the horses. His dark eyes showed approval, as well as a glittering swell of passion. His lips curved into a slight smile. There was warmth in it that almost made her giddy. Her fingers curled around his larger ones, and everything seemed sharper, more intense, more alive. The sky was bluer, the sun brighter, the breeze more sensuous, the mountains around them more magnificent.

Already the land was pulling at her heart. It always would.

Just as she knew that Ross would always pull at her heart, that it would always make that funny little skip when he was near, and that the air would always be close between them, close and heavy and electrifying like the prelude to a storm.

He hesitated, then said, "Sarah said you plan to leave tomorrow."

"If I get my business finished with Alex and I can get a flight."

"Sarah was hoping you could stay longer."

She noticed that he didn't say *he* was hoping she would stay longer. "I can't stay away from the bookstore. My partner has been covering for me, but he's trying to write a book, and it's not fair for me to be gone, and . . ." She was rambling on again. She never rambled like that. Except when she was with him. Except when she couldn't tell the whole truth.

His dark eyes seemed to know that.

"Thank you for being kind to Sarah," he said, releasing her hand.

Her world chilled.

"It's easy to do. I like her."

"You will come back again?" A muscle struggled in his cheek, and she sensed he wanted to say more.

"Now that I own a piece. You betcha."

His lips curled into a smile, a wider one now. It was more glorious for its rarity. The spare face and all its angles softened.

"I'll look forward to it," he said.

"Will you?"

"Unfortunately."

"Why unfortunately?" She was tired of his evasions.

He shrugged. "A lot of reasons."

"Name just one."

"Okay." His eyes darkened. "I have Apache blood."

"Who cares about that?"

"A lot of people in Arizona."

"I'm not one of them."

He turned away from her. "What did Sarah tell you about me?"

"Very little. Just that you came to live with them when you were twelve. That both your mother and grandmother had died. And that you were wild."

"An understatement. My mother slept with any man who would buy her a drink. You can't possibly know how many 'uncles' I had, nor how many times I heard 'Indian whore' or worse when my mother would try to rob them. In the end, I stole to keep her alive. But it didn't do any good. She didn't have a liver left."

Jessie hurt for him, ached for a boy who'd seen too much and never had a childhood.

"I was ten when she died, and I was shipped off to my grandmother, who was Indian. She was a full-blooded Apache who'd married a white man and was shunned by both races. He left her before my mother was born. Didn't want an Indian brat. I lived with her on a reservation for two years. She was forty-eight when she died, and she looked eighty. I was sent to a foster home, then another. No one kept me long, but then I didn't want to be kept. I knew that if I formed an attachment to anyone, they would die or go away or send *me* away. So I made all the trouble I could, just daring them to send me back to Social Services." He smiled, but this time it was a tight grimace.

"How did you happen to end up with Sarah?" she said.

"A social worker was at her wit's end. She finally went back and reviewed all my records, looking for a relative. She saw David's name and hunted him down. I think she went through a hundred Macleods. Then she discovered he was dead. But Sarah was interested, and they decided to give it a try.

"It wasn't easy. I hated my father. He'd left me and he'd left my mother. He'd never sent one cent. I couldn't imagine that Sarah would want her dead husband's bastard. I still don't know why she did it. Nor why she kept me. I did everything I could to discourage her."

"She loves you as if you were her own."

"It took me a long time to figure that out. Years, in fact."

"But you still call her Sarah?"

"In my experience, that was a far better word than *mother*."

She was silent. She'd learned long ago that silence was often the best prompter.

His lips curved upward again. Not exactly a smile. "You're an easy woman to be with. Has anyone told you that?"

She didn't know how to reply to that. The answer was, of course, no. But that was because she'd not been with many men.

Still, she understood what he'd just said, and the scars his childhood had left on him. She'd felt the taint of being abandoned by her mother. She knew what it felt like to be used by someone she thought she loved. But his blows had all been more powerful than hers. He'd not been able to trust anyone, not his mother, not the foster homes, not his first love. He'd built barriers to protect himself, and Sarah apparently had been the only person ever to breach them. Jessie knew how high those walls could be. She had constructed a few of her own.

She also knew what he was telling her. His barriers were still in place.

The knowledge was bitter. She'd had a fleeting glimpse of magic, and she wanted it to last. But she had seen too many women who thought they could change the man they wanted. It rarely, if ever, happened.

He was obviously still guarding his heart, and she didn't know if he would ever open it. She was right in leaving while *her* heart was still intact. Or was it?

He was watching her with those dark eyes. Speculating?

Desiring? Regretting? She didn't know. She didn't know if she would ever be able to decipher them. But the air was still charged between them, and she knew if she didn't leave now, she might never leave. "I have to get back," she said in a voice that seemed uncertain even to her.

"Yes," he said simply.

She hated that simple acquiescence. She wanted him to take her in his arms and stroke her with the gentleness she remembered. No more confidences today. Certainly no request for her to stay. That blurted-out "Then don't go" earlier didn't qualify.

But he'd turned his attention to scanning the area. He called for his dog. In seconds, Timber came in a long-legged lope and stopped beside Ross.

Jessie settled into the saddle and watched as he mounted his own horse. His face was set in hard, implacable lines as he started back down the trail. It didn't change when they met Sarah below.

The moment of magic was gone.

twenty-three

Silence met Jessie and Sarah as they entered the house—
the kind of intense, expectant silence that indicated it had
stopped just for the newcomers. Or because of them.

Marc wore his politician's face. Bland and friendly.
Cullen, however, was obviously unhappy. She watched
emotions pass over his face. Disappointment. Even resentment. Then it faded. No, she corrected herself silently.
It didn't fade. It was managed away. She had the impression of a play-dough face forced by determined hands to
transform from one expression to another. It fascinated
her. He was furious, but he was doing his damnedest to
hide it.

Sarah must have felt the tension, but she simply smiled
at each one of them, and found a seat.

Marc frowned. "Dan'l said you went for a ride. Should
you be doing that, Sarah?" There was just a touch of censure for Jessie, as if accusing her of hauling off his aunt.
Was that why the tension radiated in the room? They were
worried about Sarah?

That's what they wanted her to believe. But she wasn't
going to apologize, not for doing what Sarah wanted. Nor
for her earlier decision.

Cullen stood, his usual courtly manner back in place.
"Jessie? Sarah? Would you like a drink?"

Jessie considered the offer, then declined. "I'd better not. I have to drive into Sedona and see Alex."

Marc rose. He paced the floor. "You know we will respect any decision you make," he said. "But I wonder whether you should make it after your injury."

A new tact. "I'm in my right mind if that's what you mean," Jessie said evenly.

Marc had the grace to look embarrassed. "That's not what I meant. It's just that everything must be a little . . . overwhelming and . . ."

"It is," she interrupted before he could continue. "But I know what I want, and I want to save the Sunset. I can't miss what I haven't had, nor what I hadn't expected. I have a job and a business in Atlanta. I have everything I need."

"And want?"

"Does anyone have everything they want?"

Marc looked abashed. "I suppose not."

"The Sunset is too beautiful to destroy."

"I just want you to be sure. Once the offer is off the table . . ."

"I'm sure," she said. "In fact, I'm seeing Alex this afternoon."

Cullen shrugged. "Of course, you can do anything you want. We are just asking that you consider what the majority wants." His voice was friendly, but Jessie sensed tension within him.

She hesitated for a moment, then spoke slowly. "But I think that's why your grandfather put that provision in the will," she said. "So that the majority wouldn't prevail against a minority. He wanted the ranch to survive."

"She has you there," Marc said.

"So she does," Cullen said after only a brief hesitation. "Well, whatever you do, know that you are welcome here or at the Quest any time."

"Thank you," she said.

"We hope to see you often," Marc added with the warm

friendliness that must have brought numerous voters into his fold. "Samantha and I are leaving this afternoon for Phoenix."

"I wish I could vote for you."

"Move out here and you can." He leaned down and kissed her cheek. "I do approve of my new relative."

She left the room and went to the kitchen where she phoned Alex's office to tell him she would be there shortly. Then she went up the stairs to wash and change, pausing only to greet Ben.

Then she headed for the shower. She was dusty and smelled very much like horse. She wondered then if she and Sarah had just wandered into a brotherly conversation or whether they had been lying in wait for her.

Jessie took a quick shower. But her thoughts were crowded. Her aunt had appeared just fine when she and Ross had rejoined her at the bottom of the mountain. There was even an air of satisfaction as she eyed them. Was she really ill?

And Ross. Her body still quaked when she thought of him.

Even a cold shower didn't help that.

She turned off the shower and dressed quickly, choosing a pair of dark blue slacks and white blouse. Then she looked outside.

The sky had changed from blue to gray. Ominous-looking clouds rushed across the heavens. They'd been building all afternoon, but now looked threatening. She'd heard about the sudden, violent storms that were so prevalent over this part of Arizona. The lightning, she'd been told, was particularly dangerous.

She only hoped a storm, if it came, would spend itself out tonight. She didn't relish the trip to the airport in Phoenix in driving rain. Sighing, she took Ben downstairs for a quick romp outside. Ben looked for Timber—or was he looking for Ross? But his truck was gone.

Just as she took Ben back inside, the first drops of rain started to fall.

The rain was steady when Jessie reached Alex's office. It was an elegant yet comfortable suite of offices in a two-story complex. His back window overlooked the rock formations and she was reminded that everything in Sedona was designed to take advantage of its glorious landscape.

He introduced her to Mary Stuart, his legal secretary "and right hand," and Melissa, his receptionist. Much to her surprise, Mary was a middle-aged woman, her hair sprinkled with gray, and Melissa was probably well into her forties. For some reason, she'd expected sleek young women to inhabit his office. But then she had underestimated him before.

He guided her into a comfortable chair next to his desk. She took the opportunity to look over his office, which was quietly decorated in the browns and tans and beiges that so reflected Sedona. Very good Southwestern paintings decorated the walls. Quiet good taste prevailed, and she thought it a comfortable, nonthreatening setting.

He sat down behind a table covered with thick piles of paper. "So you've made up your mind."

"Yes. I vote not to sell."

"Marc so informed me."

"I don't suppose he's pleased."

Alex shrugged. "It doesn't matter what Marc thinks. It's your decision. You have the papers with you?"

She pulled them from her handbag and put them on his desk, then signed them.

He put both hands on his desk and looked unusually serious. "Jessie, as the attorney for the Clementses, I have to mention something else. Because the trust is so complex, I would suggest you make a will if you don't already have one. If you do, you might wish to change it."

She didn't like the prickling she felt run up and down

her spine, but he was right. She'd never made out a will, though she always meant to. Now it *was* important. She thought for a moment, then made a decision. She didn't want the ranch up for grabs. Not as long as Sarah lived.

"Then I would like to leave my share of the ranch to Sarah," she said.

He looked at her curiously. "Are you sure you don't want to think about it?"

"No," she said. "Can you do it now?"

"What about your other property?"

"The only thing I own of value is my share of the bookstore, and I want to leave that to Sol." She hesitated, then asked, "Will you prepare it for me?"

"I'll have to check the laws in Georgia."

"Can you do something that will serve temporarily?"

"Is there a reason?"

She shrugged. "I'm flying back to Atlanta. Anything can happen. I want to make sure that my wishes are observed."

He picked up a phone. "Mary, can you come in here?"

He'd barely settled the phone in its cradle when Mary came in. "I want you to draw up a will. Miss Cle . . . Clayton will leave her share of the Sunset to Sarah Macleod. Her other property is to be left to Sol Whiteman. She'll give you the address." He looked at his watch. "I know this will keep you late, but it's important. Will you ask Melissa to stay, too? I want her to witness the signatures." He turned back to Jessie. "Mary is a notary public."

Jessie gave Mary Sol's address and date of birth. She'd seen it on other documents, and it wasn't difficult to remember. January 1, 1935.

Mary disappeared again into an office next to Alex's.

Alex leaned back in his seat. "Sarah said you were planning to leave in the morning. Would you like to go to dinner tonight?"

She wouldn't. She wanted to go back to the ranch. She wanted to say good-bye to Ross.

But that would only be asking for trouble. "Yes," she said. "Can I use your phone to make my plane reservations?"

He handed the phone to her. She had the reservation number in her handbag, and it took her just a few moments to make the reservation. She had an open return and found a flight that left Phoenix at noon. Perfect. She just wished she didn't feel so lost at the prospect of returning home.

A half hour later, Mary presented a will. Jessie read it carefully, then signed it. Melissa signed as a witness and Mary as notary public. Except for her share in the ranch, she left all her worldly goods to Sol. She asked Alex to make two copies—one for her and one to be mailed to Sol.

In that hour, she'd made decisions as to whom she trusted, whom to hold at arm's length. And Alex was among the latter. He'd never been particularly helpful in answering her many questions. It had been obvious that his loyalty was to the Clements family. But to which faction?

She knew from the fleeting expression in his eyes that he understood. But if he resented it, he didn't show it. In some ways, he could be as protective of his thoughts as Ross. An attorney's stock-in-trade?

Several minutes later, they were in his car. She leaned against the door and looked at him, thinking how different he was from Ross, how easy everything seemed for him. His eyes admired her, but they did nothing to make her heart thump harder. There were no charges of electricity making crackling contact between them.

"Mexican, steak, Italian? Whatever my newest client wishes."

She thought about it for a moment. Not Mexican. She would always equate Mexican with the cantina. She wanted to keep that memory to herself.

"Italian," she said. "The restaurant we went to before."

He seemed pleased at that. "Good."

They reached the restaurant almost instantly. "So that's

another reason you like it," she observed. "It's nearly across the street."

"My home away from home," he quipped lightly, but she detected a kind of wistfulness behind it.

She looked at him curiously. "Have you ever been married?" He seemed to live for the Clementses. She wondered whether he had any kind of life of his own. She didn't feel as if she were prying. He apparently knew everything about her.

"Once," he said. "It lasted five years, until she tired of a small town and a workaholic husband. She was a big-city girl."

"How could anyone get tired of Sedona? It's magic."

"Not enough to keep *you* here."

It could if Ross . . .

But that was wistful thinking. "I love the bookstore," she said.

"Do you? Or are you just hiding?"

She glared at him. He was far too close to the mark.

"You could go any place you wish now," he said. "Paris. Europe."

"Not without selling the ranch."

"No, not without selling the ranch," he said.

The implication was there. He had dangled possibilities, leaving open the offer.

He stopped the car near the restaurant door to let her out. She waited there until he parked and sprinted through the rain to meet her at the entrance, but her appetite had faded. He hadn't accepted her decision. He'd been humoring her, obviously thinking that she would have second thoughts when she had time to consider the money.

What he didn't understand was that she couldn't even comprehend the money. It had never actually been hers. It didn't seem real to her. She didn't think it would ever seem real.

Alex put his arm around her waist in the easy, accomplished way of his, guiding her inside. She stopped and looked at him. "My answer is final. I won't sell."

Alex sighed. "The buyer has said he will increase his offer. He really wants that land."

Any lingering instinct to trust him was shattered. "And you think I should accept it?"

"It's far more than the land is worth, certainly a great deal more than the ranch will ever earn," he said noncommittally. "It's something to consider."

"I *have* considered it."

He nodded as they were greeted by the same maître d' who had seated them before. She followed him, but she felt empty. Tired.

It definitely was time to go home.

Rain was falling even harder when they left. They ran for the car, then drove in silence back to his office, where she'd left her car.

Alex felt the distance she'd put between them. It could be measured in miles rather than feet. Everything he'd gained in the past few weeks had been lost in a few moments. But Marc had insisted that he try again. The congressman just couldn't believe that someone would turn down all that money. Her refusal, Marc had claimed, was "the romance of the moment. When she gets home, she'll think about all the things the money can do."

Marc, who was usually very good at reading people, hadn't a clue about Jessica Clayton.

But then none of them had. Not a single one of them had thought she would turn down millions. And now he'd lost the one advantage he had. He'd seen the trust fade from her eyes.

He drove to his condo. Perhaps he had let his loyalty to the Clementses overtake his usual neutrality. He'd liked Jessica. He'd liked her more than any woman he'd met.

Probably for the reason she'd backed away. Her total lack of greed.

Goddammit.

He parked in the garage, then went up the steps and inside. He went right to the liquor cabinet, poured himself more whiskey than he usually did, and went out on the covered deck that overlooked the valley. Rain was like a curtain.

He sipped his drink, then went inside and called Marc. "I don't think she's going to change her mind," he said. "It was a mistake to even suggest it."

He listened for a moment to Marc. "Dammit, I'm not going to listen to you anymore. And she doesn't know anything about those damned bonds. You can tell Cullen that as well."

Alex slammed the phone down. He felt dirty, angry, frustrated. This should have been so easy.

Jessie couldn't get the conversation out of her mind as she drove down the main Sedona road. It was dark, and the rain fell in sheets. She could barely see the line down the center of the road.

She recounted each word in her mind. Damn Alex. Whenever she thought she might be able to trust him, he'd throw out another tidbit that made her reassess his role in all of this. They all thought they could manipulate her later by dangling temptation in front of her.

She fumed. *Tomorrow.* Tomorrow, she would be home. At least she knew what to expect of Sol. She knew him. He knew her.

She was still a stranger here. A stranger with something that everyone wanted. She felt betrayed. She felt empty.

Jessie shook her head, telling herself to concentrate. She didn't like driving in weather like this. She could barely discern the dividing line on the road. On a good day, it was a drive of twenty minutes or so; tonight it would take forty or more. Her fingers tightened around the steering wheel.

Lights coming from the opposite direction were diffused by the rain. They seemed to come right at her, and she instinctively swerved over to the side of the road. She fought the car for a moment, then found the road again. She breathed, and the trapped air in her lungs came out in a rush.

She was not ordinarily a timid driver, but the narrow and winding road wasn't that familiar. She leaned forward, trying to see better when she noticed a pair of headlights behind. Too close for bad weather. She looked for a place to pull over and let the car pass, but the road climbed here and there was only a dropoff on her right.

Darn it, no one was going to force her to go faster than she felt safe. Once they got over this hill, the road leveled out again and stayed that way to the turnoff toward the Sunset.

She felt a bump from behind, just enough that had she not had both hands glued to the steering wheel, it might have pushed her from the road. She speeded up just a little bit. She wanted to look back at the car behind her, but she didn't dare take her eyes from the road in front.

Another bump, this time a more forceful one. Not an accident this time. She was sure of that. Fear ratcheted upward.

She speeded up again, aware of a sharp curve ahead. She remembered a sheer dropoff at the road's edge. Her hands tightened on the steering wheel. She fought down panic. Where exactly was that curve? Where was other traffic?

She saw headlights coming toward her from the opposite direction. She pressed down on the horn, hoping against hope they would see a car too close behind her. But instead the oncoming vehicle merely splashed more water on her windshield, making it even more difficult to see. It did, however, have the effect of forcing the car behind her to back off.

But once again she sensed the car creeping back up upon her. She shot a glance in the rearview mirror but only saw a dark blob. She couldn't tell what kind of car it was, not even the exact color.

Her knuckles whitened as she searched desperately for a place to slow and stop. But if she did that, what would happen? Did her assailant have a gun? Exactly how far would they go?

She was coming to the long curve when she saw a dirt road go to the left and the faint glow of a light. A house. She made a sharp left turn, praying no one came in the opposite direction. The car started to spin, refusing to slow, missing the driveway and plowing through a fence before slamming to a stop in a ditch.

She felt the impact of the air bag as it exploded like a hammer against her chest. She lost her breath, momentarily stunned. Slowly, she started to reason again, as the bag dissolved in a cloud of white powder.

Fear clutched at her. Was someone out there? Would they come to finish what they had started? The rain was falling too hard, too loudly to hear anything. Lightning flashed nearby and the low roar of thunder rumbled across the valley.

She had to get out. Her hands fumbled at the seat belt. Her fingers were like rubber, unable to function. Finally, the belt came loose. She tried to open the door. Thank God, it gave.

She grabbed her handbag and the envelope with the wills in it and tumbled out, finding her feet sinking into mud. Then she saw a car stopped on the other side of the fence. Was it the car that had bumped her, that had tried to force her off the road?

A man was coming around it, followed by a woman in a

raincoat. Then she noticed it was a pickup, a truck. The aggressor had been in a car.

Breathe slowly, she thought. *You're safe.*

She struggled through the mud. Her chest hurt. Her body ached. The man reached her. "Are you all right?"

She wasn't. She was terrified. She hurt. Her shoes were ruined. She felt herself giggling. That was the last thing she should worry about. "I think so," she said. "Thank you for stopping."

Thank God they had.

"Did you . . . see a car following me?"

The man looked at the woman, then nodded. "I thought it curious he didn't stop. People usually help each other out here."

"Did you see what kind it was?"

The man shook his head. "I was watching your car. Come get in the truck."

He helped her over to the truck.

She turned back and looked at the wreck. She realized she wasn't going to go home tomorrow.

She also knew that she would be staying where someone wanted to hurt her. This time, it was no tap on the head, or a mussed apartment.

This time, someone wanted her dead.

twenty-four

Sarah reached for the phone when it rang. Halden had retired, and she was listening to the late news. Ben was next to her, his eyes glued to the door.

She'd thought about going to bed herself, but she wanted to wait up for Jessie. This would be her last night, and Sarah wanted to make sure all had gone well at Alex's office. Alex, she knew, might well try to change her mind.

But Sarah felt comfortable that Jessie wouldn't do that. The girl had a stubborn streak.

She'd wanted to tell Jessie everything, but everything would be too much. Perhaps when she got to know the family better, when she felt the rhythms of it, Sarah could tell her the entire truth. But then perhaps it was better that no one knew.

Only Ross knew the entire truth now, and he'd been sworn to secrecy. She'd told him in a moment of agony, when guilt became a weight she couldn't bear. He'd taught her how to live with it.

But now the events that happened fifty years ago were like a writhing nest of snakes, each capable of destruction. She could only try to protect Jessie as much as possible. At least, none of the incidents had been deadly.

She only wished she knew who was behind them. She could only guess, and guesses were worth nothing.

So the ringing of the phone startled her. She received few calls this late.

"Sarah?" Jessie's voice. Shaken. Trembling.

Sarah's heart pounded. Her chest hurt. "Jessie? What's wrong?"

"There was . . . an accident and I've been delayed. I didn't want you to worry. I'm going to call a cab . . ."

"Where are you?"

There was a silence on the other end for a moment, then a reluctant admission. "I'm not hurt, but a good Samaritan insisted that I go to the hospital."

"I'll be there immediately."

Sarah put the phone down, stood, then grabbed a table to keep her balance. The world seemed to spin for a moment. She felt weak, dizzy. *Ross.* She would call Ross.

She sat down and dialed his number.

"Macleod," he replied brusquely.

"Ross, Jessie's been in an accident. She's at the hospital. Can you go to her?" Sarah wanted to go, too, but she received the impression over the phone that the last thing Jessie wanted was a fuss.

"What happened?" His voice was rough.

"I don't know, but I talked to her. She said she was all right."

"I'm on my way."

Sarah was left holding a dead phone.

Ben whined, as if sensing something was wrong.

"It's all right," Sarah said soothingly, but Ben started pacing restlessly.

She heard Ross's pickup roar onto the road. She closed her eyes and prayed Jessie was really all right. There had been too many accidents. Perhaps it was for the best that she was going home.

• • •

Jessie saw Ross charge through the doors of the hospital. His hair was wet and mussed, his shirt partially unbuttoned, his shirttail out.

She had hoped Sarah would come, but no one should be driving on a night like this, particularly a woman who might be ill. *Might be.* Now she was questioning everything about the family and everyone in it.

Including Ross? If she didn't, perhaps she should. Black was white, and white was black. She could no long decipher the signals.

Her heart clenched at the thought as she'd waited in the waiting area. She'd planned to call a taxi, but someone at the hospital told her she might be waiting for hours on a night like this. She feared that worry might harm Sarah more than her knowing what had happened. The doctor also didn't want to release her until a friend or relative came for her. A recent concussion. Now bruised ribs and other cuts.

She hadn't wanted to talk to Alex. Or Cullen. Suspicions swam around her head. Alex was the only one who knew where she was. No, the last person she wanted to see was the attorney.

Jessie had thought about calling Ross herself but had hesitated. They hadn't parted on easy terms. She also knew what happened to her senses when she was with him. Chaos. They became complete chaos.

So she'd called Sarah.

But as she watched Ross stride up to her, his brows furrowed, his mouth grim, relief filled her. Her resistance melted. She wanted to throw herself into his arms, to feel the warmth of his body and the protection of his arms. She didn't care if her body betrayed her, or that her heart fluttered like that of a small bird.

He came right to her and stood in front of where she was sitting. "You need a bodyguard."

"Yes."

He offered a hand, and she took it and stood, a groan escaping as she did.

"Did the doctors say you could go?"

"Yes. I've already taken care of the insurance. That's always their main concern anyway." She heard the wryness in her voice. A defense. A defense against her need for him.

His expression didn't change as his eyes studied her. She couldn't even imagine what she looked like. Her slacks coated with mud, her blouse ruined by rain, her hair probably standing straight up. She'd been too sore, too dispirited, to even run a comb through her hair or check for lipstick.

An angry glint frosted his eyes. "What happened?"

"Someone ran me off the road. A few miles from the ranch road."

"On purpose?"

"Yes," she said. She was tired of looking for other explanations, tired of making excuses for accidents that were not accidents.

He reached down and touched her, then offered her his hand. When she stood, he drew her close to him. "I want to hold you," he said, "but I'm afraid I would hurt you."

The confession stunned her. Not that he was afraid he would hurt her, but that he admitted wanting to hold her.

Ignoring the pain lingering in her chest, she moved even closer to him. She wanted the warmth and comfort of his body.

His arms went around her so gently, so tenderly, that she barely felt them. She just leaned into them, feeling safe for the first time that evening.

Then and only then did he ask, "Do you know who tried to force you off the road?"

She shook her head. "It was raining too hard. I only know it was a dark car."

He swore softly. "What do you want to do?"

"Go back to the ranch," she said. "I'll have to contact

the car rental agency in the morning. I have a flight tomorrow, but . . ."

"I'll take care of everything," he said curtly. But she knew the anger wasn't aimed toward her.

Which meant he wanted her to leave. But remembering the burglaries, she wondered whether she would be any safer in Atlanta. But why? If something happened to her, her share of the ranch would go to Sarah and there would be no question of a sale. And it couldn't be the darn book. No one knew anything about it but Sol. He was the only person she completely trusted at the moment.

Still, she *wanted* to trust Ross. And did. Instinctively.

She kept telling herself, though, that he too had a motive to harm her. If she died, Sarah would have her share and there would be no question of a sale. But how would he know about her new will? For that matter, why would anyone try to run her off the road at this point? Had Alex called someone about the will? Or had someone been following them, someone who didn't know she'd left her share to Sarah?

Her head hurt with all the possibilities.

She needed to back away from all of them. She should go to the police. But then what would she say? What proof did she have? A box falling on her? Someone in too big a hurry on the road? Becoming lost? A "feeling" that her room had been searched? The burglaries back home were in a different jurisdiction.

And her suspects: a congressman, a banker, a respected rancher.

The police would laugh her out of the room. Or go after Ross.

He tipped her chin and looked into her eyes. "I can drive you and Ben to Phoenix tonight."

She was too tired and too sore to go anywhere. She shook her head. "I don't think so, but thanks."

He put an arm around her and headed her toward the

door. "I think you need a hot bath. And something to help you sleep."

"I already have that," she said with wry humor. "A prescription left over from my last visit here."

He didn't say anything until they got out to his pickup, then he helped her inside. "Why don't you and Ben stay with me tonight?" he said. "I have an extra room, and I'll be nearby."

It sounded like a very good idea. A marvelous idea, in fact. After her adventure in the attic, she no longer felt that safe in the main house. Why then did she feel she would be safe with him?

The simple fact was, she did.

When Ross settled his long body into the seat, he looked back at her. "Can you even take a guess as to who it might have been in the car?" he asked again.

She shook her head. She clutched her handbag closer to her. She'd tucked copies of the will inside. She wanted to tell him about it, but . . .

Her life was full of *but*s and *if*s. She hated it. For a moment, she even hated the Sunset.

"Could it have been Alex?"

"No, it wasn't that large a car," she said.

He was quiet then for a while, until they started along the curve where the bumping had started. "Where did it happen?"

"Probably about five miles from here. There's a dirt road to the left, leading to a house. I tried to turn in there, looking for help, but my car went into a spin and hit the fence. The air bag exploded, and then I don't know what happened. A couple came along in a truck like yours. That might have scared off whoever it was."

They rode in silence until they reached the spot. "There," she said, pointing to where part of a fence had been torn down. Rain had filled in the tread marks, and the dark rain-slicked road hid any skid marks. Her car was gone, apparently pulled out by a wrecker. She didn't even know where they would have taken it.

Suddenly, everything crowded in on her. So much to do. Accident reports. Car retrieval, no doubt a battle with the car agency and insurance company. And the feeling that she wouldn't feel comfortable driving alone again.

She felt something wet rolling down her cheek, and it wasn't rain. She moved over to the far side of the seat and looked blindly outside. She didn't want him to see the tears, to sense her fear, her bewilderment. Her sense of loss.

She was grateful for his silence.

Then he turned into the road to the Sunset. When they finally drove up to the house, he parked, then turned to her. "The Sunset's not worth it," he said harshly. "It's not worth your life."

"I made out my will at Alex's today," she said. "I left my share to Sarah. So it wouldn't benefit anyone if . . . something happened to me. It would go back to the status quo."

"Did anyone know what you planned to do?"

"No. I didn't even think about it until Alex suggested it."

His face was cloaked by the darkness. "There are copies?"

"He has one. I have two. I was going to keep one and mail the other to my partner in Atlanta. I left my share of the bookstore to him."

He moved closer to her and took her hand in his. "I don't know who would have tried to run you off the road. Or be responsible for the burglaries in Atlanta. I've had my problems with some members of this family, but I wouldn't have thought any of them capable of something like this."

"I considered going to the police, but there's no evidence of anything. I thought they might have stopped by the hospital to take a report."

"Not necessarily. Not if there wasn't evidence of another car involved. We'll report it in the morning."

"Would they believe me?"

He shrugged. "I don't know. Did anyone else see what happened?"

"I don't think so. I told you a couple stopped to help. They saw a car pass, but they didn't see it hit my car. And the car was pretty badly damaged when it went into the fence."

"Still, I think we need to notify them."

"They might blame you."

He chuckled mirthlessly at that. "I don't own a dark car."

"If I were to report it, I would merely be throwing suspicion on every member of the family. I couldn't do that, and then leave."

"What about the insurance?"

"I went into a skid."

He was silent.

"You don't agree."

"I don't know, Jess. I don't particularly care for the police. But I also don't like what's been happening."

"Damn," she said.

"Good. Now you're angry."

She wondered what prompted that remark. Had she looked cowed before? She tried to wipe away a tear before he saw it. "Rain," she tried to explain.

He merely nodded, accepting what she wanted him to accept. He got out of his side of the truck and went over to hers. She waited this time, in no rush to descend, to move, to revive that sharp pain in her chest. Then the door opened and he reached out with two strong hands, helping her down. The rain was cold and she shivered, even though it was midsummer.

"I'm going to take you to my house and put you in a bathtub," he said. "Then I'll get your dog and some clothes."

"Tell Sarah I'm all right."

"You damn well are not," he growled. "And someone's going to pay for it."

She tried to straighten, to walk alone, but she almost slipped in the grass. He put an arm around her and picked her up.

She'd read about a man picking up a woman as easily as a bag of groceries. She'd never quite believed it. She certainly never thought it would happen to her.

But neither had she ever thought that someone might intentionally try to kill her.

Her weight seem to have no effect on him and too soon they were inside his house. She felt instantly comfortable. Safe. She only hoped it wasn't an illusion.

Ross set her down carefully. Timber had been at the door and now he sniffed the mud on her clothes, then backed away.

"Oh, darn, I repulse a dog."

Ross chuckled. "Haven't lost your spunk, have you? That's what I like best about you."

She raised an eyebrow dubiously. "Because I don't run screaming when rejected by a dog?"

"No, because you don't let anything get to you."

She wasn't quite sure how much a compliment that was. It didn't say much about her femininity. She was shivering again, not quite sure whether it was because of a chill or the recent events.

He led her into a bathroom. It was larger than she would have expected in a ranch house, and she was even more surprised to discover it had a spa bath. She lowered her eyes to hide her surprise.

"After a long day in the saddle, it feels good," he explained, and she knew he didn't do that often.

He gave her a huge towel, turned on the water, then leaned down and grazed her cheek with his lips. Much to her chagrin, the tears started again, and he brushed them away. "Everything will be all right," he said. "I swear it."

Then he turned toward the door. "I'll get your clothes and Ben. Timber will stay here with you."

Guard her, he meant. She relaxed slightly. She would pit Timber against anyone.

The door closed behind her. She slipped out of her ruined clothes, then looked at herself in the mirror. A specter looked back at her. Her face was streaked with tears. Her hair had splatters of mud in it. Her midriff was already turning blue and purple from the blow of the safety bag. She looked dreadful. She closed her eyes and leaned against the sink.

After a moment, she straightened and sank into the bath.

Ross had never been so angry in his life, and he'd fought to keep it contained. He didn't want her to see it. He didn't want to frighten her more than she already was.

Those tears had nearly undone him. She'd not shed them when she was lost, nor when she told him about the rape. She'd been so damn determined and strong about everything that he had come to think of her as tough to the bone.

The vulnerability in those tears told him that she wasn't as strong as she wanted everyone to believe. He'd realized they hadn't come from fear as much as they had from the realization that someone she knew had tried to do major harm to her. It had been disillusionment, a crash from high expectations. He'd wanted to grieve with her, to share that personal agony.

His expectations had never been high. His disillusionment with life had been firmly instilled when he was little more that a toddler. But her illusions had apparently survived all her past had done to her. He didn't want them destroyed now.

He wanted to kill someone himself.

The lights were on inside the house, which meant Sarah was waiting up. He was surprised, in fact, that she hadn't already made it over to his place. The door was unlocked, as it usually was. He made a note that perhaps that should change. But then everyone in the family had a key.

Sarah was indeed up. She was sitting in a darkened part of the room. He was surprised that she hadn't stood. She was usually all energy. But now her face looked strained and white. Ben had been sitting next to her, but now he padded over to Ross, his tail wagging slowly, not with the enthusiasm that was normal. Perhaps he knew something was amiss.

"She wasn't badly hurt," he said. "Bruised ribs, a few other bruises." He paused. "It wasn't an accident. Someone forced her off the road at the curve near McNutley's place."

"Oh no," Sarah said, her face seemingly collapsing in on itself.

"She's going to stay at my place tonight," he said. "Since that attack in the attic, I don't think she feels entirely safe in the ranch house. At least at my house she has Timber to warn her."

Sarah's mouth twisted. "I had so wanted her to be happy here. I had hoped . . ."

"I don't know if she will want any part of the Clementses after this," he said, his voice hard. "I sure as hell wouldn't."

"Does she know who?"

"She only saw a blur of a dark car," he said. "Alex has that sports vehicle, which would be distinctive. Marc has a dark car, but so does Cullen and nearly every other member of the family."

"You don't think it's one of them?"

"Who else would have an interest?"

"Smith. The man trying to buy the Sunset."

"That's a hell of a stretch."

"I prefer that."

"I don't," he said bluntly. "You and I both know it's someone with a more direct connection."

"Who?"

"I don't know, but I sure as hell intend to find out."

"Are you going to the police?"

He watched her carefully. "What do you think?"

"I think we all have something to hide, but right now Jessie's safety is more important than anything."

"They could look back. A long way back."

Sarah's face paled.

"And it could wreck Marc's campaign. Not that I give a damn about him."

"But it wouldn't be fair, would it? If he's not involved."

"I don't care about fair as long as Jess is in danger."

"The police might well look at you, too."

"That's a given," he said wryly. "But I'm more worried about you."

She winced. "I never meant to put that burden on you."

"I know you didn't. But we have to be careful."

"Do you think it's the ranch? It's not worth Jessie's life. I'll sell it first."

"If that is what they're after, they've made a mistake."

"Why?"

"She made a will immediately. She left her share to you."

Sarah's mouth fell open. Then her eyes filled with tears.

"Classy lady, isn't she?" He said the words with pride.

"The book, then?" Sarah asked after a moment. "Could the attack have something to do with the book?"

"You said she didn't have it."

"I don't *think* she has it. I asked her if Harding had left her anything and she indicated he didn't."

His heart lurched. "Indicated?"

He watched as she struggled to remember exactly what Jessie had told her. Her face told Ross she couldn't.

"Well, we'll puzzle it out later. I'll talk to Jess and see what she wants to do in the morning."

"I would like to see her," Sarah said.

"She's exhausted and hurting. When I left, she was going to take a bath. I think it's best right now for her to rest. But could you get together whatever she might need in the morning?"

Sarah's face brightened at the prospect of doing something. Ross wasn't happy with the idea of her going upstairs when she looked so tired, but she needed something to do, a way to help. She didn't need to feel the guilt that he knew was building in her.

He went out to the kitchen for ice, then to the liquor cabinet and splashed a measure of bourbon into his glass. He sipped it, welcoming its warmth. He felt cold. So damned cold. Then he looked down into Ben's anxious brown eyes. He leaned down and ran his fingers through the dog's thick coat.

"We'll take care of her," he said.

He'd just finished the drink when Sarah appeared, a small suitcase in her hand. "I wanted her to love it here," she said.

"She does," he said. "That's why she voted the way she did. I don't think the last twenty-four hours has changed that. The Sunset is in her blood. I could see it today."

Sarah held out her hand to him, taking his in hers, clutching it. "Do whatever you must to protect her," she said. "I don't matter any longer."

"You matter a great deal," he said.

"Just remember what I said. Now take her things and the dog, and hurry back to her. She must be terrified."

"Not quite," he said. "Bewildered. A bit frightened. Angry. And, I think, sad that something she had so many hopes for is turning out to be a poisoned well."

Ben was reluctant to follow him. The house was the last place he'd seen his mistress. He apparently figured that was the place to which she would return. Ross finally shifted Jessie's suitcase to another hand, then picked him up, receiving an accusatory look for his pains. He liked the dog's loyalty.

The door to the bathroom was still closed when he and Ben arrived. The dog had run to it, obviously sensing that his mistress was inside. He whined, ignoring Timber, who rose from his guard post just outside.

Ross knocked. He wanted to make sure she was all right.

"Ross?" Her voice was far stronger than it had been a few moments ago.

"Yes. Can I open the door and let Ben inside? He's letting it be known it's what he wants."

Just then, Ben howled his dismay.

Then he heard a chuckle from inside. "Yep," she said.

He opened the door and Ben squeezed through immediately, barking ecstatically as he saw his mistress. Ross waited a moment until it was quiet, then told her that her clothes were in the spare room.

Ross closed the door and took her suitcase into the extra room, laying it on the bed. Then he went into the kitchen. He poured some water into a pot for tea. He wished he could do more, but she needed rest now. He glanced at the clock. It was already two.

He heard the bathroom door open, then the door to the spare room close. Several minutes later she came out. Her hair was damp from steam, and tendrils curled becomingly around her face. She was wearing a robe with a hint of a nightshirt underneath.

She found his big easy chair and folded her body inside. "Thank you," she said simply.

"You're welcome." He hesitated. "Do you want to talk about it? What you want to do?"

"About the police?"

"Yes."

She sighed. "If I was going to do something, I should have done it immediately. I didn't think anyone would believe me."

"I think they would," he said grimly. "At least, it would put them on notice."

"If anything else happens, you mean?"

He didn't like the way that sounded. But she was right.

"It could hurt Marc's campaign. Cullen's career. Your reputation. Whatever Sarah is hiding."

His head jerked back at that, and it took him several seconds before he asked, "What makes you think she's hiding something?"

"Your reaction just now."

He thought he'd been pretty quick. Apparently not quick enough.

He sat down on the arm of the chair. "Jess, this could be about the ranch. It could also be about those damned fifty-year-old bonds." He hesitated. "Do you know *anything?* Have you ever seen a book, a primer?"

Her eyes met his. They clouded. He knew she was weighing whether or not she could trust him. Hell, he wouldn't trust anyone in this family if he were she.

But she hesitated long enough that he knew.

She had the damned primer.

twenty-five

Jessie stared up at him. His face was creased with worry, his mouth in a tight thin line. She sensed a barely contained fury. He looked lethal.

Should she bank everything on him? Including her life? Give up her last ace? But then that ace had done her precious little good. Perhaps it was time that everything came out in the open. And if she couldn't trust him, if all her instincts were wrong, perhaps it was time to learn it now.

She certainly wasn't doing very well on her own. And she couldn't put Sol in danger, presumed or not. She was beginning to feel she was doing just that.

Ben was sitting at her feet. She patted her lap and he crawled up into it, one leg at a time, obviously uncertain whether it was permitted. Then he settled in her lap with a great sigh of contentment.

"Jess?"

"I have a primer," she finally said. "Seventeenth-century. But I've looked through it. I even had it appraised. There's nothing in it."

"You didn't tell Alex about it?"

"I haven't told anyone until now."

Surprise crossed his face. It disappeared quickly into a frown. "Why?"

"It's one of the few things my father gave me. He

wanted me to keep it safe. I didn't know it was important until recently, and then it was *too* important. Everyone wanted to know if my father left me anything. I just . . . well, I felt it was better to say nothing."

He shook his head in disbelief.

"I don't think it's the book everyone talks about," she added hurriedly. "I've looked through it many times. There's nothing in it. My partner looked at it. He said it was as clean a book for its age of any he's ever seen. And he knows books. I don't think it's the book Heath referred to."

Ross shrugged. "Maybe he never had time to put anything in it. I never put much stock in the tale, anyway. I didn't think anyone else in the family did, either. But then, it wasn't my treasure."

"If the bonds were found," she said, "wouldn't they be involved in the trust? Wouldn't they be split among the family?"

"I'm not a lawyer but I would think so," he said. "But that's only if someone admitted to finding them. Bearer bonds are just that. They belong to whoever has them."

"*If* they still exist," she said. "I still don't think there's a clue in the book."

"You said your home and business had been burglarized recently," he said. "Why wouldn't someone have found it if that was what they were looking for?"

She had decided to trust him. She might as well trust him all the way. Jessie knew she needed help. Wonderland had become a minefield.

"It's in a safe-deposit box."

He looked slightly dazed. Then he chuckled.

She didn't think the situation amusing at all. She scowled at him.

"I'm sorry," he said. "It's just that I doubt anyone thought about that."

"I think someone has," she said.

The amusement left his face. "What do you mean?"

"When the bookstore was burglarized, someone took an extra set of keys I kept in the desk. It had the key to the safe-deposit box."

"But they wouldn't know which bank."

"They could guess from my bank statements."

He pondered that for a moment. "No one would be able to get into it, though."

"I doubt it. Not unless I'm dead, but then I left my personal possessions, everything but the ranch, to Sol, my partner." She didn't say she'd changed the box.

"But he wouldn't know what he had," Ross said softly.

"I told him about the bonds, that there might be a clue in the book. He'd examined the book years ago and advised me to hold on to it, that it might be valuable some day, but neither of us saw anything unusual in it. One of the reasons he thought it could be worth something is the fact it was so clean."

"But obviously someone believes it will lead them to the bonds," Ross said.

She nodded, then looked up at him. "I thought I had found a perfect family."

His eyes met hers. "There is no such thing as a perfect family, Jess. And don't condemn the whole family for the actions of one person and, even then, we're guessing. There are some good people here. Sarah, Elizabeth, Halden, even April."

His comment surprised her. She knew he'd sought to stay separate from the family. His defense of them stunned her now. Was it for them? Or for her? Did he know how much she wanted the words to be true? "But is it just one? And if so, who?"

"I don't know," he said simply. "Marc would do almost anything to become senator, but murder . . . ?"

"And if I go to the police, it could ruin his career."

"Your life is worth more than his career," he said. "I'll go with you if you like."

"They could accuse you, too," she said. "They already think you were involved in shooting Marc." In fact, she thought, they would probably much rather pursue a former delinquent than a U.S. congressman.

"I don't care about that," he said.

"I do. There's absolutely no proof of a crime, except in Atlanta. And the police there couldn't care less about a simple burglary." She was quiet for a moment. "I need to get that book. Sol has a friend who is an expert in old school books. He was to be back this week. I want him to look at it."

"I'll go with you," he said. "I don't want you to be alone."

A warm feeling curled around inside her, chasing away the chill. "The ranch?"

"The ranch will be fine for a few days. Dan'l and the others can take care of the horses. Everything else can wait."

Her arms went around Ben, and she put her head against his fur. She needed time to think. How could she think in Ross's presence? She could scarcely hear him over the beat of her heart.

He stood, as if realizing too much had been thrown at her this day. "Sleep on it," he said. "You can tell me what you want to do in the morning."

Then he looked nonplussed. "I made some tea. I forgot about it."

"You? Tea?"

His lips crooked at the corner in a wry grin. "Only for you," he said.

"I'm honored. I'll take a cup."

"And I don't want you to worry. I'm leaving Timber outside your door."

"Now that really makes me feel safe."

"And I don't?"

"Fishing for compliments?"

He put a hand on her shoulder. "No," he said softly, all the affectionate amusement gone. "I just want . . . you—"

He didn't finish, but she liked it that way. She liked the sound of "I just want you." And she did feel safe with him. Secure. Happy, even.

Then he leaned down and kissed her again, softly. Protectively. It started to grow into something else. But then he stood, and she saw the struggle in his face. That muscle was jerking again.

"I'll bring the tea to your room." He offered his hand. Gratefully, she let Ross help her up. He put his arms around her for a fraction of a second, then let go when she winced. Even that gentle touch hurt the bruised ribs.

"Thank you," she said, realizing how many times she'd said those two words in the past few hours.

"Ah darlin', it was damned little."

Darlin'. She loved the sound of that. With the word echoing in her mind, she and Ben padded down the hall. She took off the robe and slipped into the bed with a sigh.

She felt safe. At the moment. But she couldn't help but wonder what tomorrow would bring, and what she had brought onto herself and, worse, onto her friends.

They made their plans the next morning, then told them to Sarah, who'd called and asked both of them to come to breakfast.

When Jessie accompanied Ross to the main house, Sarah was waiting. She came over to them, taking Jessie's hands in hers. "How are you? I wanted to come over last night, but Ross said you were exhausted and needed rest. I am so sorry. You'll never want to come back and . . ."

Jessie squeezed her hands. "I'm fine, Sarah, and I *will* come back."

Sarah blinked, then her gaze went to Ross, her eyes filling with tears. "I never wanted this to happen."

"I know," Jessie said. "It's not your fault." She gave Sarah a spontaneous hug. "We Clementses are made of stern stuff."

Sarah suddenly glowed. "That's the first time I've heard you say that, that you're a Clements."

"Ross has convinced me it's something worth fighting for," she said.

Ross coughed. "I remember hearing the word *break-fast.*"

"Of course," Sarah said, smiling fondly at her. "Rosa is making her famous French toast." Her eyes went from Ross to Jessie, then back again. "I want to hear everything that happened, but first, coffee."

She led the way into the dining room. It was already set. A steaming pot of coffee sat on the table. Sarah poured coffee into each of the cups, then sat down with them, her gaze never leaving Jessie. "What are you going to do now?"

Ross exchanged looks with Jessie. She nodded.

"Jessie has one of the primers. Her father gave it to her on her sixteenth birthday and told her to keep it safe."

Sarah started to rise, then sat back down. Her face had paled.

"But there's nothing in it," Jessie said. "I've looked through it."

"Someone must think it does, though," Ross said. "Her home and business have both been searched."

Sarah frowned. "She told me, but then . . ."

"She had the foresight to put it in a safe-deposit box."

"It's there now?"

"Yes," Jessie said. "Ross and I are flying to Atlanta today. I've called a friend. He's arranged for an expert to meet with us. At the bank."

She saw Ross and Sarah exchange glances. Quick. Apprehensive. Then Sarah nodded slightly. "Good," she said.

But Jessie saw something else in Ross's eyes. He obviously supported doing this, but he was afraid of something.

It was hard to think of him being afraid of anything.

The French toast came then, and fruit. Food to tempt an appetite dulled by fear and apprehension. And yet she felt stronger now than she'd ever felt before. She didn't intend to run and hide as she had in the past. She intended to confront.

ATLANTA, GEORGIA

The plane flew into smog as they approached Atlanta. The dirty air seemed to surround the plane.

Ross knew then and there that he could never be a city person. God, he hated what many called progress. He'd flown into other cities, of course, and Los Angeles was probably the worst among them, but this was bad enough. It always made him aware of how much he had, and how much he enjoyed the clean air and a sky unsullied by smoke and gases. But this was Jessica's city, her home, her life. She enjoyed the Sunset—that much was obvious. She could even possibly come to love it, but could she ever give up everything she had here?

He doubted it.

He leaned back and looked at Jess. She was sleeping in the seat next to his at the back of the cabin. They had gotten the last seats available and traded someone else to sit together. It had been decided to leave Ben with Sarah, since they intended to return. Dan'l would look after Timber.

At least she was getting some sleep. Her eyes had been bloodshot this morning, and he knew she hadn't slept well. He doubted he would have, had he known someone might well have tried to murder him.

They had spent the morning with paperwork on the rental car, then were able to catch an afternoon flight into Atlanta. She had called her friend in Atlanta and discovered that the book expert was back in town. They'd set up an appointment for the next morning. She'd also warned her friend to be careful.

Her eyes, when they'd looked at him last night, had been frightened yet determined. He'd known then that he had to do everything he could to help her. Even if it did put Sarah in jeopardy. And Sarah herself had been adamant. She was an old woman. Nothing mattered now except Jessie. Not her. Not the ranch. Not even the family. The latter was a measure, he knew, of how much Sarah had taken Jessica into her heart. It was far more, he knew, than atonement for past sins.

The pilot came on the intercom, warning passengers to fasten their seat belts and put their seats in the upright position. She woke at that, and her fingers inched over to find his. He found it remarkable how much he liked that feeling, the trust that had been building between them.

He wondered only briefly if it would survive his own secrets.

Then they were landing.

A half hour later, they'd picked up her car from a car valet lot. Despite her lingering soreness she suggested that she drive since she knew the way, and he'd agreed. She knew the city and his manhood did not depend on driving.

Her house, a small brick cottage, sat amid a profusion of trees and flowers. The garden was well-tended and boisterous with color. He felt immediately at home as she led the way inside. A number of carousel horses decorated the white mantel of a brick fireplace. Bookcases were everywhere, and the furniture had obviously been purchased with comfort in mind. The kitchen was bright with yellow curtains and copper pans. Hanging baskets of flowers separated the living room from the dining room. There were traces of dog—a few toys scattered on the floor, a water dish. Otherwise, it was spotless.

"Your bedroom is this way," she said, leading to a room down the hall on the left. She appeared awkward with the words. He would have much rather have shared a bed with her, but they were both tired and she must still hurt from the accident. He'd insisted, however, that he wasn't going to let her out of hearing range, even if he had to sleep on the floor. Fortunately, she did have a guest room, one that had never been used. "It's about time it was initiated," she'd told him.

Her ease with the idea of his staying pleased him. More than pleased him. He knew, though, that it would be plain hell to be in such close proximity to her. It had been last night, and only her obviously fragile condition had kept him from her. Even now she walked with a stiffness that worried him.

The guest room was as comfortable as the rest of the house. A handmade quilt covered a double bed. A rocking chair sat in a corner and a dresser in another. He hung up his clothes, then went to join her in the living room.

"I have some beer and a bottle of wine," she offered.

"A beer sounds great," he said. "Can I take you somewhere for supper?"

She grinned. "I know a perfect place."

He looked down at his jeans. "Do I need to change?"

"Nope."

She disappeared into the kitchen and fetched him a beer and herself a small glass of wine. They were both tired from a morning dealing with the authorities and the long plane trip back with a three-hour change of time.

He took off his shoes and put them up on a footstool and took the bottle. "Ah, a woman with good taste. Are you going to tell me anything more about where we're going?"

"No more than you told me about the cantina."

His brows furrowed together. "We can order a pizza. Are you sure you feel up to going out?"

"Yep, I have my second wind."

"It's not the second wind, it's those ribs I worry about."

"It's better. It really is. The one thing that will really make me better is finding out why everyone seems to want that book. Sol and his friend will meet us at the bank tomorrow at ten. It's open on Saturday morning. Then perhaps . . ."

He hesitated for a moment, then asked quietly. "You may discover things you don't really want to know."

"Such as evidence that my father killed his brother? And his wife?"

He didn't say anything.

"I think I would rather know."

He regarded her for a few moments, then nodded. He could tell her what happened, but it had never been his secret to tell. Not yet. And despite her words, he wasn't sure she really did want to know. But then would she ever forgive him for withholding the truth?

He finished the beer. "I'll wash up."

"Meet you back here in five minutes," she said.

"Five minutes?" He raised an eyebrow.

"I'm fast. And hungry."

He was, too. "I'll be here."

Jessie found herself slowly relaxing at the restaurant. It was a little Italian hole-in-the-wall restaurant with wall murals its only ambience. She loved the place and knew all the people who worked there. They had great shrimp scampi, which she ordered, and wonderful salads that came along with the meal. It was about as different from the Italian restaurant in Sedona as a hamburger joint was to a New York steakhouse.

She'd known he would like it. It was utterly without pretense, just as he was.

When he was finished, he sighed. "I like your choice," he said. He watched as the last customers left, leaving only them behind.

"I thought you would," she said. "Wait till tomorrow, and you'll have the best pizza ever made."

His steady gaze met hers. "You love Atlanta, don't you?"

She knew what he meant. "It's the only home I ever really had. My . . . father moved around a lot. We never really had a home of our own. A trailer or a tenant's home on a horse farm. Then a college dorm. The cottage . . . is my first real home. And Sol, well, he gave me something else of my own. You'll see it tomorrow." She heard the pride in her own voice.

His dark eyes were hard to read now. But his hand reached out and took hers. "And Sedona?"

"I was coming to love it, too," she said.

Was.

"I can't say I blame you," he said.

"It's not that. Remember, things happened here, too. It's just that what I have here I earned. I can't feel that way about the Sunset. I don't think I'll ever really feel that I deserve any part of it."

"Is that why you voted the way you did?"

"Partly. Another part was Sarah. And then there's the environmentalist in me. I can't bear to see that land transformed into a golf course and cookie-cutter houses."

None of it was what he wanted to hear, that perhaps one day she would make it her home, that he might have also been a factor in her decision. Then he realized that he shouldn't want that at all. She obviously hated all the deception whirling about her. How would she feel when she heard his part of it?

"And if you find nothing in the book?"

"Then I'll take it to Aunt Sarah when I go back for Ben.

She can show everyone that there is nothing in the damn thing."

He grinned at her profanity and she winced. "I try not to do that," she said.

"Then I'm surprised, since you were raised around racing stables."

"I've tried to overcome that," she said, not wanting to add how badly she'd wanted to be considered a lady then, not just "Jon's brat."

"I know the feeling," he said.

"Did *you* try?"

"No. I often wished I were someone else," he said slowly. "But no, I didn't try to be. Instead, I tried to rub everyone's nose in what I was. I wasn't a very nice kid."

"I think you were a lot better than you thought."

"I always got in fights," he contended.

"And I bet a lot of them weren't your fault."

"Do you always see the best in everyone?"

"I don't think so," she said. "I'm usually pretty cautious. But I can't see you as a bully. If you fought, it was because you were forced into it."

"Oh yeah," he said. "I wanted to show the world I wasn't Apache trash, or a bastard. I ended up proving I was both," he said wryly.

"Was that before or after you came to live with Sarah?"

"Both. Perhaps it was even worse when I came to the Sunset. I hated my father for what he'd done to my mother. I also bitterly resented Sarah. And I hated the Sunset because it and my father were tied together in my mind."

He hesitated, then continued slowly, "It took me a long time to realize Sarah had been a victim, too. My father broke Sarah's heart and she still took me in. I couldn't understand that. I always thought I would be booted out, and I was going to get myself booted out before someone did it to me. I finally learned there's no good excuse for bad behavior."

"She told me you fell in love with the horses."

"Yes," he said simply. She knew from his face that there was a lot more to it than that.

But it was enough that he had told her that much. It took trust, she knew. The same kind of trust she had given him in telling him about the rape.

He apparently thought it was enough. He rose. "Time to go."

She nodded. He had already paid the bill, and the servers were placing chairs up on tables and eyeing them hopefully.

He waited for her, and she caught his hand with her fingers. Her hands tingled with the contact, and she looked up at him just as he looked down. The heat was explosive, the attraction irresistible.

The lingering pain in her ribs seemed to fade. Too many other reactions were rocking her body.

Outside, he took the keys from her. She sat close to him as he drove, her gaze seldom leaving him. Under the streetlights, she could see his face, sharply chiseled from a side angle. His long body looked uncomfortable in her driver's seat, but he handled the wheel with complete confidence. Unlike Jessie, who would laughingly tell friends she'd get lost in her own driveway, he apparently remembered every complicated twist and turn to her house.

She'd been too shaken last night to worry about her proximity to him. She should be exhausted now, but she was alert, every sense aware and wanting. She swallowed hard, feeling the breath catch in her throat. She wanted him in more ways than she could assimilate at the moment.

He was quiet on the way back to her house. Yet she sensed his own tension. They had pulled down barriers tonight, had relaxed, and yet . . . he was still holding something back, and she didn't know whether it was part of himself or part of the puzzle that continued to elude her.

She wasn't sure which she preferred, or would dislike the least.

When they reached the cottage, she hopped out and opened the gate. She regarded the house carefully, which she'd done since the day she encountered the burglar. She wondered whether she would ever look at it the same again, and she felt a rising anger about that undeniable fact.

And with that, she realized that she *did* feel safe with Ross, safer in fact than she'd ever felt in her life. *Please God, don't let it be a mistake.*

He followed her into the house, and she thought how strange it was not to have Ben barking joyously. She would call in the morning to make sure he was all right. Before they looked at the book. No, that would be too early.

She turned on the lights while Ross checked every room before coming back. He leaned over and kissed her, his arms resting easily on her shoulders. Then his mouth moved to her ear. "I've been wanting to do that all evening."

The sensation of light breath in her ear scrambled what senses she had left. Her arms went around his neck and she licked his right ear, finding it irresistibly salty. Then, simultaneously, their lips moved, met and courted. Asking. Answering. Agreeing.

She led him to her bedroom and in seconds they'd stripped each other. Their bodies melded together. He was extraordinarily gentle, careful of every touch, watching her face to make sure he didn't unintentionally hurt her. His fingers soothed over the bruise on her chest. "I should go," he whispered. "I don't want to hurt you."

"No." She held her own hand and drew him down on the bed, her hands touching, caressing the skin drawn tightly over muscle and bone. She felt him shudder, and her own skin was alive with feeling, the core of her a mass of writhing nerve ends.

"I didn't ask to stay with you for this reason," he said harshly.

"I know," she replied, leaning over and running her tongue over his chest.

A low rumble came from deep in his throat, but the sound died as he kissed her. She felt as though she were whirling through the universe. Then he guided her down and he lowered himself, teasing her first with his body until she was almost mad with wanting him. When she thought she couldn't stand it any longer, he entered, deep and throbbing. But there was a gentleness about it, too, a caring that made her melt inside. He moved inside her like a dance of love, each stroke designed to prolong pleasure, to inflame new sensations and feelings until she burst with white-hot splendor . . .

twenty-six

They met Sol and his friend, Ames Fuller, at the bank when it opened at ten. Sol had arranged for Rob, their Emory student who worked part-time, to tend the bookstore.

After the introductions, Sol and Ross eyed each other a little warily.

"Jessie's told me a little about you," Sol told Ross. Then he looked at her face, which she felt growing hot. "But probably," he added, "not enough."

Ross held his hand out. "She told me you were like a father to her."

"Ouch," Sol winced. "I like a young uncle instead. I hope you'll come over and see the store after this. We're proud of it."

"I would like that," Ross said.

"When are you leaving?" Jessie heard just a touch of proprietorship in Sol's voice.

"I don't know. I suppose it depends on what your friend finds."

"I don't think he'll find anything. I've looked at the book before."

Ross shrugged, his eyes enigmatic. She wondered what he really thought about the book. She wondered what he really thought about her. She'd felt so warm and wonderful last night and again in the morning when she woke up next to him. But then he was silent this morning, detached again, and she couldn't help but wonder whether it had anything to do with the book and what it might reveal. Why would that bother him?

She cleared her head of the thoughts. She was imagining things.

"This is very unusual," Ames Fuller said. "I don't know if I can determine anything without examining it in laboratory conditions."

"I don't want to know about its authenticity," Jessie said. "But perhaps you can find something unusual about it. Markings. Some kind of code. My uncle indicated that he may have left a message in it."

"A message from the grave?" Ames said, his interest obviously piqued.

"Something like that," she said.

She went to a bank official and told him they needed to use the little anteroom off the safe-deposit boxes. Then she retrieved the book from the box, turning it over in her hands. The binding was intact, although the cover was faded. She held it for a moment before turning to the inside cover.

A childishly scrawled name was barely legible. She'd not paid attention to it before, because she'd known the book must have passed through many generations. But now she stared at it, trying to decipher the signature. Clayton? Clements? Definitely Clements now that she knew what to look for. She thumbed through the rest of the book. No other obvious marks.

"Daddy," she whispered. "Why did you want me to keep this?" There had to be a reason. Her father had not been sentimental. He'd apparently cut every tie to his family. So why this?

She closed the door to the box, then gingerly carried the book to the anteroom.

Sol and Ames Fuller were seated. Ross, on the other

hand, was leaning against the wall, looking for all the world like an unhappily caged mountain lion. Lithe strength. Restless energy. He ran his fingers through his hair as his gaze rested on the book in her hand, then up to her face. "The legendary book," he said softly. "I really didn't think it still existed."

"Oh, it exists," Sol said wryly. "The question is whether it's more than a primer."

Jessie handed it to Ames, watching as his hands touched it reverently. It was quite obvious he loved old books. Then she looked over at Ross. She thought she saw apprehension flit through his eyes, and she suddenly wondered if she *was* opening Pandora's box, that perhaps there were secrets meant to remain exactly that. She shook off a sudden chill. How could truth hurt?

Ames studied the signature, then ran his fingers along the binding. Then he started to leaf through the pages carefully.

Jessie had the worst craving to chew on her fingers, to do something. Sol glanced over at her, understanding in his eyes. Then they narrowed as they moved toward Ross. He obviously hadn't decided whether Ross was friend or foe. Or perhaps he worried that she would leave Atlanta. And the bookstore.

Each page was studied. Jessie looked down at her watch. An hour.

Still, Ross stood. She sensed that he wanted to pace but feared that doing so might ruin Ames Fuller's concentration.

Then Ames reached the back of the book, and his fingers ran up and down the inside back cover. She noticed that the inside back cover was backed by darker paper than the inside front. But it looked natural to her. It was certainly faded.

But his hands hovered there, feeling it, fingers running over it. "This isn't original paper," he said. "It's meant to look like it, but the texture is different." He closed his eyes, his fingers going over it again. "I think there's something under it. Most people wouldn't feel it because the back is slightly cracked."

She glanced back at Ross. He was staring at the book as if it were a rattlesnake. Her heart suddenly lurched. He was worried about something. That was obvious.

But she had to know what had been secreted in the book. "Can you look behind it?" she asked.

"I'd prefer not to do it here," Ames said. "We could devalue the book or even destroy whatever might be there. I want to work on it at my studio."

Jessie didn't care about the value of the book, but she did care about whatever secrets it might hold. She wanted an end to the mystery, to the danger, to the uncertainty. "Can we go with you?"

He looked at his watch. "I have another appointment. I won't be able to get to it until later this afternoon."

Sol looked at her. "Why don't we let him take the book and then meet him at his studio at four this afternoon?" He looked at Ames. "Will that give you time to work on it?"

The man nodded.

Jessie wasn't sure whether she wanted to let the book out of her sight, but Sol trusted Ames completely. And no one knew he was involved with them. In fact, it would probably be safer with him than with her. Reluctantly, she agreed.

Ames carefully put the book in his briefcase and locked it.

"I don't think you should walk out with us," Sol said. "We'll go first."

"Does someone want this book?" Ames asked.

"We don't know for sure, but it's best not to take chances."

Ames looked more interested than frightened. "I'll go out the side entrance several minutes after you do."

Jessie, Ross, and Sol walked outside.

"I told Ross I would introduce him to the world's best pizza. Would you like to come?"

Sol's eyes clouded. "No, I don't think so. I need to get back."

"Sol," she said softly. "I know I've really been gone a lot. I'm sorry. As soon as we know about the book . . ."

"No," he said. "If anyone deserved to take some time, you do. You've held down the fort for years while I've been roaming. Take as much time as you like." He hesitated. "But I do want you back."

Jessie looked at Ross. Remembered how she'd felt last night in his arms. But he'd said nothing about the future. He'd said nothing about love. And today he'd been almost a stranger. He'd retreated back into his private cave.

"I'll be back," she said. "Next week for sure."

Sol looked at Ross for a moment, then back to her, and she sensed he wanted to say something. But, instead, he turned away toward the other end of the parking lot.

His attitude puzzled her. Sol had always urged her to have a social life, had even tried his hand at matchmaking. Yet it was obvious he had reservations about Ross.

She got into the driver's seat of her car, Ross in the passenger side, and she drove out of the lot onto the main road. A car pulled out behind them. Don't get paranoid, she told herself.

Yet, she reminded herself, she had every reason to be paranoid.

She looked in the rearview mirror as she drove toward the strip shopping center where her shop shared space with the pizza restaurant. Just as she was beginning to relax, she noted a dark sedan that looked familiar. She made another twist, going somewhere few other drivers would follow, through a grocery store parking lot, then continuing through a residential neighborhood. No dark sedan. But when she looked several moments later, it was there again.

She only hoped that Ames didn't have a tail, too.

Tail. She was beginning to feel like a character in a book, and not one as benign as *Alice in Wonderland.* She wondered whether someone had followed them last night as well. She felt a shudder roll through her body.

"Someone *is* following us," she said.

He swore under his breath. "Then whoever tried to run you down probably has hired someone here."

She remembered that first burglary, the man in the ski mask. The terror. The violation of her sanctuary. She nodded. "But who?"

He didn't answer. She made another turn and ended up in a driveway that wound to the back of her store. "The pizza place is next door. It's loud . . . a student hangout, but the food is good."

He didn't get out right away. "Are you all right?"

"Fine," she said. It was her usual answer to the question. But then she realized she wasn't fine at all. She was angry. Very, very angry. "No," she corrected. "I'm not fine. I'm mad as hell."

He gave her a long stare. "Good," he said. "Now maybe you'll be careful."

He followed her into the restaurant, and she was relieved to see so many people there. She felt safe in a crowd. Still, she asked for a section where she could keep an eye on the door. She wanted to see who came in. She knew she would memorize every face.

Ross wolfed down the pizza. Alex, she recalled, had liked it, too, but he'd been more concerned with business. Business that had turned her world upside down. She couldn't help but think how everything had changed in little more than a month. A family. An inheritance. Danger. And Ross.

Life had been so simple then. She hadn't realized how simple. And safe. She wondered whether she would turn back the clock if she could, and realized instantly she wouldn't. You never won anything if you didn't take risks.

It had taken her until now to discover that. She hadn't really lived until now. She'd just marked time.

If only she knew the source of the risks.

She took a bite of the pizza and thought of Alex again. Could he have anything to do with this? He knew where she lived. The burglary happened only three days before he'd showed up on her doorstep. Perhaps he'd been there longer than he'd said. She tried to remember the burglar. He'd been tall, bulkier than Alex, but that could be deceptive.

Where had he been when she'd been run off the road near Sedona ? She'd just left him. He could have climbed back into his car and followed her. But her assailant had been driving a car, not a sports vehicle.

"Jess?" Ross's expression was concerned.

She fought to keep her expression neutral, then she rested her elbow on the table and used her hand to prop her chin. "Something is worrying you," she said, "and it's connected to the book." She paused. "I know you said that whatever you're withholding doesn't involve me, that it's not your secret to divulge." She continued in a spurt of words, "But whatever is connected to that book occurred fifty years ago. How can it hurt anyone today?"

A muscle in his cheek twitched, but he didn't say anything. He didn't deny it. And that hurt. She wanted to trust him completely, to wash away that last lingering doubt. Not that he would hurt her. She wouldn't be here if she believed that. But he was playing some part in this, and that small missing piece could possibly complete the picture.

She pushed away her plate. She realized he wasn't going to answer.

Maybe this afternoon she would have her own answers.

The waiter came with the bill. Frustrated with him and determined to show her independence, she reached for her handbag. Ross shook his head and had a credit card out before she could dig down deep enough for her wallet. As she started to protest, he silenced her with a question. "Have you seen anyone?"

Startled, she replied, "What do you mean?"

"Your eyes have been glued to the door. See anyone who looked interesting?"

She shook her head.

"They're missing great pizza then. You were right. I've never tasted better."

"Don't do that," she said.

He looked puzzled. "Don't do what?"

"Don't think you can change the subject so easily."

He didn't reply. Instead, he looked out the window until the server returned with his card. He signed the receipt and stood.

She watched his face carefully, then stood stiffly. "Would you like to see the shop?" she asked.

His expression lightened and he seemed to relax. "Yes," he said simply.

Avoiding any contact with him, she stood and led the way to her store next door.

He had known the questions were going to come up again. She couldn't let it go. But then he probably wouldn't be able to, either. Still, he hated that doubt in her eyes. He particularly despised himself for being unable to alleviate some of her fear. If only . . .

But there were no *if onlys*. He had no options. He'd come to Atlanta with her because he wanted her safe, but also because he knew she was going after that damned book. He had to know what was in it, to limit, if possible, the damage. He knew he was endangering any future with her, but how could he build anything on the funeral pyre of someone he loved?

Apprehension twisted his stomach as he followed her into the bookstore next door to the restaurant. Events were moving downward like an avalanche. He just didn't know who was going to be swept down with them.

He did know he wasn't eager to see Sol again. He'd felt the man's antipathy and knew he'd seen something he didn't like, that he'd sensed that Ross wasn't being entirely honest. The fact that Sol was right didn't help at all.

The shop was narrow, with books lining both walls and every available inch of space. He saw Jess visibly relax as she entered and headed toward the back, where Sol sat. Halfway across the store, a young man was unpacking volumes. Jess stopped, stooped, and looked at them, her hands running over the books, and he felt the outsider, a role he'd felt so many times before. This was *her* place. Her *world.*

The Clementses had torn apart everything it represented, everything she'd had before Sarah had launched her search for her brother. Jess had been happy. Content. Safe. Most of all, safe.

A lump filled his throat. She obviously loved this shop, and Atlanta, as much as he loved every inch of the Sunset. Sol knew that.

Sol stood and came over to him. "Forgive the musty smell," he said.

"I like it," Ross said simply.

Sol looked a little surprised.

Ross wanted to say something sharp, something like, "I do read." He wondered whether Sol *wanted* to think of him as little more than an illiterate cowboy because then he wouldn't be a threat. He could literally feel Sol's protectiveness.

And he had reason for it, Ross thought as he tried to mask his uneasiness. No one had been honest with Jess, not even him. Damn. He wasn't used to worrying about people. And now he was nearly frantic with worry about two people with conflicting needs. How could he sacrifice one for the other?

He looked at his watch. Three more hours. Three more

hours before they discovered whether there were answers to a fifty-year-old mystery. An ugly mystery. A tragic mystery that could have tragic consequences.

Jessie seemed to notice his discomfort. "I'll show you around a bit more," she said. Then turned to Sol. "Will you be there this afternoon?"

"I wouldn't miss it," he said.

She nodded. "Be careful. I think we were followed."

"Rob will be here with me," he said, "and he'll tend the shop this afternoon."

She leaned over and kissed him on the cheek. "Thank you for everything," she said.

Sol had at least thirty years on Jessie, but Ross still felt a knot of jealousy bunch in his gut. He knew it was as much for her life here as it was the man himself. Then he harnessed it as he'd harnessed such feelings in the past, fencing them in someplace where they couldn't hurt. Much.

Ames Fuller's studio was in the basement of a large, rambling Victorian house in an old residential section of Atlanta. The street was full of restored homes with stained-glass windows and elaborate gingerbread trim. She realized immediately, however, that Ames's home was protected by a state-of-the-art security system. A high, ornate wrought-iron fence surrounded the house, and the gate featured an intercom. Only a buzzer would admit a visitor.

She knew why. Ames had a priceless collection of old books and he often sold them from his home.

Jessie was sure they had lost anyone who might have tried to follow them. Ross had driven this time, twisting and turning, shooting through yellow lights. With her directions, he'd even circled through the nearby zoo's labyrinthine roads, emerging out of one of its seldom-used service roads. But she took one last look around. No dark sedan.

She pressed the button, identified herself, and was buzzed in. Someone could probably climb the fence, but the windows had the kind of wrought-iron work that substituted for iron bars.

Jessie felt her heart pound as she was admitted by Ames, who had a satisfied smile on his face. Sol was already there. He looked worried.

"I found what you were looking for," Ames said. "Come with me."

He led the way downstairs to a room flooded with powerful recessed lighting. One wall was lined with bookcases made of some kind of metal and protected by thick glass cases. Inside were leather-bound volumes.

A worktable sat in the center of the room, a stool in front of it. She saw her book there. It was open at the back, a piece of parchment-type paper next to it, along with the back inside cover page of the book.

Ames picked up the thin parchment. "I found this under the cover," he said. "It's so thin no one would notice it unless they had reason to look." He paused. "It had your name on it, so I didn't read it."

A kind of dread, an inevitability, filled her. She wasn't sure now that she wanted answers. She looked at Ross. His face was tense.

She picked up the letter. The ink was fading, but she recognized her father's scrawl. She had to strain to read it. He'd never been good at penmanship. A lump settled in her throat as she remembered how difficult it had often been to decipher his writing.

Jessica,

I don't know whether you will find this letter. Part of me wishes you will. Another . . . well, you'll understand when I finish.

I had hoped you would never need to sell this book. Since you've found this letter, I suppose you did. Only a dealer would notice the back cover. And so I am, finally, leaving you a legacy.

It is a mixed one, for at last you will know your true roots and the events that led me to abandon them. Please do not judge me harshly.

Your real name is Clements. I was one of six children born to Hall and Mary Louise Clements in the Sedona area of Arizona. I helped manage the family ranch until 1950, when I discovered that one of my brothers, Heath, had stolen family money and planned to leave Arizona with my wife. I won't justify what happened next. I found them in our family's cabin. I had a rifle with me, and I threatened to use it. He tried to take it. It went off, and the bullet hit him in the heart. Lori, my wife, attacked me, accused me of murder. I pushed her away. She fell and hit her head on the stone fireplace. She was unconscious when I left, but I knew she would go to the police. I couldn't think of anything but running.

One of the two people I loved most was dead; the other hated me. I feared the family's reaction, the humiliation and scandal I had brought to them. To be honest, I also feared the law. I couldn't bear the thought of a cage.

My brother had used the stolen money to buy bearer bonds—and a partnership—in a new company. Before he died, Heath told me he'd hidden the bonds and that the location could be found in the primer. When I left the cabin, I picked up his briefcase on the way out, knowing I would need money and suspecting he had some of the stolen money with him. Instead, I found the book.

The bonds had no value then, and I discounted the possibility that they would ever have any. Then several years ago I happened to hear someone mention the name of the company and I realized it had succeeded beyond anyone's dreams. I've been following its progress ever since, and I expect those bonds are now worth a great deal of money.

I discovered the location of the bonds on the inside of

the back cover. They are buried under the hearth of the fireplace in the family cabin at Oak Creek. There is a loose stone there, a cache where Heath and his twin and I used to hide treasures.

I wish I'd had the courage to tell you earlier, but I could never force myself to reveal the truth about your father, to see even more disappointment in your eyes. I allowed the days to go by. And now, coward that I am, that I have always been, I know I'll never have the words . . .

Perhaps some day you will find this letter and return to the family what belongs to them. I know Heath meant them to have the money.

I leave it to you to redeem both of us.

And forgive me.

Always remember, I loved you.

> *Jon Clayton (Harding Clements)*
> *April 1988*

Jessie stared at the date. It was the month she'd turned sixteen. He must have written it before he'd given it to her on her birthday. The line on the page blurred from the sudden moisture in her eyes. Then she read it again. *One of the two people I loved most was dead; the other hated me.*

But Lori died that day. Had her father been mistaken? And he said nothing about a fire. If his brother had died of a rifle bullet, then wouldn't a coroner have discovered it, and called it by an ugly name? Murder?

Her father wasn't very old then. A little younger than she was now. She couldn't even imagine what had gone through his mind that day. The panic. Fear. Grief. Betrayal.

She felt that grief now. She wished she'd known. Maybe she could have done something . . .

"Jess?" Ross's voice. She felt the concern in it.

Wordlessly, she handed it to him.

She watched his face as he read it. No surprise there. Her heart sank precipitously. She wanted surprise. Shock.

It would have been there if he'd not already known at least a good part of the story. But there was none. He'd known about her father. He'd known that he had killed his brother. He'd known that Harding had left his wife alive.

She struggled for an explanation. Perhaps her father had been wrong. Perhaps Lori had died from the fall. But then what of the fire? Surely since her father was confessing murder, he would have confessed to it all.

Not my secret to tell. Ross's words.

Yet it was the key to much that had happened. It had to be. Betrayal ate at her. She almost doubled up with the pain of it. Ross had known she suspected that her father could have murdered both his brother and wife. Instead, it had been an accident, and he'd left his wife alive. And Ross *knew.*

What else did he know?

Bile rose in her throat and she fought to keep it down, to maintain her composure, to do what had to be done, to accomplish what her father had wanted.

She turned away from him, freezing him with the icy shock she herself felt. She took the letter from him and passed it to Sol. She had no secrets from him, and he was involved now since the store had been burglarized.

When he finished, his eyes flickered from her to Ross and back again. His lips thinned and she knew he'd picked up on her feelings. "Is there anything I can do?" he asked gently.

She shook her head and took back the letter. She stared at it blindly, fighting to keep tears at bay.

She turned to Ames, who was watching curiously. "Can you make a copy of this?"

He nodded. He took the fragile sheet of paper and disappeared, returning shortly with the original and copy.

She put the original in the book and handed it to him.

"The bank is closed. Will you keep the book for me for a few days?"

"Of course," he said. "I'll put it in my vault."

She reached out her hand, hoping it wasn't trembling. "Thank you. You've been extraordinarily kind."

"It's been a pleasure. But in return, I ask that you tell me the ending of this story."

"I will," she promised. Then she gave Sol a hug. He clasped her tight, and she knew he sensed her tumultuous feelings. The grief for her father. For his regret. His lost years. Then the anger. The sense of betrayal. Betrayal from all of them. All of her so-called family who'd kept so much from her. Even Ross. She'd given him all her trust. He'd given her none.

She carefully folded up the letter. She would reread it. Again and again.

She didn't look at Ross. She wanted to be alone, to grieve by herself for a man she'd never really known.

But she couldn't do that. She couldn't leave him in the middle of a city he didn't know. Instead, she put the folded paper into the pockets of her slacks. She wanted it on her. Then she nodded to the men and walked toward the door. Ross fell in next to her, matching stride for stride. But she didn't want to look at him. She didn't want him to see how wounded she was.

"Would you like me to drive?" he asked at the car.

"No," she said shortly.

She did look at him then. His dark eyes were steady. His mouth was grim. A muscle flexed in his cheek. That was always the only sign that he felt anything. But he didn't say anything more. No excuse. No explanation. Did he even know what he had given away by his silence?

She didn't know. She only knew there was one more person she could no longer trust.

twenty-seven

Ross didn't say anything on the way back to her house. He knew what he'd just lost in those few seconds. He knew he'd lost the trust, the closeness that had developed between them. He'd seen comprehension dawn in her eyes when he'd stopped reading the letter.

And he had no defense. He couldn't say why he'd withheld information she'd wanted so badly, because then he would be betraying someone else. He'd thought his heart immune to wreckage. It wasn't. He consoled himself with the fact that he hadn't been tossed out on the street. At least, she realized he wouldn't harm her in any physical way.

He turned slightly and watched her. He also occasionally glanced backward. No dark sedan. They'd definitely thrown whoever had been following them. *If* they had been followed.

He looked at her, at her set face, the chin jutting forward in that determined way of hers. She wouldn't look at him, and when she did her eyes were like ice. He'd not seen that side of her before. It was formidable. It said, "Don't touch, don't approach."

He had no idea how to do either. He accepted that she wanted him to leave her alone, just as he accepted that he could not. She was probably in more danger than ever. If whoever wanted those bonds knew she had the information leading to them, she would be a prime target. Damn it all to hell.

They arrived at her cottage at close to seven. Atlanta traffic had consumed nearly an hour and a half. He didn't know how she tolerated it, the traffic and the smog that hovered over the city. He already longed for the clean skies of northern Arizona.

They got out of the car. The air was muggy and hot. Great bulbous clouds filled the sky, and he smelled the coming rain. The denseness of the air seemed to heighten the aroma of the garden, spreading the sweet scent of magnolia and lilies and other flowers he didn't recognize.

The garden was visible evidence of her affection for the house, for this place she'd made her own. He hated the way she hesitated at the door, as if her one haven had been irretrievably spoiled. He saw her glance apprehensively up and down the street.

Nothing. No suspicious cars. No suspicious people.

Ross took the house key from her and motioned for her to let him go in first. He checked all the rooms. Nothing seemed disturbed. He appreciated the fact that she didn't ask if such precautions were necessary. She'd simply accepted that they were. Nor did she quarrel with his self-appointed role of protector. She didn't seem to notice him at all, in fact. She had tuned him out as completely as he'd done to others.

When he'd satisfied himself that everything was as they had left it, he joined her in the living room. "What do you plan to do now?"

She looked at him with cool eyes. That hurt more than angry ones would. "What do *you* think I should do?"

He stilled. There was a coldness about the question. Even an accusation.

He knew what he *wanted* her to do. Burn the goddamn book and the letter. The Clementses didn't need an opening of an investigation of a murder—murders—fifty years earlier. There was no statute of limitations on murder.

"Whatever you think should be done," he finally said. "It's your call."

"It's my father's call. He wanted the money returned."

"All right. How do you want to start? Go to the police?"

She looked up at him. "You don't want that, do you?" Her eyes had narrowed.

"It's the safest way to handle it."

"You didn't answer my question."

"No," he said flatly.

"No, you didn't answer my question, or no, you don't want me to go to the police?"

He shrugged. "No, I'm not going to answer that question."

"Because of Sarah?"

He turned away.

She persisted. "She was involved in some way, wasn't she?"

"Only in making sure the family . . . wasn't hurt," he finally said. *Part of the truth.*

"What do you mean?"

"She used her . . . the family's influence to convince the authorities that autopsies weren't necessary. She'd known what had happened when she found Heath's note and Harding disappeared. She suspected they would find murder if they looked. Her favorite brother would be hunted like an animal."

"That was all?"

"The facts can still destroy the family," he said, realizing how weak the argument sounded.

"Did she—did you—think I would run to the police with a fifty-year-old crime my father committed?" She was outraged. And hurt that she hadn't been trusted.

"She didn't want you to know, either," he said. "She was

still trying to protect your father. I swore to her years ago I would never say anything."

"My father said Lori was still alive when he left her."

He shrugged. "He was frantic, Jess. He may not have realized how badly he'd hurt her."

"And the fire? Was that just convenient?"

He shrugged. "I don't know. Perhaps a spark from a gun. There were fires all over that summer, and authorities assumed one trapped Lori and Heath. A fire crew found the bodies."

"And Sarah's role in all this?"

"She suspected what had happened, and she diverted the attention of the police. She told them that Harding had left on a business trip. When she reached him by phone and when he heard about his brother and wife, he said he needed to get away."

"Then my father killed two people," she said, her voice breaking slightly.

He wanted to take her in his arms, but he couldn't. Not now. He wasn't that much of a bastard.

Her eyes seemed to stare through him. She wasn't accepting everything he said. But neither was she rejecting it.

"I want to finish this," she said. "But I don't want to destroy everyone in doing so. If we just get the bonds and give them to the family, then . . . all this should stop."

"But then you'll never know who tried to run you off the road." Ross was acting the devil's advocate now, arguing first one side, then another. He wanted her to be sure, to have no doubts. Or as few as possible. Damn it, she had a way of turning him into knots.

"Do you think I'll really find that out if I go to the police?"

He doubted it. He shrugged. "It's up to you."

"*I* don't," she said, then went to the phone. "I think we should go to Sedona tomorrow and see if the bonds are still there."

He liked that "we." He nodded, taking the phone from her hands. God only knew how much she'd already spent in plane fares. This was one time the ranch could pay. She had, after all, saved it. He made the reservations, however, for Las Vegas. "We'll rent a car there," he said. "If we disappear from here, someone might watch the Phoenix airport."

She listened as he made all the arrangements, using the ranch credit card, but her face seemed frozen. She looked as if she would break into a thousand pieces if she allowed her emotions off a very tight leash. And yet she had still thought of the Clementses first. He was baffled at that.

"Would you like a drink?" she asked when he hung up the receiver.

He shook his head. "Would you like dinner?"

"No," she said. "I'm not hungry. I'm going to bed. Make yourself at home. Help yourself to anything."

Anything but her. The words were unsaid but he felt them. She disappeared down the hall, but he knew he would always remember the way her lips trembled. The break in her voice. Everyone in her life had let her down.

Including him. Perhaps especially him.

Jessie had to be alone. She had to reread the letter. She had to think about her father. She had to weigh what Ross had said. It sounded so logical. And yet she didn't believe him. At least she didn't believe everything. Or maybe it would be hard for her to believe anyone at this point. She just wanted it all to be over.

But her father had given her a charge. She now knew only a little of the agony he must have gone through. She wiped a tear from her eye. He'd obviously loved the ranch, loved the other members of the family. Loved his wife. Regret and anguish had been in every word of that letter. No wonder he'd sought solace in drink. No wonder he'd barred his heart.

She wished Ben were here. She wished it with all her heart. She desperately needed to love something at the moment. And needed to receive it. Unconditional, uncomplicated, honest love.

Jessie didn't know how long she stayed in her room, remembering, thinking.

She looked at the clock. It was after one, and their plane left at eight in the morning. They would have to leave the house at six. Yet she knew she couldn't sleep. Perhaps a glass of milk would help.

She put on a robe and went to the kitchen, padding silently on bare feet past Ross's room. She paused for a moment, wanting to knock, then bury herself in his arms, but she couldn't tonight. He was still holding something back. She felt it to the marrow of her bones.

How can you have love without trust?

And yet she trusted him with her life, if not her heart.

The house was dark, and it took several minutes for her eyes to adjust. Before going to the kitchen, though, she looked out the window. A dark sedan was parked down the street. Chills ran through her. Was she really doing the right thing in not going to the police? And yet she still didn't have evidence of a crime in Arizona, except for the one her father committed fifty years earlier.

Then she felt Ross's presence next to her.

"Jess?"

"Someone is out there."

He looked out. "We don't know it's the same car."

"I do," she said.

He moved behind her and put his arms around her, pulling her back to lean into his body. He felt so good. So solid. She knew then she wanted to stay there. Maybe he *had* told her everything. His hands massaged the back of her neck. Gentle hands. Loving hands.

Yet she couldn't trust them. She gently pulled away. "I came out to get a glass of milk."

"I'll stay up," he said. His hand caught hers.

She held it for a moment, feeling its warmth, its strength. The now-familiar heated tension stretched between them. His finger traced the contours of her face. But then he dropped it. "Get your milk," he said gently.

Jessie nodded. It wasn't what she wanted. But she knew he was right. She was emotionally volatile. But she knew she wouldn't sleep now. Instead of milk, she made a pot of coffee, and together they silently watched throughout the night.

The ease between them was gone as she prepared a quick breakfast of toast and jam. Electricity continued to shimmer between them, though, and the emotional distance Jessie tried to establish made that attraction even more compelling—the human foible of wanting what you can't, or shouldn't, have.

The sedan was still there in the morning, but there was no sight of occupants. But after they pulled away and went several blocks, they saw the car again. They had discussed that earlier, though, and she had called Sol. They arranged to meet at a busy restaurant. Sol parked on the other side of the restaurant, and Ross and Jessie went through one of one set of doors to another, got in his car, and drove away.

Jessie knew that it wouldn't take long for someone to discover they'd returned to Sedona, but hopefully it would be too late.

She tried not to glance at Ross, but it was impossible. Neither of them had packed any clothes. She had a toothbrush in her handbag. She would buy whatever was needed in Sedona, but she didn't expect to be there that long. Just long enough to see whether they could find the bonds, or whether they'd been destroyed in the fire. And pick up Ben.

She and Ross had talked during the night about alternatives. Should they add several people to their trip into Oak

Creek Canyon? Sarah? Alex? But neither of them could completely eliminate Alex from the list of suspects, nor did they want to put Sarah in danger. Someone had gone to a lot of expense, and the danger of exposure, to find those bonds.

If they dragged the police in, the whole sorry story would come to light. It could ruin Marc and others. And there could be nothing there at all. Why raise hopes? Or scandal?

He'd then suggested that he go alone. Her flat "No" had ended that discussion quickly. If there was danger, she would share it.

The skies had cleared and the flight to Las Vegas was uneventful. They quickly obtained the rental car. "It'll just take us an hour longer than it took to get to Sedona from Phoenix," he assured her.

Jessie nodded, and slept part of the way, then offered to drive while he did the same. To her surprise, he agreed.

They neared Sedona at three, having gained several hours in time changes. Ross took over the wheel and drove to the cantina. He led her inside, ordered food, then went over to huddle with his friend, the owner. Then they both disappeared.

Jessie sat and waited, then she rose and walked around, stretching her legs. It was an odd hour, and few people were inside. She went to the window and looked out, wondering whether she'd ever stop looking again.

Nothing unusual. Then her gaze went to a bowl full of matches. She snatched several books, as she usually did in restaurants, and dropped them into the pocket of her slacks. A souvenir. A memory, too. Though she wasn't entirely sure how many memories she wanted of this summer.

Both the food and Ross appeared at the same time, and she went back to the table. They both ate quickly and without many words. The tacos were probably wonderful, but now they were tasteless. She ate because she knew it would be a long day, not because of appetite.

When he'd paid the bill, they walked out to the car. As she stepped inside the passenger side, she saw a shovel and other tools in the backseat. And a rifle.

Ross apparently saw concern on her face. "Just a precaution," he assured her. "There are snakes in that canyon."

Jessie wondered whether he referred to the two-legged kind or those that crawled. But the sight of the rifle was reassuring. All her pacifist inclinations had faded that night when she was almost run off the road.

He drove down the main road to Oak Creek, keeping his eyes open again for a tail. He didn't see one.

"Tell me about the cabin," she said.

"There's damn little left."

"Is any of it still there?"

"The chimney," he said. "I'm not sure about how much of the hearth survived. The heat must have been terrific. It could well have incinerated anything close to the surface." He paused, then continued, "The Clementses still own the land. They've never thought of rebuilding, though. Too many ghosts there. But no one has suggested selling it, either. I think the specter of those bonds kept the property in the family. I always thought it rather futile." He shrugged.

"Was it large?"

"Just a two-room cabin from what I understand," he said. "Old Hall Clements built it as a retreat *from* the family, not for it. This was all wilderness then, a great place for hunting."

"But everyone knew about it?"

"Oh, the family, certainly. But unless they were invited, it was off-limits. Perhaps that's why Heath selected it. He planned to bury the bonds there, then meet Lori for their getaway. Your father must have seen Lori leave and followed her."

A chill ran down Jessie's back as she imagined her father on this same road, following his wife, wondering whether she was going to betray him. She remembered his rages. He must have been in a towering one then.

Ross didn't say anything more as they drove approximately five more miles, then he turned off onto a dirt road that ran beside the creek and crossed a narrow, rickety-looking bridge. All signs of civilization disappeared as they bounced along an old overgrown drive. He turned again into a barely visible track.

The car bounced along overgrown weeds. "I wish I had my truck," he said. But he deftly maneuvered the car between branches and over rough ruts.

"I'm glad *you* rented it," she said. "If it were me, I'd probably never be able to rent a car again. Not after destroying the last one, too."

He chuckled. The sound warmed the chill inside her.

Then the overgrowth became too much, even for his driving. He parked the car. "We'll walk the rest of the way."

She nodded. She slung her handbag over her shoulder and stepped outside. She watched as he stood beside the car, listening. A buzz of insects. The rustle of branches as a squirrel retreated to a higher limb. Then he opened the back door, hesitated, then took out the shovel and a large box of tools.

She reached over to take the shovel. He gave that to her, but kept the box of tools. "It's heavy," he said. Then he took the rifle out and shouldered it with his other hand.

He led the way to the ruined cabin. Piles of stone lay in heaps. Remains of a fireplace. She hesitated at what once might have been a doorway. An eerie sensation ran through her. She shivered. Her father had stood here, or near here. He'd done something that had forever changed his life.

"Jess."

She turned around. Ross was directly behind her. He

rested the rifle against a large cottonwood, then put the box of tools down. She was holding the shovel like a rifle, and he took it from her. He put an arm on her shoulder. "Are you all right?"

"No," she said honestly.

He pulled her to him. "When I was a kid, Cullen's twins, Hugh and Heath, brought me up here to 'treasure hunt.' I was thirteen. They were three years older. We dug up all sorts of unlikely places. Then they left me here. I was scared out of my wits, though I would be damned before I would admit it. I saw ghosts everywhere."

Jessie was surprised. First of all, she couldn't imagine him scared. Secondly, she was surprised he admitted to it. Nothing about him had endeared him to her more.

For the first time since yesterday afternoon, she reached out and took his hand. "What happened?"

"Sarah drove out. When I didn't come home, she'd pried the information out of the twins. It was the first time I was glad to see her."

"But you didn't show it?"

"No. That wouldn't have been manly," he said with a wry twist to his lips. "But I think she knew it. Several days later, she gave me a horse of my own. I knew how to ride. Every kid on the reservation did, but I'd never owned one. Hell, I never owned more than two pairs of pants at a time."

His fingers closed tightly around hers.

She looked up at him. "You love her very much, don't you?"

"Yes." So simply said. Yet with so much feeling. He'd thrown her off in the beginning with his reserve, with his reluctance to join in any family activities, his insistence on calling Sarah by her given name. She should have known better. She should have sensed how much feeling lay underneath the exterior.

And she knew then that whatever he hadn't said had

been to protect Sarah. Had Sarah sought to cover up her brother's crime by starting a fire?

She leaned into his arms, feeling the strength in him. He didn't love easily, but he loved powerfully.

It was he who pulled away, but not before his hand lingered on her arm, and she saw the warmth in his eyes. "I think we'd better look for those bonds before it gets dark. There really are spirits here. I saw them," he said seriously with only the smallest trace of humor showing. He hesitated, the amusement fading, then added, "Maybe we can put those ghosts to rest once and for all."

She nodded. "I just want to end the speculation. I have no expectations of finding anything."

"You've never had any, have you?" he said, his fingers touching her chin. "I've never met anyone like you before."

His touch burned all the way through her. She felt as if she were melting. All her anger, all the hurt faded. He hadn't done anything to hurt her; he had done what he had to do to protect someone he loved. How could she fault that?

He leaned down and kissed her lightly. Except for the promise. She felt that promise with every beat of her heart.

Then she backed away. It was getting late. Perhaps if they found those bonds, her father would rest easier.

She watched as he walked over to what was left of the chimney. A huge pile of rock lay around it. He leaned down and started to toss away the rocks that had tumbled down during the past fifty years. She joined him in throwing the rocks aside.

Not a breath of air stirred. The sun had lowered but the temperature was still hot. *Fool's errand,* she told herself as sweat pooled on her face. When she thought she couldn't stoop one more time, they reached the bottom of the pile.

Ross kneeled and brushed away dirt from what must have been the fireplace foundation. They found burned fragments of brick, and she knew it must have been an extremely hot fire. Ross used a spade to dig under the rubble. How large a package could be secreted under a hole in the hearth?

Minutes seemed to turn into hours, then she heard a clank. Metal on metal. Ross worked a few more moments, then started pulling on something. His hands emerged with a long, narrow metal box. Heath must have hunted long and hard for something that would fit into the opening. It looked like a long safe-deposit box with a cover.

Ross just held it for a moment, and she stared at it. Part of her had never believed the bonds could have survived all these years. She looked around. The walls of the canyon rose up in back of them. The river gurgled in the late afternoon. Several birds flew from their perches in the trees. So peaceful. Yet echoes of violence seemed to linger. She tried to shake off the feeling.

Ross was still kneeling, looking down at the box. Pandora's box, she thought. She'd had the image earlier and she'd been right. Then he looked at her and, surprisingly, he winked. It was so out of character, so whimsical at the moment that her heart lightened.

Ross picked up the box, finding a key in the lock. The metal box apparently was not meant to keep anyone out, but to protect the contents from the elements. "Should we?" he asked.

"We should," she said. She felt the stirrings of excitement.

He stood, straightening his long, lean body, and she knew he was a far greater treasure than anything they might find in a box. He'd rolled up the sleeves of the white shirt he'd worn all day. Sweat had dampened the shirt and also the unruly dark hair. He used one of his hands to run his fingers through it, leaving a small trail of dirt on his forehead. He was really quite irresistible, and she fought to turn her attention back to the box that had caused so much tragedy.

He led the way to a log where they could sit. He looked at her again, his hand touching hers briefly, then opened the metal box. A sheaf of papers were rolled up inside. He carefully unrolled them to find elaborately designed certificates. He looked closely at one, then handed one over to her.

Just as she started to take it, she heard a loud crack, then an oath from Ross. Red flowered his shirtsleeve. Before she had time to think, he took her hand and practically threw her behind the log, throwing himself over her. They hunched down as another shot whizzed by them, then another.

Their rifle. They had left it leaning against a tree near the chimney.

He whispered into her ear. "Can you crawl into the underbrush? I'll try to circle around and get the rifle."

She started to protest. "You're hit."

"A scratch," he replied. "Do as I say." This time he didn't give her a chance to protest. He started snaking away behind her. A bullet hit near her and she tried to merge herself with the ground. Then she saw Ross move from tree to tree. So apparently did the shooter. He would never make it. She remembered Marc's wound. A rifle, too. Whoever was shooting was a good shot. She moved behind a rotted log, then looked up. Ross was systematically moving toward the rifle, but there was an open space he would have to cross. He would be in the open with no protection.

Her stomach clenched. He would never make it. She felt in her pocket for the matches she'd picked up earlier. The bonds were beside her, spilling over across the ground; Ross had apparently let them go as he'd grabbed her.

Another shot. The shooter's attention was all on Ross now.

He was almost to the clearing. *Now.* She spread the bonds out on the log. Then she took one and rolled it up. She lit the end and watched it flame like a torch. She stood up, holding the flaming bond over the others. It might buy Ross a few seconds.

"I'll burn them," she yelled.

The shooter turned toward her. "Noooooo," he yelled. *Cullen!*

A silence. The flame was eating its way through print, its heat singeing her fingers. When it went out . . .

The gun was aimed at her now.

"Blow it out or I'll kill you," Cullen said.

"No. Not until you put the gun down." She saw his face turn toward Ross's direction as he started to sprint across to the rifle.

The blaze burned her skin. Ross needed more time. She did the only thing she could. She dropped the torch and another bond flamed up. The rifle wavered, then Cullen aimed again. Toward her. A loud crack. Pain ripped through her. Then as she started to fall, another crack.

Everything went black.

Light crept into her consciousness. She wanted it to go away. She wanted to sink back into darkness, into nothingness.

But a voice wouldn't let her. "Jess," it called. Over and over again.

Go away. It hurts too much. She could scarcely breathe. Every small breath was agony.

"Jessie." A softer voice. But just as insistent.

Go away.

"Dammit, Jess. Don't go being a coward on me now."

She opened her eyes, slowly at first, Reluctantly, certainly. The light was painful. Dissolving shapes.

Then she felt her hand. It was clasped tightly, even painfully.

"Come on, Jess." Coaxing now.

Her eyes finally found and deciphered Ross. He was wearing a sling. His face was haggard. Unshaved. His thick hair looked as if it hadn't been combed in a week. His shirt wasn't stained, so he must have changed it, but it looked wrinkled. Slept in.

But he was alive.

He bent down and brushed a kiss along her cheek. "No coward here," he said, and she saw something like mist in his eyes. *But maybe it was just her eyes. They weren't focusing very well.*

"Little idiot," he said. "Didn't anyone ever tell you not to taunt a killer?"

"He was going to . . . shoot you."

His fingers tightened around hers.

"Cullen," she said. "It was Cullen."

"Yes."

"Where . . ."

"He's dead," Ross said as his fingers tightened around hers. "He died yesterday of a gunshot wound, but first he admitted to shooting Marc, trying to run you off the road. For what's it's worth, he claimed he didn't want to kill you. Only scare you off. At the cabin, too. He'd hoped we would just run for it and leave the bonds. When we didn't, he panicked."

"But why . . . shoot Marc?"

"He hoped it would be blamed on me. If I were jailed, Sarah would have to sell the ranch. And it might well make you decide to sell. He was in deep financial trouble, deeper than anyone knew, with some very high-interest loans. He was about to lose the Quest. If you had agreed to sell the ranch, he could have stayed afloat awhile. Probably not long, though. Those bonds were his key to survival. He wanted them all."

"The attic?"

"Cullen again. He'd stolen back into the house to get the letter. He was sure you knew more than you were saying. That's the reason Timber didn't bark that night. He knows Cullen."

"But how did he know I had the book?"

"He hired some thugs in Atlanta. He'd borrowed money from a dubious source and they put him in touch with these people. They put a bug in the bookshop. He was convinced you knew more than you told Alex or the family."

"And Alex?"

"Not involved at all. He was just keeping all his options open. I think he feels guilty as hell now that he didn't realize how desperate Cullen was."

She closed her eyes. She knew about desperation. Her father had been desperate. He'd set in motion consequences that continued until this day. She tried to move, and pain shot through her.

He leaned over and she felt his lips on her face. Tender. Loving. "Get some rest," he whispered. "You were hit twice. One bullet hit your lung, the other your hip. Your lung collapsed and you had a touch of pneumonia."

She remembered clouds of pain, a tube, suffocating. Her throat still hurt. So did her side whenever she moved. She also felt fuzzy, sedated. And tired. So tired.

But first she had to know one more thing. "The bonds?" she asked. "Were any of them saved?"

"Most of them," he said. "According to Alex, the remaining bonds are probably worth a little more than the ranch would have brought. You seem to be an heiress again."

"I don't want any," she said. "If I have a share, I want it to go to the others."

"Are you sure?" he asked.

"Yes. It's fruit of a poisoned tree. They destroyed my father. If Heath hadn't taken the money . . ."

"He might still have taken Lori."

A shiver passed through Jessie. "Maybe. But my father never would have gone to the cabin that day. He never would have taken a gun. I can't help but feel that money is more a curse than a blessing. At least for me. Not for the others."

He nodded. His gaze was wondering. "You're the only woman I've ever met that keeps turning down fortunes."

"I still have a share in the Sunset. That's a great deal more than I had a month ago." She hoped she had something else. Something far more important.

With that thought in mind, she allowed her eyes to close. She was still so tired, so weak.

His fingers still clutched hers. It was all she needed at the moment.

Jessie didn't know how long she slept this time. Some of the pain had faded, though. Her chest still burned, hurt, but she could breathe easier. When she woke again, Sarah was beside her.

Sarah. Marc and Samantha. Alex. Even Elizabeth, who must have flown in.

Marc came over and sat beside her. "We all wanted to tell you how sorry we are. If we had known how desperate Cullen was, we might have been able to help. I only hope that this doesn't affect the way you feel about the rest of the family. We've all come to care for you."

The grief in his eyes was unmistakable. Cullen was his brother. And now surely Marc knew that Cullen had been the one who shot him. History repeating itself. And greed had been at the bottom of both tragedies.

She held out her hand, took his, and squeezed it tightly. "If only I had told Sarah and Alex about the book sooner. He would have had his share of the bonds."

"No," he said. "None of it was your doing. He made his own decisions. The twins were unaware. They . . . were afraid you wouldn't want to see them, or they would have been here."

"There's been too much grief already," she said. "Of course, I don't blame them."

He hesitated, then added, "Thank you. Ross told us you wanted us to have the remaining bonds. I still think you should take your share."

"I burned mine," she said wryly. "My father should have told you about them long ago."

His brows furrowed. "Still . . ."

"No. I have what I want," she said. "I have a family." She moved slightly, and winced as pain drove through her.

"We can talk about it later." A smile lit his face. "I think Ross plans to stay nearby." He ushered the others out. All except Sarah, who lingered at her bedside, a nervous smile on her face.

Her aunt tried to smile. "Ross went down for some coffee. All of them had been waiting to see you for hours. Marc even canceled some fund-raising event. And Alex has been haunting the corridors."

"Some of the bonds were destroyed," she said cautiously, wondering whether that had made a difference.

"You saved Ross's life in doing so. Cullen rushed over to stamp out the flames, giving Ross enough time to get the rifle. No one faults you for that."

Still, Jessie couldn't let it go. "My father wanted me to get them all back to the family."

"Ross told me about the letter." She hesitated a moment. "I know . . . you believed Ross wasn't honest with you."

Jessie felt her stomach constrict.

"I was the one who had your home burglarized before you came here," Sarah said slowly. "You weren't supposed to know anything about it, much less come home early."

"But Ross said Cullen . . ."

"He said he put a bug on your phone in the bookstore. He got the idea after Alex told him you'd been burglarized. He thought it more likely you would have left whatever it was in the bookstore."

"But why . . . ?"

"I thought your father might have left you some clue to

those bonds. We knew they had never been redeemed. Those damnable things almost destroyed the family. Heath. Harding. And . . . I was afraid the sheriff's office might revive the investigation into those deaths fifty years ago. But now I'm tired of secrets."

Jessie waited.

Sarah's eyes filled with tears. "My brothers meant everything to me. Each one of them. They had protected me and looked after me since I was a baby. But your father was always my favorite. I would . . . have done anything for him." Her fingers tightened around Jessie's. "That day . . . that terrible day, I saw Harding rush out of the house. I knew something was wrong and followed him. But I lost him along the way. He was going too fast. I could only guess that he was going to the cabin.

"When I neared the turnoff, I saw his car turn out into the main road. I don't think he saw me. I drove on in. I found Heath dead of a rifle bullet and Lori . . . hurt. She regained consciousness, though, and demanded I call the police. She kept saying Harding had killed Heath and he would pay for it. I knew I couldn't let Harding go to prison . . . or be executed. It was all Lori's fault. She set one brother against another brother. I was wild with grief and anger and I knew that if she lived she would destroy Harding. I . . . couldn't let that happen. She started for the door. I picked up the rifle and told her to stop. She wouldn't. The rifle . . . went off."

Her head fell. She was silent for a moment, then continued. "I went after Halden. We started a fire near the cabin, knowing it would spread and consume the cabin. It was easy to convince the law that Lori and Heath had been careless and must have been trapped inside. There were any number of fires that summer and once we were sure the cabin was destroyed, we stopped and phoned in an anonymous report.

"After that, no one was really surprised that Harding left

town. His wife and brother were dead. It was only natural he would want to get away.

"You know the rest," she continued. "We found the letter from Heath in his room. No one looked for the bonds because they weren't worth anything at that time."

"But the company became successful," Jessie said.

"Beyond anyone's wildest dreams. My brothers searched for the bonds over the years, then my nephews. I thought, hoped, everyone had given up on it. I . . . was afraid that if the book was found, it might raise questions and open an investigation. An autopsy would reveal bullet wounds."

"Ross knew."

"He knew I had covered up a murder," Sarah said. "When he got in trouble once, I told him we all had our sins, actions we regretted. I was consumed with guilt and told him part of the story. I suspect he knew I did more than start a fire."

She paused. "I tried for years to find Harding, tell him that it was safe to come home. That I had made it safe for him. Then Alex found you for me, and I wanted to make everything right. I just wanted to make sure you didn't have that book, that it wouldn't lead to you learning what happened with your father.

"Then I saw you and Ross together and thought perhaps I could ensure his future, too. But Cullen believed you might know something about those bonds. He was obsessed with them. I just never thought he would go so . . . far."

Sarah's confession was like new blows to Jessie's stomach. They pounded far deeper than Cullen's culpability. She remembered that photo, the old photo, with the six happy siblings. Part of her understood the horror of that confrontation in the cabin so many years earlier. If they had been *her* brothers, how far would she have gone to protect them?

"I'm sorry," Sarah finished. "I am so sorry for everything." She rose slowly and walked from the room. The energy was gone, the life. She looked like an old woman.

She'd left Jessie with choices. She could tell the police about the murder fifty years ago.

Or she could keep silent, as Halden had all these years. Had that silence infected his son, caused *him* to commit murder?

How many lies and secrets could the family endure?

A knock at the door. Then Ross came in. His face was troubled.

He sat on the side of her bed and took her hand again. "Sarah told me what she told you," he said. "I'm so damned sorry about all of it. I should have told you everything I knew."

She brought his hand to her mouth and kissed it. "You were protecting the one person who had protected you," she said. "It was fifty years ago. There's nothing to be gained to prosecuting an old woman."

"She doesn't have long to live," Ross said. "The doctors say no longer than six months."

Grief flowed through her. No matter what Sarah had done in one moment of anger so long ago, Jessie had come to love her. She had obviously paid for that decision over the years.

Jessie nodded.

Ross hesitated. "You have to do what you think is right. That's what I love about you. What Sarah so admires about you. It wouldn't change anything."

Love. It was the first time he'd actually said the word.

In that moment, she felt free. And she knew that what she was doing was right.

"I love you," she said.

His fingers tightened around hers. "If you want to leave here, I can try to find a job around Atlanta," he said.

She knew how much that offer cost him. She loved him

even more for making it. But the Sunset was her future, as it had been responsible for so much of her past. She wasn't going to run from it again.

"No," she said softly. "The ranch is staying in the hands of the family. It's what Heath and . . . my father would have wanted. I think he somehow meant for me to decipher the mystery of the primer and go home. And," she added, "there's no Sunset without you."

A slow grin came to his face. "Will you marry me? I think it's the only way I can keep you safe."

"I like that," she said.

"We'd both be getting one hell of a family," he said.

"And enlarging it."

"A dreadful thought," he replied sternly, but a smile played around his eyes.

"A marvelous thought," she corrected.

He leaned down, this rough cowboy of hers. His lips touched hers with a tenderness so sweet her heart swelled to near bursting. It was a promise, a melding of spirits.

And she knew it to be true and real and strong. As strong as the land and as true as its beauty. She was, at last, home.

epilogue

Jessie had never been so tired in her life.

Nor as content. Happy. *Euphoric.*

Her arms went around the tiny bundles. Twins. Both alive. Both well. Both with ten fingers and ten toes each. *Twins run in the family.*

Ross had been in the delivery room with her, his hand holding hers throughout labor, breathing with her, encouraging her. Sharing the pain. She even felt that his was greater than hers, because he'd felt so helpless against it.

He'd hated feeling helpless. She knew that about him. And now so much more. She knew how big his heart was, how fine his mind, and especially how loving his soul.

She heard the door open and looked up. She saw Ross standing there. He'd left after the delivery to make a few phone calls and now he was beaming at her, grinning like the proverbial cat who ate the canary.

She relished the smile on his face. It came so easily now. He came over to her, and together they looked down at one red face, then the other. Both had fuzzy knobs of dark hair. And dark, dark blue eyes. She was told that might well change but she hoped not. She loved dark hair, their father's hair.

The twins were not a surprise. They'd known for months, just as they'd known it would be a boy and girl.

But the reality was something else, something so profound and glorious that she could scarcely contain the joy inside her.

She'd never known she had a maternal streak. But ever since she discovered she was pregnant, she'd felt a fierce protectiveness she'd never imagined possible. These children would never know a moment's insecurity. Not if she could help it.

Nor her husband.

She smiled as she recalled how many times he'd touched her stomach with such awe, such reverence.

Jessie only wished that Sarah had not died two months earlier, one month after Halden—her last brother—died. But at least she'd known. She'd known about the twins, and she'd rejoiced with them. They'd shared a bottle of sparkling juice and watched the sunset together.

Ross had announced then they planned to name the twins Sarah and Harding.

They'd discovered Sarah the next day. She'd died in her sleep with a smile on her face.

Ross leaned down and kissed Jessie. "They're wonderful," he said. "Little miracles."

"Take one," she challenged.

He hesitated, but then he had taken child-care classes with her. He'd learned to hold babies. "I take it this is Sarah," he said as he picked up the pink-blanketed baby, holding her gingerly. He'd practiced with dolls, and the remembrance brought a smile to her face. He'd been so big, so awkward, yet so tender.

"Hi, Sarah," he said in a soft voice. "We did all right, you know, your mother and me. And your great-aunt. You wouldn't be here without her."

Then he turned back to Jessie. "Alex has called the rest of the family. Marc is delighted. And not only with our news. Our new senator just got his first bill passed." He hesitated. "Alex said that both Heath and his brother send their best wishes."

"Good," Jessie said softly. "Perhaps they'll come to the christening."

"Alex believes they will." The twins hadn't attended their wedding ten months earlier, but had sent a congratulatory note. Alex explained that they felt guilty about their father's actions and thought they wouldn't be welcome. Sondra had taken what was in Cullen's account after he died and disappeared, leaving the twins to clean up their father's mess. They had inherited half of Halden's share in the ranch and sold it to Jessie in exchange for her portion of the bonds; that money and their own share allowed them to pay off Cullen's debts. She'd never wanted the bond money anyway, and this way she ensured the future of the Sunset.

Now Hugh managed the Quest, and Cullen's dream had survived after all. As had Sarah's to keep the family together . . .

Ross replaced Sarah into a nook under her arm, and he sat on the bed, his fingers touching her cheek. "You are so incredibly beautiful," he said softly.

She was no such thing. She'd been in labor for the last six hours. But she knew he believed it, and that was all that mattered.

"I love you," she said.

His eyes glistened, and she wondered how she'd even thought him aloof. He had filled her with love.

She looked down at the twins again. For a split second, she remembered the photo of five brothers and a sister: the laughing faces, the affection that had been so obvious before the war.

"He would be happy, wouldn't he?" she asked.

His mouth creased into a tender smile. He didn't have to ask who. He knew. It was part of the knowledge between them.

"Yes, love, he would," he said. "We've all come home."